CW00340953

The Saint Who Loved Me

The Saint Who Loved Me

MIMI THEBO

First published in Great Britain in 2002 by
Allison & Busby Limited
Bon Marche Centre
241-251 Ferndale Road
Brixton, London SW9 8BJ
http://www.allisonandbusby.com

A catalogue record for this book is available from the British Library

ISBN 0 7490 0504 1

Printed and bound in Spain by
Liberdúplex, s. l. Barcelona

To Andy

Chapter One

There are five or six ways I can get into work in the morning, but none of them actually get me there on time. My general rule is to hop on the first thing moving and hope for the best. This morning, I jumped on a bus outside the door, changed at Dalston Junction for the 38 and then, at the Angel, made a historic run down the centre of three lanes of traffic to throw myself onto the 73. People were actually cheering. A brass plaque will probably be screwed into the tarmac at the site. Pity I hadn't noticed it was only going to Euston. Now here I am, stranded on a white line in the middle of Euston Road at rush hour, trying with equal fervour to both survive and to flag a cab.

I don't want to be late for this meeting. I don't want to die, either. Too late, I remember that I might be pregnant. If we're successful this month, conception should be happening yesterday or today. And here I am, breathless, sweaty, swaying on a painted line so that the lorry behind me and the coach in front of me can both pass me at forty miles an hour. Euston Road shakes under my feet. Being inside my womb must be like being in a cocktail shaker in an unpresssurised cabin at about 30,000 feet.

The light has to change soon. That's all I can think. It can't stay green forever. Now, I start to get frightened. This is typical of me, to hurl myself off the bus in a mad rush and then to get frightened later, when I am already committed to this painted line. Through the traffic, I can only intermittently see the bus stop I intended to reach. There's no way I can get across. Everything's picked up speed, and everything passing me seems to be big. I'm sure the drivers can't see me until they're nearly on top of me.

Gusts of wind come from under the buses and lorries and

make the tail of my mac flap. Bumpers and grilles seem to be getting closer, and they must be doing at least fifty now. I flatten my case across my knees and try and wrap my mac tighter to my body in case it catches on something and drags me under the wheels. At the thought, I close my eyes, and for the first time in I don't know how long, I pray.

'Oh, sweet Jesus,' I say out loud, 'please help me in my stupidity.'

Immediately there is a lull in the constant noise. I open my eyes and the traffic has stopped. Right in front of me is a black cab with its amber light showing me welcome. Hope, shelter, success, and life itself are now all mine for less than a fiver. I sink back into the seat and let my long legs and my belongings sprawl. Just for a moment, I am a child again, home and safe. Then I pull my skirt down over my stocking tops, adjust my jacket and mac, and gather my belongings neatly. I will check my lipstick again, and my watch. Both will look good.

I am not the only one in my office frightened of our office manager, Anya. This morning, I need to see her straight away, yet I don't get to assert my authority by bellowing for her as I come in the door. She is already there, waiting for me, lips pursed disapprovingly, glancing at the clock as I shrug my mac into the cupboard.

'Well,' she says by way of greeting, 'at least they aren't here yet.'

I follow her into the best meeting room, the Wedgwood blue one with the audiovisual suite. The one with the little panels in the bleached oak table that slide back to reveal computer monitor screens. I have no idea how to work any of this equipment since before this none of my clients have warranted it. Anya is sure of herself with all of the technology. As I follow the instructions on how to use only what I will need this morning, I look at the back of her strong little neck. The muscles are rigid with some strong negative emotion and in contrast, the little line of dark

10

hair crawling down from under her upsweep seems absurdly vulnerable.

I master the controls and she escapes. I am alone for a few precious moments. I could be checking my notes. I could be getting my messages. My email has probably built up to the size of the Bible over the last few days. Instead, I think about Anya and what I do for a living. She hates her job, but I like mine. It's not the salary that makes the difference, I think. I find that the larger salary comes from the liking, not the other way around.

I blagged my way into this job. Writing press releases for friends' bands was how I started. Of course, I had my English degree. Of course, I had written for loads of magazines, freelancing. But I had no real experience when I came here, and Anya knew it. She took pity on me. I would have never made it if it wasn't for her. But from this morning, everything is different and she is dependent on me, now. No wonder her neck is rigid.

The huge window in the suite is cold and I want to lean my forehead on it, but I know that would leave a mark. Instead I look at the city stirring into full morning panic. Up here the little running ants are amusing. I wonder if any of them will die the way I nearly did this morning while I look down, remote and a little amused. You could have died, I tell myself sternly, and for what? For this meeting. To launch a new tampon.

Is a new tampon worth your life? But it is my life, it is how I am spending it, how I will spend it for the next few months. I'm working such long hours that my home life consists only of bathing and sleep.

On each side of my bed there are large blue candles. When one of us is working late, we light a candle for the other. We find that we can sleep with the candles lit and yet they give enough light to crawl into bed by. Usually, my candle looks much bigger than Simon's. This morning, as I struggled into my corsetry and hosiery, I noticed that my candle was burnt lower than his. I can't

11

remember the last time we were both in the bed and awake.

Like I said, this is my life.

I check my watch. If I start a task, I will only have to abandon it halfway. They will be here any second.

Still, I would welcome some distraction, which does not come. This morning, no one will disturb me. I am preparing. I am the pitcher on the mound, the golfer lining up the tricky tee shot. A hush will perforce envelop me, leaving me to my thoughts.

Why is it worth living to bring a new tampon to the market? I think about this tampon. It is a good tampon. It works well, and expands widthways. Originally, tampons were designed by men, and expanded lengthways. They don't work so well. There have been widthways tampons on the market for about thirty years, but they don't have applicators. That's what I use. But some women, and, as it turns out, quite a lot of them, don't like to touch themselves down there, especially during a period. So, the company invented an applicator for them.

Simple. But you can't break out the big splashy television campaign about it, because you are aiming it at women who are squeamish. You need a softly-softly. A market saturating softly-softly. You need me.

And so I am spending this part of my life, really, making some poor sad women who are obviously completely repressed a little less sad by saving their dignity and their panties. Yes, and making them more productive and better citizens in the bargain. It's my little bit of world changing, the bit that God gave me to do.

I check my nails, shoot my cuffs and face the door. I hear footsteps coming down the hall. My last thought is, what is this God shit this morning?

I went home that night early, with twenty-seven unread email messages flashing their more and more strident reminders on my screen. Early means I left the office at seven, before the cleaners had arrived. Early meant that I picked up some horribly overpriced garlic and olive oil in Liverpool Street station and told Simon that I was going to cook.

'What are you going to make?'

'I don't know. I don't think there is much.'

He laughed, 'Good,' he said, 'you always make something fab when there's nothing. I'll try to be home at a reasonable hour. Red or white?'

'I don't know. You'll have to guess.'

'I'll see what's in the tasting room. I'm looking forward to seeing you. It feels like a date.'

That was at 4:00.

At 8:00, when I finally arrive home (train delayed), there is a message blinking on the answer phone.

'Sweetie, I'm so sorry, but the buyers have got back to me. There's about a thousand amendments on the price list copy. It's gonna be a late one.'

I punch in his number when I hear the 'I'm sorry.'

'Marketing.'

'When did you know?'

'About the list? About five, I guess.'

'Simon! Damn you! Why didn't you tell me at five, then?'

Silence.

'I came home early. To be with you. I have this job thing, too, you know.'

'Honey, I'm sorry I can't make it.'

'That's not why I'm angry.' And I am angry, very angry, kneeling on the desk chair with one leg, jamming that knee into the cushion. 'I'm angry because you didn't let me know early enough that I could keep on with my work. My work! Remember? The stuff that makes the mortgage payments while you piss about playing with the wine boys?'

'I'm putting the phone down, now,' Simon says, and then I am only listening to the click and the buzz.

13

I slump down onto the floor, completely defeated, fighting the urge to call back and apologise. It has been a hell of a day. I might not move again. I might stay right here forever. I might indulge in a nervous breakdown. I look at the hardwood floor that I stripped myself. It's not nearly as good as the one downstairs that we hired someone to do. And it's not doing my suit any good.

This last is the motivating factor not to fall completely apart. And the tampon. I mustn't forget the tampon. I hang my suit up carefully and wrap a big fluffy towel around me. I start the bath and eat some yoghurt. If Simon thinks I'm cooking for him, he'll find he's mistaken.

I watch *EastEnders*, or at least the last ten minutes. I fall into bed before nine and sleep as if I was dead.

It's a dream. I'm sure it is. But there's an overwhelming smell that I can hardly place, and my brain reminds me that I seldom smell things in my dreams. Before I roll over and open my eyes, I try to place it. Water. I smell water, lots of it. But there's no dripping sound. Of course, I can't see that well without my glasses, even when it is after midnight and my neighbour has turned on his new security light. Even so, it's a man's shape, bulky at the shoulders, looking out at my garden. I know it isn't Simon.

I am awake. Or dreaming myself awake. I am one or the other. Sometimes the cat brings in strange things, strange smells. But not this one. How long has it been since I scented water? In London, in England, most of the year I am surrounded by it. I am remembering something, almost. I close my eyes to think. And then the alarm is going off.

I immediately reach out for Simon, and encounter his hand, reaching for me. 'I'm sorry,' he says. 'I was so looking forward to seeing you.'

I am angry again, almost immediately. I do not have the life of a woman dependent on her man for anything, and I am not going

14

to have the patronising that goes with it. 'That isn't the point, you idiot,' I snarl.

'I know. Your work. I know.' Simon swings his legs out to the side of the bed and talks with his back to me. I scramble for my glasses, so that I can at least get clues from the back of him.

'Well?' I say, propping myself up on one elbow.

'I don't know. Maybe I didn't tell you because I didn't want it to be true.' Now he turns to me. I have forgotten again how handsome he is. He's male model handsome, Simon, complete with broad forehead and cleft chin. His elegant jawline cuts deep into the muscular neck which joins to the long shoulders perfectly. Absolutely perfectly, as if he'd been moulded out of plastic. Simon is Ken. He's Action Man. He's a Dream Date. My breath catches in my throat, just looking at him. I never really get used to it.

His sandy hair falls in a flop over his eye, and he pushes it back impatiently. I am looking into those soft brown eyes, drowning in chocolate. My body warms from my chest down.

Finally, I remember to argue. I say, 'That's stupid.' And then I lunge across the bed and hold him tight. I am so afraid we are going to lose each other, that we will just lose track of each other. That one night I'll come home and realise that his candle has burnt away and I haven't seen him for a few months. And then he'll love somebody else, but I never will. I never will. I hold on to him for perhaps too long.

'Maggie,' he says at last, kissing the top of my head. 'What's wrong?'

We get up, make the bed, start our morning routine. 'I don't know. I was so strung out last night that I felt... And I had a dream about a river or a man or something. Powerful.'

'Take care of yourself,' he says, and then we start grooming in earnest. It's not a bad marriage. There's just not enough of it.

Four minute run to Rectory Road train station. Train is late, so I walk to the end. It makes it more possible to get a seat on the last

15

carriages. I play with the paving stones on the way, trying to find the one which rocks the most. Simon and I used to do that when we caught the train together. Now he is always out the door first, working farther away. Perhaps we should move closer to his work. I don't know.

The train is supposed to take seven minutes and seldom takes more than fifteen. I have snuck a book into my case this morning, even though I have less than no time for personal reading. I'm embarrassed by it. It's a one pound classic special, a Louisa May Alcott book, the sequel to *Little Women*. If I am reading something cool and trendy on the train, I feel it looks better. I'm sure reading *Good Wives* makes me look unhip. But I'm enjoying it.

So much that when I look up we are at Bethnal Green. Liverpool Street and the Central Line next stop. A little later, I look up again. Still Bethnal Green. I notice people near me are looking pissed off. I look at my book and then at my watch. I begin to make up fantasy disasters contained in the twenty-seven unread emails. Some people get off. I am racking my brain for Bethnal Green connections. I could catch the number 8. But it's so slow by Bank.

The doors tinkle and slam and we move off, only ten minutes delayed. But after we clear the platform, we stop again. Without the option of leaving, the air in the carriage vibrates with our scarcely contained frustration. A stupid message will come on in a minute - there it is. 'Ladies and gentlemen, we apologise for the delay. There is a signal failure. We will be proceeding to Liverpool Street station in five minutes.'

This last is a lie, and we all know it. We groan and shuffle our feet, but we made the wrong decision and are now trapped. The Central Line. Hell. I could have got the Central Line from Bethnal Green. What was I thinking? I pick up my book again, escaping into Jo's world, which is so much better than mine.

I emerge at Tottenham Court Road, at last, feeling like I've just survived a forced march. The first thing I do is check my stockings, but, by some miracle, no one's briefcase has snagged them. That's two quid saved, I think as I pass Boots. My blouse, however, is crushed, and it seems like the whole of humanity has pushed into and over me this morning. It is eight-thirty and I am already running late.

Anya tells me good morning as I shove my mac away, and then tells me that an old client has been trying to reach me. This is all I need, and I work hard not to scowl at her, to say, 'Oh, Jesus,' with a smile and to ask her how she is. She looks tired. She probably is tired. There are new flowers on reception, cream lilies fat, and waxy. 'I'll ring Donald this morning,' I promise. I must read those emails, I think. I must read them now.

My desk is down a sea-green wall, textured to look like a vastly inflated square of shantung silk. If I run a finger down it, the plaster bits can cut, but sometimes I do it anyway. Today, I consciously enjoy the colour, slowing down. Trying to breathe deeply. It is only four or five steps, but it is after reception and before my desk and nothing can happen to me here.

'Maggie! What happened?'

It's Henry. I had forgotten about Henry. 'I'm sorry,' I say. 'Delays at Bethnal Green.'

'Do you want to meet now? I've got to go in an hour. Or we could meet about 6:00?'

Not at six, my brain screams. It will run on forever. You and Simon need to see each other. But seeing Simon needs Simon as well, and I can't control that. I can't also keep working myself to death to make it possible to see someone who might not bother to show up. Henry is watching me while I stand there with my mouth open.

'Now,' I say, choosing marriage again. The thought of the emails brings a deep, frightening unease, but instead I walk directly into Henry's office and begin listening to how he's handling my

17

old deodorant account. He's doing, I think, a much better job than I ever did.

A journalist cancels lunch with many sincere apologies. I am extremely nice about it, which should make us mates for a while, and reschedule without a whimper. At 11:30, a kid comes around with a basket of sandwiches, crisps, chocolate and drinks. I choose what I hope are the healthiest options and keep going, pushing through the day, pushing towards my goal of being home early, before eight o'clock. I emailed Simon about 10, but I haven't got anything back, so I ring. He's in a meeting.

Push on, push on, push on. Don't for godsakes start thinking about it. You don't have time to think.

In the end, I am home by eight-thirty. I stumble into sweats, hang up my suit carefully, and start to cook. Just as it is nearly ready, Simon's key is in the lock. We don't say much. He hangs his jacket up on a kitchen chair and we sit with the wicker trays on our laps watching a mindless situation comedy. We drink maybe a half a bottle of wine that Simon has brought home from the tasting room. We chase the cat upstairs to bed and then all three of us collapse in a heap, together. It feels like mending something, but not very well, knowing that it will soon need mending again.

But tonight, as my eyes pull shut, I feel blood run into the muscles in my shoulders that have not relaxed for days. It tingles pleasurably, and I arc closer into the warm smell of love.

It must be about two o'clock in the morning. My eyes fly open when I smell it again, water. I smell water. The man with the big shoulders is standing by the window again, looking out at my garden. I am proud of my garden, even though I don't have the time or the money to do what I want to it. It's well planned and fairly tidy and, above all, I think it's interesting. I am happy that someone likes the look of it.

Tonight, as last night, I am not very worried about this stranger in my bedroom. His hair is white, but his body is active,

18

virile. It pulses with energy, just standing there. His breathing is steady and even. He is wearing some sort of robe. I can't tell more without my glasses. With my astigmatism, everything is just a vague impression. I want to reach for the case, but I am afraid of scaring him away.

Simon is sleeping, as always, like the dead. I often wonder what midnight feedings will be like with Simon, who will probably never even hear a baby crying. At the thought of a baby, my eyes swoon shut with desire, and then the alarm is shrieking in my ear and it's time to do it again.

Chapter Two

Walk down Leswin Road and catch the 73 at the corner. Get the best seat (left, top, front). Continue reading *Good Wives*. We are making good progress, sailing down Essex Road. I look up and we are nearly at the Angel. I look up and we are at the Angel. I look up and we are still at the Angel. And again.

I snatch up book, case and bag. Run down the stairs to the platform for another look. The Angel is a parking lot. People are hooting their horns with frustration, but no one is going anywhere. The lights in our direction are green, but the driver hasn't even bothered to put the bus into gear. In front of me is a metal safety fence about three and a half feet high. Beyond that is the pavement and then the entrance of Angel Station.

I grab *Good Wives* between my teeth and stick my bag over my arm and my hand all the way through my case handle and vault the fence, scissoring my legs over the top rail since I am not fit enough to jump it. My stocking tops and cellulite are thus shared with the whole of the population, but I don't care. Through the gate and it's the run down the zillion steps of the Angel escalator.

It's been years since I lived in the Angel, years since I trusted the Northern Line for transportation. I plan to change to the Victoria Line at Kings Cross. Kings Cross is South from the Angel, so I get on the Southbound train. Unfortunately, Kings Cross is on the Northbound train. Change at Old Street, walking across the platform. Extremely trendy young girl doing the same snorts at me and says, 'I thought I was the only one stupid enough to do that.'

I smile at her and start to say something, but she walks away haughtily, as though she has a perfect right to be stupid, but I have infringed on it. I end up changing at Euston and running to the office from Oxford Circus.

My day is flying by. I get a call from Simon at 12:00 which I return at 4:00. It is Thursday, he reminds me. Only one more day after this. He will be late. So will I. We'll grab something to eat around work. We'll see each other in the morning.

The company pays for another taxi and I feed the cat, take out my contacts, brush my teeth and crawl into bed. Almost asleep, I light Simon's candle.

At three o'clock in the morning I don't want to smell water again. I burrow back into the covers. The bed is so warm that Simon must be in it. I push my nose underneath the covers so that I can smell only him.

I am not a very curious person, which is why I never made it in journalism. I could never think to ask all of those intrusive questions. I don't think I really wanted to know the answers. But when a strange man clears his throat in my bedroom at three o'clock in the morning, I do sit up and take notice. And I put on my glasses.

I'm not afraid at all, and I'm more than half sure that I'm dreaming. But dreams are not usually this vivid, this detailed. The man is looking at me, now, not out at the garden. He has turned. He's massive in his upper body, but he's not that tall. He's dressed in coarse brown material with a bit of a shine, like linen. This is made into some sort of vaguely ceremonial robe, like a dashiki or something. He is wearing something on a thong around his neck, but this, whatever it is, is hidden down the slit which forms the opening of his garment.

His hair is pure white, but there's a lot of it missing. He wears a neat beard, white like his hair. He stands like a brickie. My eyes are blurring as I try to make out his features. Everything seems to be shifting. The hair, it stays white, what's left of it. The beard, it stays white and neatly trimmed. But the features seem to kind of swim.

Simon is snoring softly. I don't even think to wake him.

It is the stranger that smells of water. As he moves from the window towards the bed, great wafts of the scent fly from him. I scoot over and pat the bed, in a reflex, and he sits down at the level of my hips, looking at me.

'What are you doing here?' I whisper.

'Don't whisper, ' he says. 'Your man won't wake up.' His voice is heavily accented, but I can't quite place the accent. It might be Greek. It might be Iranian.

I am vaguely uneasy, and then think that something is wrong, that he has killed Simon or plans to hurt me. The fear which has been completely absent now slams into my chest with panic. I start to push myself up, out of bed, and when he reaches out for my shoulder, a strange squeezed sound comes out of my throat. But then he touches me and immediately the panic vanishes again and I slide back down under the duvet, covering my breasts.

'I will not hurt you.'

'Who are you? And what the hell are you doing in my bedroom?'

'You should not call to hell. You never know who is listening.'

The gravity in his voice sends a chill down my exposed spine. Sitting up in bed like this suddenly seems ridiculous.

'Who are you?'

I am staring at his face, watching the nose widen and lengthen and then shrink again, the eyes flashing from black to brown, the lips thicken and thin.

Before he can answer my first question, I say, 'What's happening with your face?'

He puts one heavy hand on my head and closes his eyes. When he opens them, his face has stabilised. It looks vaguely familiar.

'Is that better?' His voice now sounds familiar as well.

I nod, trying to think.

'Now. For your first question. I was called Simon. The Master

22

gave me another name, he called me...' Here my visitor screws up his lips, 'Peeeter. Peter. I do not like it.'

His forehead bunches into knots. 'English. I hate it. It has no grace of its own. Bits and pieces of everything slammed together, like a bad stew. And the worst of it is Peeeter. I understand men use this name for their manhood. This,' he points into his lap, 'is my Peeeter. I do not like it. It is supposed to mean rock, but nobody knows that anymore. Rock, you know. Like Pierre. Ah, I wish the Gauls had gained the ascendancy of the world! But they were always too busy with the flesh.'

He sighs, gazing out much farther than my bedroom wall allows. 'Do not call me this Peter,' he decides. 'Call me Rock. You can call me Saint Rock.'

I haven't been to Mass for ten years. I haven't been to Mass since the month after my wedding day. I can think of no reason why I should fantasise about Saint Peter seeing my tits. And I can also think of no reason why Saint Peter should choose me for a visitation. Whichever it is.

I look at him, and my horror must show on my face.

He makes a face, a little supplicating smile, and raises the massive shoulders to indicate irony. In an instant, in that gesture, he looks a caricature Jew. The smell, I think, he is a fisherman. My mind reels with collaborating detail and I arch back away from him, closing my eyes.

I intend to say, 'No, it can't be,' but I am asleep again before I can.

7:41. I can just make the 7:45 from Rectory Road. Out the door, twist the key for the mortise lock. Run halfway up the street. Realise I have forgotten the cleaner's money. Back home, open both locks. Search in purse and pull out twenty pound note. Pet cat, who has come down from her morning sun spot on the bed to see if I would like to stay home with her today. Tell her I would indeed and leave again. Remember my grandmother's superstition and go back in. Sit down. Stand up and leave for the third time, locking the mortise again. Cat now completely confused.

76 to the 38. Or at least that was the plan. Busily reading *Good Wives*, I miss my stop. Am halfway to Bank before I notice. Decide to stay on and get Central Line at Bank.

Marmee has just given Meg some good advice. She has told her to be the first one to apologise to her husband when they quarrel. I also was always the first one to apologise, every time. I got heartily sick of it, and wonder if Meg will get sick of it, too. I expect Simon to want to talk things out. I expect Simon to give in sometimes, too. The other morning, he did it well. But something just wasn't in it. Thinking about clutching him like that in bed is vaguely disturbing, vaguely humiliating.

I tuck *Good Wives* away in my bag and watch the bus route. It's a strange one, hiding down the backstreets of Islington. This is my old race walk route when I lived here. When I had time to exercise. When my hips didn't threaten to take over the universe.

At Bank I am, as always, intimidated by the Financial Sector. They all look so sure of themselves and so deeply conservative. Even dressed in one of my soberest suits I still feel frivolous and useless, a parasite.

Oh, yeah, I find myself thinking. Well, if you're all so wonderful, why did Saint Peter appear to me?

And then I look worse than frivolous, I look mad. I'm all by myself and laughing like a fool.

Friday night we do not work late. Friday night we get away as early as we can and meet by 7:00 at the latest at a big old pub on the high street. There is a wonderful Balti House across the way and whoever gets there first puts in the order and buys the beer. There are always guest beers, so we try one of each.

Tonight I'm so early that I go home to change first, since the neighbourhood is still a bit unfriendly to suits. As I sweep past the kitchen table to feed the cat, I see the cleaner's note. The striped princess is clamouring for her food, so I take the scrap of paper upstairs and end up shoving it in the pocket of my leather jeans as I grab bus pass, mobile, lipstick and keys and run down the street to meet Simon.

When I open the door to the Balti House they wave me away, so I know he has already ordered. As I stand there and wait for the traffic, I shove my hands into my jeans pockets and find the cleaner's note. I pull it out and look at it in the yellow light of the restaurant window.

> Miss
> There was terrible lot of sand in bedroom carpet. I think I get it all but you going to need new bags for Hoover.

A heavy weight settles on my head. My neck feels too weak to hold it all. There is also a crushing weight on my chest. I stare out into the passing traffic and allow the strip of paper to fall from my fingers and mingle with the crisp packets, newspaper pages and cauliflower leaves.

'I do not want to know,' I find myself saying. I just do not want to know.

Chapter Three

What happens to the weekends? Simon has been very, very kind to me this weekend. He has done all of the things he knows I like, both in and out of bed. I don't really understand it. Is it because of the rise in my pay-packet, the fact that I'm under a lot of stress? Has he realised that we need to work harder to save our relationship? I try to broach the subject several times, once at Katie and Steve's party, but I am deflected.

He just smiles at me, beam full on, dimple displayed. He's full of himself sexually these days. He reaches down the back of my dress where no one can see and subtly strokes the skin where my bra would be if I was wearing one. I hear Steve in the kitchen rummaging for more wine and Phil flushing the upstairs loo.

I've asked, 'Why are you giving in to me over everything?' and this is my answer.

And although I'm being pampered, I feel abandoned. There's just one of us here, I think. There's just my agenda. Where are you really and what did you do with yours?

I start my period on Monday morning. It's a strange terminology, I start. As if it is my choice, my action. When I see the blood, I start to cry, great tearing sobs coming from my throat. Simon has already gone to work. The cat comes in to see if I am alright. How can I explain to her when we spayed her? I feel guilty. We should have at least had one fertile thing in the house.

I locate silver tampon holder and load up for the day. Finish grooming. Case always seems heavy on Monday mornings.

The 7:45 train arrives without incident at Liverpool Street at 7:59, which these days is a bit of a minor miracle.

When I first moved to this town I used to love being in Liverpool Street station in the morning. For me it is the perfect example of how good British society can be. Consider this: There are people coming into the station by rail to connect to the Central Line to go West or the Circle Line to go South. There are people coming in from the West to go East, to Aldgate. And then, there are the people who are just coming into Liverpool Street, the Eastern edge of the Square Mile, the City, one of the busiest financial centres in the world.

All of them are walking as quickly as they can across vast expanses of white tile flooring under a huge, dwarfingly high arch of a ceiling. They are travelling in all different directions and even different trajectories in those directions. Now, nearly all these people are silent, and if they talk, they keep their voices down. All you can hear is the feet. Feet pounding and clicking, feet shuffling slightly to correct speed to avoid a collision. Because this is the amazing thing: No one runs into each other. No one shouts at each other.

In this chaos, co-operation reigns. There is nobody to enforce it, it just happens. We all watch out for each other. It is an impossibly complicated bit of choreography as we all dance through the space carefully, getting to work. London is getting to work.

Or not, as it happens. Once on the Central Line, the magic quickly disappears. Security alert at Holborn. We won't be stopping. Selfishly, this is fine for me, it means we will get into Tottenham Court Road that much quicker. Once past Chancery Lane, however, we wait in the tunnel for clearance while the squad checks out a 'suspect package'.

I think about the chances of a bomb actually going off while we are in the tunnel. I know that the 'suspect package' is probably only someone's lunch that they've left behind on the platform, but that doesn't stop the thought of flames licking down the side of the carriage, glass exploding. It doesn't matter how long you have travelled by tube, how many 'suspect packages' you hear about. You still think about it, if only for an instant.

It was my choice to move to London. Simon gave me a shortlist of New York, LA, Seattle, or London. All places where he could get a job and a career going. I hate New York and LA. Seattle's okay, and the hiking and biking and canoeing possibilities made it very attractive. But Simon is English and he has tons of friends here in London and since what he was trying to do was quite difficult I plumped for London.

I had no particular plans. I had been writing quite a lot then, placing some short stories in some good university magazines. I had been working on a novel. I don't really want to think about that. Anyway, Simon needed support, and financial support as well. So I started working at whatever I could find, making as much money as I could.

And so I am here, arriving at last at Tottenham Court Road Station. I have arrived, I think, as I check my immaculate black suit. I have arrived.

Monday morning hits me like an express train and before I know it it's eight o'clock. Post meridian. Another black cab for Maggie.

I sent Simon an email around noon, but I never heard anything back. The house is cold when I get home and while cat whines at me for her supper, I risk smart black jacket on the recycling while I let in more water to the central heating system and restart the boiler.

I remember spooning pasta out of an aluminium carton at some point in my last meeting, so that's okay. Although I know it will slow me down tomorrow, I can't face a bath. I wash my face and brush my teeth, light Simon's candle and fall into bed, to die more than to fall asleep. I am unconscious in mid-air as I lurch towards the pillow.

The looming presence is what wakes me up, I only smell water later. I pat the bed and he sits down.

28

'Hello,' is what I can think of to say.

Automatically, I have put out my hand. He takes it and holds it. I think my hands are my weak point. All those years of camping, waiting tables for a living, travelling third class in the third world, climbing - it takes its toll. All of the other female consultants have elegant, pampered hands. Mine always look rough.

But not compared to his. Compared to his, mine are Marie Antoinette's. It is almost like not feeling skin at all, like he has a rough glove on.

He senses what I am thinking. 'I worked with them,' he says. 'Not like your man. He uses just his head, keeps his fingers soft for you.'

He lets go of my fingers and traces a short line under my jaw with his forefinger and smiles. A shadow of fear stalks my heart, even now. I do not smile back. His touch was too sexual to belong to a saint.

'Don't be afraid. But I am only a man. I am sorry. You did not ask for me to be here.'

'Why are you here?'

A short, brisk sound is made through his nose. 'I wish I could tell you this. The Master sent me. To you I must come. I don't know why.'

I think I'm going to need my glasses for this. I scrabble them out of their case and push them on.

And then I see what he looks like.

It's Sean Connery. It's Sean Connery sitting on my bed, calling himself Saint Peter. I don't know why I didn't recognise him last night. I must have been half-asleep or something. And all that swimming around of features, it must have put me off. The accent! It's not Arabic. It's not Greek. It's his distinctive mix of West Highlands, Jermyn Street and Hollywood.

My head hurts.

Desperately, I try and continue the conversation. I half mumble, 'Jesus Christ sent you to visit me?'

And then I realise what I've said. Jesus Christ has sent Saint Peter to my bed?

Saint Peter shrugs his massive shoulders. 'Yes. This makes you unhappy?'

I gulp for a moment, trying to feel if I am unhappy, but all I feel is astonished. 'Why? And why do you look like Double O Seven?'

In answer, Peter grins. 'You like it? I try to find something you like.'

'What do you really look like?'

He says, 'This is not important,' but he must be able to see that it is to me, because he then says, 'I really look like a bag filled with crumbling bones.' He does that shrugging thing again. 'It's a velvet bag in a pretty box. Would you rather talk to that?'

My head doesn't just hurt. It's going to explode. 'You're dead. And you're using Sean Connery's body to...'

'No.' Peter cuts in decisively. 'No. I am not using his body. This man is using his own body. I am copying some things about him, that is all, in the image I am giving you.'

I put my hands around the top of my skull to try and hold everything in. 'It's all so complicated.'

He blows out his lips with a little puffing laugh. 'You can not imagine!'

'And you are doing all of this to speak to me? And it's important to Jesus? Why on earth is speaking to me all that important to Jesus Christ?'

Again the massive shoulders gesture. 'I do not know why.' He sighs. 'I never know why. Well, maybe, sometimes I do. But, Maggie, I do not know why I am to visit you. I only know that you called to the Master-'

The taxi, I think, Euston Road. 'But-' I start to say.

'He heard you.'

My head feels so heavy I can't possibly hold it up anymore. I sink down further into bed. 'I can't believe this,' I mutter.

'The Master believes that we need to spend time together. I do not know why.' And then Saint Peter slumps. He actually seems to shrink into himself. He starts to chew on his lip.

He stares at my bedroom wall as though it wasn't there, as though he could see ten thousand miles through it. He says, 'I do not know why,' again. I can suddenly believe he is two thousand years old. It's an even sadder and older look than Arthur in *First Knight*.

As pity goes out from my heart, he gives himself a brisk shake and, seeming to realise he is staring at my wallpaper, he turns back to me.

'So,' he says, 'how are things with you?'

This is ridiculous. How are things with me? I can almost get my head around Saint Peter coming to visit me. I can almost kind of deal with Sean Connery sitting on my bed to play him. But I don't think I can actually participate in it, if you know what I mean.

I know if I just hold my eyes closed for a moment, I will go back to sleep. Simon's candle is spitting. By its light I can see that it is only midnight. I am used to functioning on little sleep, but I need more than two hours. I take my time thinking about all this, incidentally wondering where Simon is.

'Look,' I say, 'it's great to see you and everything, and I'm terribly grateful to Jesus for making the arrangements and all, but I'm in the middle of something a bit special at work, and I really need to get my sleep.'

'This you do not have to worry about. There is no time when I visit you.'

'No time?'

'It would be hard to explain it. You maybe should trust me.'

And for some reason this makes me angry. 'Trust you? You've

31

just come into my bedroom, for what, three, four nights now? And now you tell me you're Saint bloody Peter and that Jesus sent you? And meanwhile, you've morphed into my favourite James Bond? I don't know why I haven't called the police!'

'So? Why are you not calling the police?'

'I don't know! You did something when you touched my shoulder.'

'And the robbers, they can do this thing, too? And robbers, they too can make themselves to look like your friend?'

His voice is heavy with irony, too heavy, too dramatic. Not civilised, not European. In a way, this makes me feel more at ease, as if we share our crudity from a common past.

I struggle against it, but then I am giggling. I say, 'Sean Connery is not my friend. He's a movie star.'

Saint Peter snorts through his nose and looks back out at my wallpaper. I seem to have embarrassed him.

'I'm sorry,' I say. 'The whole thing's just a bit-' I can't think of a word to fit it. I just waggle my hands around.

'I do not know why I am here,' he says again. 'But there is a reason. And if you will not work with me, then…'

He looks so sad that my hand automatically reaches out and rests on his leg. He looks at it lying there on his thigh and then looks into my eyes. It's like a shutter has gone up and I can see into him for the first time. There is an eternity of sorrow there, a burden made heavy not only by time but by sheer immensity. And I forget about how crazy the whole thing is. I just want to help him. I squeeze his thigh. I try to pass some energy to him, to give him some sort of help.

When his hand moves to mine, his eyes change. Now I also see something I haven't seen in a man's face for years, frank and open desire. He gently detaches my hand and pushes it towards me.

'I am only a man, Maggie. Think about what I see here. A beautiful woman in a warm bed. She has no clothing and her hair

32

is tumbled on her face. Her body is soft and glows of pink. It has known no sun, no hard labour.'

I start to protest about the sun and the labour, but the rough hand covers my lips softly.

'I see you and your man much apart. I see you are lonely. And then you touch me that way and I...' He sighs. 'This is not easy for me, Maggie. So...please.'

Abashed, I put my arms under the duvet and wriggle deeper, covering my shoulders. 'I was only trying to comfort you. You seemed so sad. Are you going to tell me that I am an occasion of sin?'

I smile, but he is not amused. 'It takes two to make the sin,' he said. 'You did not know how you tempted me.'

But I wonder. Even the thought of someone aroused merely by my hand on their leg makes me flush with pleasure, and perhaps with something more. The thought of the years of desire penned inside that powerful frame makes my stomach nearly cramp with want. And after all, it's Sean Connery. I can't remember a time before I fancied Sean Connery. I think as soon as I could focus my little eyes on a screen I fancied Sean Connery. Like millions of other women, I had no trouble whatsoever believing Catherine Zeta-Jones could fall for him in *Entrapment*.

I am glad to be able to squeeze my tampon. It gives me some relief.

Mentally, I give myself a shake. Saint Peter is sitting on my bed. He needs to talk to me on the orders of Jesus Christ. And all I can think about is what a good fuck he would be. What is wrong with me? I roll my eyes in exasperation, and the next thing I know the alarm is shrieking in my ear.

Chapter Four

'Good morning.'

Simon is leaning over me, stroking my hair out of my face. 'You were completely out of it when I got home. You still had your glasses on. I took them off for you.'

'Thanks. What time did you get home?'

He smiles. 'Late, I'm afraid. Had to be nearly eleven.'

I don't want to tell him that I know it was later. I don't want to have an argument. I want him to go on stroking my head. I want him to go on smiling at me. 'What about this new assistant?'

'Sandy.'

'Sandy. I thought it was all going to be easier, now, that you'd be home more.'

For an answer, he kisses me. It's lovely. I throw my arms around his neck and hold him tight. 'It's good to see you,' I say, and then, 'I started my period.'

His immediate expression of blissful relief is soon thoughtfully changed to disappointed concern. 'Don't worry about it,' he says. 'I certainly don't mind trying again.' I get another kiss.

'What time train are you catching?'

'I worked so late that I'm not going in until ten.'

This is excellent news. I use the telephone and leave a message for someone I was supposed to speak to this morning. I remember when I was an account handler how I could never get the consultants to speak to me on time. I suppose that I will just continue in this tradition. If I don't get into the office until ten o'clock today, I'll just have to somehow work harder to catch up. This is impossible, but I'll do it anyway.

We take the 73 into the Angel and have breakfast at Alfredo's, dirty great fry-ups. The staff still remember us from when we lived around the corner. When we used to be together all the time. When it didn't seem such hard work just to have a good time together for an hour. When my husband smiling at me didn't seem like some kind of a victory.

I smile back and put my hand on his leg under the table. I can feel the muscle tense with the effort of not pulling away.

My mobile rings. Anya. One of the partners wants to see me in a half an hour. Simon gets a quick, deep, sexy kiss that he seems to enjoy without too much effort and then I am running towards the green, backwards, looking for cabs.

Five or six hours later and I am deep into a meeting with Creative, who are currently having a problem with the tight perimeters of the brief. It is a delegation, really, headed by Roberto to try and get me to open up the client to another direction. We are an integrated agency, which means that the PR and the advertising are under one roof. Usually, the direction of a campaign is led by advertising, and I am more or less told how to approach a product. With this one it is the other way around, and I can tell that they're all uneasy about it.

I am trying to explain that it is the target market which is so closed, not the client, and therefore can not be 'opened up' for Roberto's great idea. Now they think it is just me standing in the way, and the pressure is starting to get heavy. I find that other women's attitudes towards their bleeding vaginas is not an easy subject for me to talk about in mixed company. This is laughable, really, but true.

As I listen to them warble amongst themselves, I realise I haven't changed my own tampon in perhaps too long and excuse myself. Down the hall to my office for my silver tampon case and then towards the ladies' loo. Anya ambushes me halfway and tells me that Simon will be home by eight tonight.

My hands shake as I reach for my tampon string, holding back my urine so that it doesn't explode all over my hand as the pressure of the tampon is released. There is blood on my yellow panties, a brown spot and a bright red one swimming in a paler pool of fluid. I mop at it with toilet paper while I release my urine in a grateful stream.

Simon will be home at eight. Well, isn't that nice for him. I will be home about midnight. I'm supporting Henry at a deodorant party, an early evening event, but knowing the journalists involved, likely to run much later. We've rented out a couple of hours of Madame Jo Jo's and booked four drag artistes. They'll be running through several energetic dance numbers, but their underarms will be fully protected by the product, which has a unisex scent. What better way to demonstrate that the product is fit for both a man and a woman? Stroke of genius on Henry's part. The journos have been fairly baying for tickets.

Insert tampon and stagger to the sink with my skirt up around my thighs and my panties around my knees. Wash self with paper towels to prevent any other stains. Luckily no one else comes in during this hasty operation. Wash hands, pull knickers up and skirt down. I'm ready for another four hours. Take case back to office and make telephone call to Simon. Sandy answers. Tell her that I have a function tonight I must have forgotten to mention and won't be home until late.

She is a bright, personable thing who always talks to me with much sympathy in her voice. She also seems actually interested in what I have to say about my scheduling and so I trust that this message will get through. I go back to Roberto and company in the pen. As I open the door, everybody looks up and I decide to press this natural advantage.

I walk to the table and don't sit down, I just lean with my fists supporting me and look at them until they all get quiet.

'Those of you,' I say, 'who have never had a bloody cunt and tried to get through the day might not know that it is highly

36

embarrassing, even to women like myself.' I am pleased to see them all wince.

I point to Roberto. 'How would you like to hear about my blood, Roberto?'

He puts up his hands in surrender, looking slightly sick.

'I can tell you what colour it is, how many clots it had today...'

Now they are all frankly grimacing. Several close their eyes.

'This campaign is for people much more squeamish than we are, and we can't even talk about the issues of the product amongst ourselves. Keep that in mind. I'll see you Thursday morning.' Dismissed.

In silence, they gather their belongings and depart. And I? I sit down for a minute and tell myself that I am utterly brilliant.

I am dealing with the caterers and the venue and the audio-visual folks so that Henry can concentrate on his star turn. Although I'm sat on Russell's left hand, I've left my mobile on vibrate in my lap and they all have the number. When the Ru Paul wannabe starts doing vintage Chaka Khan, the thing begins to shake like her hips and I, bent double to be unobtrusive, scurry out to the service hall.

It's Simon at the deli, wondering which pasta I would prefer for tonight.

I ask him if Sandy gave him the message that I left at four o'clock and he seems embarrassed to say that she didn't.

What can I do? My man goes silent on the other end of the connection. He hears the disco music blaring in the background.

'I'm working, Sweetie. I'm helping Henry deal with Russell. It's his first campaign launch and we've spent a small fortune. I've got to help make sure it goes well, and you know what these journalists are like once they've had a glass or eight.'

'I understand.' I can picture him in the doorway of the deli with one of their wicker baskets on his arm and his briefcase at his feet. He'll hang his head and kick at an imaginary ball. He'll have to shake his hair out of his eyes.

'I would much rather be with you. I would much rather be having pasta tonight with you than be here.'

The connection is crystal clear. I wouldn't think the reception would be so good here. I can even hear him sigh. 'I know,' he says. And then that lovely connection is severed and I get to crawl back to my seat and beam at the utterly delighted Russell.

It's one o'clock when I finally crawl into bed. My candle is looking very small and I remind myself to change them on Saturday. Simon is laying curled up in a ball. He has pushed his pillows off onto the floor and instead is resting his head on his bicep. The duvet has slipped around his chest. I tiptoe around the bed and rescue his pillows. By just nudging his neck with them, he realises on some level that they're there and rolls over, towards my side, pulling the pillows under his head. I then cover him up, and tiptoe back around. I ease myself under the duvet and die of exhaustion.

Two hours later, I start to surface. I whimper, 'I need more sleep than this.'

'I have told you. I am not stealing your sleep. There is no time in a visitation. Everything stops.'

I yawn and reach for my glasses. 'What do you mean everything stops? The whole world stops so that you and I can have these little chats?'

'World?' He sniffs. 'More than that.'

I settle my glasses on the bridge of my nose, thinking that I really should clean them one of these years. There he is again, Sean Connery, in my bedroom and looking worried.

'Why are you doing all this to see me?'

'You know I can not tell you this.'

I tuck the covers firmly under my arms and settle back into the

38

pillows. 'I still find it hard to believe that you are Saint Peter...let alone that you are here, on bequest of the Host of Hosts, to ask how my day went.'

Sean Connery's face folds itself into a grimace. 'I think you should just call him Jesus.'

'That seems a little informal for the Son of God.'

'Please.'

'Okay, Jesus,' I say. He stands up and paces the two steps my bedroom allows and back again. He is rubbing his sternum and looking worried again, and I begin to feel guilty.

'Oh,' he says. 'You do not know how this kind of thing...'

I can feel his anguish almost palpably, almost like another presence in the room. I still want to help him. I still don't know how. I pat the bed again and he sits down. 'Perhaps it would be better if you wore some old clothing to bed,' he says.

I've done it again, flashed my tits. I snuggle down under the duvet, apologising.

He gives me a brief smile and looks away to collect himself. After awhile he says, 'I need your help to find why I am here with you.'

'What do you need me to do?'

'I don't know.'

'Great.'

We look at each other for a moment. I can see from his expression that his real body must also have had deep lines incised on the forehead. He finally says, 'We will have something in common, some problem or something.'

'We will?'

He opens his hands in reply.

'Well, what do you know about me so far?' I ask.

'That you are beautiful. That you have trouble with this man. That you work very hard.'

Of the three, the latter seems to be the safest topic. 'Yes,' I say, 'but it isn't always like this, my work. I'm in the middle of a product launch.'

He thinks for a moment and his forehead contracts again.

'Launch,' he finally says, 'is putting a boat in the water, is it not?' His face suddenly clears. 'Do you help with fishing boats?'

I hate to say no. 'No,' I say, 'it's nothing about fishing or boats. It's a metaphor, I guess. I am helping to put a brand new product, a brand new thing, on the market, in front of all the people in this country.'

This is clearly less than helpful. He jumps to his feet and begins pacing around my bed in a horseshoe pattern, rubbing his sternum again. 'What is this brand new thing?'

'It's a tampon.'

He looks blank.

And I really don't like having to say, 'It's for women? When they bleed? It goes inside them to absorb the blood so that-'

He holds up one hand. His eyes are closed. The look of disgust on his face is so strong I think he might vomit. My voice trails off.

After a while he opens his eyes and swallows. 'This is unclean to me,' he says.

'What do you mean?'

'Menstruation.' He gulps again like he's just had half a kebab on top of ten pints of lager. Again, the hand goes up in front of his chest, as if he's warding the subject off. 'My people,' he finally manages, 'find it unclean.'

'You mean half your people,' I say coldly, and at this his head jerks up and his eyes open, again giving his face that sudden luminous clarity. He drops his other fingers and just holds up his index finger now, raising it in front of his face.

'Ah!' he says, and there is great hope in his voice. 'This is no doubt true!' He waits for a moment and then slumps against my footboard. 'True,' he mutters, 'but not true enough, clearly.'

Defeated, the actor playing Saint Peter drags himself around

40

the bed and sits down heavily by my hips. I toy with the idea of telling him I'm bleeding right now, but decide I can't be so cruel.

I say, 'What did you think would happen? Are you just going to go whoosh when we get it right?'

He gets very serious. 'I am not allowed to tell you this,' he says.

'Oh, pooh.' He raises one eyebrow at me. Was this one of his requirements for a body as well? White hair, white beard, dark eyes and a trick eyebrow? No wonder it took him so long to find something suitable.

I say, 'Well, I don't understand any of this. You were obviously hoping something would happen when your did you "Eureka!" pose just then.'

This makes him smile. Of course he knows what I meant by 'Eureka'. My little joke is closer to his time and culture than to my own. Or does he get some cultural references along with the body? Thinking like this makes my head hurt again.

He says, 'Maggie, I am here to learn something. You are here to learn as well.'

'What do you mean by "here"?' I ask. 'Do you mean here in this bed "here", or here in whatever kind of time warp you've got going "here", or do you mean here on earth "here"?'

He makes that blowing gesture with his lips. 'Well,' he says, 'I think it is all three.'

I think about that for a moment, trying to ignore the chilling of my spine this information brings. 'Is everybody on earth here to learn something?'

He shrugs this one off. 'Of course. When the Master came back from India…' he begins, but I'm not with him.

'Jesus was in India?'

'Yes, of course. When the Master came back from India…'

'When? When was Jesus in India?'

He puffs again. 'Maybe fifteen, sixteen years. Why?'

'Why did he go to India? Hell, how did he get to India? It's not like there were regularly scheduled flights, were there?'

'There was the Silk Route. It was not that uncommon. He went with his uncle, Mary's brother. You know, after the trouble at the temple in Jerusalem. Mary thought he would be better off out of the reach of the elders for awhile.'

'All I remember is something about money changers.'

The saint makes an impatient gesture. 'No, when he was twelve,' he says, 'and anyway, this is not important. What I am trying to tell you is that when the Master came back from India, he had much knowledge about how we learn here, how we come here to learn.'

He keeps talking, but I'm not with him. This whole thing is getting more and more bizarre. If this is all coming out of my imagination, then I am either a creative genius or completely insane. It's too weird to even be a dream. I refuse to waste any more time on this nonsense, I think, and I close my eyes.

'Maggie?'

Simon is leaning over me, concern furrowing his brow.

'Hiya,' I say, stretching. 'What's up?'

'You didn't hear the alarm.'

'Oh.' I drape one arm around his neck. 'Sorry. And sorry again about last night. I'm surprised that Sandy didn't tell you.'

'It's been really busy. I think she forgot.' His eyes grow, if anything, more open and loving as he says this. I slide my hand down his back, feeling it tense as I go. He can't lie with all of his body yet, only his eyes. This makes mine fill with tears.

'Don't.' Simon slides to lay by my side, pillowing his head on my shoulder. 'Don't let's, Maggie, okay?'

I try to agree, but all that comes out of my throat is a croak. My neck feels wet, and I realise I am crying. Simon makes a small sound and I feel a small trickle also in my left armpit. He is crying, too.

76 to the 38. 38 to the Angel. Change for the 73. All in a dream, all in a daze. I am reading nothing. I am not even sure what I am wearing. I'm not completely convinced that I am here, that I am alive. I love Simon and Simon loves me. I know this as much as I know anything else in the world. So, what, exactly is happening? What in the world is happening to us?

The 73 arrives and when I come to, I am in the middle of a stream of people, all getting on the bus around me. I almost don't even get a seat. Just as I open my case to fish out my diary, which I forgot to check this morning, my telephone rings. Simon.

'What time can you be home?' he asks.

'You must be psychic. I'm just checking my diary.' I look at it critically. 'Seven, if I push.'

'Push.'

'Okay. We aren't going to have a big talk, are we?'

'Oh, God, no. I thought we could go to Meditterano. If they've got a table, should we go straight there?'

I ache for time at home, in front of the fire, but he is trying so hard that I do, as well. 'Let me know if they don't,' is what I say. 'Otherwise I'll see you there.'

'I love you, Maggie.'

'I know,' I nearly wail. Half the bus turns to look at me. 'Me, too, you know.'

'Okay,' is what he says. 'Okay.'

One of the partners grabs me in the hall. 'I hear you're pretty good at getting your point across to Creative,' he says, smiling. 'I've always found a gun works well with Roberto.'

This is meant as a big compliment, and I smile in a way I hope comes across as deprecating. 'Roberto is brilliant,' I say. 'He does want a bit of extra management time, though, doesn't he?'

'He wants a choke chain. Good work.'

'Thank you, Quentin.'

43

What with that and my date with Simon, I fairly dance through my day. Extra energy seems to come from nowhere, and I am juggling all of my balls effortlessly. I have even kept on top of both my tampon and my email account, so that when I cut out the door at six with Anya, both my conscience and my panties are spotless.

It's sardine city on the Central Line platform at Tottenham Court Road. No problem, I'll take the 73 instead. I run up the stairs only to find that traffic is strangely stationary. Down to the corner, where I can scope out approaching buses. They're too far away to see the numbers, but I can tell the distinctive, rounded shape of the Routemasters from miles away. And there aren't any.

Back down to the Central Line, I think. I push through a crowd of German students consulting maps on the corner and shoulder my way into a mass of people congregating outside the locked tube stairs. Stupidly, I stare at the gate for a few moments, I guess because I think it shouldn't really be there. Then it's back through the crowd to peer at the other entrances. All of them also have crowds gathering. Bad news. It's not just the platform then, it's the trains.

In the middle of this, I am vaguely aware of a disturbance – someone extra shouting. It's two men on the corner, arguing over a taxi. Traffic is still inching both ways, and it's the only cab in sight. There are several strategies here, but time is awasting. It's already 6:15. I dig out my mobile to ring Simon's, but he must be in a tunnel. I leave a message, 'Darling, chaos reigns at Tottenham Court Road. I'll be there as soon as poss.'

I evaluate and discard several strategies and then ring the taxi firm that the office uses. We spend a fortune with them every year, and you can hear the dispatcher cringing as she informs me that it's at least an hour's wait. So, it's a walk, but which way? There's a lot of hotels in Russell Square. I reckon a tourist might be getting out of a cab somewhere around there, and if not, I can always hit Kings Cross for a taxi or a bus or even a tube up the Angel and then a bus. I'm already walking.

There's four of us doing this right now, but I'm the only woman, the only one doing it in kitten heels. The guy ahead is about fifty, in perfectly cut pinstripes. He is really moving and I'm struggling to keep him in sight, because I figure he'll know all the tricks. Two guys follow me, and I'm trying to make sure they don't pass me, that they don't get the taxi I know will be waiting for me there. Under my mac, I hitch up my tight skirt and start to motor.

I arrive at Meditterano at seven-thirty. In the cab I have reapplied lipstick and aired my sweaty silk blouse the best I can. It's a slow night in a small restaurant. It doesn't take me long to see that Simon's not there. 'Are you Mrs. White?' an elegant young person asks me, and I nod.

'Your husband had to go home, he said you might find him there.'

I nod, smiling tightly. Might? I might find him there? My cab is still waiting to pull out into Church Street. I engage him again, dialling the home number as I crawl into the back.

When Simon answers, for a moment I don't know what to say. He has to say hello twice. 'It's me,' is what I come up with.

'Where are you?'

'I've just left the restaurant. I'm in a cab.'

A long pause.

'Did you get my message?'

'Yes, it was crazy at the office. It's always crazy at your place, Maggie.'

By now we are in front of the house, and I fish out another fiver to the cabbie. 'Simon, you idiot, it wasn't the office that was crazy. It was the transport. There wasn't any.'

Another silence. I am fumbling with my keys. 'I left the office

45

at six, with the secretaries. Tottenham Court Road station was closed and there weren't any buses. I can't tell you how hard I worked to be here anywhere near time.'

Nothing is coming from the phone. I walk up the stairs until I see him in the bedroom, standing with the phone in one hand and a pile of shirts in the other. 'Simon?' I say.

'I'm still here.'

Another turn in the spiral also lets me see the open suitcase on the floor. 'But only just,' I say, and he turns around to face me. We both still have the phones to our heads.

'Yes,' he says. 'Only just.'

My legs give way and I sink down to sit on the floorboards again. I can't stop looking at him with the shirts in his hand. Finally, I realise that the phone is still on and I remove it from my ear and switch it off.

Simon has crouched down next to me. The shirts are now on the chair. Not in the suitcase, but then, not quite back in the drawer yet, either. Two fat tears ooze out of each of my eyes. 'Jesus, Simon,' I say, 'It was only thirty minutes.'

He commits himself to sitting on the floor with me. My hopeful heart sees this as a good sign. 'Only thirty minutes,' he echoes. 'But when it's the hundred and fiftieth time…'

I look in his eyes. If it was a suffering competition, I think I would be losing. He seems much, much more unhappy than I am. 'You're so unhappy,' I say stupidly.

He nods. 'Yeah, I know.'

'Why?'

'Let's order a pizza. Let's go downstairs. Take your suit off. I'll open some wine.'

'Will you tell me then?' I sound about ten years old, but I can't help it.

My husband tells me yes and leans over to wipe under both my eyes.

'And,' my chin collapses and I struggle to speak, 'and will you put your shirts back in the drawer?'

His expression hardens slightly, and I hurry to amend, 'Just for now?'

'Just for now.'

My hand shakes as I light the fire, but Simon is in the kitchen dialling a pizza and doesn't notice. I can't believe that I've stayed calm, that I'm not absolutely going mad. I feel like if I start to go mad he won't talk to me and what I want most in the world is for Simon to talk to me. If he only talks to me I feel sure I can put this right. But I also hear the phone go down softly, as my husband dials another number to explain, I know (I think I always knew), why he's not moving in with Sandy tonight.

It's a gas fire. The flames dance blue for the first half hour, and the pattern they make is the same, not interesting, not like a real fire. I watch them anyway.

A glass of white comes over my shoulder. 'I thought we'd start with this,' he said. 'It'll be a half an hour before the pizza arrives. I've got a Super-Tuscan left for that.'

All I say is, 'Thank you.' Again, he looks unfeasible handsome to me, unnaturally attractive. It is as if I am falling in love with him again, now, when it's too late.

He sits down opposite me on the rug. 'It's been a couple of years since I've been happy,' he says. 'And I haven't wanted to talk to you about it because I guess even I can see it's not fair.'

'What's not fair?'

He takes a sip of wine, which spills his hair forward. He takes his time smoothing it back. 'I wanted you to get a job. You know. Four years ago. I wanted you to work at something steady. I know that.'

'Well...' I'm surprised by how much thinking about that time hurts.

'I guess I just didn't think you'd do so well.'

I was taking a sip when he said that and started to laugh, choking myself. 'Oh, thanks,' I say with sarcasm as I cough.

Simon reminds me that this isn't easy, you know, and I compose myself. 'Well, what did you think would happen?'

'I thought you'd, I don't know, type or something for a couple of years and then when I was making more money, quit.'

'And?'

'Oh, hell, Maggie. Have babies, I guess, go back to writing for fun. Do whatever you used to do.'

'And instead?'

'Instead you did brilliantly and made a great career. You've got a job that about ten thousand people want, you've bought us this house.'

'I sense a but.'

'But I hate it. I never see you anymore. And when I do, you're all, I don't know. You're different. You used to be so soft and sweet and now you're all hard.' There is a long pause while I try to let myself die. 'Don't cry,' he says. 'Oh, Maggie, please don't cry.'

As if I could help it. 'I was just doing what you wanted. You were the one that always needed nice things. You were the one that used to sniff at my clothes.' I don't feel like I'm breathing. 'Simon, you were the one that complained that our flat was too small. That was all you.'

Simon stumbles to his feet and turns to the window. 'I told you it wasn't fair,' he said. 'But I still can't help it.'

'And with Sandy you could have a nice soft sweet woman again?'

'Don't.'

I know that he will walk out if I keep on. I don't want him to go. I think that I might be able to breathe if I get flat, so I lay back on the rug and stare up at the ceiling that cost me seven hundred pounds to plaster.

'Babies?' I say. 'I don't know that I could want them any more than I do.'

'And then pop them into a nursery and go back to the office?'

'We have enough room for a nanny. I could take out a loan and fit another shower room.'

'What about that?' Simon comes back from the window. He hasn't been looking for the pizza, he's been crying. 'Won't that be great? We'll be able to see them on the weekends. They won't be people to us, they'll just be another logistical problem.'

'Well, what do you want me to do about it?' I can't help it, the pain bubbles over and I'm crying heatedly now, angrily dabbing at my eyes with the backs of my hands. 'This life wasn't my idea, Simon. I've just been trying to make you happy. I've spent the last ten years of my life trying to make you happy.'

'Well, you must be pretty crap at it.' This is a joke and I recognise it and hold out my arms. Silently, Simon comes into them and we sit like that, in front of the fire, waiting for inspiration and for Pizza Go-Go.

But we only got one of them.

'Your eyes are swollen.'

I don't open the eyes in question. 'Is that you?'

And Sean Connery's voice answers, 'Yes, Maggie.'

Bloody hell. 'Can we skip tonight?'

'Did he beat you?'

'What?' I start to laugh. Amazingly, I am laughing, and in thanks I reach for my glasses. 'No, Simon doesn't beat me.' The events of the evening come back and my laughter cuts out like a flooded engine. 'I imagine he wants to sometimes, though.'

'Do you not want to talk tonight?'

'I'm awake now.' I put on my glasses. Who I suppose I will have to admit is Saint Peter is sitting on the edge of my bed, looking composed. This is, I remind myself, a fairly rare opportunity.

And to be honest, I welcome the distraction. Simon's complaints still ring in my ears. I can hear him snoring softly next to us, but I don't want to look at him. I drink some water out of my bedside bottle. The Father of Our Church watches it slide down my throat.

'So, do you think we're getting close? To whatever it is?'

The Fisher of Men blows out his lips. 'Maybe,' he says, and then, seeing the expression this engenders on my face, 'No. I do not.'

I push my hair out of my face. I feel a bit guilty for not taking him more seriously. 'Look,' I start. 'I haven't been much help, here. Let me tell you about what I do for a living, okay?'

Peter nods, and I'm away. I simplify the agency structure, but I pretty much get across just what we do for clients on the PR side. He asks a few questions here and there, but he is remarkably quick on the uptake for someone who comes from a time and place so far away.

'...and then the sales will tell us whether or not we got it right,' I finish.

The saint is sucking his teeth, thinking. 'What if the thing itself is not a good thing?' he asks. 'If it is not a good thing, then people will not buy it anyway, will they?'

'Ah!' I say with enthusiasm. 'I have to depend on my bosses not to take on a duff product. But if we do by mistake, if the initial...' I've learned how Peter looks when he's puzzled and amend this, '...if people buy it to try it and then never buy it again because they don't like it, then that's still a success for me, you see? I got them to try it. Then it's up to the people who make the thing to be sure it's good enough for people to buy again.'

'So you do not make anything yourself.'

'No.'

'You just talk about someone else's work.'

'Yes.'

50

Peter swallows and looks at the floor. 'Maggie,' he says, 'I think I know why I am here.'

My jaw drops open. 'Jesus surely didn't send you to me in my capacity of a public relations consultant.'

Peter is silent. 'Peter?' my voice screeches on the last syllable.

'Do not call me this,' he says. 'Call me Rock.' His eyes still haven't left my floorboards.

'Rock, what has this got to do with me being a PR?' The whole idea makes me so uncomfortable I want to crawl out of my own skin.

He turns to face me, the luminous clarity in his face somewhat dimmed by an expression of misery. 'This, too, was my work,' he said. 'And very bad at it I was.'

I make a sound which comes out like, 'Whaaaaaaaaa?'

Peter stands up and begins to pace. 'The Master entrusted me with the word,' he said. 'He gave me transmission. You know?'

I can't say anything. I can barely hear him. This must be what it's like to be a dog or a cat or some other animal without a complex neo-cortex. Peter is making sounds, but they're not really registering anywhere because my brain has shut down.

'I made mistakes, Maggie. Many, many mistakes. And the word was changed, was lost. And now it is dying. This is my fault, do you understand?'

I nod, but I'm lying. I might understand later, if I have a brain again, but right now I'm just kind of storing what he says to think about then.

Peter sits down and takes my hand. Warmth flows up my arteries, in the returning blood. I can feel my arm, and then my shoulder and then my chest. My head clears.

'You're saying you were Jesus's PR man.'

'Yes, Maggie.'

'You're saying you were crap.'

He drops my hand and jumps to his feet to pace a few more

times. Finally he says, 'When I had my father's boat, Andrew and I worked together with our men. I could feel the wood under my hand. I could feel the ropes of my nets. The fish were alive in my hands, their blood ran down my arms.' He's holding up his hands as though he could feel it still.

It's my turn to grimace.

'It was a real thing, Maggie. You know?'

I suddenly recall waiting the lunch shift at Lake Yellowstone Hotel, in the middle of two and a half million acres of wilderness, how heavy the tray was, how the ketchup bottle I had stuffed in my skirt pocket banged against my hip. I say, 'I know.'

'And then, so quickly, the Master was gone and I had this other work, and what was it? It was just words, this work. And it was more slippery than a fresh catch. Nothing, nothing I could hold onto. You know?'

It strikes me that even in my weakened state I know exactly what he's talking about. PR is unsubstantial, no doubt about it. You're playing with rumours and shadows, trying to create something out of nothing, weaving air into illusions of stability. Not a reasonable career move for a fisherman, really.

And I thought *I* took a big risk, getting into the business.

I take one of his huge pumice paws and pull him back down to sit. 'I know,' I say. 'Of course I know.'

His eyes look into mine, and the burden of his sorrow is so heavy, that even to witness it makes me feel as if a lead weight has been placed on the top of my head. Still holding his hand, I lie down to think about all this. 'Give me a second,' I say, 'I need to think.'

And then the alarm drills into my ear.

Coming out of the shower, I see Simon shaving. 'Do you think we ought to go to Relate or something?' I say.

He thinks about it, face half foam, half skin. 'I don't know,' he says. 'It seems to me that we can talk to each other pretty well. This is just a logical problem, really. I mean, this is economics, really, isn't it?'

It is on the tip of my tongue to ask him if fucking his assistant is a logical solution. But I can see his eyes begging me to agree with him. 'Okay,' I say. 'So do you think we'll find an answer?'

'I don't know.' The razor drips a gobbet of foam onto his foot and he turns back to the mirror.

I don't really know how I got to the escalator in the Angel. My umbrella is out of my bag and collapsed, yet unfurled, its cord around my wrist. It drips, so it must be raining. I am standing on the right, so that's okay. I don't even think about running down the stairs. My watch shows that it's only 7:30 and that means I must have a morning meeting. I don't know what it is. I'll check my diary on the Northern Line, and decide whether or not to take the Victoria Line at Euston.

I think I probably have to face the fact that I'm having a nervous breakdown. The whole thing is just too much for me, would be too much for anyone. The strange dreams about Saint Peter are growing more and more upsetting. On the other hand, what if it's true? What if it really is Saint Peter, using the image of Sean Connery to talk to me on behalf of Jesus Christ about his PR problems? This is so ridiculous that it makes me smile and I make an effort to pull myself together, to take this minute advantage of feeling a fraction better and run with it, into my work and away from everything else.

I realise I am late on the train. I'm supposed to be meeting with the Creative team and my two Account handlers for an all day session which I have stressed is vital. This is when Roberto comes up with the goods. This is when they are to get the lead out. It's supposed to start at 8:00 and I will have to run like hell to be in the meeting room in time. I charge down Oxford Street like a woman possessed and blast by Anya at the desk, who is saying someone called and it's urgent. I just cannot deal with any more shit today, I think, tossing my mac into a corner of my office and grabbing a plastic wallet full of notes. I was going to collate them last night, but left early. I was going to collate them this morning, but I forgot.

I spend thirty seconds smoothing my hair and slowing my breathing and then walk down the hall.

At 9:45 I realise they've got it. A mail out, combined with advertorials in *Bella*, *Take a Break*, *New Woman* and *Look*. Promos. Shelf wobblies for the supers. No TV, no radio, no outdoor. Softly, softly. Roberto shows me some lovely wispy images which none of us like, but which we all reckon are the business. Anne's got the bones of copy and a few slogan ideas. It's lunchtime, now, and we buzz out for sandwiches.

At four o'clock I get back to my office and immediately grab my tampon case and head for the toilet. I don't even want to tell you the state my knickers are in. I remind myself of the existence of pantyliners for perhaps the fortieth time, muttering it while I mop up as best I can. Finally I make it into my office for long enough to utilise the chair.

It's the first time I can remember sitting down since the Victoria Line. My email notifier is flashing like Las Vegas, and there is a big post-it in Anya's handwriting on the screen. 'Call Simon, Urgent!' I look at the corner, where 8 am is neatly noted inside a circle. Fuck. Fuck, fuck, fuck!

I ring his direct line and almost faint with relief when I hear his voice. 'It's me,' I say and listen to him breathe. 'I just got your message. I've been in a meeting all day. What's up?'

He sighs. 'Nothing, I guess. I was just thinking about Relate again on the train and rang them. They had a free appointment this afternoon, but nothing again for a month.'

'What time this afternoon?'

'It's too late, Maggie.'

I fumble for the water bottle on my desk and undo the cap. I feel my throat closing off and water helps with that. 'What time was it for?'

'That's not what I'm talking about. It's just too late, I think.'

Anger slams into me without warning. I push it down my throat with the water, and try to speak in even tones. 'You only told me what was wrong last night, Honey. Don't you think you're being a little unfair?'

'You're doing it again, talking like a children's television presenter.'

The tempo of his breathing increases. We sit and listen to each other fume. Then he puts the phone down. If I start to cry, that will be it. They will find me in here and I will be off to some nice place with good food and plenty of Prozac. I can feel my sanity as a thin filament, stretched to breaking, like a trout line hooking a salmon.

Ah, Alaska. Where our only dangers were glaciers and bears, things you could get to grips with. My window looks out onto a light well. In the offices of the engineers opposite, three men look up as they see me highlighted against the glass, backlit from my desklight. It's already getting dark. Fall. I seem to have missed it. Kodiak would be colder than hell right now. I sit back down and click on my emails.

At 8:00 I realise that I am no longer able to do any constructive work. I also need food.

Oxford Street is busy with late night shoppers. I round the corner slowly and find myself staring into Knickerbox. A nightgown. I'll buy a nightgown. I don't feel like being naked and vulnerable in my bed anymore, and besides, Saint Peter asked me to put something on. I sift through textures, colours and take an armful back to their little closet of a dressing room. Although I look to me as if I am about to collapse, I am still good looking. My hair is thinner, but it was too thick anyway, and the tears which are always threatening these days make my eyes shine.

I have just bought a nightgown for a hallucination. What if the apostle was a client? What if I was bringing his business into the office? Would I be so easy to convince? So eager to please?

Back in my now-familiar daze, I go back to the office, speaking briefly with the cleaner as I come in. Mine is the only light on, now, nine o'clock on a Thursday night. My modem seems loud in the empty suite of offices, with only Demeter's vac humming in the background. Right, search engine. Jesus, India comes up with four pages for missionaries. What am I doing? In disgust, I push off the PC without exiting the system or shutting down. That will slow things down tomorrow.

The cab service apologises again. I'm going to have to speak to Anya about this, they've let me down now two nights on the trot. Bag, case, mac, and Knickerbox carrier secured about my person, I scurry back down Oxford Street. At Tottenham Court Road, I veer into Waterstones without telling myself about it and head straight for the religion section. I'll buy a Bible, I think, at least keep track of what I *do* know. As I scan the forty or so different varieties of holy truth on offer, a table stack catches my eye. When I see the title, the shop starts to spin. In two inch letters on the cover it reads 'Jesus Lived In India'.

Chapter Six

'Are you alright, miss?' I'm sitting on the floor in Waterstones, belongings strewn in everyone's way. A member of staff has my elbow.

'I'm sorry,' I say, thus immediately establishing my sanity. In England, I discovered years ago, whenever anyone speaks to you, the first thing you do is apologise. 'I haven't eaten and I came over funny.'

He smiles and hauls me to my feet. If I'd been wearing something else it might have been different, but in my Joseph trouser suit, my explanation is taken at face value. After wolfing down a Subway sandwich from next door, I flag a cab on the corner and remember my own address without any help from anyone.

Pay cabbie. Open door. Feed cat. Take great care with clothes, contacts and teeth. Cut tags off nightgown and brush hair one hundred times, leaving masses on the brush. Don't light Simon's candle. Burrow down into bed as though I could squirm through it to somewhere better with enough effort. I wake up again, and from the level of darkness when I open my eyes, it must be about three. I come out of my sleeping curl and lie on my back, yawning.

Someone clears their throat.

He is standing by the window, the way he did when he first came to visit me.

'Maggie?' he says. 'Are you alright?'

I pat the bed. 'Please sit down.'

His face lights up with a sudden and blinding smile. 'Last night, you asked me to wait and then...I waited for a while.'

'I'm sorry. I fell asleep.'

'I realised that after a time, yes.'

'Sorry.'

Saint Peter shrugs and comes to sit down on the bed. We look at each other for a moment. I think I'm getting used to the whole Sean Connery thing. It doesn't hit me quite as hard tonight. He looks more ordinary tonight, more harmless. Kind of like he did in *Indiana Jones and the Last Crusade*.

I say, 'Sorry,' again and Peter sighs, staring out at my light socket.

'Can you see anything?'

'Hmm?'

I take his hand and give it a bit of a tug. 'You're always staring through my wallpaper. Can you see something?'

Peter looks surprised. 'I did not think it was so… obvious,' he says.

'That's not an answer.'

He cocks his head on one side and considers for a bit. Finally he answers, 'Yes. Yes, I see things.'

'What kinds of things?'

He shrugs his massive shoulders. I'm sure he's meatier than Sean Connery. And I'll bet Connery's manicurist would faint dead away if she saw his hands in the kind of state Peter's are in. 'Things from my past,' he says, after another long pause.

'Like a movie?'

His eyes narrow. He reaches out and lays one of his unkempt hands on my head. It strikes me that this isn't the first time he's done this. It also strikes me that when he can't be bothered to ask me something, he just reaches out and trawls about in my brain.

It doesn't hurt or anything. In fact it feels kind of nice. It's the blessing pose, I recognise. I suppose I'm receiving a blessing every time he does it. Maybe it'll give me some time off in purgatory.

Saint Peter snorts, laughing. 'Maggie,' he says, 'hold your thoughts still. I can not concentrate when you are being funny.'

This serves to pretty much stop me dead in my tracks. I can't think of anything. I'm too busy gulping air like a beached guppy.

'Yes,' he says at length, taking his hand away.

'Yes, what?'

'Yes, it is like a movie, what I see.'

I stare at him for a moment, still doing my guppy impersonation. Slowly, I close my mouth. And then open it to ask, 'Can you show me?'

Peter stands up and starts pacing the floor again. He's also muttering again in that guttural tongue he uses when he's cursing. He flings out one hand and looks at it, muttering a steady stream and then flings out the other one and mutters some more, with a rising inflection. I think he might be about to explode.

'Forget about that,' I say. 'I'm sorry I asked. Come sit down.'

Obediently, Saint Peter comes to sit back down on my bed. He sighs and rubs his eyes.

'When you were talking about being in public relations-'

He makes his little puffing sound. 'Yes, and how I failed in it.'

I think about the huge stack of bibles in Waterstones and say, 'You know, Rock, I think that's bullshit. It was probably the most successful product launch in the history of the world.'

He rubs his eyes again, this time with such force that an opthamologist would have told him off.

I say, 'Well?'

'Oh!' is the answer. He groans. 'You know nothing, Maggie. The Master says that you can help me, but…there is so much that you do not know!'

I think about this for a moment. I actually enjoy these visits. I think it's the only time I really relax. I say, 'It's not like we've got time constraints, is it? And look!' I sit up and pull down the covers, 'Ta da!'

His brow instantly furrows. 'What is this?'

'Look,' I say again, hauling at the straps, 'a nightgown. I bought it for you. You know, for our talks.'

His laugh is far too big for my little bedroom. The Apostle laughs long and hard, and I start to feel, entirely at my expense. When he stops, he wipes his eyes and sees that I am hurt. 'Oh, Maggie,' he says. 'I am sorry. But you buy this thing, for why? To hide your nakedness from me, so that I do not desire you?'

'Well…yeah.'

His face and posture change. He's not harmless any more. Now he looks like *Entrapment* again, with that same smouldering sexuality. The merest breath of air could bring it into flame.

He says, 'Have you no glass, Maggie? It is so soft, this cloth, that my hands itch to touch it. The colour is the same as your eyes. And I still know that there is a warm woman inside of it. If you are more comfortable, I am happy, but if this is to make me more comfortable, to make me want you less, it is a failure.'

Joy rushes into my heart with such force I find it hard to breathe. Guiltily, I glance over at Simon, but he is not there.

'Your man did not come home tonight.'

The answerphone is blinking, but I don't really want to hear the excuse. On some level the pain registers, to be dealt with later. I shrug my shoulders. 'I see,' I say, trying to hold onto the joy which rapidly leaks out of my heart.

'Maggie, I come here because this work is important. It is not easy for me. And it will not be easy for you.'

I don't hear this, but I do see the old pain on his face. With the nightgown I can sit up when I want. I want to now, I want to touch him.

I want to help him, I tell myself, but really I just want to tap into the warmth of his desire. I reach out for him and my hand goes to cradle his face. There is a sharp intake of breath on his side, which is echoed on mine as a flush begins in my chest. I drop my hand from his cheek, but it lands on his massive shoulders and I can't help myself from then on, I close my eyes and reach out my other hand, stroking the mass of his shoulders and arms.

They are like stone. He truly is a rock. The chest now, the slit of his garment reveals a shocking contact of oiled skin, then the biceps. My hands stroke down, to where the massive chest tapers into a waist. Suddenly my hands are captured by the pumice of his own. He has stopped me.

I open my eyes to find him gazing into them. A long, long minute passes. Some part of me is screaming, What are you doing? But it is faint, in the heat of his eyes. 'Maggie,' he says, but I don't care what he has to say, I don't care about anything now, but this.

Kneeling on the bed in front of him, I press my lips to his. His hands are on my shoulders now, the rough skin catching on the nylon. I make a mental note to invest in silk and then I realise he is pushing me away.

'Sit down, Maggie!' His voice thunders in my tiny bedroom and I am suddenly afraid. He stands up and paces around the bed. 'Woman, you do not know what you are doing. You are so eager to please me...'

The pain hits me first below the notch of my throat. It burns. It is nothing to do with Peter, or what he is saying, not really. Simon did not come home. He did not come home tonight. I know that there's nothing really wrong, that he isn't hurt. I would have felt that somehow. Still, I twist out of bed and go into the study to hit the answerphone button.

He's been drinking. I would say this is a five glass or three pints voice. Probably five glasses, because the atmosphere behind him is quiet, not a pub, and most probably not an office either.

All I have heard is 'Sweetheart,' and I'm already angry.

'Sweetheart,' he says, 'It's the en primeur leaflet. We have to completely re-write the damn thing and it looks like it might be an all-nighter. I'm going to go over to Sandy's in Tooting and bash it out in her home office. We'll get a pizza or something. I may just as well kip here. It just makes sense tonight. Call you in the morning.'

I'm finding it hard to breathe. Tidily, I push the button on the answerphone to rewind and erase the message. There was only the one. There is only ever the one for me. I remember when I used to have friends, then they disappeared and I only had Simon. Now, I only have, it seems, me.

Hearing her daddy's voice, the cat has come up from downstairs. She looks up at me as if I could explain to her if I wanted. 'I'm sorry,' I try to say to her, but my voice isn't coming out right.

Peter stands in the doorway of the bedroom. He holds out his arms and I run into them. I can't remember how long it has been since I cried like this. Great gobbets of tears are running out of my eyes. My nose runs, my mouth, open in a rictus of grief, is even salivating. Saint Peter seems to take all this in his stride, using a corner of a pillowcase to dry my face as I go. When the sobs start to fade, he tidies me one last time, and then pushes me away from him.

'Maggie,' he says. 'I will come back again.'

'Don't go!' I wail, threatening the water production again.

'I don't think you can work right now.'

I dash two recalcitrant tears away with the flat of my hand. 'You keep saying things like that - I can't understand or I can't work.' I take one of his rough hands in both of mine. 'How do you know so much about my abilities, Mr Rock? I can work no matter what is going on in my personal life.'

Peter shrugs. 'But you...'

'I know, I know.' I feel my shoulders slump. 'It seems like everything I do these days is wrong.'

'No, Maggie. But you are having trouble with your man. You are not wrong or bad, but you are like any other woman having trouble with her man.'

'If you wait to talk to me until my relationship with Simon is stable, well...' I rub the burning point in my clavicle and force myself to take a deep breath. 'I don't know when that's going to happen. I don't even know if it will. But I don't want to lose this, too.'

Peter hesitates, 'I don't know if-'

I make what must be a visible effort to pull myself together.

'Look,' I say in my best boardroom manner. 'I'm not going to be able to sleep tonight anyway. Can you drink, eat?' Peter nods. 'Can you leave the bedroom?'

He winces. 'That's a little more difficult. There is a fulcrum, you see, and it is set for this location.'

'Are you telling me that my bedroom is currently the centre of the universe?'

'It is one way of putting it.'

My mind goes blank for a moment as it tries to accommodate this. Then I give myself a little shake.

I say, 'In that case, I'll get a tray.'

Red wine, white wine, goats cheese, grapes. There is a French stick left, a long one. I don't want to waste time cutting it up and just plonk the whole thing on one side of the tray. Olives, I think, and open a tin of Spanish ones, lemon stuffed. I also dig out some hummus and put it into a small bowl. Two wineglasses and napkins and we are in business. I notice, as I pass the living room, that the VCR is not blinking. 3:00 it still says.

Peter is on Simon's side of the bed. He's sitting propped up against the foot of the sleighbed, and has pinched Simon's pillows for comfort. I pop the tray onto the bed and pass him a napkin, a knife and a plate, which he takes solemnly. Then I turn my attention to opening the white. 'I thought we could start with some Sauvignon Blanc,' I say, stupidly. 'Some white wine,' I correct myself, sloshing some Cloudy Bay into the glasses.

'You know,' Peter says, 'No one has ever offered me food before. No one has ever even asked. It has been over nineteen hundred years since my last glass of wine.' He tastes it, holding the big balloon of glass in both his huge hands.

'Do you like it?'

'It is wonderful.' Peter smiles. 'I am almost glad I am here.'

My throat starts to burn again, and I hurriedly take another drink. The chill seems to ease it. 'So,' I say, 'You think you flubbed the launch.' He looks a question at me. 'Did not do the launch correctly, I mean.'

Peter dabs a bit of bread at the goats cheese, and gobbles it. 'It is hard to know where to begin.'

'Start with the worst bits.'

He gulps some wine and brushes crumbs out of his beard. 'Maggie, this is very difficult to say. You know so little.'

Do I need this? Do I really need to be told how ignorant I am right now? I'm surprised by how much Peter's disapproval hurts. I blink back tears that seem dangerously close to falling.

'Oh, Maggie, I am sorry.' He waves his glass around a little and makes a 'tsking' sound. 'Oh,' he says again. 'You have given me this feast and you are so kind and you want to help, and I need your help, surely.' He indulges in a bit more muttering and then says, 'It is just so difficult. It gets more and more difficult as time goes on. You see, you know nothing about my time. You know nothing about how things were done then. What I have to tell you, I don't think it will make any sense to you without your knowing these things. I must somehow tell you everything.'

I manage to look at his face. He's all earnest. It makes me want to giggle. I say, 'Well, don't tell me then. Show me.'

He stares at me for a moment. He eats one olive and then takes a handful.

'You know,' I remind him, 'Show me your movies.'

'Maggie, I know what you have said. I am just unsure about…'

'Oh, come on. You were going to tell me everything, anyway, weren't you?'

64

Peter sighs. 'I suppose I would,' he says, 'I suppose I have to.'

'Well, then?'

'These olives are wonderful.' He tears off some bread and dips it into the hummus. He says, 'I am thinking about how to do this thing.' And then, 'Give me your foot.'

I just look at him.

'Move the bedclothes and let me feel your foot.'

I stick my right leg out from under the duvet and cross it over my left ankle. Peter stuffs the last of the bread in his hand into his mouth and chews noisily and all too visibly. He licks his fingers clean and then rests his sticky hand on my ankle. I can feel the left one push deeper into the bed under the weight. 'Well?' he asks me, 'Can you see?'

I look at the wallpaper by the light socket and a dim yellow square seems to appear. It's not really like a screen, it's more like a tunnel, but I can see it.

'It's there,' I say, 'but I can't see people or anything, just light.'

'What do you see now?'

A spit of land leads into water. The water is impossibly clear, a slightly shimmering blue. There are hills to the right, blue as well with distance. In fact, although the land up close is burnt-looking with yellow grasses and tough little dusty green shrubs, it too fades into that same shade of blue. The air seems to shimmer with it.

'It's the air,' I say out loud. 'I've never seen blue air before.'

Peter's voice rounds and lowers, 'Capernaum,' he says, 'On the shore of Lake Kinneret. It is afternoon. The water, it turns the air blue on a still day. Over those hills is Tiberius.'

None of this means anything to me. 'Peter,' I say, 'I don't know where this is, even with all those names.'

'It's the Sea of Galilee, Maggie. My home.'

'It's beautiful.'

'I know. It broke my heart to leave it.'

A boat appears, a small enough thing, about the size of a

dinghy, but deeper, wider and clumsier. There are four men inside, rowing. I am standing on a stone construction at the shore, filled with water. When the boat comes near, my hands catch at a rope. I pull and it turns out to be a net. I spill silver fish into the big box of water.

'We built those. One year when the water was very low. We could keep our catch fresh that way, you see?'

I guess.

The screen wipes blank. I look at Peter, who is stony faced. He slugs back the rest of his Cloudy Bay and I fill his glass again. 'Here,' he says, 'look.'

We are in another, dustier place.

'Nazareth,' Peter says.

It's a small church. We look through the door. Inside is an uproar. Everyone is shouting, waving their hands about. Only one person is calm. He really does have reddish brown hair. And lighter eyes. He's terribly thin. And he's standing near the front of the church, where you'd expect an altar, but they've only got a kind of stand. He's wearing plain white robes. He's got the dignity of Ghandi and stands almost eerily still amidst the chaos.

I look at the other faces. There are others there just as pale. 'Why are some of you so white-looking?'

Peter sighs. 'We were occupied by the Romans,' he says. 'Many of them were fair.'

It takes a moment for this to sink in. I guess my mind is pretty far away from copulation, for once. 'Jesus was the son of a soldier? What happened to Joseph? What happened to God, for that matter?'

'This is not important. Look.'

The outrage in the church is growing. An older man comes up to Jesus and starts hauling on his arm, shouting at him. Jesus says something and for a moment they all freeze. Then they all start shouting at him. They surround him and start shoving him. He's obviously in a great deal of danger, but he doesn't respond to it, really. He just kind of lets them shove him to the door, where he walks outside, followed by what is now a muttering mob. He then kind of glides away from them, leaving them staring at him.

'That was before it got bad,' Peter says. 'It got much, much worse. And he wouldn't listen. He just did not seem to see what was going to happen.'

'I thought they were going to kill him,' I said.

'Yes. Me, too.'

Now I see Jesus again, laughing. I see Peter's hand, it must be, grabbing Jesus by the arm and shaking him.

'Argument,' Peter says.

Jesus jerks his arm away and speaks sharply. And then he reaches out a hand to touch my face.

'What was that about?'

'I wanted the Master to call himself the Messiah.' The scene fades.

Peter is eating goats cheese off his finger. He puts his head on one side. 'I suppose I should tell you that although I know now that he was the Messiah, I did not know then. And I did not care.' He shrugged. 'I wanted the Romans gone. I wanted the elders to see some sense. Jesus was the man to do it all.'

'So why did you want him to call himself the Messiah?'

'To try and save his life. Look!'

The heavy hand comes back to my ankle. I see the same Jesus and the same shouting men, this time at the top of a cliff. Several of them are dragging Jesus to the edge and threatening to throw him off. They are shaking him and shouting at him. But they are also shouting amongst themselves. Jesus is putting up no resistance whatsoever, but while they are shouting about something or other, he shakes himself free of the hands that have bound him and slips away out the back of the crowd.

'That was close,' I say.

'In your Bible I think he sprouts wings and flies down,' says Peter.

This is the first interior scene. I am sitting with Jesus and a few other people at a rough table. 'Who's that?' I ask, pointing towards someone writing on a wax tablet. I realise that I recognise what it is from the Museum of London's Roman Britain exhibition.

'John.'

Everyone starts to laugh. The woman at the table covers her mouth with her hand. 'Who's the girl?'

'Mary from Migda.'

Mary Magdalene? She points to a symbol on the tablet. There is brief discussion. Then I see my hands, which must be Peter's hands, waving before me in speech. John laboriously rolls an area of the tablet flat and scratches in something new. 'What are you guys talking about?'

'Matching up prophecies.' I look at Peter, who shrugs. 'It was crazy,' he said.

I must still look blank because Peter takes his hand away from my ankle and the tunnel closes. 'That time at the clifftop, it was close. Even the Master, he is convinced to declare himself the Messiah. But there are all these prophecies about how to recognise the Messiah. And so, we must match them all up, you see.'

'This is the beginning of your public relations career.'

Peter starts to spit on my floorboards, catches himself, and wipes his mouth with the back of his hand.

I can't take it anymore. I wave my napkin at him and say, 'Use this.'

He flushes. 'Sorry.' He fishes around in the bedclothes and ostentatiously wipes his hands and lips. I feel like a complete cow. And then he says, 'Yes,' heavily. 'This was the beginning of my new job.'

He stares out at the fleur-de-lis near my light socket again. And then he grabs my ankle again, harder than before.

There they are at the table, but now he freezes the frames. Slowly, while Peter and Mary laugh, I see John look at Jesus. There is a question in his eyes, and there is also great love and great pity. Jesus stares back at him and then gives a little half smile and a shrug. Then they break eye contact and laugh at something else Peter has said.

'What was that all about?'

'There was a prophecy I did not know about.' Peter jumps to his feet and starts his pacing. 'I was a fisherman. I wasn't lettered. I couldn't read or write. I didn't have good manners.' He waves the napkin at me. 'Now, the Master, when he was young, spent all his time at the temple. Reading. And John, too, in the mornings. They knew all these things.

'But how could I know, Maggie? I was fisherman. From the time I could walk I was on my father's boat. And before I could take a woman, he was dead and the boat was mine. How could I know?'

'I don't understand.'

He makes a sound like 'arach' and clenches his fists. 'The prophecies, there was one–'

'I don't get the prophecy thing,' I admit. 'Like what, exactly, what prophecies were there? And what do you mean, matching up?'

He makes a dismissive gesture. 'Oh,' he says, 'you know these things.'

If I do, I'm not telling myself. 'Well, just give me one.'

He scratches his head above his ear. 'I will. I will. Okay.' There is a pause, and then he turns to look at me. 'There was a prophecy which said that the Messiah must be from the House of David, right?'

I nod.

'So, in your Bible, it traces the ancestry of Jesus from Joseph, do you see? Because Joseph was of the House of David.'

I nod again. But Peter waits for a reaction which doesn't come. He makes another little strangled noise and continues. 'But Jesus is meant to be the son of God, right? Not from Joseph's seed. And anyway, he has this hair. You've seen it.'

'Which might mean that Mary had been fooling around with a Roman.'

'Oh, it was all crazy!' Peter sinks back down on the bed. 'So we say, Mary is a virgin, you know, before Joseph. Which takes care of that. But then, we still need Joseph's seed to make him from the House of David. John says, no one will notice. And they do not. But it was all crazy. And then in the Bible now Mary is virgin all her life! What about Thomas? Eh? And the other brothers of the Master? And anyway, have these people never seen a child born? How could a maidenhead survive that? Crazy!'

I say, 'What a nightmare.' He looks at me, startled. So I say, 'What?'

He says, 'Nothing. It is just…' he smiles at me, tossing the napkin back towards the tray.

'What?'

'It is just…' he starts again. He shrugs. 'I don't think anyone has ever heard me tell this and thought about my part in it. They are always thinking about the Master's part. You know, was he right to say he was the Messiah? Was he wrong?'

I brush this aside. 'What's the prophecy you didn't know about?'

'Oh.' It's a long, drawn-out sound. Peter rubs his eyes again and speaks to me while he's doing this. 'He will be put to death and buried? And on the third day he will rise again?'

I say, 'Oh, shit.'

Peter looks at me. My brain is whirring like a gyroscope. He's waiting for me to make the connection that, with an almost audible snap, I suddenly make. I say, 'You faked the crucifixion?'

He blows out his lips. 'I wish!'

70

'You faked the Resurrection?' He doesn't meet my eye. 'You did! You faked the Resurrection!' My head feels completely empty and I'm having trouble breathing. I get out of bed in a daze and go and open the French window, sucking in the cold air as if I were under water and it was my only chance at survival.

I don't know why this is hitting me so hard. It's not like I'm a born-again Christian or even a practising Catholic. I don't suppose I really believed the whole thing. But there's a difference between it being there to believe or not and not having it to believe at all. I lean out the window to look at the square of light on the patio coming from the utility room window. I must have left the kitchen light on.

My bedroom is an extension and it's a bit bigger than the utility room below it. I lean out to see the underpinnings. Underpinnings. I don't know that I want to live without underpinnings.

Whether or not this story is real to me, it is really the basis of my entire civilisation. I don't know that I want to know that the whole of the Western World was founded on a cheap fraud. My head is suddenly full again, and when I reach to close the window, I find that my hand is shaking with anger.

'Jesus went along with all this?'

'You see?' Peter says. 'The Master. Always about the Master. I suppose it is only natural.'

'Peter, answer me!'

'Do not call me this name.'

'Just fucking answer me!'

Peter sighs and stand up to face me. He spreads his hands wide in front of him. 'What do you want me to say? Of course he knows about it, Maggie!' He blows his lips out at me as I sag against the window frame. 'You are looking at this thing from your end of time! From our end of time, it was just another prophecy. Tricky, yes! Dangerous, yes! But just another prophecy! And the

71

Master had his work to do. Work that must be done! And it was my work now, as well.'

He lowers his hands. 'You do not know what it was like, Maggie. You do not know how it was for us. The Romans, and the elders! The elders were worse than the Romans! The temple, it had us by the balls! It was money here, money there. You could not eat but a certain way, you could not drink but a certain way! I swear there was a law how to make water! And if you got it wrong, you pay. And if you can not pay, you suffer. Sometimes people die. A woman speaks to a man not her husband, the next thing her neighbour throws a stone, the next thing she is dead!' He looks at my face and subsides into muttering.

The anger I felt is leaching from me, just watching him try and speak to me. He is in such torment, and it sounds like it's not new. I don't really understand much of what he's said, except that he thought it was worth it, that it was all worth it. And it sounds like Jesus did, too. And maybe he's right about the time thing. Hindsight is 20/20. It's not so easy when you're caught up in the middle of it all.

I'm walking back to the bed when the anger goes, and with it the adrenaline. My knees let me slide down the wall where my hand comes to rest on the burgundy, Aloxe Corton, 1986. I say, 'Throw me the tool.'

Saint Peter slides the tray out of his way and leans over the edge of the bed to hand it to me. I wrestle with the impenetrable foil.

'Do you want me to help you?'

'I can handle it.' I look up at him. I say, 'Sorry.' I say, 'It's just a lot to take in.'

'I know.' He reaches over and shoves a grape in my mouth. 'You are doing well, Maggie.'

I answer, 'Fanks,' and realise now he's got me doing it, talking with my mouth full.

72

I lever the long cork out gently. Peter has already retrieved his glass and I pour the precious fluid into our glasses. We raise them briefly to each other and drink. 'Oh!' he says, 'Oh my!'

I couldn't have put it better myself. It's a great one. It hits my palate like a velvet-covered pinball, caressing every taste bud I have and creating, it feels like, a few others just for the occasion. Iron and blood, that's all that's left of it, the tannins have mellowed away to hold the fruit that gently. It's absolutely fantastic. And it gives me great and guilty pleasure watching Simon's carefully hoarded wine going down the neck of a peasant like Peter.

Which reminds me.

'Rock?'

He props his head up on his hand. 'Yes?'

'Why was Jesus so much more educated than you were? I mean, you say you were just the son of a fisherman, but surely he was just the son of a carpenter?'

Peter laughs and wipes his mouth with the back of his hand. 'Carpenter is wrong word,' he says. 'Builder is perhaps the better word. Joseph built half of Tiberius. He raised his sons like princes.' He laughs again. 'And Mary, she has much ambition, you know?'

It's weird to think of the Virgin Mary this way, as perhaps not so virginal, as a social climber. Peter has dripped wine into his beard, staining it. No wonder she didn't like Jesus hanging around with him, he's a lout.

'Why were they going to throw Jesus off the cliff?'

'It was after he'd helped Lazarus. After Lazarus had his stroke.'

'Stroke?'

'The Master had learned much about health in the east.' Peter sits up and rubs the small of his back. 'Before he found his Master, he studied many things. But then he met his Master and studied only the way.'

'The way?' My mind is doing it again, spinning madly. 'Jesus was a Zen Buddhist?'

73

Peter is busily stuffing more olives into his mouth. He talks around them. 'I do not know these names. He could never have survived it all if he had not studied all these things. I could not do it, as strong as I was. I did not know how to shut off pain. Of course, the Master taught us all how to be still, but he could sit like a rock, for many hours. These things are what helped him.'

'I think you'd better show me the rest.'

Chapter Seven

I get up and sit on the bed and Peter takes my hand. In front of me, the tunnel opens up again. I am in the desert, or what looks kind of like a desert. I guess it can't really be desert because there's some trees. They're twisted and tortured, but trees nonetheless.

'Where is this?'

'Judea. Look.'

It's dark. My point of view seems to be giving money to someone. It looks just like a drug deal. 'It looks like a drug deal.'

'It is a drug deal.' Peter lets go of my hand to hold up two fingers. 'There are two drugs that could make you "die". One is dangerous, very dangerous, and it works right away. The other one is much safer, and it works slowly – you have maybe five, ten, fifteen hours, maybe more. That man was a friend of mine, Syrian trader.' Peter shrugs. 'Mary from Migda, she knows him, too. He could get second kind of drug. For the Master. For the cross.'

'You had it all planned.'

'Oh, yes.' Peter takes another drink of wine. 'Oh yes. I thought I was great general. I thought I could plan it all.' He raises his eyes to heaven and mutters something in his own language. 'Here,' he says. 'This you know.'

It's the Last Supper. It must be. There's Jesus standing up and talking, and wine cups and bits of food on the table in front of everyone else. For a second I'm kind of overwhelmed by just seeing it. Then someone else stands up and starts to answer Jesus.

'Who's that?'

'Judas the Iscariot.'

'What's he saying?'

Peter swallows hard. I look at him and tears have filled his eyes. 'He is saying that he is the one who should "betray" the Master.

That none of us trusted him at first anyway, and that it would look natural to the Sanhedrim.'

'What's a Sanhedrim?'

'Council of elders. The judges of our law.'

'Everyone is arguing with him.'

'It was a hard thing for anyone to do, but harder for Judas. You see, he was right, for a long time none of us did trust him. No one wanted him to take on that burden.'

The argument subsides and now I see Peter's hands in front of me again. He is counting off five as he speaks. My attention wanders.

'Why did Jesus always wear white clothes? Isn't that a little impractical? In such a dusty environment?'

Peter answers, 'It's an Essene idea.' As if that's going to be informative.

'Essene?'

The picture falters and the tunnel closes. Peter lets go my hand. 'They had, um…' He reaches over and trawls in my brain. 'Communes,' he finally says. 'They had communes and did things a certain way. They hoped to overthrow Rome and the elders.'

'Jesus was one of them?'

Peter takes another handful of olives. I'm starting to feel hungry too, and break off some bread for hummus.

'Not really,' he said, 'I don't think he ever meant to stay with them. But he spent time with them, and they loved him. And they thought him the Messiah. Really believed it.'

'Show me more.'

Judas kneels at Jesus' feet, throws some cloth over his head, and edges out the door.

'That was the last time I spoke to him.'

Peter's weary pain seems to have settled on him again. I start to ask what happened, and then I remember. 'He killed himself, didn't he?'

Peter nods, sighing and looking at the floor.

'But why? If everyone wanted him to do it?'

'It was too early.' He lets go my hand and the scene fades. 'We thought he would go to them and they would call a council the next day and talk long about whether or not to take the Master. Then we would hear that they were coming and the Master could take the drug, and...survive his ordeal.'

'And instead?'

He fumbles for my hand again. They all go outside, still talking, walking in the dark through city walls and across a bridge. There is a big hill in front of them, blocking out the stars. Trees appear, proper things, tall and lush looking. There is a fountain and flowers. Jesus says something and then sits down by the fountain, settling into the lotus position.

'He wanted to begin his readiness for his ordeal.'

Some of the others keep going up the hill. Some sit with him, a few with their legs bent, some with their legs tucked under them.

It's eerie, watching this. For the first time, I feel I am intruding. A yawn splits one of the faces, and the sitter makes a low seated bow and then stretches out to sleep. My view becomes intermittent, as Peter's eyes dip shut again and again.

Suddenly, they are wide open. Armed men shove Judas into the garden. He is bleeding and his arms are bound behind him. He is shouting. Tears are running down his cheeks.

Jesus stands up and goes to him, kissing him full on the lips, while Judas sobs brokenly.

'It is too early,' Peter says.

There's a brief fight, but it's over in seconds. And then Jesus is gone.

You can feel the panic in the rest of the men. Some of them start running up the hill, shouting. A few sit on the ground again, stunned. One of these is Judas. He doesn't even look up when some disciple cuts his hands free.

Peter, who is what I think of as my camera, seems to move one way and then the other, towards safety, I presume, and then back in the direction of the arresting party. And then there is a hand on his arm. It's the Syrian drug dealer, who passes him something small in a scrap of cloth. In the next shot we are running.

We pound back through the city walls and into a compound, just squeaking by the closing gates. Jesus is being led through an archway. We sidle towards it. My view is now somewhat occluded. Peter must have covered his own face, just like Judas did. We look at other doors, all closed. There is a fire in the compound, and people are drinking. It's like a party. Faces swim in and out of vision. There's now a guard on the archway. And then three or four faces. Jabbing fingers. A hand on our sleeve. There is no way to achieve the archway. There is no way to get the drug to Jesus. We edge back and back, until our back is at the gate, and then we lift the bolt and slide through, running back across the bridge.

Everything swims. Peter is weeping. In the garden, one of the graceful trees seems compromised, knobbly as a desert olive. The sky lightens as we get close enough to see Judas, naked, hung by his own clothes. A puddle of silver pennies lies under his feet, mixing with the shit which has streaked down his legs. From his purple face, his tongue protrudes obscenely. And then we are running up the hill.

I don't know what to say.

I look at Peter, who is still staring out at the wall, swallowing. I pour some more wine in his glass, and he raises it mechanically. 'It was too early,' he says again. 'We thought all was lost. I did not know then how my Master's mind worked, strand upon strand, like the web of a spider.' He drinks again. 'If one strand breaks, well, you have the others. But I did not know this then. And how I suffered that night! There were times I envied Judas his tree.'

He turns to me. 'You know scourging?'

'Some kind of torture?'

Peter nods. 'Yes. The Master thought he could survive this, with his skills. But not the cross. No one survived the cross. They kept a mallet on the hill, the Romans did. And if you did not die quick enough, they shattered the bones of your legs. Then you died.'

'And Jesus didn't have the drug to look dead.'

'No.'

'What about the great whacking holes in his hands and feet? Didn't you think that might be a little tricky?'

Peter grimaces. 'There was an art to the cross. They liked them to die slowly. They liked to use the mallet. And so, if they did it correctly, little was broken by the nails, so that little would bleed.' He stares out at the wall a little more and then takes my hand again.

The first thing that strikes me is how few folks have turned out for the occasion. I suppose I'm still thinking in hindsight. It must be a bit like Woodstock. Afterwards so many people will say that they were there. I'm looking at the ground, where Jesus, terrifyingly conscious, is being nailed onto what looks like a fallen tree. There's a hole at the base of it and some big rocks waiting to steady it once it gets hauled upright.

There's only two Roman soldiers doing this, and the one who is doing the actual nailing seems to be concentrating quite hard. I'm watching the second hand nail going in, but it's not a nail, it's a spike.

'It was when I first had a little hope,' Peter says, 'Look. It is missing the main bones and the tendons.'

I would look, but I feel I might be sick. I lean over to put my wine glass on the floor. Iron and blood, indeed. Will I ever drink great Burgundy again without thinking of this?

'Look at this,' Peter freezes the frame again. The hammering soldier has looked up, making eye contact with us. His mouth gives a little quick grin, and he drops one eyelid in a wink. 'I get this big stupid feeling of hope. This part is not important, the feet go in same way.'

He does what we would call fast-forwarding. 'Here,' he says.

The air has changed in some way, and I realise the sky is yellower. It's afternoon, and some of the small crowd are having a little picnic, watching Jesus die. Occasionally someone might yell at him a bit, shaking their fists and shouting something that makes their mates laugh. Otherwise it doesn't seem like great entertainment.

Suddenly Jesus screams. The soldier who did the nails has a little pot with him. He says something to the other soldier, who guffaws. The nailing soldier pulls a sponge out of the pot and sticks it on his spear. He lifts the sponge to Jesus' lips and Jesus sucks greedily.

'Your bible says, "They gave him bitter herbs to drink".'

Jesus's face convulses with disgust. The spectators have a good giggle at that.

Half a minute later, Jesus sags on the cross. The nail soldier removes the sponge from his spear and then shoves the point deep into Jesus, right under his ribcage on the side. Water and blood pour out, but Jesus doesn't so much as twitch. The other soldier yawns and gets to his feet. The small crowd pack up to go. They look rather sullen, as if they're disappointed.

A fat guy in nice clothes comes up to the soldiers and presses some coinage in their hands. They lower the cross and cut the body down. The fat guy's servants take it away.

The scene fades.

'Was the soldier a Christian?'

'What?' Peter laughs. 'Him? No. He used to go to the cockfights with the Master. He owed him money.'

'Jesus bet on cockfights?'

'Maggie, do not be like that!' Peter looks disappointed in me. 'Of course he goes to cockfights. He goes among the people, to where they go. He knows everyone - soldiers, whores, everyone!'

I reach for my glass and drain it while I think about this for a moment. 'So, who was the fat guy? A wrestler?'

'Joseph of Aremethia. A Pharisee.' Peter looks at my blank expression. 'Important man, but followed the Master.'

'The sponge thing, it was the second kind of drug, the one that works right away?'

'That's right.'

'But the spear wound?'

'Was in the kidney. Evidently you have two. And the herbs made it clean.'

'Did you know all this then?'

Peter makes his puffing sound. 'Are you crazy? No! I knew nothing! None of us did. We hoped, that's all.' He looks meaningfully at the wine bottle, but it's empty.

'I'll get some more,' I say, and pound down the spiral staircase.

I rummage around in Simon's cellar and finally come up with a 1996 Montrachet and some non-vintage Billecart-Salmon Champagne. I grab the quick chiller out of the freezer and run back up the stairs.

I don't want to look at the VCR. I don't want to think about the real world. And I especially don't want to think about Simon spending the night in Tooting with his girlfriend. Though it occurs to me I'm no longer all that jealous of him. Out of the two of us, I'm sure I'm having the more interesting evening.

Peter is leaning back on Simon's pillows again, against the foot of my sleighbed. He has his eyes closed. I put the Montrachet in the quick chiller and then see the glasses, which are streaked and spotted and generally look horrible. 'I'm going to go wash these,' I say, holding them up. Peter opens one eye and nods.

I rinse them out with shampoo in the upstairs bathroom and then realise I need a wee badly. I wee, change my tampon, dry the glasses first with a towel and then with toilet paper and go back into the bedroom. I say, 'The wine won't be a moment. I'm just chilling it.'

Peter smiles to himself. 'You live like a queen,' he says. 'You must have cool wine for your soft tongue.'

I ignore this, looking at the tray of food, which is pretty much destroyed. I slide it under the bed. 'Do you need to use the toilet?'

'Hmmm?'

'Do you need to wee? To make water?'

He thinks about this for a moment. 'Ah,' he finally says. 'Yes, that must be the pressure.'

'Go ahead and use the toilet. It's right through there.'

Peter looks embarrassed. 'No. That's all right.'

'What's the matter? I'll show you how to use it, if that's the problem.'

'No. I am fine.' But as he says this, he squirms, squinting his eyes.

'You can't leave the bedroom! I forgot.' And for some reason, this is what's making him embarrassed.

'It is very difficult, a visitation,' he says, bristling. He's all affront-ed pride. It reminds me of that film Connery did with Nicholas Cage. I can't remember the name. But he looked just the same at one point, all drawn up to his full height and touchy. 'Not every-one can do even so much as me.'

'I believe you, I believe you!' I am terribly amused to see that the needs of the male ego do not fade after two thousand years in a box. 'Here,' I say, opening up both French windows. 'You can go out here.'

Peter comes to stand beside me and peers dubiously down. 'There are tiles,' he says doubtfully.

'It doesn't matter. It will probably rain tonight anyway.'

And there's no show of modesty whatsoever. I haven't even turned away when he's hitching up his dress whatsit and going for

82

it. He gives a moan of satisfaction and then there's a large splashing noise down below. I'm not looking. In order to keep not looking I go back to the bathroom and wet a flannel in hot water, rubbing some soap onto one side. I also get a little handtowel.

He's done when I come back, and is competently working out how to close and lock the window catch. 'Here,' I say. He looks at me. 'Hands,' I say, and he holds them out. I put the flannel in one, and he cottons on, using it thoroughly. I then give him the towel and he uses that, too.

I go back to the bathroom and rinse out the flannel, trying very hard not to think about that big groan of satisfaction and what I almost saw beneath his robes. Yet I find myself brushing my hair and tinting my lips carmine with a lip pencil. I stare at myself in the mirror, saying, You've just seen Jesus die on the cross. You've got no shame in you, none whatsoever. And then I go back.

I feel the neck of the Montrachet, and then sit down on the floor to open it.

'One thing I forgot to say, Maggie, is this is Passover time. And the Sabbath, too. You need to know this.'

'Okay.' Like it means anything to me.

Peter comes to lean over the bed. 'We could not leave the house. We could not journey, nor cook, nor care for a dead body that maybe wasn't so dead. From sundown to sundown. Do you understand?'

'What did you do?'

Peter shrugs his shoulders up to his ears. 'We worried, is what we did.' I pour the wine and hand him a glass. He takes a big slug. 'This is truly a blessing, these wines,' he says. 'You know, it makes all the work much easier.'

'You're just getting pissed. Concentrate,' is what I say, but when I taste it, he's right, it's another corker. A great white Bordeaux is a glorious thing, like winter sunshine in a bottle, tasting of austere fruit, with hints of honey. It's as unlike a big fat

Australian Chardonnay as Kate Moss is to Pamela Anderson. When Peter starts speaking again, it's me that needs to concentrate.

'Well, the Marys, they went with the body to the tomb, and they had time to wrap him up a bit and to spread the herbs and oils he had given us onto his body. But he was badly hurt, Maggie. Very badly hurt. And they had to watch them roll the stone over the entrance and they had to leave him there in a cold tomb, with all his wounds.'

I think about this, about leaving, knowing your son was still alive, but being unable to stay with him and nurse him. 'She must have cried buckets, Mary.'

'They both had hearts of eagles. She would not shame her son with tears. Her anger burned as bright as the sun.'

'So you had to wait all day?'

'And all night. And when the women went to the tomb on the third day, I did not go. But Mary from Migda, she comes running back and tells us that an Essene had been waiting for her in the tomb, that the Master was alive and that he would visit us in Gallilee.' Peter takes another drink and sighs. 'I can not tell you how happy we were. We sang! Oh, my! And then also, it was good to leave Judea with our skins…'

He has yet another drink, this time chewing the mouthful a bit before he swallows. 'Oh! That is good.' And then he says, 'In your Bible, you know, is all this. In your Bible, the Essene is "young man in white", and then I think another of your scribes puts in that he is angel with wings. Very big on the wings, that scribe, he put them in wherever he could.'

'So the stunt was successful.'

Peter shrugs again, 'You could say so, I suppose.'

He reaches out his hand to me and pulls me up to my feet. 'Come back to bed,' he says, 'the floor is hard and it is a cold night.'

I do as I'm told. 'And so you all went back to Galilee, spreading the good news that the Messiah had fulfilled the prophecy.'

'Well,' Peter looks shifty at this, as if he is embarrassed again. 'We went back to Galilee, yes.'

'And spread the news?'

He has been leaning near me, and now he pushes himself away, back to the footboard, in an angry movement. 'No,' he says. 'No, we did not spread the news.'

'What? Why not? Wasn't that the whole point of the poor sap getting crucified?'

Peter puffs out his lips again, this time with some force. And then he does that shrinking thing, as he stares into his glass. 'We were frightened,' he admits in a soft voice. 'We feared for our lives.'

'So,' I can't quite get my head around this, 'So what did you all do?'

He doesn't meet my eye. 'Andrew and I went back to our boat, to help our men. Mary, her father was ill, and she goes back to Migda to nurse him, even after how he treated her. John could not do anything, John. He just dragged himself around my house, waiting like a dog.' There is a long pause.

I'm having a hard time not being judgmental here. It seems rather shitty of them, I can't help but think, that Jesus gets himself tortured and crucified and they almost screw it up and kill him and then they just run away after he's actually done it and don't even tell anyone. Some of this must show in my face.

'I am not proud of this, Maggie.'

And I can see why not. 'Well, what happened then? How did the Bible even get written? If you all bolted back to your ratholes?'

'Give me your foot.'

It's Capernaum again. I can tell, the air has that blue look again. Peter, my camera, has been looking out the window at the

85

lake. Then he turns around, dollying in an arc shot around the round stone walls of his house. They all seem to be here, the Last Supper bunch, and Mary Magdalene, too.

'I thought she was at Migda with her ailing father.'

'It is not far, Migda.'

John really does look like hell. Classic case of depression, I'd say. He's unkempt and he slumps in a bed, silent, while they all talk. There's some sort of argument going on. Then the door creaks open, and they all freeze.

It's Jesus, and if I thought John looked like shit, this guy really has changed. He's so skinny he looks as though a strong wind could blow him through the window and out into the lake. John throws himself down at Jesus' feet, while Andrew, it must be (I saw him on the boat) comes and pushes a chair over, into which Jesus sinks gratefully.

Jesus says something, and Mary jumps up and busies herself around a hearth, returning with a pottery beaker and some dried fish. She then wipes her hands on her skirt and begins examining her Master's wounds as he eats and drinks.

'He looks barely alive, even now,' I said.

'Well, that is what he will be saying,' Peter says, 'He was dead for some minutes, you know. The Essenes had to pound on his heart to start it again. He had broken ribs from this.'

Broken ribs, a scalp full of sharp cuts, whacking great holes in his feet and hands, a pierced kidney, and whatever the after-effects of that drug were…I guess he's looking about right, considering all that.

I'm watching the screen. Jesus' face is filled with joy. Peter must rush over and fall to his knees in front of him, because now I am seeing Jesus forgiving me, placing his hand on my head and smiling down at me with love. It affects me so much that my eyes fill with tears.

I blink these away during a long scene with Jesus talking. He must be talking softly, because they all gather around him in a tight knot, kneeling and sitting at his feet. He is waving his hands around a bit, as he gets excited.

But it's the look on everyone else's faces that I can't get over. It's like someone's given them some sort of drug. Over the course of five minutes, they've completely changed. They even seem taller.

There must be a sound at the door because they all look to it, but not with the panicky fear they exhibited when Jesus knocked. Mary goes to open it, and it's a couple of guys in white robes, Essenes, I guess, and they kind of collect Jesus and take him away. The scene fades and I look at Peter, who is smiling.

'I'll bet you all went and preached like the dickens after that.'

Peter laughs. 'You are right, Maggie. That is just what we did.'

'I could see what he said fired you all up. What was it?'

'He had been dead. He told us not to fear death, that there was a place for us when we died. He had been there, and it was glorious.'

I'm waiting for something else. But that appears to be it. 'That was your pep talk? Go ahead, guys, and if you die, you'll like it?'

Peter shrugs. 'We had not known this before.'

'You didn't know it then!' I stand up and start pacing around the bed. I need to walk. I need to move. I need some fresh air, too. I crack one of the French windows and put it on the snick. 'He was ill, Peter. And he'd been really sick and whacked out on whatever was on that stick! You knew that! How did you just believe him and then charge out and maybe get killed?'

In answer, Peter smiles. 'Maggie. I am dead now. And Jesus was not wrong.'

I am by the bed when he says this and I sink back down onto the floor again. I don't know how much of this I can really take. One hand lands on my wineglass, and I automatically drink from it, as if that's going to help me any.

It's all a bit too much, that's the problem. Of course Peter is dead. If he's actually here. How can I argue with him about life after death? And he's probably really not even here. It's probably just me, making it all up, in some sort of sick dream concocted out of stress.

Whatever is not here takes my glass from me and heaves me up off the floor with indecent ease. He cradles me in his lap and strokes my hair. He makes 'shushing' sounds, like you do to a baby or an overwrought horse.

My voice croaks when I say, 'It's scary.'

'I know.' I get another few strokes on my hair. It feels wonderful. He feels wonderful. And I want him to be there, whether or not he actually is.

I say, 'I want you to be here.'

And I'm so close to him, I can almost feel him smile. He kisses the top of my head. He says, 'This is it, Maggie, this is it exactly.'

I twist around to look at his face, steadying myself with one hand on his massive shoulder. He says, 'Faith, it is called. But really, you know, you make your own world. You choose what to have in it.' I must look as bewildered as I feel. He tries to explain. 'The leap of faith. You say this?'

I say, 'Well, I don't, personally, but people do.'

This time I can see him smile.

'It is this jump of the faith. If I did not believe the Master, then I had been following a madman. I had thrown away my year with him, I was very stupid, and, even more, there would be no deliverance from God. My people would be the prey of the elders the whole of my life.' Peter makes a sweeping motion with his free hand. 'Finish.'

'But if I did believe? If I did believe then all was worth it. If I did believe, then I had been following the Messiah of Israel who had come with the New Covenant to set his people free. If I did believe, then the spirit of fire in my heart was real and could be shared by all men-'

'People,' I automatically correct.

'That's what I meant. And sins would be forgiven. And I had been a part of this And I had nothing to fear.'

Nothing to fear. I want to live in a world where there is nothing to fear. His confidence is powerful, transferring itself to me. I am suddenly aware of where my body touches his, my buttocks soft on his thighs, his shoulder rock-like under my hand. It makes my hand seem so little and weak.

Peter reaches for the wine bottle and fills his glass, crushing me slightly to do so. He holds me to him with one massive hand so that I don't tumble onto the floor. This wraps his hand around my waist, where it remains.

He holds his glass to my mouth and I drink as fast as I can, but he's tilting it too much, and some runs past my lips. His sandpaper finger goes to catch the drop, which has slid down my throat.

It follows the line of wine back to my lips, and then, as his eyes burn into mine, it pushes past them. I suck the drop from the end of his finger.

And then it happens so fast. The wine glass is gone and my arms have circled his neck and then he is kissing me, his fist tangled in my hair, kissing me harder than I have ever been kissed in my life. I taste blood as my teeth break the skin of my lips. And then my eyes close.

'What in heaven's name happened here last night?' Simon is standing at the head of the bed surveying the carnage.

My water bottle has a quarter inch of water left in the bottom. I fumble with the Ibuprofen cap and somehow swill three tablets down my throat. Then I grope for my glasses. I've slept through the alarm again. It's eight o'clock. I pad to the phone and ring the office, dialling Anya's voice mail when no one picks up. 'Anya, it's Maggie. I feel dreadful. I'll be home if anyone needs me and I don't think there's anything to cancel. Thanks.' I put the phone back down. My voice is certainly convincing. It has even convinced me. This could be the world's first terminal hangover.

'Maggie!'

Simon is still standing by the bed. Even though I can now see food smeared all over it, it still looks attractive and I climb back in.

'Be quiet, darling,' I say. 'There's a good boy.'

Having spied the wine bottles under the bed, he starts examining labels. There is a sharp intake of breath.

'Will you answer my question, please?'

'Go away, Simon.'

'Maggie, for fuck's sake!'

I still have my glasses on. I sit up and look at his white face. 'You have no right to question me about last night, Simon.' I am amazed at how even my voice sounds, and I realise I'm not even angry. I suppose my new client helps me put things in perspective.

To Simon, though, his love affairs are still the most important things in the world and he stares at me as if I am a stranger.

'Where did you get that nightgown?' he sneers.

'Knickerbox.'

'I don't understand what's going on.'

'I'm extremely hungover and tired.'

'I can see that much. And I can see you had company last night. Who was it, someone you picked up at the pub after you got my phone call?'

It's like he's from another planet. I'm processing his words, but they don't make any sense to me. 'No. It's a private client. I've seen him before.' This sounds reasonable to me, in my current state, but Simon goes ballistic.

'You're seeing someone else? You're bloody seeing someone else? You let me feel so fucking guilty when all the time-'

I stop him in mid rant with one upstretched hand. 'Client is the operative word here, Simon. Not lover. Client.' Only because I fell asleep, I think, but still, it's true.

'Why are you seeing a client in our bedroom, Maggie?'

I shake my head, wishing I hadn't told him anything now, caught back up in the messy emotions of want and lack from which I had just had such a brief holiday.

'How's the leaflet?'

'Done. I have to go to the printers this afternoon to check the first run.'

'So you've got the morning off?'

'To sleep. I really did end up working all night.'

'Me, too. Honest.'

'Who's this private client, Maggie?'

Fuck, now it's all starting to hurt. My eyes start to leak. 'Shit, Simon. I know you're not going to believe me. I can't tell you.'

'What?'

'It's really secret. And I can't tell anyone. Not even you.'

'I'm supposed to believe that you had a client up here in our bed, swilling my best wines, eating and it looks like rolling about a bit as well. And you aren't going to tell me who it is?'

He is shaking so much that he holds onto the headboard. I shrug at him, still crying. 'And I'm supposed to believe that you and Sandy worked all night on a leaflet at her flat and the only reason you didn't have much sleep was because the work was so difficult?'

He seizes a handful of his own hair and looks at me. 'It's true,' he says. 'Maggie, it's really true. I don't want... We've got enough to think about without... You just have to believe me.'

You just have to believe me. Peter's 'jump of the faith'. I can hear his voice in my ear, telling me that we choose the worlds we live in. God my head hurts. I would like to choose a world in which my husband loves me. Where I can trust him and he can trust me. And where I can go back to sleep. Is it that easy? Can I just choose that now?

I swallow and the taste in my mouth is disgusting. Simon's waiting for me to say something and he looks like he's about to have a fit. 'Okay,' I say. 'Okay. I believe you. I believe you, Simon.'

We look at each other for a moment. And then I ask, 'But can you believe me?'

He starts to shout at me, but stops. He rubs his eyes and softly swears instead. When he finally speaks, it's only to say, 'You look like shit.'

'You do, too. You're white as several ghosts.'

We grin at each other. It feels marvellous.

'That bed is disgusting. Come down the hall to the spare room. It's Ravinder's day, isn't it? We'll bung her a couple of extra quid.'

He's talking as we walk down the hall. He's undoing his shirt buttons and his cuffs. He fiddles with his watch alarm and then we sink into each other's arms and sleep, under the old duvet we had when we were first married, and had to clean up our messes ourselves.

Chapter Eight

We get up at two and shower, dress, as if everything is fine, as if this is a normal day. I check into the office, but it seems that the whole company doesn't collapse the minute I'm out of the door – nobody needs me. It is Simon's idea to go down to Alfredo's for a fry up and this we do, catching them just after the lunch rush. Both of us are still tired, and neither one of us chatters brightly, but that doesn't seem to matter.

The physical ease that was so missing on our last visit has somehow returned and Simon does not jerk away from my touch. In fact, when he feeds me one of his chips, he pushes the tip of his finger in my mouth and smiles into my eyes. It's as if this is the first time he has seen me in a long while. We kiss goodbye outside across from the green before he hops on to the 171A, and he nearly misses the bus, bending back my head and putting one hand up my jacket just to touch where my jumper has ridden up from my jeans.

The plan was to go back to bed, but the three glasses of orange juice and double beans on toast seem to have revived me a bit. It wasn't that I drank so much, I reckon, because it wasn't that much. It was the fact that I drank it all at 3:00 am. As far as my body is concerned, I just chugged a bottle and a half of wine in a nano-second. I am thinking this out logically, as if it's true that Saint Peter appears on my bed and stops time.

Hmmm.

I look in the window of AuraAuraAuraAura, at the hundreds of pairs of silver earrings on display while I think. I could be going crazy. This is true. But then wouldn't I have just dreamed drinking all that wine? The bottles wouldn't have actually gone, would they? I don't even like those lemon stuffed olives that much.

Certainly not enough to eat two tins of them. Surely I couldn't have drunk three bottles of wine on my own? I would be worse than this if I had, much worse.

I realise that the proprietor is looking at me and shuffle along to stare at the menu for the Afghan Kitchen.

You have to decide what to believe. Peter said that. Peter said a lot of things, I think. At least I could find out if some of them are true.

I fumble in the pocket of my Gore-tex jacket for my wallet and search for the pink edge of a plastic card. Good, I have it. Back at the bus stop, I wait for the 73 that will take me to the British Library and, hopefully, some answers.

It is my first time in the new building and I find it somewhat intimidating. The signage is also less than helpful, and I wander around a bit before trudging up the gleaming white staircase to the security guard who waits there. Without a bag I have little to show, and he just glances at my pass and waves me through with disinterest. After wandering about a bit more, I find the Humanities One reading room.

The old murmur of feet, pages and pens is the same. It is a little after three, prime working time for the scholars. I find my way to one of the catalogue computers and choose Subject. At first I type in Saint Peter, but then backspace out of it. No. Jesus, I type, and hit return.

There are 2,645 matches for my search. Grimly, I begin to plow through them.

In the pub a few hours later, Simon goggles at me over his pint of Flowers. 'You're going where tomorrow?' he asks.

'Back to the British Library. I'm researching something.'

'And you can't tell me what it is.'

I grin, shaking my head. 'Sorry.'

Thoughtfully, he sips, his fringe falling into his eyes. 'I'm going to get a haircut, then,' he says, pushing it back.

'Good idea.'

I raise my glass, too, and we sit looking at each other for a second. 'Listen,' I say, 'I'm going to Mass on Sunday morning. Would you like to come along? We could go down to Columbia Road afterwards, buy some winter pansies for the window box. I'll treat you to a bagel.'

'Mass?'

'Yeah.' Again, I can't really explain without going into the whole Saint Peter thing. I want to go to Mass. It's been ages. I can't quite remember how the church puts all the things that Peter's been telling me. I don't think I'm so far gone to think that I will find the truth in a Roman Catholic service. But I feel compelled to go, in any case. I guess if Peter really was a client, one of the first things I'd do is check out past campaigns.

Simon is still looking at me strangely, but he is intrigued, I can tell.

'You don't have to bribe me,' he says. 'I'll come or I won't come, but not for pansies and a bagel.'

'Even if I throw in a latte?' This makes his eyes crinkle into half moons.

'Okay,' he said. 'I'll come with you.'

And this makes me feel much better, although I don't have any idea why.

The new library has these nifty little lights that pop on when your books are ready. I've ordered the limit for yesterday and again for today and mine is flashing like the emergency services. The serious scholars on either side seem disgruntled when I keep hopping up. They also seem contemptuous of my scholarship methods, diving into the indexes to check individual facts and then pounding away on my laptop. They are much more thorough. Their folios turn with infinite slowness as they cover page after page of notebooks with neatly indented scrawl.

I'm looking at things that deal with the historicity of Jesus as well as contextual historical studies and things that analyse the gospel critically. This has narrowed down my search to about three hundred books. Of course I haven't anything like time to read them. Again, I'm not really sure what I'm doing. Trying to find out if I'm going absolutely crazy, I suppose.

I push *Jesus Lived In India* to the corner of the desk and take up *Christ As Criminal*. In the back of my mind as I read is always an awareness that I could find something which will discount Peter's story, even Peter's existence. *Christ as Criminal* lolls shut around my finger as I stare across all the bent heads.

I open another file in Word and list out the possibilities as neatly as my neighbours would. One. Saint Peter could be visiting me. Two. I could be going mad. I star this one with an asterisk as most likely. Three. My visitor could not be Saint Peter at all, but someone else. Who? A burglar with a strange dress sense and a bizarre biblical knowledge who is uninterested in material goods? A rapist who desists and neatly covers my unconscious body when I fall asleep during the rape? Who could it be?

I backspace over the last entry until it reads, Visitor could not be Saint Peter, and hit return thoughtfully. It is Word '97, so another number helpfully pops up. Visitor could be Satan, I type, and shiver. I'm reconsidering the dangers of a life without underpinnings. The world without God seems much less chilling than a world with both God and the Devil. I close the file without saving it and go back to *Christ As Criminal*.

It is strange how it all comes back to you. The smell of beeswax and incense smacked me in the face when I opened the door and I groped for the holy water blindly. Now Simon and I are reciting the Profession of Faith nearly without a stumble, as if our last time in church was last week, as though ten years is nothing.

'…the creator of all that is seen and unseen.' I glance at him without turning my head and he stands sturdily, head and shoulders back, looking at the altar. Knowing Simon, he is probably evaluating the architecture and ornamentation, but to the casual observer he looks to be in a manly dialogue with the bloke on the cross. '...of the Virgin Mary, he suffered, died and was buried. On the third day he rose again, in fulfilment of the scriptures and is seated at the right hand of the Father.'

Personally, I'm finding it hard to look at the cross. Every time I do, I think about the nails going in just right, and Peter's big stupid feeling. In a way, I respect Jesus more for not being a supernatural power. I suppose that's because I now believe he really did die for our sins to be forgiven. Just in a different way. And also to save his own neck, of course.

But he could have just run away. That's the thing. And instead he chose to do that, and that is pretty damned impressive. It's a plaster Jesus, this one, and a good, no-nonsense Catholic one, painted with no regard for restraint or good taste. Red blood runs down from the hands and feet. Jesus's eyes are open. The poor bastard is waiting for his kidney to be punctured. Of course, he also was waiting for the stick to get stoned enough not to care too much about it. I'll bet the time he spent waiting for that stick seemed like a fucking eternity.

We sit down and start listening to the readings. The first one is something from the Old Testament. The woman reading it is speaking every word with the same intonation. I find her impossible to listen to. Besides, I keep looking at the damn cross. Three or four days. That's how long it usually took them to die. The Romans were pretty proud of their ability to keep people suffering. And when they got tired of it, they could always shatter their legs. It was the thighbone they shattered, I discovered yesterday, so the femoral artery was punctured.

I found lots of stuff out yesterday in my research. The sword thrust itself was just a way of making sure that the victim really was dead. Jesus died so quickly. It really must have looked a bit dodgy. But then, they'd probably beat him up pretty good before. Scourging. Flaying the back with thorn bundles. Sometimes they put salt on, if they had enough salt and felt like it. Sometimes they poured on vinegar.

It's not until the Epistle that I can concentrate. It's Paul, an excerpt from his speech to the Athenians. He's trying to talk about everlasting life, but he loses them when he mentions Jesus rising from the dead. He only gets two converts.

Paul does wick on a bit, and makes the concept of immortality which Peter was talking about sound terribly complicated. I start flicking through the little paper missals they give you these days and all the Epistles seem to be Paul. I can't imagine why. To me, he doesn't seem much of a public speaker.

Simon has to nudge me to stand for the Gospel. I hardly hear it, thinking.

We sit down and the priest starts talking about how we can live forever through Jesus. It doesn't seem much like what Peter was talking about at all. Now he's saying something about the new covenant, but he's not talking about the old Jewish law at all.

It doesn't sound right. It doesn't sound like anything Peter told me. The priest says something about how Paul said you can only have life after death if you believe in Jesus. I don't think Jesus said that. I just don't think he would.

My head's starting to hurt again, and I wish I'd stayed awake in the Philosophy lectures at university.

People are starting to fumble in their bags and jackets for money anyway, so it's not really that obvious when I fumble for my notepad and start to write. Simon gives me a bit of a funny look, but I'm not going to worry about that.

The offerings go up to the altar, and this is an old fashioned church where they put the collection money there, as well. My fiver is about to get blessed. It's a nice idea, and I wonder if there really is some juju that makes it impossible for the later owner of my fiver to spend it on child porn or badger baiting.

I like all of the Eucharist, I always have. I like the poetry of what the priest says to the bread and wine. I like the prayers. I like shaking each other's hand and saying, 'Peace be with you.' It's just nice, I can't explain it. It's such a homely way of preparing for the weekly miracle.

Now we kneel down again.

I was in Notre Dame for Mass one Sunday, ages ago, and at the moment of transubstantiation, when us Catholics are meant to believe that the bread and wine become Jesus' body and blood, flashbulbs erupted from a coachload of Japanese tourists. It reminded me that this moment was meant to be of some consequence. As I kneel for it today, I remember being a little girl, peeking up from my folded hands, trying to see the exact second when it happened.

It makes me feel old.

I am tired from all of this. My shoulders ache from too many hours hunched over some desk or table somewhere – the office, the library, the study at home. Simon had to call me three times last night for *Blind Date*.

'Lord, I am not worthy to receive you, but only say the word and I shall be healed.'

Only say the word. And I shall be healed. It is lovely. It is. It's so very personal.

You hear a lot about how the church is dying, but this place is pretty crowded. Looking for the words that heal, I guess. Simon and I aren't shriven, so we watch the others file down the aisle to eat God.

It's such a scrum over here. Back home there are ushers that let you out of your pew row by row, and every church has a kind of traffic pattern that takes people up to the altar and back to their seats in the pews in perfect order. Here folks just seem to go for it.

You can take the Host into your hand, now. That was just starting the last time I did this, but it seems to have caught on. Even the old folks do it. And you can chew the Host these days, as well. You used to have to let it kind of dissolve. It was forever sticking to the roof of your mouth, and you'd have to try and pry it off with your tongue. Simon says that's why Catholic boys are so good at cunnilingus.

I sit there, watching them all go up and come back. I envy them so much it burns in my throat. I wish I thought I could be saved by eating the Host. I wish I could kneel back down. I wish I thought there was something there to heal me, heal us. Heal Peter, too.

Chapter Nine

Peter never visits me on a weekend, but it seems I'm not used to sleeping through the night anymore. I wake up Monday morning at 5:00, full of energy and raring to go. Sleep is suddenly hopeless, so I ease quietly out of our bed and, pulling on the sweats I was wearing the night before, go into the study. My laptop comes on with a whirr and a flash, which seems to echo through the house, and I pull the door closed.

This is the quietest hour of all the twenty-four in London. The worthy still sleep and the villains have had enough and crawled home by now. The energetic CEOs who will be at their desks by seven are still in Surrey, having their showers and listening to the shipping forecast and the farming news on Radio Four. Even the cats in the squares are curled up under the shrubbery.

I open up my notebook and read through it for maybe the twentieth time. And then I open another file and begin listing out questions. One. What happened to Jesus and why didn't he keep going with his preaching? Two. How did the whole 'believing in Jesus' idea start? Three. Explain Paul.

I look critically at this last entry, but open up my new Bible to Corinthians, reading through chapter fifteen, trying to make some sense of it. Impossible. Why was he representing them at all? I leave number three standing.

That's probably enough for one night. I switch on the printer and wait while it warms up. It's nearly six o'clock. The alarm is set for six-thirty. I have an idea. My trainers are by the door and my bag is in the living room. I burgle myself and tie on my Nikes, letting myself out quietly.

When the alarm goes off, Simon wakes up to a tray of coffee, orange juice and croissants from the bakery on the corner, still warm from the oven. His smile still devastates me, almost as much as the appeal of those chocolate eyes. 'What's all this?'

'We call it breakfast in English.'

'Yum. Pass the jam.'

God, I don't want to lose him. If I lose Simon, what have those ten years been about? If I lose Simon and we never had children together, it would be like someone had stolen a chunk of my life. I have to look away and blink back tears. 'Darling?' I finally manage to say fairly steadily.

'Umph?'

'Do you reckon we actually could go to Relate?'

I turn around in time to watch him put down the knife and consider. 'I guess,' he says. 'Although we've been doing alright, haven't we?'

'Well, maybe I'll just go see someone, if you aren't keen.'

'Maggie? Are you okay?'

But his voice sounds so far away. I feel a pressure on my arm that I find difficult for a moment to connect with the voice. 'Maggie!'

'Yeah?'

'I'll go. It's not a problem. I'll even arrange it,' and then I'm looking at him, but I can't really see him. I just see the clock and know I have to shower.

7:45 to Liverpool Street. Central Line in. Although I walk to the end of the platform, the train is heaving with Essex commuters and I don't get a seat. We are all crammed into the entrance area because some twit standing and talking to her girlfriend in the first seat won't move down the carriage. I'm in between two city types, the wide boy in the chalk stripe suit and somebody from middle management in grey slip-on loafers. I've had enough of this, I think, and shoulder down the entrance to where Chatty Kathy has blocked access to the carriage.

I mutter 'excuse me,' as I push by her, climbing over her bags, and go to lean at the very far end, against the door. Emboldened, now Chalky and a mousy little thing I hadn't noticed earlier do the same. Chatty is looking daggers at me and says something to her mate which makes them both giggle. Lovely.

Most mornings I wouldn't even notice but this morning I fight back tears over it. I'm obviously losing it. Whether Simon gets it together with Relate or not, I should probably go and see some competent human somewhere or another. It's not like it won't happen if I pretend not to notice. This morning I tucked a laser printed list of questions, neatly folded, into my pillow slip so that I could remember to ask Saint Peter all about them when he wakes me up in the middle of the night. Saint Peter played by Sean Connery, of course.

That just can't be healthy.

At St Pauls, there is a flurry of disembarkation, and I get a seat, as do Chalky and Little Mouse. All three of us give Chatty Kathy the same tight little smile as we sit down and she continues to stand. She scowls at the whole carriage. It's stupid and petty, but this cheers me up no end.

When I get to the top of the Tottenham Court Road staircase, I check my stockings. Somewhere in my scramble I hit something pointy, and I check my watch and dive into Boots for another pair. I'll keep the spare one in my case until another disaster strikes, I think. Or maybe in my desk. It occurs to me that I've had this thought before.

Anya isn't even there yet when I arrive. I love that. I shrug the mac into the closet and think I'll go right into the Ladies and see to my stocking. But Quentin hears my heels tapping by and comes out of the boardroom, where the Monday morning part-ners meeting is in full swing. 'Can you pop in here for a moment?' he asks me. I mumble something about client meeting at 9:30 and follow him in, as if I had any choice. I am utterly mystified when Rob motions me to a seat at the table.

A selection of pastries is there with two half-empty cafetieres. Everyone is drinking coffee. While I wonder what's going on, I also can't help but realise that they do this themselves, that one of them must be the one that swings by the patisserie and someone else must set the table and someone else must grind and brew the coffee. I look around the table at Martin, Crispin, Samantha, Rob and Quentin trying to figure out who does what. They all smile at me, and Martin pushes a spare cup and saucer my way. Smiling, I decline with my hand.

Rob clears his throat. 'Maggie, you're American,' he begins, and then stalls.

'Yup,' I say. 'Though I think I hide it pretty well.'

This elicits another group smile.

Rob gathers himself up to try again. 'Well,' he says, and then is reduced to fiddling with his mechanical pencil.

Quentin clears his throat. 'We've got a problem, well, it's not really a problem yet. We have a niggle, about our health insurance and absenteeism.'

I jerk myself into the meeting. They're trying to sack me! They're trying to get ready to sack me! 'It was only one day,' I say, with what I hope is a calm and confident manner.

'What?' Quentin shakes his head. 'Oh, Friday. No. No.'

They aren't trying to sack me. So that's alright.

'Still,' he says, 'It makes the point – that was your first sick day, I think, since you started, wasn't it? Some people hardly get a full week in for sickies. Stress is really what it's about. Seems like if someone gets stressed out enough, under new EU regulations, they can sue us. Sue us!'

Everyone shakes their heads and looks glum at this. Rob gets up and starts walking around the table. 'It's ridiculous,' he says. 'It's not as if there's some sort of stressometer you can hook people up to. Some people crack under the word deadline, and some people – like you, Maggie, and us around this table – just love it. Pile it on, and we just go faster!'

We all chuckle at this, and I wonder if everyone else also feels as though they are dancing on the ledge of insanity working this hard. Quentin clears his throat. 'Quite,' he says, and leans forward.

'Oh, tell her what she's here for, boys,' Samantha says. 'She's got a client meeting in an hour. And for that matter, we still have half the agenda to work through.'

I can't keep my eyebrows from raising.

Quentin smiles at me and leans across the table. 'We have to hire a head doctor,' he said. 'We're all going to go and see whoever it is, all of us, whether we feel like we need it or not, every week.'

That's a bit jammy. That's a bit too damn jammy. I immediately suspect Peter. Then I notice everyone is waiting for me to say something, so I try and find a reason I've been sitting there thinking and say, 'She or he will of course not report to management?'

Samantha snorts. 'Nothing as useful as that, dear. No, Charlie just told us that if we do this and someone does end up doolally, they can't have us in court.'

Everyone looks at me for something. Approval, I finally guess, and I nod thoughtfully.

Rob sat back down. 'Seeing as you're American and probably know more about this type of thing than we do, we wondered if you would manage the project.'

'Me?'

He shoved a clear plastic wallet across the table. 'Charlie's got a sort of shortlist. They're all accredited, have done company-wide work before. You know the company culture, Maggie. You see them. You pick one out, would you? Set up the facility? Get everyone on board?'

I try and look reluctant. 'If you really think I'm the right person for the job, I'd be glad to take it off your hands.'

'Good gal,' Samantha says, reaching for the pain au chocolat she's been eyeing intermittently since I arrived.

I show myself out.

When I finally get to my desk after changing my stocking, I put the other one in the big bottom drawer that I don't use for anything. Or at least, that's what I mean to do. When I open it up, it's bursting with packets exactly like the one I have in my hand. I must have been putting spare stockings in there for six months or maybe even a year. Carefully, I close my open door policy door and sit back down in my chair. I really have to get a grip, here. I really have to pull myself together.

I take the shortlist into my hands as if it was a lifesaving ring and stare at it intently, as if even reading the names and telephone numbers would drag me back in to safety. The jamminess of the whole thing is still bothering me. Maybe the board noticed I was working myself round the bend. Maybe that's why they handed it to me.

Maybe that's paranoia. Like about getting sacked. God, paranoid tendencies. Jesus, what is wrong with me?

But this can't just be luck. It's way too neat for luck. It's all very well thinking about Jesus not being supernatural. But then how is Peter getting to my bedside in Sean Connery's body? If he is. But then where did the olives go, if it's a dream?

Oh, bloody hell.

Say Saint Peter really is appearing on my bed every night. Every week night. I roll my eyes to the textured ceiling tiles. Just say that Saint Peter has a highly developed knowledge of work habits in the Western World and appears to me in my bedroom. Just say.

And say he really does want my help with PR. Wouldn't he and his gang want to keep me from going completely loony? Wouldn't they want me in good working order? And if they can arrange people rising from the dead and borrow bodies and things, surely arranging counselling for one of their team wouldn't take that much effort.

What? I ask myself, EU regulations inspired by divine guidance? Highly unlikely. I've read some of them, and they sound more like the work of the other side.

I open my bottom drawer and have another look at my stocking mountain. Evidence of insanity, right there. Who am I to try and reason this out? And I need to collect some stuff from Roberto's team and print out some notes I'd been working on.

I decide to take a working view. My working view is that if the board had noticed I was cracking and still gave me this assignment, it was a good thing and shows that they want me to recover. On the other hand, if there is a God meddling in my life, that could only be a good thing, too. Right now I need all the help I can get. 'Divine intervention', I mutter to myself, 'is good.' And then I open my door before anybody notices.

Simon rings while I'm out, asking me to ring him and when I do, of course, he's in a meeting, or at least that's what Sandy tells me. I wonder if she knows I know? We finally talk about 4:30, when he gives me three Relate appointments in December to choose from. We pick Friday nights, so all we have to do is go to the pub an hour and a half later than normal. Simon says that's brilliant and that we'll probably need the drink and we both laugh and then both fall silent at the same time.

I clear my throat and say, 'Thanks for organising that.'

And he says, 'Well, it's important, isn't it?'

And then we just sit and breathe to each other for a few minutes, before my other line starts blinking and I have to go.

It's the end of the month and I have to give my reports on the personal hygiene accounts. I waylay Henry and drag him in for a chat. He did his memo on time, but it's only his second one and he left a bunch of things out, and so we go through the report system again. He sulks just a little bit, so I tease him into interest by showing him what I do for Quentin, just to remind him that he will have my job one day if he keeps working hard.

By the time we finish this, it's about seven o'clock. I finish writing the thing about 8:30 and copy it onto diskette as an ASCII file. This I take down to reception to print off the Mac in colour after redoing all the headings and stuff. I use reception to collate and staple and then go back down to Quentin's office to slip the report into his in-tray. I am shocked to find Quentin still there, sitting in the dark, looking out his window with a glass in his hand.

'Sorry,' I say immediately. 'Just came in to get this to you tonight.' I wave the little plastic wallet in the air and then plop it into his in-tray.

'Maggie?'

'Yes?'

'Have you got anywhere with those counsellors?'

'No. I'll start tomorrow.'

I can't see his face, can't see if that's okay or not. I stare at the back of his head, watch his hand around the squat tumbler as it rests on the arm of his leather chair, trying to get clues.

'Sometimes-' he starts, and then sighs.

'Quentin?'

He spins around in his chair and switches on the desk lamp. He looks terrible, is my first thought, but then I correct myself. It's just the halogen light so close to his face. It bleaches out the permanent tan and shows all the lines.

'I stopped driving home on the weeknights, oh, must be six years ago, now.'

'That's right,' I say, 'I nearly forgot. You've got that little flat in Pimlico, don't you?'

I say this brightly and clearly, as if trying to drag him away from any confidences in me. I don't want to hear about Quentin's misery. I don't even want to think of him as truly human.

'Yeah.' He turns halfway towards the window. 'But every Monday night I think, What the hell am I doing here? You know?'

I look at my watch creeping towards nine o'clock. 'I know,' I say. 'It's going to take me a good half hour or forty-five minutes to get home, and I'm in Zone Two. I'm up early tomorrow. Not much marriage, is it?'

'Did it for the kids, really, moved to Berks. And now I hardly even see the little beasts.'

I can't take this. I really can't. I just stand there, shifting from foot to foot, like a schoolgirl waiting to be dismissed.

'Anyway.' He stands up and shoots the last swallow of Scotch down his throat. 'We should get out of here, don't you think? I'll order your cab, too, while you get your things.'

Cab home. Go to feed cat. Simon is standing in the kitchen over the sink with his overcoat still on, spooning rice out of an aluminium container. 'Want some?' he asks.

I'm suddenly ravenous, and get a spoon myself.

'Why do you still have your coat on?' I ask indistinctly.

'Heat's out again.'

Still chewing, I go into the utility room to inspect the boiler. No pilot light. That door needs replacing, might as well just hang a sheet over the doorway for all the good it is.

Simon comes in and watches as I manipulate the three switches needed to relight it. When I get to the stage where I have to hold the gas knob in, he spoons more rice into my mouth.

The boiler roars into action.

'My hero,' he says, applauding with the spoon on the side of the rice.

'Simon, you've watched me do that a hundred times, surely –

'I know, but it just gets better and better every time you do it.'

He smiles at me impishly, but I'm not having any of it.

'Come here.' He pettishly slings the carton into the sink and slumps over to the boiler. 'If there's no blue fire here, it means the pilot light is out. You have to turn this off, and then hold this down while you flick this, see?'

He nods. He's not looking. He's not bending over to see where the ignition switch is.

'Oh forget it,' I say. And I go upstairs and hang up my suit, brushing it before I put it in the wardrobe, and rubbing a cloth over my court shoes. Then I go into the bathroom and brush and wash and floss the rest of my façade and crawl into bed. Simon comes in with me and kisses me goodnight, but neither of us mean it at all. I toy with the idea of crying, but I can't be bothered and then I am asleep.

The smell of him wakes me up. He is standing, the way he used to when he first came to visit me, looking out at the garden. Too late, I remember that I should have worn the nightgown. I grab my glasses and look at his back for a moment. He seems monumental standing there. You know that scene in *Robin Hood*, when Sean Connery plays Richard the Lionheart and they shoot the whole thing up at him from about knee level? How imposing he looked? It's like that.

'Rock?'

He doesn't speak, but he snorts through his nose. I can't see all that much, I realise. Where's my neighbour's damn security light when I need it? I look at the clock. It's only 11:35.

'You're early.'

Nothing.

I can't get out of bed and go to him, I'm starkers. I just lay there and wait for him to say something.

He turns, and his front is even more awe-inspiring than his

back. He says, 'I should not have kissed you in that way. It will not happen again.'

I'd almost forgotten.

'It doesn't matter. Don't worry about it.'

He moves to the side of the bed and I can see his face. He's not a happy apostle. He says, 'I know you want a child badly, Maggie, but I will not make this child with you.'

I feel my jaw slack open. 'I don't want you to make a baby with me, thank you very much.'

It flits through my mind to wonder what I would do if it needed bone marrow or something, with Saint Peter as the genetic father. Or would Sean Connery be the genetic father? The whole idea is ridiculous.

'No, Rock. I want my baby to have both mother and father from the real world.'

He says, 'Mmm.' He clearly doesn't believe me.

He's such a bulky shadow, and in this mood, he's truly terrifying. The memory of that savage kiss is disturbing.

I used to have this fantasy of being staked out on a garden bench and a man coming along and using my helpless body. I know, I know, but sexual fantasies aren't really that amazingly original. And that was mine.

I told Simon about it one night, and he arranged it so that we could act it out. It was horrible. I hated it, even though I knew it was Simon, really, and that he loved me, really. I felt so dirty and hurt that I didn't even go through with it all the way. Just thinking about it makes me sick.

And the way Peter grabbed me by my hair when he kissed me makes me think that making love to a first century fisherman might be the same. I don't think it would feel much like making love, to be honest. I think it would feel like rape. It strikes me that I just liked him wanting me.

There's a word for girls like that. I say, 'Rock? I think I've been

111

a…' But it sticks in my throat. I sigh and try again. 'Look, sit down. The kisses were my fault. It won't happen again.'

'You still have trouble with this man.' Peter looks at Simon sleeping with an expression of distaste.

I don't say anything. I don't even want to look at Simon.

Now it is his turn to sigh. 'I am spending too much time here.' He sits down on the bed, on the very edge.

'The body, it is so strong. When you are dead, you forget how difficult it is to control this,' he makes a wide gesture which takes in his entire height, 'this meat.'

'Meat?'

'Yes! It has it's own ideas, the meat. Always you must rise above, rise above. So tiresome. I had forgotten.'

I say, 'Maybe the wine was a mistake.'

But he's still talking and says, 'But the Master, he says I must return. And so here I am! Jesus says go, and I must go. Maggie says sit and I sit!' He cups his hands around his face and begins to mutter something. The only word I can understand out of it all is 'dog.'

My hand automatically goes out to pat his shoulder, and the duvet slips down, exposing one breast. I refrain, and as I slide back down I hear the pillowcase crinkle.

I clear my throat. 'I've been, ah, doing a bit of research over the weekend.'

He doesn't answer, so I slip out my list. The unfamiliar rattle of the paper makes him look up.

'What is this?'

'It's just some questions I have for you.'

'Wonderful.'

'Look, do you want to do this or not?'

He snorts. A bit of snot flies out from his nose and settles on my skirting board. 'What does it matter what I want? Nobody cares what I want!'

112

'I do.'

He raises his head to look me in the eye. It's a long moment. I say, 'I'm really sorry, Rock, about coming onto you,' but he waves my apology away.

His voice thunders in my tiny bedroom. 'This fault is not yours, Maggie! I am the saint! I am the Boddhisatva! I came to you!' I am frozen at the violence in his voice. He snatches the bit of A4 from my hand and looks at it, running his finger over the smooth surface of the laser printing. 'Tell me what this says.'

My voice shakes when I ask, 'Why didn't Jesus do anything much after the resurrection?'

'Ha!'

'There's all that stuff he says and you guys say about him coming again, but he never does.'

'Yes.'

I wait for a moment, but that's all I'm getting. I swallow, 'Well?'

'Well, he was very sick. And also, he was depressed.'

Jesus Christ needed counselling? 'How do you mean, depressed?'

Peter shrugs, 'You know. Down in his mind.'

'Why?'

'Why? Why? Why? I do not know all these whys!' He stands up and starts to pace. 'It is not easy to be tortured. It is not easy when the people you came home to save say, No, Do not give us the rabbi, Give us the rapist Barabas. It is not easy to be lamed, to have the spikes go through your flesh-'

He's never shouted like this before. I really don't like it. I find myself rigid in the bed, pushed as far up against the headboard as I can get.

He sees this, and kind of deflates on his feet. He says, 'Maggie, I hate this.'

My mouth is dry. 'I can tell.'

'I am sorry. I have not been good to you tonight. No wonder you prefer him.' Peter motions his head towards Simon's side of the bed.

'He hasn't been that great to me tonight, either.'

This makes him smile. 'Poor Maggie.'

He sits down by me and takes my hand. 'Look.' A faint glimmer of light appears on the second fleur-de-lis from my light socket, and the tunnel opens up again.

Well, at least the poor bastard has gained some weight. That's the first thing I see, when I see Jesus. He's up on a cliff top. This isn't Gallilee. The earth is terracotta and the sun is fierce. There are goats behind him, grazing on the sparse grass of the top of what I would call in my own country a mesa.

Jesus is in the lotus position. His eyes are shielded, looking down.

Again, I am Peter. I must be talking, because my hands intermittently come into view. Jesus does not answer.

I look over the cliff edge to spit. The rock is honeycombed with little caves. Other guys in white scurry from chamber to chamber on the narrow paths. Down below, there are irrigated fields and people working in them, in what might be a wine press, in what looks to be a big laundry. Everyone wears white. Laundry must be pretty crucial to the Essenes.

'Qu'mran,' Peter says. I guess that's what it's called.

'What are you saying to Jesus?'

'I am trying to convince him to come home. I have travelled a long way and I want to bring him back with me.'

'And what does he say?'

'He says nothing, as you see.'

We watch Jesus sit a little more.

'Does he ever say anything?'

Peter fast forwards. 'Three days later.'

'You talked to him for three days?'

Images blur past me, some interiors. I see Jesus on a dais above a big table. And then I'm back on the clifftop, shouting, by the look of my hands. When Jesus turns his head to face me, he snaps it, and snaps his eyes open. They burn with anger. He starts to shout.

'What's he saying?'

'He's asking me how I can be so cruel. He's asking me hasn't he done enough. He's telling me to leave him alone, that he can not help me, that he has lost his way.' And then I see my arms go around Jesus, who lays his head on Peter's shoulder and cries like a child.

Rock clears his throat. 'He says he thought he was a Buddha, but he was not. He says that he failed his people. He says that he wants his Master.'

Jesus is sobbing as if his heart is breaking in his chest.

'What did you say?'

Rock stands up and the picture fades. 'I said that he should have his Master. I said we would find the money, we would hire a caravan, we would send him back to Hemis.'

Tears fill Rock's eyes. 'What could I do?' he asks me. 'What else could I do? You see how he was.'

And then something strikes me. 'You said you didn't know anything about Buddhism. And now you're saying Buddha and Boddhisatva and stuff.'

He shrugs. 'I did not, so I asked the Master. It is just words.'

'Jesus Christ being some kind of Zen Master is not just words, Rock. It's big, it's really big.'

He shrugs again. 'So, I am Saint Peeeeter, right? I stand at the gate, right? Well, you can call me gate-keeper or you can call me Boddhisatva. They both wait at the gate, to enter last, do they not? It is just names.'

We look at each other while I try to take this in. I shake my head a bit, as if I've just come out of a pool with water in my ears, as if that will help. Suddenly, talking about Jesus' breakdown seems an easier option. So I say, 'And did you manage it? Did he go back to India?'

'With most of his family. It was like a royal progress. Many had heard of his teaching. Unfortunately, Mary died on the way.'

Okay, now that's too weird to talk about, as well. In desperation, I reach for my list. I say, 'I went to Mass on Sunday, and I've been reading a bit of Paul.'

Peter sighs again. 'Go on.'

'Well, it's this whole idea of believing in Jesus. In. Not believing what he had to say, but believing in him as a God.'

Peter is perfectly still.

'Do you know what I mean?'

'Yes, Maggie.'

'Well, what's that all about? I've been reading Paul, but frankly I can't make heads or tails out of most of it.'

I look up from the paper and he's swelling with anger again. He scares me when he's like this.

'No more!' he roars.

'Stop it!' We glare at each other. 'Stop shouting at me. I hate it!'

He stalks over to the bed, where I cower against the headboard. I might have sounded brave, but my heart is beating like an overwound metronome.

When he sees how frightened I am, Peter sort of collapses. He sits back down on the bed. 'I am sorry, Maggie. It is as I said. This meat, it is so difficult. I have no control.' He reaches for my hand, but I leave it under the duvet. I don't want to touch him. I don't even want him here.

I say, 'I didn't ask for this. I've got enough going on. It was nice last week, but if you're going to be horrible…' and then to my shame, two tears leak out of my eyes.

Peter sighs again, this time with enough force to break a rib.

116

The hand I left empty wipes a thumb under each of my eyes. This actually hurts like hell, with all his callouses, and dislodges my glasses off one ear, but I don't complain. He rests his hand on my head in the blessing pose for a moment, and then strokes my hair back out of my face.

'Maggie, you are my friend.' He strikes his chest. 'I know this, here.'

He seems to be waiting for something, so I nod. 'But this is not easy for me. I have to live through bad times again, and look at all my mistakes.' He strikes his chest again. 'It hurts me.' He opens his hands and looks at me with that misery weighing in his eyes. He says, 'I am not angry at you. I am angry at my past self.' And then he mumbles something, of which I can only hear, 'woman'.

'What was that last bit?'

He says, 'I do not like to show you my mistakes.' He can't meet my eye.

And that's when I twig. He's embarrassed. I say, 'Hell, we all make mistakes, Rock.'

He's staring out at my lightsocket again. 'Not like mine, Maggie,' he says in a voice that seems to come from a million miles away.

I say, 'Are you going to tell me about Paul?'

But he says, 'No more tonight, Maggie,' in such a tone of voice that I don't dare argue.

I just lay there, looking at him. Finally, he smiles, sadly, sweetly. He bends down and kisses me on my forehead. Warmth courses through my body, relaxing all the muscles I tensed when he was shouting. He strokes my hair a few more times.

Then Saint Peter takes off my glasses and puts them in my case. Gently but firmly, he closes my eyes.

Chapter Ten

It must be something about sleep patterns that has me waking up so early. If Peter had visited me at two or three, I would probably have slept till the alarm, but since he came at 11:30, I am raring to go again at 5:00. Of course that may also be the rain.

Today, there will be no breakfast in bed for Simon. I glance at him sleeping for a second when I get up and my heart hurts in my chest just looking at him. The boiler. I can't believe we argued about the damn boiler. But still, it is his boiler, too. It's the whole thing, I think, the cheap rice takeaway, the cold house. If I went to the takeaway, I'd get something nice for both of us. When I come home to a cold house, I fix the boiler. At least he fed the cat, I'll give him that much. He looks after her and partially himself, but I don't think he's ever even considered looking after me.

This last thought comes when I'm already in the shower, so I don't have to notice that I'm crying again and can pretend it's just the shampoo in my eyes.

Half an hour later and I'm walking down Leswin Road, watching the sensible sleep. An older man, hips rolling smoothly, racewalks by me and I sigh with envy. I could have done that this morning, I could have gone for a racewalk instead of going in early. I didn't even consider it.

The 73 takes me all the way in and the traffic is dependably minimal at this time of the morning. I look through my case for something to read and come up with my copy of *Good Wives*. I catch myself about to sigh again and stifle it. I have to stop this. I sound like a boiler with a problem myself.

I can't remember where I am in the book, so I open it and random and start reading. Daisy and Demi are born and afterwards

Meg has more trouble with John. Or it seems, John with Meg. She doesn't have time to hang out with him in the evenings any more, so he starts spending his evenings away from home. That seems familiar.

Marmee's advice is to make a little more of a fuss over him and to allow him more scope in dealing with the children, which does the trick nicely.

What would Marmee say about my situation? The only woman who ends up working for a living in this thing is Jo, and she's got wonderful Professor Baer, who doesn't mind about washing and socks and no doubt about boilers. Meg and Amy married poor and rich respectively, but both of them just help their men and look after the children. My problem is that I married poor, but with rich tastes. He wants me to be like a stay-at-home wife, but he wants my income, too.

I slam the book closed. The last thing I need to read about is other people's arguments. I have enough of my own. I can even argue with a saint. I smile, thinking of Peter. It always makes me smile to think about him. Strange that. It's not like it's a laugh a minute when I'm with him.

We're already at the Angel. Why am I always arguing with Simon? Maybe that's something we'll work out in Relate. My smile fades.

I'll bet he doesn't spend any time worrying about it. It's just me fretting here. I look at my watch. He's still asleep, the bastard.

And the thought of him in that bed, his hair tangled and his shoulders bare, makes me nearly cry again, this time with longing and frustration. He is my one true love, the only one. And how I hate him sometimes, just for that.

Twenty minutes later, I get out the shrink folder. Charlie, our man at Brandon and Son Solicitors, has done his homework, or rather, his PA Tracy has. In a neat table are five names, with addresses, telephone numbers, qualifications and association memberships, practice specialities and method/theory leanings. I discount the one without BAC accreditation right away, and that leaves four. One of the four lives in Hertfordshire. The others are in Shepherds Bush, Finchley, and Hackney. I decide against the country practice, as well. Now I only have to see three.

Have to see? I open my bottom drawer again and show myself the stocking mountain. I remind myself that I have a date with Saint Peter in my sleep to talk about Saint Paul so as to get more background on a PR job I'm doing for Jesus Christ. I let myself feel, only for a second, the incredible anguish of Simon leaving me. Country Practice comes back in.

As the office slowly builds to its usual hum, I push the folder to one side and write twenty or so emails, sending them to grocery and pharmacy trade journalists about the new tampon. I don't actually spell out what is so new about the product, this is just a teaser, but in a chatty, personal way, I let them know that something big is about to happen and that there will be largish money thrown at the campaign. A few of them actually got invites to the Madam Jo Jo's do, even though it was meant to be for consumer glossies only, and I subtly remind them that they owe me large.

About nine o'clock, Quentin comes in with my report and we spend a few minutes going over some of the trickier points. He seems fairly pleased about the way things are going. Before he goes, I tell him that I've made a start on the counselling project. He gives me a searching look at this, but then just nods at me and tells me to keep up the good work, whatever that means. Anya sends Melanie to me on the coffee and croissant round that is usually confined to the board and those who are working extremely hard, and I order breakfast.

Out of the four, all can come in some time this week, and Country Practice can actually see me that afternoon, having had a cancellation. When Melanie comes in with the coffee, I ask her to stay in my office and recite the lyrics to the 'God Save The Queen', while I close the door and see if I can hear anything. I can't, and so I don't book any conference rooms for the interviews. Melanie looks at me a bit funny, but I'm pretty sure she thinks we're all crackers anyway, so that's alright.

Country Practice turns out to be a fairly good looking man in his late forties, all elegant in a slightly informal way, zip neck cashmere jumper, Italian trousers, square toed boots. He takes command of the interview quite early on, and I, amused, let him. He has a fairly impressive list of other company-wide consultancies and has a typed sheet of different scheduling and billing options which he takes out of a scuffed Mulberry satchel.

I wait for him to wind down, looking at his theory/practice entry 'mainly Jungian' and wracking my brain for old information from my freshman Psychology lectures. At last he determines that it's my turn to say something, and I give him one of my 'I hope you're happy with yourself after all that' smiles and lean forward over my desk.

'Let's say that I was having a problem,' I said. 'What would your approach to me be like?'

He runs a manicured hand through his silvering hair. 'Of course, it depends on the problem and the type of person you are.'

I smile again, and he gets a little more nervous. 'Let's say that the person is me,' I say, leaning back in my chair and swinging my legs out in front of me. 'Let's say that I believe...oh, I don't know. Let's say that I believe Saint Peter is visiting me in my sleep. Coming and sitting on my bed and having great long chats with me. How's that? Is that something to work with?'

Country Practice snorts and leans forward. 'Usually the problems are a little less dramatic,' he says. 'Usually a woman in your position has a hard time balancing family commitments and work commitments. Somewhere, they show the strain, either in their marriage or their parenting or in their work. These are the kinds of issues we deal with. And though the image, the concept, of Saint Peter may prove to be of use, it's not generally central to the real problem.'

I nod thoughtfully. 'And how would you approach what you feel is the real problem?'

'If we were talking about a woman in your position, with these heavy and conflicting commitments, we would probably try to work out ways of reaching out for help, setting boundaries, finding priorities...' Confident again, he scoots his chair forward, until he can put his elbows actually on my desk. 'It's all too easy to take on too much,' he begins. He keeps talking, but he's lost me.

I pull the file off my desk and tilt it onto my lap so that he can't see what I'm writing. 'Sexist, Pushy, Bit of a snob, Jungians are supposed to be keen on imagery, but he let a whopper of one just slip right by him, makes you wonder about what else is on his sheets. Dunno about this one. Seems dodgy.'

Just as I'm making the full stop on 'dodgy', he winds down and I look up and smile again, watching the wilting effect this has on him.

'That's fascinating,' I say, standing up. 'You can imagine what a complicated process it is for a company to choose the right person for them. Well, you've been through it all before, haven't you?'

He smiles deprecatingly.

I turn the folder over when I slide it onto the desk and he knows right then that he's blown it. He takes it well, though, buckling up his satchel without making small talk or trying to sell himself any more. We walk down the shantung hallway and I press the lift button for him. 'Thanks so much for coming in,' I say. 'I'll be in touch.'

When he turns around in the lift, he looks down his nose at

122

me, and lets his arrogance shine through. I have not made a mistake, I decide. He really is horrible.

Anya is in reception, and I take a moment to thank her for the coffee run. I also tell her that I used the colour printer last night and hope I didn't run it out of anything. She also disapproved of Country Practice, and this makes me feel better. Then I look at my watch, shocked at the time it all took, and start to run again.

Body Mist trauma at five, and by the time I get Celia straightened out, it's seven o'clock. Muttering sullenly, I ring Simon just because I haven't spoken to him all day. He's left the office. I ring his mobile. It starts to ring and then I get the message service. That either means he's on the Underground or he saw my number and switched it off. Although it's a bit early I ring for a cab. Get one right away. Home by 7:30.

It's cold. There's only one light on in the place and that's in the utility room. Cat comes to whine for her supper, but first I follow the light in there, where I hear something. Something turns out to be Simon, with brown rubber piping and a staple gun, draughtproofing the door. He looks at me briefly, no appeal in those eyes. He's not doing this to make me happy. He's doing this so as not to feel such a shit.

Feed cat. Upstairs to brush suit, look critically at it and put it in dry cleaning basket. Polish shoes. Wash hands, take out contacts, don sweats. Downstairs. Door is closed. Boiler is started. Without speaking to me, Simon shoves a glass of something white into my hand. It is delicious. A Sauvignon Blanc of some description, vaguely vegetal on the finish, but in a nice way.

I get two giant potatoes and turn on the oven to heat while I spear them with a fork. Then I throw them in to bake, and open the fridge again to rummage, pulling out half an onion, a bit of brie, a soft avocado, a bag of salad that doesn't look too bad.

Simon takes off his overcoat and his suit jacket and lays them over a kitchen chair.

'I sorted it,' he says.

'I see,' I say. I wait for a moment, and then go back to sorting through the salad bag.

'Is that all you're going to say?' This is said with a rising inflection of both tone and volume.

I sigh. Yet again. I turn back away from my salad bag. 'What do you want me to say, Simon? You hardly applaud every time I light the damn thing.'

'I've done more than light it. I've stopped the draught, well, cut it down anyway.'

'Thank you.'

I raise an eyebrow at him, asking him if he's quite finished, and he looks away. I go back to sorting through the salad bag. He pushes the chair back and the next thing I hear is the television, up too loud.

I putz around in the kitchen the entire forty-five minutes it takes the potatoes to cook. Then I bring Simon in his tray. It looks wonderful, I must say. The giant potato steams and the chunk of brie melts into the butter like an advertisement. He looks at it and says, 'No thanks.'

I know this one. I say. 'Oh, sorry,' and put it just out of his reach, on the coffee table, and take my own napkin and fluff it out on my chest. 'Is there any wine left?' I ask, and he furiously jumps up and gets it, his hand shaking with rage as he pours me a glass.

'Thanks.'

He goes to put the wine on the coffee table and then comes face to face with the brie, the potato, the salad, the home-made sundried tomato and olive tapenade on the garlic bread. Grumbling, he seizes his tray. I'm not sure at first whether he's going to eat it or throw it across the room, but then he sits abruptly down and shakes out the napkin.

'Ohmmnzerliane.'

'Pardon me?'

'I'm not going to let this go to waste.'

'Jolly good,' I say, in my children's television presenter's voice he so hates, and then I relent and go for the full Blue Peter. 'It's one I made earlier.'

He's taken a bite of potato, and when he looks at me so furiously, with that bulge in his cheek, he's like an angry squirrel. This makes me giggle and then we are both laughing, at the whole situation. It is one of those laughs that makes you think about how long it has been since you laughed like that. My ribs ache.

When we finally stop, Simon has to use his napkin to wipe potato out of his nose. This sends us off into giggles again, but he finally calms down enough to say, 'I'm sorry about last night, I was an ass.'

And I say, 'I was an ass tonight. So we're even.'

Cat comes in and flops down heavily in front of the fire, looking from face to face. She's not interested in our food tonight, but she is here. Perhaps she's been worried. I don't know. Can cats sense these things?

In bed by 9:00. Simon makes love to me fiercely and thoroughly. Asleep by 9:45, smiling.

'Maggie?'

'Hmmmm?'

'Maggie, it is me.'

'Oh, hang on.' I give myself a brisk shake and grab my glasses, turning on the light afterwards.

Peter's already sitting on my bed. It's one o'clock. I rub my eyes behind my lenses. 'Sorry,' I say. 'I must have been really out of it.'

'I am sorry to wake you.'

'It's okay.'

We look at each other for a moment. I don't know what he sees, but whatever it is makes him smile, and when his eyes crinkle up, I reach out and pat his knee, which juts out where he sits on his foot. 'Hi,' I say.

His smile fades. 'I am also sorry that I frightened you last visit.'

It strikes me that I'm terribly glad to see him. I must have been worried that he would never come back. I mumble the gist of this to Peter, who says, 'You are very kind to help me, Maggie, and I should not be angry with you. None of this is your fault.'

He says this quickly and in a sort of sing-song voice that makes me think, 'You memorised that little speech, didn't you?'

He looks embarrassed again.

'Did Jesus make you tell me that?'

'The Master was not pleased with my behaviour.'

Which means Jesus is somehow monitoring these discussions? I look around. 'Is he here?'

This makes Peter grin again. 'No,' he says. 'I am Boddhisatva. I know the gate. I go back and forth.'

'From where to where?'

'You would not understand.'

I start to protest, but then think that I've probably got enough to deal with. I lay back down on the pillows.

'So tonight,' Rock continues, 'We must talk about Saul.'

'Who's Saul?' Now he's completely lost me.

'Paul, then.'

'How many of these buggers are there?'

'It is the same man.'

'Oh.'

We look at each other for a moment. 'Saul was a big problem.' Peter thinks for a moment. 'Give me your hand, and I will show you.'

It's a town, but it's not Jerusalem. There's a market and it seems early. People are rushing about a bit.

'Tiberius,' Peter says.

We're talking to the owner of a fish stall and the owner is

126

laughing and clapping us on what must be Peter's shoulder. And then everybody freezes. Slowly, we dolly to face whatever has come up behind us. It's six Roman soldiers, who have marched into town. They're like an honour guard. In the middle of them is a weedy bloke in nice clothes. He clears his throat and begins to read from a scroll. He's got a supercilious expression on his face, as if he could smell the fish and didn't think much of them.

'What's he saying?'

'He's saying he has the power to put the heretics to death. He's saying Jesus was not the Messiah and anyone who says he was will be killed.'

'Oh, shit.'

'Exactly.'

People are looking at Peter covertly, but nobody says anything.

'You've got good friends there.'

Peter starts to spit and catches himself in time. One of these days, though, my floorboards are going to get spattered with saint loogie. He says, 'Saul was like a weasel. He could smell his quarry.'

Sure enough, the weasel's eyes rest speculatively on Peter, who turns his back. The scene fades.

'Had Jesus left for the Himalayas yet?'

'No. I had just begun to raise the money.'

'Was he still in that Essene place?'

'Yes. In Qu'mran. South of Judea.'

'Well, that's good.'

'Look.'

It's a man, walking along. He's kind of skinny and a bit bent. Nothing much to look at.

'Stephen.' Peter says.

He might be familiar. I can't remember if I've seen him before.

'Where are we?'

'Jerusalem. I had gone to talk to James about this problem.'

I should have recognised it. It's got rather distinctive architecture

127

and is a bit built up for Galilee. And then Saul comes into the frame, his face distorted by shouting.

He's exhorting a group of people. He bends and with a strength you wouldn't expect in his weedy little body, he hurls a good sized rock at Stephen, which catches him in the face. Everyone near Saul does the same and they keep pelting him with the things. Stephen's face is bleeding and he raises his arms to try and protect it, which throws him off balance and he falls to his knees. And that's the end, really. The men are egged on by Saul, who is watching to make sure they're all throwing. It doesn't take long for Stephen to die.

I mean, one minute he was just walking along. And the next minute he's like sponge. Bloody sponge.

Peter says bitterly, 'Jerusalem Sanhedrim. They would have licked Saul's feet like dogs. He was a Roman Citizen, you know.' We sit and look at them all congratulating each other. 'I could not even get his body.'

'Shit, Peter.' I drop his hand, sickened. I reach for my water bottle and offer some to him, but he waves it away. 'Saul was like the Inquisition.'

'Yes,' Peter seizes on this. 'Yes, exactly like.'

'What did you do?'

'I did not know what to do, Maggie. James was useless. So I sent to the Master to ask his advice.' This bothers him and he jumps to his feet. 'Advice only is what I wanted, Maggie. Do you understand?'

'Sure.' I can't really see why he's getting all worked up.

He sighs and sits back down. 'It was a tricky time,' he said. 'Only a few of us knew of the Master's plans. The Essenes, they did not know. They thought he was going to help them build a new Judea. And now we have many hundreds of followers, and they do not know. We told them Jesus was going to ascend into heaven.'

I give him a sharp look and he shrugs. 'Those mountains near Hemis were very high,' he says, 'it was not much of a lie, truly.'

'Bullshit.'

'Well,' he shrugs again, 'anyway.'

'So what did Jesus advise?'

He does that puffing thing with his lips again and waves for my hand. He says, 'This is not my memory. I can only show you my thoughts.'

And I think, so? But when the tunnel appears, I can see what he means. All the detail is gone. The land, the vegetation is like a child's drawing, one clump of grass in the foreground and a lot of white space. It's the difference between a movie and a stage play. Peter says, 'Saul was on his way back to Damascus.' And then I see him, Saul. He's walking with a little bag over one shoulder. Scroll tops protrude. He's kind of mincing along. I wonder how much of that is Saul's real walk and how much is what Peter thinks of him.

We pull back along the road and there are his honour guard. They're all relaxed, laughing and joking amongst themselves. One of them pulls a wine pouch out from under his breastplate and they all get excited and sit down for a moment, pulling off their helmets. Saul continues to mince. He's way out of sight and earshot.

Suddenly, Jesus jumps out of the vegetation and into Saul's path. He waves his arms around and shouts.

Saul's little weasel mouth drops open and he falls to his knees. Jesus dances around him, shouting, and then disappears into the brush again. Saul appears to be having some kind of stroke or seizure. He pisses himself, jerking around on the path, frothing up mud to stain his clothes. When the soldiers finally arrive, he's holding onto to his head and moaning. He can't seem to open his eyes in the sunlight.

Peter drops my hand.

I say, 'I can't believe Jesus did that.'

Peter snorts. '*You* can't believe it? I wanted to kill him!'

'What happened?'

'Saul had seen the risen Christ! He converted overnight.'

'And when did he start calling himself Paul?'

'When he knew the Master had given me a new name, he wanted one for himself,' Peter smiles wryly. 'He was ambitious.'

'You didn't like him.'

'Like him? I hated him!' Peter jumps to his feet and begins to pace again. 'If I had not hated him, things would not have gone so wrong. If I had been a bigger man. If I could forgive. If I could have opened my heart…'

As he says the word heart, he strikes his breast with his fist and he stands there, doing this until I say, 'I don't get it.'

It's like he's forgotten I'm there. 'What do you mean?' he asks.

'I don't understand the problem. I mean, you wanted him to stop killing you guys and he did. Sooooooo…?'

'Tomorrow night.'

'Aw!'

'Tomorrow night, Maggie!' His thundery voice is back.

'You can't just keep bullying me, Rock. It's not fair.'

'Sorry, sorry, sorry.' Saint Peter sinks down onto my bed again and looks at the wall. In profile, in the lamplight, the wrinkles and lines on his tanned face are etched so deeply. How does Sean Connery get so tanned? Does he play a lot of golf? Or is the tan Peter's? I lay there trying to remember if Connery is always tanned. Was he tanned in *The Name of the Rose*?

And the next thing I know the alarm is drilling my eardrum again.

Chapter Eleven

67 to Dalston Junction, 38 to Holborn, 10 up Oxford Street. Traffic slow, bored to tears, resort to *Good Wives* again. This morning Marmee's advice simply seems sound, and I am touched nearly to tears when Beth comes to realise she will not live much longer.

So, what's changed? It's clearly not the book.

It's the whole trust issue again, I suppose, but it's more than that, too. It's like in the modern world we have forgotten how to give, really give to each other. We're good at racking up relationship points by appearing to give in, but we don't really give up anything. Not really. Not anything important.

Of course, when Meg gives in over something, she knows John will be giving, too. She has this… Shit, we're back to trust again. The jump of the faith, or however Peter mangled it. I could be as 'soft' as Simon wants me, if only I knew he was giving too. If only I could make that jump.

Even when I do make the jump and it works, I still find myself back over on the other side. I wake up, or I'm on the bus or something, and discover I've wandered back to my side of the crevice, and need to jump again. And it takes a terrible amount of trust to keep doing that. A terrible, terrible amount.

I'm not sure I've got it.

Clickety-clicking down Oxford Street, I am made to pause at a corner and can't help but see myself reflected in a large plate of glass opposite me. My hair gleams, my makeup is faultless, my suit fits perfectly and everything matches. Nothing is obviously last year's, nothing is too remarkable, everything looks as though it cost much more than it did. Nonetheless I am dissatisfied, and even when the traffic clears, I still stand, looking, wondering why.

There are new flowers on reception, obese pom-poms of carnations. It's almost time to think about buying a poppy, I remind myself, looking at the calendar. I usually buy four or five, so that I always have one looking nice against my lapel. They tend to bend up and look crumpled, and then you look cheap. Some people have really nice floppy ones, not like the cardboard ones, and I wonder, as I put my mac in the cupboard, where they get them. I've always wanted to know, but never wanted to emphasise my foreignness by asking. Anya comes to the door while I'm picking my case back up and I buzz her in.

Down the shantung hallway to my office. Email notifier going bananas. I sit and click.

Shepherd's Bush is a Freudian, and is ushered in to me at 10:00. A woman, this one, tweed jacket, corduroy skirt, low heeled boots, jumper, glasses. She is so quiet as we shake hands and order coffees that I find myself nearly gabbling in my efforts to make things look like they're going well. This is a reflex, I think to myself, and let the room fall silent.

The coffee arrives and I decide to let her doctor her own. Again, silence devolves and the rustles and clinks of bodies and spoons are loud with the door closed. I smile. 'Would you like to tell me a bit about your practice?' I ask. 'Experience, approach, that sort of thing?'

She concisely lists out her previous experience, which includes several media companies. I nod encouragingly, as if speaking was not her natural way of communication and I need to help her. And then I stop that, as well. She is just unnaturally self-possessed. I have never seen anyone less awkward in my life. The nervousness which most people feel in such a meeting is so obviously absent that I find myself wanting to supply it.

I give her a quick briefing on why we are interested in hiring a counsellor, which, from the look on her face, is entirely unnecessary. Under the ledge of my desk, I look at my watch. It has been four minutes.

I ask her how she modifies her approach for a corporate setting, given the obvious time limitations, and she gives me another dense little speech about therapeutic methods that seems terribly sound to me. I really don't know what else to ask her. My foot starts to jiggle, and I bark it on the rough underside of my desk, which makes me think about my stocking, which makes me think about my stocking mountain, my marriage and Saint Peter.

'Would it be all right if I were at this point to give you a hypothetical situation?'

She nods.

'Suppose you were our counsellor and I had a problem that I wanted to talk to you about?'

She leans back a little and settles her glasses more firmly on her nose. 'Yes?' she says. 'And what would this problem be?'

'Suppose I told you that Saint Peter is visiting me every night - I correct myself, '- every weeknight, and talking to me about his public relations problems.'

I would have bet money that Shepherd's Bush had never laughed in her life, but this produces a wry grin. 'Is this the problem you want to talk about?' she asks me.

'Well, yes.'

'Why is it a problem?'

Because it means I'm going crazy, I think, but I don't say it. Instead I think back to try and find something more tangible. 'Well, for one reason, I don't wear anything to bed and it's driving Saint Peter crazy.'

'Why don't you wear a nightie, then?'

'Because my husband hates it when I wear anything to bed. He says it's unhygienic, but I think he just likes me to be naked with him.'

This gets another wry grin.

133

'So you have to choose between, what, tempting Saint Peter? And irritating your husband.'

'Yes.'

'And how do you choose?'

'So far I have mostly tempted Saint Peter. Although one night I did wear the nightgown.'

'And how did your husband react?'

'He wasn't there.'

'Ah!' she says, as bends over eagerly in her chair, reminding me of a dog scenting a trail. 'Where was he?'

Ah, yourself, I think, and then figure I might as well tell her. 'With his assistant, working late,' I say. I make little quotations marks in the air around the 'working late.'

'Tell me about the assistant.'

I shrug, squirming in my chair. 'I don't know that much about her. Her name is Sandy. She's younger than I am by about ten years. And she's sleeping with my husband.'

'Wow.' Shepherd's Bush obviously didn't expect this on her interview. But what strikes me is how much she's enjoying herself, how much she likes what she does. I check my watch. We've still got another fifteen, twenty minutes.

I clear my throat. 'So,' I say, 'if this were my problem, how would you approach it?'

She is sitting now like a wren, her head on one side, her eyes brightly blinking behind their small metal frames. She gives herself a little shake and smiles at me.

'Well,' she says, 'I suppose I would want to find out a bit more about both relationships, and what Saint Peter means to you, both in your nightly relationship and as an image. And at the same time, if we could explore a bit about your family relationships, that might be helpful.'

I nod, feeling terribly exposed now. I make a conscious effort not to let my body language reflect this.

'How do you think this problem might affect my work performance?'

Here she is on safer ground and she snuggles back into the chair. 'Well, of course, when someone is preoccupied with a problem of this magnitude, it is bound to have an effect on their performance.' Now she makes a little darting motion with her neck, like the wren has seen a tasty insect, but decided not to go for it. Weird. 'But of course, it could be the other way around as well. Often when there is trouble at home, people tend to spend more and more time in the office. If the workload isn't sufficient to excuse that sort of behaviour, often they will take on more projects or even subconsciously sabotage their own work in order to mask this behaviour.' We get another little darting neck movement.

'And, presumably, if the person is in enough of an autonomous position, no one would realise the sabotage?'

'Oh, of course. It is a short-lived phenomenon, in any case, but it can do much damage.'

'I'll bet.' At least I haven't been doing that. At least I've been doing my work properly.

'But the danger for the employer can be that they overload their employee with projects far past their capacity.'

'Because they seem to want them.'

'Exactly.'

We beam at each other for a second.

'That's really interesting.'

'And very difficult to detect.'

I think about Quentin sitting in the dark swilling Scotch. He doesn't even go home any more, except on the weekends. From what I know of his social life he must be hard pressed to find time to deal with any home problems. Maybe he schedules them in for Sunday afternoons.

'This is really interesting,' I say again.

'I think so!'

I can't believe it. Shepherd's Bush has made a little joke. I glance back down at my watch and then say, 'Well, I'm afraid our time is up,' which makes her smile.

At the lift I tell her that I'll be in touch and turn thoughtfully to walk back to my office.

'What did you think of that one?' Anya asks me.

'I liked her.'

'We did, too.' Anya is talking to me while her hands are busy collating something shiny and important looking. 'She's a bit spooky though, isn't she?'

She is a bit spooky, Anya's absolutely right. And when I do go down the hall to notate her CV, it's the only word I can think of. Interesting, Acute, Keen as mustard, but Spooky.

Lunch with Russell at Mezzo, shouting over the noise and our pasta. I'm mock drinking, lifting and lowering my wine glass while only barely wetting my lips each time because I have another appointment at three-thirty. Russell's in full flow, more for the benefit of the extremely attractive waiter than for me. Henry's doing a great job, we both agree. This makes me happy on three points. One, for the sheer professional pride of the account. Two, because I have taught Henry so well. Three, because it means that I will perhaps never have to lunch with Russell again.

Pour client into cab and hie self up street to the Berners Hotel, clickety-click. Helen was an editor when I was an account handler. Now she has jumped over into the strata of publishing where real money starts to be made. She still exercises much editorial control over the four or five women's titles in her stable and is perhaps my most important contact. Both of us must power lunch and both of us have homes, hers complete with two children. I dreamt up afternoon tea meetings as a way of both giving her an unusual treat and getting the two of us out of the office and home by five-thirty. She loves me for it.

You don't really want to use the word leak on a tampon campaign, but that is what I do, tell her what the client is up to and tell her that it is going to be a huge PR campaign. When I mention the product mail-out, her little eyes light up, and she starts mentioning advertorial effectiveness, especially bolstered with a mention in the health sections. By the time we've worked our way up the cake trays to the strawberry tarts, we have some sort of a deal worked out and she swears that her lips are sealed.

Tube home, change at Liverpool Street for train. I'm so early I get a seat all the way.

I could have gone back to the office, but the voice of Shepherd's Bush lingers in my ears. I go home to face my problems and my life, but all that is waiting for me is the cat, who comes tearing in her flap when she hears me. She rubs up against my legs as though it is the biggest holiday in the world and I am her present.

I pour myself a hot bath and just as I step into it, I hear my mobile go. Back out, and dripping, run through the house naked like a mad woman, trying to find the damn thing, which I finally locate in my mac pocket by the front door. As I fumble with the buttons it stops ringing, but I hit reply list and see that it was Simon. I pad back to the bath, ringing him on the way.

He asks if I can be home early and I tell him I'm in the bath already.

'That's handy. I'm making dinner.'

'You're what?'

'Don't argue. Just soak. I'm already on the train.'

I'm just at that point of a bath when you lazily contemplate actually using the soap and shampoo when I hear the key in the lock. The next thing I know, Simon is there, looking at me in my nest of bubbles.

'Ummm,' he says. 'Just in time!' He slides his satchel and

shopping under the towels and leans over to kiss me. It is a nice, deep, penetrating kiss, which makes my back arch and my breasts bob out of the water. He reaches for them, but he still has his overcoat on and I stop him.

'Simon! You'll get soaked!'

'Yeah. Yeah, you're right. I'll get dinner on, shall I?' And then I am left to hate myself as he slumps back to the door to hang up his things properly. What is wrong with me? Why should his overcoat be more important than our sex life?

I bought that overcoat. Cashmere, Armani. Even in the sales it cost me £530. But he'd sacrifice it for a novel shag.

This is a new little circle of pain. The overcoat circle. I should have been more receptive, he should take care of the things I buy him, I should be more receptive, but he should take care of the things I buy him. Aaaargh! I sink under the water to get my hair wet for a shampoo, and perhaps to drown myself as well.

As I get out of the bath, I notice a strange tinge to the steam on the mirror. I blow my nose on some toilet paper and flush it and then I can smell it. Onions and garlic. Burning in olive oil. It's filling the house, any moment now the smoke alarm – there it goes. And there I go, upstairs, to pretend to get the sweats which I'd remembered to take down with me. The cat follows me, and we retreat into the bedroom, where I open the French windows a crack. We both stand there, she on her back legs, balancing her front ones on the little sill, noses to the fresh wind. When I look down at her, she looks up at me, and it makes me smile.

He's trying so hard, poor lad. He's trying so very, very hard.

I lather moisturiser all over my body and face and towel the excess back into the skin until I have a moist pink glow. I put lipliner all over my lips and blot until I have a sexy wine mouth that no food or kisses will remove. I soak my neck, my wrists and my thighs in Coco, one of his favourites, and pull a strapless black velvet gown out of the closet. I leave my hair wet, just gloss it up with hair serum, and my feet bare. I take off every bit of jewellery, except for my wedding ring.

'Maggie? Dinner's ready!'

He's sweating furiously as he builds his masterpieces onto plates. I turn the spiral staircase quickly and come to stand in the doorway. He doesn't look up. 'I thought we'd have them on trays because *Animal Hospital* comes on soon.'

'Fine,' I say.

When he looks up and sees me, he blinks a couple of times before it registers. He makes a strangled sound in the back of his throat.

'What did you make?' I ask him.

'Mushroom omelettes.'

'Do you like them cold?'

'They're much better cold,' he says. He's already pulling out his cuff links.

It was the kitchen table in the end, a strangely exhilarating experience, with the kitchen door still open for the smoke and no curtain on that window but a row of plants. Afterwards we sat wrapped in the chenille throw in front of the fire, watching Rolf Harris and eating cold omelettes with warm Muscadet. Heaven.

Cat came down when she heard the ruckus, took one look, and went back upstairs. When we go up, she shifts a bit more to the middle of the bed and we all fall asleep at the same time.

I must feel his weight on the bed, because I wake up to find him sitting in the dark. He's breathing extremely slowly and sits completely motionless. And then I notice his hands on his knees, cupped into little circles. Sean Connery is meditating on my bed.

Just as I resolve not to disturb him, a yawn cracks my face.

He puts his hands together and makes a low sitting bow. I take my glasses out of the case and switch on the light.

'I'm sorry. I didn't want to disturb you.'

He shrugs. 'It helps with the meat. If I'm going to spend so long in it, I should discipline it once more.'

I yawn again. I can't help it. And when I do, I ask, 'Where's the cat? Is she here?'

'No. She goes out to hunt frogs about this time.'

It's three o'clock.

'Where is she when you come earlier?'

'She goes down to eat and then lies on the kitchen table over the heating device.'

'She's not supposed to do that.'

'That's why she waits until you're asleep. She is a very mannerly cat.'

'It sounds like you know her.'

'We have met.'

'I never see you together.'

He shrugs.

'Does it freak her out?'

'I helped her with that.' He stretches his back, considering. 'She does not enjoy my visits. She knows the laws of her world and does not like to see them broken.'

'Cats are like that. She doesn't even like it when I move furniture.'

This makes him smile.

I rub my eyes under my glasses. I yawn again. 'Where were we? Oh, yeah, Paul.'

His smile goes as quickly as if his mouth was a drawstring bag and someone had pulled it tight.

'Look,' I say, after yet another splitting yawn, 'if you don't want to do this, it's cool. I don't mind sleeping through the night. At all.'

He puffs out his lips. 'It is my work, Maggie.' He shrugs again. 'It is a heavy burden, these mistakes. I can not rest.'

And again, in his eyes, I see that ancient pain, so palpable it's

140

nearly a third presence in the conversation. The voice and the gestures might be Connery's, but the pain is all Peter's. Saint Peter's. And whether these are dreams or hallucinations or visitations organised by some sort of God, they must be important *somehow*, or they wouldn't seem so real. It must be important for me to try and help this poor bastard with what he thinks are his PR problems. I catch myself starting to yawn again, and instead drink some water and try to assume a more professional air.

'Where were we?' I say. 'As far as I understand it so far, you were after a change in, what, the legal system?'

Peter nods.

'And when Jesus came along talking about a New Covenant,' I use air quotes, 'you decided he was the goods. But you had to make him the Messiah to save his skin and to launch the product, which in this case is Jesus' teachings.'

Peter has turned to face me. Something is dawning in his eyes.

'In order to make him the Messiah, you had to fake some of the prophecies, including the Resurrection. You also planned to fake his ascension into heaven.'

He winces. 'The Transfiguration. We said he went up into high mountains and turned into a beam of light.'

'And they bought it?'

He nods. It's my turn to raise my eyebrows at him. Still, if it worked, who am I to argue?

'Anyway, Jesus has fucked off back to India and left you holding the baby.'

Peter gasps and says, 'You should not-', but I wave this aside.

'But before he goes, he terrorises this little Saul guy, who then reckons he's had a transcendental religious experience.'

Peter looks horrified, but I can now recognise the something in his eyes. It's hope.

'Now what happens? Show me a movie.' I thrust out my hand.

Dazed, Peter takes it, and the tunnel starts to open up on my wall.

I don't know where this is. It looks kind of like Galilee. Lusher than Judea, anyway, and lusher than that red place Jesus was hanging out that started with a Q. Paul is wearing white, which is a bit of a comedown from the gold embroidered stuff he used to sport. He's hectoring folks in a marketplace and has gathered quite a crowd. Of course I don't get any sound and my ancient Greek or Hebrew or whatever he's spouting is a little rusty anyway, so it's not much use.

Peter says nothing.

But the scene cuts and we're in Capernaum again. Peter's sitting on the steps of what must be the synagogue, talking with some folks who are sitting on the ground near his feet. They ask questions, he answers them. Sometimes he spreads his hands wide in that 'I haven't the foggiest' gesture I've come to know so well.

'Do you see?' he asks me.

'It would help if I knew what you both were saying.'

He snorts. 'Paul was saying that if you believe in Jesus Christ you will never die.' His head bends forward and shakes slowly from side to side. 'He said that–'

But I'm still in work-mode and cut in, 'So he talked all kinds of crap. Why couldn't you tell him to shut up?'

'He thought he knew best.'

'Why didn't you hit him with the facts?'

Peter jumps to his feet and faces me. 'Why do you think? He was a Roman Citizen, Saul. He was also rabboni. He had connections. He could have denounced us. Imagine how angry he would be, if he knew he had been tricked? He might have gone back to persecuting us, and that after knowing who we all were!'

I say, 'Oh,' but it doesn't sound like much.

'Even though he converted, he still has his friends and his family. His cousin the this, his cousin the that.' Peter is making a little flapping mouth with his hand. 'I could not trust him. And James was terrified, after Stephen.'

'So what did you do?'

'I tried to reason with him. I tried to tell him he does not always know best.' Peter runs out of words for a moment and puffs at me two or three times with much frantic arm waving. 'But it is like trying to reason with a flood or a fire! On he goes! On he goes, the great Apostle Paul!' His sarcasm booms around my tiny bedroom, finally dying into echoes.

He sinks down onto my bed.

'How long did this go on?'

He mumbles something.

'Rock?'

'Twenty years.'

I start to laugh. 'Don't you think you could have cut loose with the truth sometime? I mean after a year or two, he'd be in so deep that even his cousins-'

'Yes, yes, yes, Maggie.' The pain in his voice is so sharp that my laughter cuts out. 'It's very funny, isn't it?' He buries his hands in what's left of his hair.

'Well, why didn't you?'

'Because I hated him.' His voice is barely audible. 'We all hated him, but I hated him the most. Everything came easy to Saul. He was lettered, he was wise, he could manage his flocks so well. Clearly, this should have been his burden. And I should have given it to him. But instead, I clutched my burden to me like a child. I would not share it.'

'For that long?'

'For that long.' He raises his head. Tears are streaming down his cheeks. 'Even when we died together. I told him nothing.'

'Shit, Peter.'

He nods soberly. He says, 'Shit indeed.'

'And meanwhile, he's converting up a storm. Look at the size of that crowd he had gathered!'

Peter's face folds into a grimace of pain so grotesque that even if Connery could make it, he'd be directed not to. 'I know! And many were gentiles! What could the New Convenant mean to a gentile?' He dries his eyes on what I guess I could call his sleeve and then blows his nose on it as well. 'It was crazy,' he says, neatly folding over the fabric so that the snot doesn't show.

I lay there for a moment. It's a lot to take in.

Finally I ask him, 'So, what have you done about it since you've been dead?'

Saint Peter gives a ribcracking sigh and settles down against the footboard, swinging his feet onto the bed. 'I have done many visitations.'

'To who?'

He shrugs. 'To the powerful. Presidents, Premiers. I appear to every Pope…'

Oh, they must love that. No wonder they often pop their clogs so quickly. First of all there's all that stress with the white smoke business and then they get Saint Peter coming to tell them that the whole Christ thing is pretty much a hoax.

But Peter's still talking, 'philosophers…' he mumbles an aside, 'though that is tricky, many of them go mad,' and then continues counting the others off on his fingers, 'writers, musicians, artists…' his voice finally trails to a stop.

'And?' I ask.

'And nothing, Maggie. If any of it had worked, you would already know the truth. I would not have had to tell you, would I?'

'Is that what you want? For everyone to know the truth?'

'Yes!' Peter gets out of bed and begins to pace. 'You know how an unruly vine can cover a tree?'

I nod.

'And then, the tree can not live?'

I nod again.

'And so the tree collapses? And with it the vine?'

I refuse to nod any more. I ask, 'What's with the horticulture?'

And Peter says, 'The Master's word is the tree. Paul's words are the vine. And they are both dying.'

He comes to my bedside and reaches out for my hand. 'Maggie, we must cut the vine to save the tree. We must save the Master's words.'

And for the first time I realise what he's asking of me. A heavy weight descends on my head. I can nearly hear the discs in my neck grinding together.

I say, 'Oh, shit,' and close my eyes.

I am tired when I wake up. I refuse to think about Peter's visit. I want to concentrate on my nice warm bed. It is lovely in my nice warm bed. It's nearly impossible to get out of my nice warm bed when Simon's in it.

When the alarm goes off and he kisses me good morning, our hands automatically reach for each other and we are halfway to making love before we even think about it. 'I can't, I can't, I can't,' he murmurs against my lips, and neck, and with a wrench, he heaves himself upright. He has an erection you could hang a towel on.

'We should move closer to my office,' he says, as I help to make the bed. 'It doesn't matter for you, does it? All roads lead to Oxford Circus.'

'We just got this place done!' All I can think of is all the work, the days and days and days of work.

He comes up behind me, the rat, pressing himself into my buttocks and kneading my breasts. 'But if we lived closer to my office, I wouldn't have to leave you right now.'

The images of boxes and floor sanders fade as my back arches and I lay my head on his shoulder. 'I'll think about it.'

In the end, we are out the door fairly early. I run down Leswin Road to catch the 73 all the way in. I leave *Good Wives* in my case, and stare out the window in a pleasurable glow. I don't have a meeting until 11:00. I don't have much on my plate today at all. It's nice, this, just sitting here, looking out the window. Today I put my mac in the dry cleaning basket and am wearing my overcoat. I feel snug, rolling along, wrapped up in my own private blanket.

Traffic is still light, and the bus isn't busy. We're cracking along at a good rate. I'm halfway down the bus upstairs, not because my favourite seat was taken, but because I just couldn't be bothered to go any further. Two women, five years younger than myself, come to sit in front of me. They're both dressed like Anya and her team, trendy black bits of clothing, layered jumpers, leather jackets, chic little trainers.

They look behind them as they sit down and somehow mutually decide to discount my presence and continue their conversation as if I wasn't there. They're talking about some club that's on tonight and whether or not to go and whether or not if they do go some guy will be there. I only half-heartedly eavesdrop, still finding the window entertaining, until I hear the brand name of my tampon account.

I imagine my ears must have pricked up like a horse's hearing oats going into a bucket. 'But I don't like those,' one hipster says, 'they're good, but they get your hands all messy.'

Ah, I think to myself, but I'm about to change all that.

'True,' says hipster two, 'but what I don't like about them is you can't have a poo around them. They're just too big. It says on the leaflet that you can, but you can't.'

'It says that? I can't even wee around them. Not properly. I'm always changing them. Costs a fortune.'

'They are good, though, for like going out and things.'
'Yeah.'

'But you don't really want to pull, do you? I mean, if I go, and he's there, well this time I can't say no, really, can I? Not after last week, he'll think –'

'Yeah.'

'So, I might as well just use a pad, really, and have an early night.'

Hipster one giggles. 'Yeah, okay. I might still go.'

'If you see him, right, tell him I'm sick or something. Tell him I said to say hello.'

'Yeah, alright.'

'But only if he comes over to you.'

More giggles. 'He will.'

'I hope so. Did you see what...'

I stop listening, and go into a panic, heart racing, breathing quickly. I'm suddenly colder and I wrap my coat closer. It's not going to work, I think. The launch won't work.

If other women are like that girl, then all the applicators in the world won't switch her over. It's the whole concept of the tampon that they don't want. They would rather leak than suffer a bit of discomfort, that's the truth of it. I can't imagine that myself. I'm just not like that.

But then none of us are in my business. None of us in the Sanitary Sector, either. No professional woman can risk leaks and smells while she's menstruating for the sake of expense and comfort. No way. I mean, just imagine the state of my underwear after a meeting if I wore a traditional tampon!

But we aren't everybody. We aren't even typical, perhaps. Oh, good Lord!

I could kick myself.

'Insight into other people's priorities.' That's the basis of what I do. And I've completely got this one wrong. Hell, the manufacturer got it wrong, too. Market research in this area is notoriously sketchy. It's impossible to get people to talk as frankly to an interviewer as that girl just did to her mate. Oh, Jesus!

I don't even want to think about the money involved. Quentin. I've got to tell Quentin.

And tell him what, exactly? Tell him I overheard two girls talking?

Holborn passes by me as I sit, watching my life disintegrate.

Shit.

I don't know how I get through the morning. Quentin is actually out, so even though I think I should talk to him, I don't have to actually think about doing it. I don't actually think about anything. It is like my brain's gone dead again, flatlining down to some lower primate structure. I move paper around, answer emails, take a few phone calls; all without using a cell of my neocortex.

Finally, some part of me surfaces, and I show a slight interest in life by looking at my desk diary to see who my 11:00 is with. Oh, hell, it's Finchley. I have to pull myself together or they'll put me in the loony bin. Air. I need air.

I go to reception and tell Anya that I'm going out for something to eat. She offers Melanie, but I decline, heaving my big coat over my shoulders and checking that the pockets have something jingling and rustling in them. 'I'll only be a minute,' I say.

Henry comes running into reception. 'You're not leaving are you?' he asks breathlessly. 'Only I wanted you to brief me on your lunch with Russell.'

Fuck Russell. Fuck you, Henry. 'I'm just going out for something to eat!' I say, perhaps too loudly. 'Is that a problem? Can I not leave for ten fucking minutes?'

It's like a game of statues. Everybody freezes.

And then Henry does what any other English person would do. He says, 'Sorry.'

I don't even wait for the lift. I take the stairs.

Clickety-click, clickety-click. What the hell is happening to me? Clickety-click, clickety-click. I pass DeLorcas. I pass Ninyas. I pass Pret A Manger. So I don't really want something to eat.

148

Clickety-click. I turn sharply and find myself pounding down to Soho Square. It isn't until I am standing by the statue of Charles that I realise I haven't the faintest clue of where I'm going.

And that is when I really lose it, because it's not just where I'm going to eat or where I'm going with this damn tampon campaign. It's where I'm going at all. I don't know what I'm doing. I don't even know what I want anymore. Do I want a bagel and some orange juice at Delorcas? Or a cappuccino and pain au chocolate from Pret? Or maybe some early sushi from Ninyas? What? What? What?

Or maybe I could go down that path to the Living Room and hang out with the hipsters, drink a latte. Or maybe I could go down that path into Piccadilly and hit Dunkin Donuts. Or maybe I could go to the groovy fifties café on Charing Cross Road, that way. And now, I am standing in the middle of Soho Square, revolving. I stop this as soon as I notice it, and I am facing the sooty edifice of what looks to be a Catholic church. I leave that way and push into the doors, past the notices to keep a close eye on my belongings. A pound coin will buy me, what, five candles at least? I take all of them and then wander around, trying to decide which saint to light them to. At last I just choose Jesus, because from what Peter tells me he might actually be listening. I nearly burn my gloves getting the damn things lit and when I kneel down, I just stay there for a moment.

Five candles. So what do I want? Strength. Please give me the strength to deal with all the shite you lot throw at me.

Ten minutes later I walk back in with a bag full of goodies from Valeries which both explains my long absence and apologises for my outburst in one swoop. I know Henry loves cream cheese and I take him his tartlet on a little plate from the cabinet that only reception have the key to. That way he knows that my apology is as public as if I had done it over the PA system.

I've put my hand around the opening of his cubicle and

waggled the tartlet until he has sighed and said, 'Come in.' Now I am standing in front of his desk.

'I'm sorry I was such a cow,' I say. 'I've been feeling a little over-worked lately and I just snapped. You were the straw, I'm afraid.'

He sees what the tart is filled with and smiles at me, completely sunnily. How can he do that? He looks… happy, damn it. It almost makes me want to snap his head off again.

'That's what we were saying when you left.' He can't resist. He takes a bite and then talks around it. 'At reception. Anya mentioned the hours you've been putting in.'

That's another favour I owe the girl.

'Anyway. Russell had nearly nothing to say yesterday except for what a good job you're doing and how cute the waiter's ass was.'

'Hmmm. Which waiter?'

I laugh dutifully. 'No briefing needed. And I don't think I'll see him for another six months at least. If there's a problem he'll ring me. But I don't think he will. You've made him happy, Henry. Well done.'

The boy actually blushes. I look away to give him time to collect himself and then see the clock, 10:55. I yelp. I excuse myself. I run like hell.

Tear through papers on desk. Find shrink folder. Push desk into some semblance of order. Phone buzzes. Melanie. I've got the time it takes for them to walk down the hall to glance over Finchley's file. I don't get it. Mainly Reikian, with Freudian background and Transactional methodology? What? Too late, the door opens and I stand up and do my perfectly collected act.

I needn't have bothered. Finchley turns out to be a bit of a hippie chick. Mel disappears to get coffee and Finchley just kind of oozes into a chair. She's wearing a long, flowing skirt which emphasises her flat narrow hips. Above that is a chunky blue plain knit jumper displaying some sort of Celtic silver whatsit on a thick chain. Her hair is long and curls into millions of ringlets. Her smoky brown eyes dart around my office, looking at books, art, plants.

Coffee arrives and while I continue to introduce self and company, Finchley interrupts to ask Melanie for some mineral water instead. When this arrives, she pours herself a glass and then sits back in the chair, waiting for me to run down.

I do this fairly quickly and then she launches into her set speech. I am surprised by what she's done. She has a variety of company-wide experience, and currently is working for a women's magazine title which I know. We make connections, mentioning names. I get a feel for how far she will go discussing her clients. Reassuringly, it isn't very far. My tiny room is soon silent.

Neither of us fidget. Me, because I ruthlessly suppress it. She, because, I am coming to recognise, doesn't feel the need. She is almost as collected as the Freudian, but with a warmth old Shepherd's Bush lacked. She's not spooky.

Might as well get it over with.

As is my wont of late, I give a little sigh before speaking, damn it. And then I say, 'I don't really understand your methods. Can I give you a hypothetical situation?'

'Of course.' If possible, she grows even more comfortable.

'Suppose I was to come and to tell you, oh, I don't know…' I pretend to look at the ceiling and think. 'Suppose I was to come to you and say that Saint Peter is visiting me every night. What would you say?'

Finchley's eyes narrow as she regards me carefully.

'Is he, Mrs White?'

I gulp, automatically correct, 'Maggie.'

'Is he, Maggie?'

I pretend not to understand. 'Pardon?'

151

'Is Saint Peter visiting you every night?'

Those brown eyes shine with compassion. And I completely blow it, starting to shake. 'Yes,' I say, 'he is.'

Chapter Thirteen

She's at my side in an instant. 'Hey,' she says, kneeling down by my desk. 'It's okay.'

She puts out her hand and I put mine into it. Hers is warm and dry. It feels good.

'I-' I start.

She waits.

'I haven't told anyone else about this.'

'I'm honoured.'

'Well, actually, I have told two other people, two psychologists interviewing for this job. They just didn't believe me.'

I catch her eye, which is amused, and then we are both laughing. She goes back to her chair. 'How long has he been coming to see you?'

'Over a month, now.'

'Every night?'

'Every weeknight.' She is nodding, as if this isn't anything which particularly bothers her. 'He looks like Sean Connery.' I gulp a little bit. 'I think I might be losing it.'

She smiles. 'I think I might feel the same way if it were happening to me.'

'There's other stuff going on as well.' Briefly, I detail my stocking mountain and my husband's affair. She keeps nodding. She's not looking at me with any less respect than she did when we were introduced. I look at my watch, it's almost 11:30.

'Look,' I say. 'Do you want this job?'

'I think I'd like it very much. I'd especially like to continue our discussion.'

'I'm going to recommend that you be hired.' I pick up her folder and bounce it on my crossed leg. 'I think I need to see you quite soon, perhaps under the guise of setting up a program, though I think we could do that as well? Would that be okay, or does it seem sneaky to you?'

'That sounds sensible to me. That's fine.' She immediately withdraws a brown leather diary from her bag and flips over pages. 'How does Tuesday sound? I could give you two hours from ten, maybe a half an hour on the set-up and the rest for you?'

'Lovely.'

'And I think I'd like another hour on Thursday, as well?'

I consult my desk diary. 'Can you do afternoon? Two-ish?'

She nods. I nod. We smile at each other.

'I feel good about this,' she says, as she stands, settles her bag back on her shoulder.

'You do? That's great.' I pull myself further together, ready to face the walk to the lift. 'That's great,' I say again.

Finchley gives me a secret little smile as the door closes that I find terribly empowering. Anya leans over reception to stage whisper, 'You've got to hire that one. She was really, really nice.'

'I think you're right.'

Anya preens herself in my approval and I decide to let her know a little of how much I appreciate her by saying, 'You know, you've been right on all of them. I could have saved myself the trouble of interviewing them, just had them sit in reception.'

'Get back to work, Maggie,' she says sternly, terribly pleased.

I run my finger down the textured wall, feeling it bump and catch.

'Quentin, I'm a bit worried about the tampon launch.'

I'm saying this to myself in an empty office, just to imagine what it would be like to say it to him. I pretend that he asks me why.

'I overheard a conversation on the bus today that gave me great pause.'

Oh, yeah. Brilliant. I'm sure he'd be impressed by that. And it'll be even easier telling him about peeing and pooing around a fanny plug. God! Why does everything have to be so damn difficult?

I sit down at my desk and stare into my screen saver. There is no way I can tell him and not look a complete idiot. But I really should tell him. I really, really should. But I absolutely can't.

I bang my hands on my desk and thus jiggle my mouse a micron so that my email notifier pops up. 11 messages. I'll think about it later. I'll sleep on it, that's what I'll do. And as I start clicking I think Jesus, I'm turning into Scarlett fucking O'Hara.

At six o'clock I face the fact that I've been fairly useless all day, and decide to go home early. Most of the office seem to have had the same idea. By the time I emerge about twenty minutes later, I can hear myself walk down the carpet. This is so spooky that I check the big clock behind reception, but it's alright, it's only six-thirty.

As I walk down to Tottenham Court Road station, I pass a pub. It's getting really dark now, at this time of night, and the yellow light of the windows attracts my eyes. Everyone is in there, Anya, Henry, Melanie, Roberto. I stop still and peer through the glass on a diagonal, so that I can see in, but cannot be seen. Even Quentin's there, getting a round in at the bar.

I can't believe they didn't ask me. Was I that much of a shit today?

I decide I don't care, cut across the street and keep going to the tube station, but I can't stop thinking about it all the way to Liverpool Street.

Train in ten minutes and I wander into Knickerbox, thinking about nightgowns, Saint Peter, stuff like that. I am transfixed in the window by a knickers set in midnight blue, Simon's favourite colour. Panties, bra, suspender belt. All embroidered in a deep burgundy. They look fabulous. I don't even think about it, I just buy them.

I still have loads of time for the train. It is one of the old ones, this train, with seats that work like a tube train's, facing inwards in rows. I sit in one of these, thinking about the knickers, and hoping I'll look good in them. I think I will, it's a style that usually flatters me, even these days, as I age.

A man gets on. I don't really look up at him or anything, but he registers as fanciable even so. He's hot enough that I refrain from looking any closer, just to avoid temptation. Still, when he turns into my carriage, I am delighted. The delight turns to a frisson of fear when he sits right down next to me in the middle of a row of empty seats.

'Hey, Gorgeous, what you got in the bag?'

I look up in shock at this fanciable man who has spoken to me in Simon's voice only to find that my husband has boarded the same train as me. He leans over and kisses me, probably shocked by the way I kiss him back with fervor. Even the sight of his knees still sends me, still gets my endorphins racing. It's so nice to know that the most fanciable man I've seen all day is already mine.

I fold the neck of the bag over. 'You'll see soon enough,' I tell him. 'If you're good.'

He smiles.

'What are you doing home so early?'

'What are you doing home so early?'

We've spoken at the same time. I shrug. 'I've had something weird happen to me with my campaign. I don't know how to handle it and it's distracting me. I wasn't doing anything remotely useful, so I came on home.'

'Do you want to talk about it?'

The train was filling up.

'Not here.' He nods in return.

'What about you?'

156

He lets go of me to fish in his case. 'I went by a couple of estate agents. I got these.'

They are pictures of blocks of flats with details underneath. I stare at them stupidly.

'Streatham looks like the place,' Simon says. 'That's what everyone was telling me at work. Just on the other side of Tooting Common.'

'From what?'

'From Tooting.'

'Where is Tooting, anyway?' The only thing I've ever been interested in south of the river is the National Theatre and a couple of restaurants.

Simon sighs. 'Look,' he says, removing an A-Z from his case. What else does he have in there, I wonder?

'Here's my office. Here's Wimbledon. Too expensive. Here's Clapham. That's really high now, too.'

'What, worse than Stokie?'

He shrugs. 'I was going to say…'

He trails off and I look at the particulars again. They're all in the 90-105K range. Our house is 280K. I read. Two bedrooms, communal gardens. Porter. 'Are these ex-council?'

'No, I was going to say…'

We pull up to Bethnal Green. 'What are you going to say, Simon?'

My voice sounds cold, even to me.

'These are places I can afford. Just on my salary.'

I look at him as if this will all make sense if I can just read it from his face.

'Look, Maggie, what's up with Streatham is that it had a really bad reputation, was really rough for a while, but it's being cleaned up.'

'Like Stokie.'

'Yeah. These are private blocks. In the thirties, Streatham was the place to live, the trendiest, coolest locale in London. They built all these private flats to really high specifications. Parquet floors, big diner kitchens, really nice gardens, thick walls, you know?'

'You want me to quit my job?'

'No!' His tone has such anguish that everyone in the carriage turns to look at us. Cambridge Heath.

'No,' he says more quietly. 'But I want the pressure to be off you. And on me, where it belongs.'

'Belongs?' Now I'm the one screeching.

We glare back at the passengers and they all develop an intense interest in their *Evening Standards*.

'I know, I know,' Simon rubs his eyes. 'Bin them if you want. But, Maggie, you don't have to prove anything to anybody. If you want to take some time out, have a family, that's cool, too, you know.'

Part of me is screaming Yes! Yes! At last! He's taking responsibility at last! I'm free, free! Part of me is saying, Hey, wait a minute. Why don't *you* stay home? Then we can live someplace nice.

Hackney Downs. London Fields.

'Look,' I finally say. 'It's a lot to think about.' He nods, giving me that. 'But I think it's really cool that you've come up with this plan. I think that you thinking about all this and coming up with a plan is really, really cool.'

He kisses me so hard and so long that we nearly miss our station and he has to wrestle his case out of the door before the train takes off.

I never even got a chance to try on my sexy undies. We went straight to bed and ordered a pizza about nine o'clock. I missed *EastEnders* and we forgot to feed the cat.

'Maggie.'

I am dreaming of some pasture I know well. It sits outside my home town of Lawrence, Kansas, up just where rolling prairie hills flatten out into the plains which stretch clear to the Rockies. There's a horse between my legs, and, although he's been dead seven years now, I know him, too. Frodo is what I named him. Before you start, it was the end of the seventies and I was just a kid. So give me a break.

'Maggie?'

This word someone is saying has some kind of significance. Suddenly I remember it's my name. I blink a bit. Frodo and the Flory's land wisp away like smoke.

I open my eyes. Saint Peter is sitting on my bed in the meditation pose again. 'Oh,' I say, 'Hi.' I fumble with glasses, lamp and water bottle.

'You were very deeply asleep.'

'I was dreaming of home.'

'Ah.' This is said with a wealth of understanding. 'Then I am sorry to wake you.'

'It's okay. I mean, I can go home whenever I want. You know, it's not like Capernaum was to you.'

He nods. 'When were you last there?'

I think for a moment. 'God. It's been nearly five years.'

'And you can go whenever you like?' His voice drips with irony again, in his too-emphatic way.

'Look, we aren't here to talk about me.'

He shrugs, but I can tell he's terribly pleased to have struck a nerve. I say, 'Stop it,' and he grins, which makes me grin as well. For a moment, we just sit there, enjoying how well we know each other.

'So,' I finally say, 'do you have a movie for me tonight?'

He smiles sadly. 'I think the movies are over, Maggie. You know everything now. Now, we must get to work, eh?'

My head flops back onto my pillow. 'I don't think I know enough,' I say. 'I don't feel like I know enough.'

Peter is silent.

I say, 'Rock, this is really big. I have to get my head around it, you know, before I can give you any advice.'

He blows out his lips in that puffing gesture and says, 'it is all in your Bible, what you need to know.'

'Well...' I feel my face wrinkle into a grimace, 'I don't really know my Bible all that well, Rock. What with growing up Catholic and one thing and another, I just...'

'Why does Catholic make it hard?'

'Well, you know, the Baptist kids, they had to practically memorise the damn thing.'

Peter shakes his head with impatience. 'It is not difficult, Maggie. There is the story I have told you, the movies you have seen. Then there is what is in this book, and all the things Paul said. They are not the same. We have to separate one from the other, you see?'

I say, 'I think I need to read a bit more before I can...'

'Fine.'

'It's just that-'

'No. Read. I shall not come again this week.'

Great. Now I've got Sean Connery sulking on the edge of my bed. I start to say something, but there's nothing to say. He seems a million miles away.

I feel terrible about closing my eyes. Still, I do it with the hope that when I open them again, Saint Peter won't be there.

'Oh, shit.'

'What?' Simon's tousled head rises from his pillow. 'What did I do, now?'

Sweetie lamb. 'Nothing,' I say. 'It was a dream, kind of.'

'Oh.' He raises himself up on an elbow. 'As long as it's not me.'

'No, not you.'

'I'm still okay.'

He's looking at me cheekily now and I slide across the bed so that he can kiss me. 'You're better than okay, Simon, and you know it.'

When you're a little kid and you smell grownups in the morning, you never think that you would ever kiss someone that smells like that. Then you grow up.

Snuggling costs us dear and I am furiously brushing my teeth while Simon wet-combs his hair into submission when I ask, foamily, 'What are we doing this weekend? Are there any parties, or anything? Isn't it Amanda's birthday?' It strikes me that we haven't seen his mates in ages.

He frowns in the mirror at me. 'I meant to say,' he says, then stops himself. 'I meant to ask,' he corrects.

I rinse and spit. 'Ask what?'

'I thought we could go and look at flats.'

'What, way down there?'

He nods.

'It's just that I've got some reading to do.'

'For work?'

'For this special project.' I really should tell him something about Peter sometime, I guess, but I can't even think about it now. In fact, by now, we're shouting the conversation, because he's getting dressed while I'm still washing.

'Is it portable?'

It's the Bible, I think. 'Well, yes,' I say.

'Take it with you.' His head peeps back around the doorway, appearing in the mirror. 'Problem solved?'

'Okay,' I say, 'okay.'

Although I'm in a hurry, I've missed the 7:15 and don't want to wait for the 7:30. Nothing is coming down our road at all, I wait ages and all I see is one of those weird three-wheeled cars. I decide to walk down to Leswin Road for the 73 and just as I get within can't-possibly-make-it distance, I see one glide by the stop. Shit.

I look at my watch and get panicky. I don't know why. I don't have any big meeting this morning or anything. It's last night, I figure. It's everybody going out for a drink without me. Bastards. I'd better work harder and be nicer to everyone. I really had.

The 102 is a squat single decker, but it's empty. I decide to get on and ride to Highbury and Islington, where I can catch the Victoria Line. Traffic is still light in Stoke Newington and I keep checking my watch, thinking that something must be wrong, but when we get closer to Islington, London swings into the full morning crush and the bus fills up. Everyone, except for one old lady with a red plaid shopping trolley, gets off at Highbury and Islington and we all shuffle across the two crosswalks together, lucky this morning, no waits.

I shove my ticket in the machine like everyone else, but it tweedles at me, and flashes red, telling me that something is wrong with my card. Can't be. I keep it in a special pocket in my nice green leather card holder I got from John Lewis, so the magnetic strip never gets scratched or anything. A queue builds up behind me instantly as I look stupidly at it and shove it in again. Tweedle. Fuck.

I excuse myself out of my queue and look in vain for a barrier official. There's always one or two standing around just to deal with this kind of thing, and you'd think that as soon as they heard the tweedle, they'd prance over and eliminate your discomfort.

But you'd think wrong. There's two of them, but they're on the other side of the barrier, chatting, and the Royal Philharmonic could tweedle in unison before they'd even look up. I shout, wave my pass around and generally act demented before they deign to notice me and one nods, finishes his thought, enjoys the good giggle with his mate and then leisurely detaches himself and strolls over to me. By now I am a seething mass of fury.

'I don't know what's wrong with this,' I say to him.

People are still using the machine. To talk to him, I have to

162

keep dancing out of their way. He gives it a cursory glance. 'I know,' is all he says.

What? 'What?'

'It's out of date, madam,' he intones, loud enough for everyone in the hall to hear. I go instantly from posture of outraged customer to posture of cringing supplicant. I do the English thing and say, 'Oh, sorry.' As I turn around to go to the ticket window, everyone smirks at me.

I can't believe it's November. Of course I can, I wrote October 31st on yesterday's letters, and wondered about Halloween and how it had started to catch on in Europe. I did wonder that didn't I, or was that last year? Was that why everyone was at the pub? Was there some kind of Halloween do and they didn't ask me, since they thought it would be too lame for an American? What was I anyway, last time I went out on Halloween? Oh, yeah, Simon and I went as Bonnie and Clyde. I remember.

November. Shit. We're launching soon. Of course I knew this, intellectually, but it's not the same as actually knowing it. Do I have to wait until Tuesday before I can see my shrink? I'm really losing it, I tell myself. I'm really cracking up.

I have plenty of time to think of all this, because although I can see four or five people in the ticket counter walking around behind the glass windows with mugs and biscuits in their hands, there is only one person serving. And, as it's the first of the month, there's lots of other people like me, caught out on a Friday getting new passes. And of course, once I actually get up there, I've never bought a pass at Highbury and Islington before, so I have to fill out a huge card that asks me for everything but my blood type and a urine sample and then wait again for a break in the service (what there is of it) to push my card through and get my pass. All in all, I'm now another twenty minutes late.

I clatter down the escalator and the stairs and then suddenly understand Tokyo and their white-gloved attendants. I wish there was somebody to shove me on a car. The entryways are packed, even though I can see that no one is standing in the middle of half of the carriages, despite repeated pleas from the driver to 'move right down inside the cars.'

I think about bursting into tears, but instead, I just decide to take the next train, which is actually waiting right behind. I don't get a seat, that would be asking too much, but I do get a place to stand where I can put my case between my feet and sway in peace, with no one pressed up against me. Today, that seems like the only satisfaction my journey in will allow me. The amount of money I've just paid to suffer this pain keeps ringing in my brain like an old fashioned cash register. 'I give up', I say to myself, and then realise I've said it out loud. The pinstripe gent in front of me rattles his paper and looks at me warningly. I feel like saying, I don't need the warning, bub, I know I'm losing it. But we all know that, now, don't we?

When I finally emerge at Oxford Circus, I am determined to tell Quentin about my doubts. He's had to have gone through this before. And besides, it's not just our campaign that will be at fault. Some products bomb. Even with a great campaign. But those usually have good initial sales. This won't. I cut down the side of C&A and see myself in the mirrored pillar. I've chewed all the lipstick off my bottom lip. As I walk, I take my little green leather lipstick case out and repair it. With a good jacket on my back, and a bit of lipstick, I try and tell myself, there's nothing I can't handle.

It's after eight when I walk in and I put my coat in the closet without witnesses. I like being in the office, I think, because everything looks so clean. Ravinder will be doing our place today, but it won't look like this. Only I can clean it so that it looks like this. Ravinder doesn't do skirting boards, doesn't do window sills, doesn't do any of the little details that really make a place shine. I used to like making our place perfect when we lived in Packington

Street. It was too small, Simon used to complain. But it was just right to clean. You could see a result in no time.

There's nothing on my email. It's weird, that. Some days you have a million and some days nothing. I've even rung up and checked with our server before.

I put my jacket on the back of my chair and roll up my sleeves. And that's when I realise that I'm finally pretty much caught up. I have time to go over the launch details that Celia put together. I have time to read Henry's monthly report on Russell's account, and start to plan my own monthly report. I have time to actually do my job.

I have forgotten how boring that is. Twenty minutes into it and I'm dying for the post, for an emergency of some sort. Is that how I keep going, I ask myself? Is it only the adrenaline rush that keeps me awake, here? I've got the launch stuff spread out on my desk and it's just like I asked for. Two days of small groups. The suite at Claridges. We only have to pay for one night, the Texas oil money who are in before us are going home BA First Class and will vacate by seven. Claridges staff will whisk in and do their thing before nine. Our first meeting that day is at half-nine and we'll be out the next afternoon. Claridges are brilliant that way. Of course, they'll be making money on the catering, and we come back again and again, but still. So flexible. Amazing.

And it'll just be me and Celia behind the teapot and the sandwich trays. She'll be serving and I'll be smiling and showing slides on the highpower laptop all day. There's breakfast and then brunch and then lunch and then late lunch and then tea. By that time, I might actually use the bed. Then there's early breakfast, late breakfast, brunch and lunch the following day. I'll see fifty people, maybe fifty-five. I will have taken the important folks aside earlier. It's softly-softly with impact. It's harder work than hiring a hall and whacking on a slide show, but it's meant to get the concept of discretion into the heads of journalists. If I put it that way, I'm sure you can see why it's not so easy.

I make a few notes about who to invite for when, for Celia. Get the hard drinkers in for one of the brunches and then they can lie in with a good excuse. Get the ladies with kids in for the tea, so that they can go home early. Get best mates around for the early lunches so that they can hit the pub together afterwards. Make it attractive for everyone, that's the key. Make sure everyone associates your product with pleasure.

Pleasure. I look at my watch. Only twenty minutes have passed. It's not even nine o'clock yet. I go down the hall to Celia's cubicle and pop the report with my notes and my red pencilled changes to this and that into her in-tray.

And then I look at Henry's monthly report. Yatada, yatada, yatada, ya. What am I supposed to say about it? Everything's going well, the campaign is going great, sales figures from Russell look good. New product is already on track and it looks like we'll secure that, no problems. I make a few random notes in the margins, just to show I've read the damn thing. And then find something wrong, a stupid little something, a colour reference that is wrong in an old campaign, and annotate the text with the right reference. Big deal. That's why I get paid? My chair could do that. And it's back down the hall five minutes later to Henry's cubicle and in-tray.

Only Henry is there, working. Hasn't been there long, though, his coffee cup is still full. He must have just sat down. He grins at me. 'That's a little late coming back to me, Maggie. The ink must be just about dry by now.'

'I think I'm just about caught up in tampon land, so I thought I'd pretend to be your boss for awhile.'

He grins more. 'Want some coffee?'

I've left the house without breakfast again. 'And toast,' I say, 'and beans, egg, chips, mushroom and tomato.'

'I can do coffee.'

'Coffee's good.' I sit down and he flies out the door, and reappears seemingly instantly with a steaming mug. Forget the account, he's even better at making coffee than I am. I barely had time to look around his cubicle and notice how neat it was and how he'd pinned up an Egon Schiele drawing of a tree before he was back.

'Henry? What do you know about Streatham?' I'm working on the premise that all gay men know everything there is to know about trends. It's a horrible generalisation, I know, but it's the same generalisation that got Henry his job. He sits down and thinks for a minute.

'It's close to Brixton, isn't it?"

'Brixton? As in "Guns Of" ?'

'That was a long time ago, Maggie.'

I must be getting old. 'Simon wants us to move there.'

'I'll ask Blaine, he'll know.'

I don't ask who Blaine is, I'm sure he's a friend or a lover or the boy who cleans the windows or something. I'm sure I've probably even met him. I'm sure if I ask, Henry will be horrified that I don't remember. I just say, 'Thanks, Henry, I'd appreciate that.'

I nod towards the monthly report in his in-tray. 'Do you know what the new product is, yet?'

'I think it's a body spray.'

We haven't ever handled that side of Russell's stuff before, and I show myself to be impressed. 'Well done!' I say, and watch Henry glow.

And then I remember him in the pub, talking to Roberto, and the smile fades off my face.

'Is something wrong, Maggie?'

I shrug and then take a sip of the coffee. 'You tell me, Henry.'

'I think you've been working too hard,' he says, and then we grin at each other again, because this really isn't that much of a revelation. It feels good just to be sitting in his chair and grinning at Henry. I drink my coffee and decide not to worry about the pub, to take whatever feels good to me at the time and enjoy it. Whatever evil is coming my way will get to me soon enough.

When I get back to my office, Anya is waiting for me. Well, now I pay, I think, for that five minutes in Henry's cubicle. Something must be wrong. But she's only checking that I haven't made any luncheon plans overnight. I reassure her, an she tells me that Quentin wants to see me in the boardroom at half-twelve.

'Boardroom?' I ask. 'He said boardroom?'

She shrugs and walks away, as if she didn't want to talk to me about it. Quentin can't type anything, not even an email, without breaking into a sweat. If he's reprimanding me, or firing me or something, Anya will know because she'll have to type the documents. I get a cold feeling in my stomach.

While I wait for Melanie to bring me my post, I decide to go ahead and write the psychologist report for the board, as well as finish up my monthly report. That way, if something is wrong and they try to lambast me, I'll at least have something in my hand, something that tells them that I might have been pushed too far. Maybe if I can subtly remind them of the new EU ruling, they won't sack me for fear of a lawsuit.

Now, I know, somewhere in the back of my mind, that I can't be sacked, that I'm doing fine, but that is the small, soft voice of Reason. Panic is a much louder voice, and that's coming through fine. I scatter the contents of the folder across my desk and begin to type.

Henry's head appears around the doorway. 'Saint Reatham,' he says, archly.

I look at him blankly. 'Pardon?'

'Saint Reatham. If you move to Streatham, that's how you say it.' He wanders around to my guest chair and settles himself into it. 'There's a new generation of genteel moving in, evidently,' he

168

says, pleased with himself for knowing all this. 'It seems there are all these fabulous properties, some of them Listed, some of them have pools in the basement, porters. It sounds pretty posh, really.'

I get it together enough to thank him. It might be my last chance.

'Tell Simon to beware the service charges. Some of them are as high as 2K a year.'

'Wow!' I try and emote convincingly. I nod. I thank him again. About fifty million years later, he leaves me alone, and I start typing again.

I've answered my post. I never did get any emails. I've printed out the psychologist report, which details my findings on the candidates, my hiring of Finchley, and the schedule to which I plan to work in order to get the counselling sessions going throughout the office. It's pretty damn hot, if I do say so myself, and it's only two pages. I had to put a cover on it just to give the stapler something to grab. I've even summarised it in a little one para box under the heading, for people like Samantha, who are busier than God.

My monthly report was easy, since we haven't started any new projects this month. Anya gave me Melanie to do the printing on the Mac and the collating. I tried to sound her out about Quentin again, but there was nothing doing.

Clutching a stack of shiny things in plastic envelopes makes me feel a little better as I walk down the shantung hallway to the boardroom. Reception seems quiet. Everything seems quiet. I can't see anyone.

I give a cursory knock on the closed door and then open it.

'Surprise!'

When twenty people shout something like that, it makes a bit of an impact. I rock back on my heels so hard, I'm only caught by the doorjamb.

Everybody is there, and there's sandwiches and cake and crisps and things on the boardroom table. Everyone's talking at once. Anya comes up and puts a glass of white wine in my hand as loads of people, including Roberto, come and draw me in the room, take my redundant reports away from me. The wine is an indifferent Australian Chardonnay, put through so much malolactic fermentation that it's like drinking a pound of butter, but I down a good half a glass in one gulp.

Quentin clears his throat and it all gets quiet. He turns to me and says something about hours and appreciation and taking the rest of the day off. He spreads his arms to incorporate the whole staff and talks about appreciation again, and what a lucky bastard he is. Everyone applauds, and turns to me, as if they expect me to answer.

Somehow, I smile and say thank you. Somehow, I grin and say that I thought PR was going to be glamorous. Somehow, I manage to say something about teamwork and being glad to help. There is more applause. Now I see onion dip, and I walk over to it in a daze. This is all really nice. Having the afternoon off is really nice. Knowing that they were all in the pub planning this is really nice, and knowing I'm not going to get the sack just yet is really nice, as well. So why do I still feel like I want to cry?

Chapter Fourteen

I am gloomy on the train. That launch is like a time bomb. Once it goes off, no one's going to be throwing me parties any more. It's not even three o'clock when I get home. Henry and Celia fairly shoved me out the door, and, although there's more of us in this carriage than I'd expected, everything in London Transport seems to be running well.

Cat is all excited. I feed her and go upstairs to change, but don't, I just take off my suit and lie down on the bed in my blouse and stockings, reaching for the Bible I now keep on my nightstand. Cat follows me up. The sun shines into this window in the afternoon and she stretches herself by me, luxuriating in both her bath of yellow light and my presence. Why do I seem to be able to make everyone happy but myself?

Paul doesn't seem really loony until I get to I Corinthians, when he starts bitching about the working conditions of the apostles. That's when he starts going off about sex, and laying down the law as if he was a prophet of old with a hotline to God. I read his strictures several times, but he sounds to me like a comic character in a pub, trying to decide the issues of the day through sheer force of will. Somehow, this makes me start to kind of like him, grudgingly. I can see him as someone not unlike myself, worn to a frazzle and trying to control the world.

Which, of course, he somewhat did. This makes me shiver, and I slide under the duvet. Cat is so disturbed by this, she nearly rolls over, but in the end is able to settle again. I wonder, watching her get into an even more comfortable position, if everyone envies their cats.

A ranting and raving control freak is human and somehow likeable, in a way. But the idea that one was taken seriously as a mouthpiece of the Lord is not likeable at all. Over and over, the poor man tells us how hard he is working, how he faces death every day. Can't anyone see that someone under that kind of stress is bound to make mistakes?

I'm not thinking about Paul, I'm thinking about me again. Or maybe I am thinking about Paul. Maybe we've just got a lot in common. I don't know. I just don't know. I can't read this anymore, it hurts my head. I look down at Cat and eventually, she slits her eyes against the sun and looks back. She seems to be asking why I'm still awake, and I don't have any answers for her. I set the alarm so I won't be late to the pub to meet Simon and then I take a nap myself, curling around her and making her purr so loudly I think I'll never drift off.

'Maggie.'

'Hmmmmmm?' It's Saturday morning and we're in Liverpool Street station, waiting for the Central Line.

Simon is speaking to me. I'm reading Paul and just catch the end, '...not that I've got anything against religion, but you know what I mean.'

I put my finger in my page. 'It's research.'

He looks at me blankly. His collar is all rucked up under his jumper. I straighten it.

'I told you I needed to do some research this weekend,' I say, and watch him remember.

'What is this special project?' he asks. 'Are you using Revelations to sell kitchen towel or something?'

'No, but I might end up using kitchen towel to sell Revelations.'

'What?'

'Doesn't matter.'

The tube arrives. We're only going one stop. This trip is a pain in the butt. I can see why Simon's not thrilled about doing it every day. I say something to that effect.

172

'There's something fun coming up at Bank.'

The something fun is a moving ramp, like an escalator without stairs. Since we're alone on it, Simon shows me that it bounces. We run down it, moon walkers on our way to the Waterloo and City Line, trampolining from foot to foot, taking giant steps for just ourselves. My hair flies up behind me and I laugh. At the bottom, Simon lifts me in the air, and whirls me around. I try to believe I am weightless.

Change at Clapham Junction for Streatham Hill. When we emerge, traffic is thick down the large main street. Even so, I'm struck with how clean it is, and how quiet, after Hackney. It looks to be about the same ethnic mix. As we walk to the estate agent's we pass a greengrocer with yams outside in boxes, Greek restaurants, Turkish restaurants, even Mexican. Simon seems to take note of a pub announcing guest ales.

I start to like the places in spite of myself. The first flat is on the fifth floor above a busy intersection, and it needs new windows, of which it has many. I mention this to Simon and he makes a note. 'What do you think,' he asks, 'three thousand for new windows, or four?'

'Say three and a half.' He scribbles. It's a galley kitchen, and another slit for a bathroom, but the bedrooms are huge and the living room is a pie-shaped wodge, with windows on two sides of the slice. There are two balconies, both currently used for plastic bikes, but I can imagine planting them up. One is right outside the Master bedroom. Simon points to the window embrasure. 'You could stick a desk there, he says, 'write in the mornings, like you used to.'

We peel back the carpet and find that the whole place has parquet floors. But it is the hall I like, with all the cupboard space. I go out on the balcony and can see forever. The estate agent is talking about service charges and co-operative ownership and the lack of parking. Simon nods, he's writing all of this down. I still feel like

I can fly, like I could soar off the balcony over the trees of Tooting Bec Common.

We see a few more. One is in a Grade II listed building, very groovy and deco indeed, but the security isn't brilliant. We could install something, Simon says, writing down a figure. The glass doors that shut off the living room are elegant and plain. I think I would buy a Vespa if I lived there, and dress in PVC.

The next one is a lovely little place, parquet again, and this one already has central heating installed. It needs a new kitchen and windows. The communal gardens are small, but well kept. The balcony shows the roofing, old terracotta tiles which have aged beautifully. I keep going back out to look at them.

We walk up the hill with another estate agent, who keeps talking about the common, though we are walking away from it. Finally I see more trees, and realise that there is another huge park nearby. Streatham Common. This place is a little smaller than the others. The second bedroom is more like a glorified closet. It's also more expensive, but comes with an elegant garage that has double doors and leaded windows. This is set in the acres of immaculate gardens. It's just across the road from the common. It needs radiators, a new kitchen and flooring. Simon scribbles. The maintenance is expensive. Simon scribbles some more.

I wander around while they talk. There's tons of oak panelling in the front staircase and there are also back stairs, so Cat could go out. When I come back in, Simon's looking at the fireplace, where something electric and open bar sits. Another scribble.

We are quiet as we walk to the pub. Simon is adding and subtracting in his head, and he keeps hauling out his little notebook. I am looking at the bus stops. I know that the Streatham Hill rail line goes to Victoria, but I'm thinking about tube strikes, leaves on line, that sort of thing. Me missing the train, that's the one most likely and the one I left out. While we wait at the crosswalk, a Routemaster lumbers by. I look at its destination board. It's the

159 for Oxford Circus. Simon raises his eyebrows at me, and it makes me laugh.

In the pub, I keep saying, 'Any of them. I could live in any of them. But they'd need to be done out first. I don't want to live out of boxes for two years again.'

'Don't you like any of them best?'

'I guess I like the last one best. But I liked the next to last one, too.' Simon looks at me. 'You know that we'll make money on your house,' he says.

I nod.

'Would you put down the deposit?'

'If we do this, of course.' I hadn't even considered not doing so.

Simon looks relieved. 'I think we'll be able to buy a car,' he says. 'And maybe even some new furniture.'

'And go on holiday.'

'And still have money in the bank.'

'Yes?'

'Oh, yes.' He whips out his notebook and looks over the figures again. 'I'm not so sure I can afford the last one,' he confesses. 'The service charge is really high.'

'How high?'

'Eighteen hundred pounds a year.'

I whistle. 'They can raise it, too, can't they, any time they want?'

He nods grimly, and pulls out his phone. 'Let's look at the next to last one again.'

It is small, I think, but very nice. All the walls are straight. All the ceilings are flat. The parquet is in good shape, under the layers of lino and carpet. It has terracotta window ledges. I go back out to the balcony, which is getting a bit of afternoon sun. The communal gardens are small, but very nice. If I live here, my whole life will be smaller. But it might be very nice.

It takes us twenty-two minutes to get to Kings Cross station in

North London. It takes us forty-five minutes on the bus to get the three and a half miles from there to home. We could have almost walked it faster. I am starting to see Simon's reasoning.

'Saint Reatham,' I say.

He looks at the Bible on my lap. 'I've never heard of him.'

'God, what time is it?'

I was trying to be silent, but I've knocked my glasses case clattering to the floor and it's woken him. 'It's early. Go back to sleep.'

'What are you doing?'

'I'm going to Mass.'

Simon pops his head up from the pillows. 'What,' he says, 'again?'

I go into the bathroom and have a quick wash. He's still awake when I come out and start rummaging for something to shove on.

'Maggie, have you been born again or something?'

I tell him not to start and that I'm late. He shakes his head, disgusted, and snuggles down under the covers.

Nearly nine on a Sunday morning and the streets of Stoke Newington are filthy. Crisp packets, half-eaten kebabs and the attendant pools of vomit, crates of inedible vegetable bits, newspapers, flimsy striped carrier bags. I don't so much walk down the street as wade down. Why did I want to live here? I can't even remember.

It was trendy. It was cool. My friends thought I was really amazing to have found a whole house and bought it. And where are those friends, now that I'm paying for the house? I kick at a rotten canteloupe and watch with some satisfaction as the 73 bus crushes it to butter.

I'm not really in the right frame of mind for church. It's the nine o'clock no-singing-no-dancing Mass, and it's being led by some priest so old that his skin is translucent. If I painted him, I would use a lot of blue in the flesh tones, and I would try to get that fading look in his eye. He seems determined to be useful, but the parish priest hovers around the sacristy, watchful. It would be easier for him to do it himself, you can tell.

There's about twenty of us in for early Mass. I actually recognise two or three. I'm going through the responses on autopilot, which amazes me so much once I realise it that I stumble and have to find my place in the book to read it, instead. Then we finish and sit down for the readings. 'A reading from the letters of Paul to the-'

It's all I can do not to groan. I leaf through the missal for another reading, but they all seem to be Paul, Paul, Paul. I'm at this so long, I almost miss the petitions.

The parish priest pumps my hand as I leave, holding on to me, asking me if I want to come for a cup of tea in the church hall. I excuse myself, but it's an odd experience. I must look posh in my good jacket and loafers, in spite of my jeans, or maybe he's just that nice to all newcomers. Of course he is, I berate myself, walking down the street. Being nice is his job.

They've swept the streets in the intervening hour. It's quicker going on the way back. I pick up some bagels and croissants on the corner and then start down my street. It's not busy at this hour on Sunday, and you can cross without risking your life. The road has a curve, and I can see my house for ages as I walk, see the nice bright render, see the shiny black window boxes and the yellow door. The ivy waves attractively in the slight breeze. I'm glad we got the winter pansies in early this year, they do better when I don't shove them in under subzero conditions.

I don't want to leave my house, my neighbourhood. I know where everything is. I even know the priest, now. I don't want to leave my garden. It seems like ever since I met Simon, I've been leaving places. I don't want to do it again.

I've stopped walking. My hands are cold. I let myself into the house and talk to Cat, who immediately takes me to her bowls in the kitchen, as if I might have forgotten where they are. Simon is in his dressing gown, making a pot of tea.

'You too holy for Earl Grey?' he asks me.

I hand him the bag from the bakery and sink down at the table.

'What's up?' he asks me. 'Bad sermon?'

It was, actually. Dreadful. The old guy got off on some tricky bit of doctrine concerning free will that completely lost me. He kind of meandered around the subject, poking it with sticks, until it got angry. Then we had a short prayer. I tell some of this to Simon.

'Why did you go? Have you made some kind of deal with God?'

'No. I'm just doing some research. I told you.'

'Not much. What exactly is this project, anyway?'

'I can't really tell you all that much, Simon.'

He stands, teapot in his hand, and looks at me for a second. Then he pours. 'Okay,' he says, 'Change subject. When do you want to move? I think this place will sell so fast that I don't want it to interfere with the launch or whatever.'

I get up and get a big plate out of the cupboard. I start arranging the things from the bag on it. He's waiting for an answer, but I keep on messing with the croissants and the pain au chocolat, stacking them different ways. I can see he is getting angry, but I don't know what to say.

'Maggie? Are we going to communicate at all this morning?'

'Simon, I don't want to sell my house.'

That's not exactly what I meant, but he just says. 'Oh. Fine.' He takes his bagel from the plate and starts upstairs.

'Simon, don't go! I meant...'

He stops. He waits.

'It's all so sudden,' I say. 'And when I was walking back from church the house looked so nice.'

He leans over the railing. I can see how hard he's gripping it, his knuckles are white. 'But that's just bollocks, Maggie. How nice it looks. This fucking house! Every weekend we worked on it like slaves. Every single weekend, and some nights, as well. It takes all of our money. We can't even afford to furnish it all! And what about us, Maggie?'

It's making me shake, this shouting. I just stand there, and start to cry.

'Oh, hell!' Simon shouts this very loudly, and then he comes back down and slams his bagel on the plate I am still holding. I slide it onto the table, and he takes me in his arms.

'What?' he says. 'Can you just tell me what's going on in that fuzzy little head of yours?'

'It's mine, this house.' He doesn't look any more enlightened. 'I don't have anything else, Simon. Just this house.'

'What about me? What about Cat?'

I shrug and his arms fall away. 'I'm not that sure of you, am I?'

He looks at the floorboards. They were stupid in a kitchen, bits of food always get stuck in between, but we couldn't afford quarry tiles when we were doing it. He says, 'I'm sorry about that.'

And then we are at the table together, eating breakfast, as if everything was okay, and this was just one day out of a whole life together, and not a shaky truce that depended on things neither of us fully understand. The sun comes out and shines on the pine table like it was in on the joke, and wants the atmosphere to be even more perfect, so that the irony is even more cutting.

'Can you tell me in a week?' Simon finally asked. And I nodded. My bagel was sticking in my throat. I don't know why I bothered with it, anyway. It tasted like paste in my mouth.

Monday morning. 67 outside the door. Balls Pond Road is perfectly stationary, so I stay on for Liverpool Street. All I've got in my case to read is that damn *Good Wives* and I can't face it at all, I'd rather sit and brood. We're stuck behind a cyclist all the way through Dalston and the big bus crawls along. I have plenty of time to think.

Why not do it? Why not just go with everyone's flow and let Simon take over the bills and the mortgage and everything? Then when the campaign fails and I get the sack, I can just stay at home.

I think that this should sound idyllic to me and I wonder why it doesn't. I try to conjure up images of myself doing Jocasta Innes effects on the walls of the next-to-last flat and making complicated dinners in the new kitchen we could put in, but the images refuse to come. We've finally come as far as the canal. A very drunken Irishman lurches up the stairs, cursing loudly, and sits behind me. There's no doubt that he slept rough the night before, he is damp from the dew. I would feel sorry for him if he wasn't clutching a fresh can of Special Brew and stinking to high heaven of things I try not to identify, but can anyway.

He mutters to himself, but the alcohol has weakened his hearing, and it comes out as more of a low roar. The smell is making my eyes water, but I don't dare stand up to move away. I don't want to insult him, true, but I'm also afraid to insult him. I'm also deeply ashamed of myself, that this revulsion is all I can feel. I don't want to help him – I don't think he can be helped. I just don't want to see him. If he has to suffer like this, I want him to suffer somewhere else. Now my revulsion is doubled. There is the original one, at him, and the new one, at me.

The cyclist finally turns off, and the bus picks up speed. We hurtle through Shoreditch, past all the inexplicable shoe importer's shops and strip clubs. Suddenly, we see the City. It's like the fairy godmother hit the next street with a wand and turned the sagging signage and grimy bricks into gleaming white pillars and shiny steel. We can see the station when we come to a complete stop. It's the Ring of Steel, the police cordon around the City, checking folks out for being terrorists. I've no idea how they do this. I think they just stop all vans and have a quick peek in the back for Semtex. The queue stretches blocks.

Now, if this was a Routemaster, I could just hop out and continue merrily on my journey. But it's not. Behind me, Special Brew starts cursing louder. It's not his language so much as his breath that makes me get up and go down the stairs. I stand there, by the doors, and wait for them to open. They've got to open sometime.

Taking off three hours on Friday afternoon shouldn't make that much of a difference. But it does. I'm behind again. I keep smiling at everyone and thanking them, as well, which by lunchtime is really starting to piss me off. I look at Tuesday, to see how much I can push off on tomorrow's schedule, and see Finchley's appointment shining out from the pages of my diary. I figure I can have my breakdown then, if I'm nippy about it.

Quentin sticks his head in my door about six and asks me how I'm doing and I act all calm and collected. He stays, chats a bit about the party and what someone said to Mandy about her new trousers and what she said back. I remember that during the week Quentin doesn't have a home to go to, and I try and seem interested and amused.

Then a lull comes and I find myself saying, 'Have you ever had a really bad feeling right before a launch?'

'About what?'

'About the product itself.' I hold up pretty well when he looks at me, even though I had no idea I was going to say anything like this.

'That's not really your business, is it?' he says. 'I mean, I've done great work on some flops.'

'I'm just afraid—'

'That's it, you know. You're just *afraid*, Maggie.' He looks at me meaningfully and I try to seem enlightened by this. He must see through that though, because he walks over to my desk and touches me, lays his hand on my shoulder. It's warm through my blouse. And then he spins around and walks out my door. I suppose that's all the mentoring I'm going to get today.

I finish what I was doing and leave before seven. Central Line, for a miracle, is running smoothly and a train is just about to leave Liverpool Street. I look at my watch as we hit Hackney Downs. Twenty-four minutes. Amazing.

The downs themselves are shrouded in darkness, heaps of leaves raked under trees look faintly ominous in the glow of the lamps. When I get off the train at Rectory Road, the wind whistles down the platform, cutting in chill. I need to dig out my gloves and muffler. Winter is here.

Chapter Fifteen

Saint Peter is late. My clock shows three-fifteen when I wake up to find him sitting on the edge of the bed. When I click on my light, he looks worried sick. You know in the *Untouchables*, when Connery's character knows all about the police corruption in Chicago, and Kevin Costner's character hasn't got a clue? And Sean's trying to impress on Costner all about what they're up against? He looks like that.

When he turns to me, he says, 'Well?'

And I say, 'Well, what?' which makes him sigh.

'Well, now you have read your Bible. Have you had an idea about what you should do?'

'You mean an idea about what you guys should do.'

He blinks. 'No, Maggie. What *you* are to do. I am dead.'

I don't know what he sees in my face, but whatever it is makes him keep talking.

'When you use this PR of yours. To save the words of the Master.' He pauses and then bursts out with, 'Of course! Maggie, what is wrong with you tonight?'

My brain starts whirring but my face is frozen in shock. I can't seem to move my mouth, which is hanging open, and I can feel my eyes start to hurt from not blinking.

He just waits.

And meanwhile, some ridiculous images spring to mind. I see Bibles in tubs with 'I Can't Believe He's Not Risen' printed on the top, imagine the makeup lady from *Richard and Judy* confiding to the camera during a makeover that she's never been a big fan of Saint Paul, picture an advertorial in *Bella* headed 'What You Don't Know About The Crucifixion'. I manage to shake my head and this breaks my paralysis enough so that I'm able to tell him, 'Rock, I'm just not qualified to mount-'

'You have been chosen, Maggie.'

'But I'm in FMCG. I don't even know anyone in religion.'

'The Master has called you. You will come.' He sighs. 'I just hoped you would come tonight. These things weigh heavy on me, more so since I have spoken them to you.'

But for once my own emotions interest me far more than Peter's. 'I *can't*,' I try to say forcefully. 'It's not that I won't. I *can't*.' I think about this for a moment. 'I might come up with a few ideas, if I think about it for awhile, but you're going to need someone in the sector, Peter.'

'Do not call me-'

I say, 'Sorry,' automatically. I'm not getting through to him. He's on my bed, stolid as a garden gnome. And he's waiting for me to come up with some sort of...campaign. To pull story boards from under the mattress and pitch the whole thing to him. This makes my head feel heavy.

Perhaps I've been naïve, but it never occurred to me that... I've got to try and explain it to him.

I say, 'Look, I'm *nobody* in the religious world, Rock. And if I start spouting off about what,' air quotes, ' "really happened" with Jesus, they're going to lock me away.'

He uses Connery's trick eyebrow, so I rephrase this, 'People will think I am mad. I'll lose my livelihood, and most likely my husband...'

This has made him smile. For some reason, he's found that amusing. We're just not communicating. In desperation, I speed up. I also get a great deal more emphatic.

'I mean, *nobody's* going to *listen*, Rock. *Nobody* will believe *me*. I've got *no* credibility in this area. Now, if it was a new bikini wax, I'd be your girl, but *this*...'

I'm not making any impression on him whatsoever. Indeed, his smile is now a big toothy grin. 'You will do it, Maggie.'

This serves to make my jaw drop again. 'Rock, have you heard a word I've said?'

'What? That you will lose your way of life? That you may be imprisoned? That you will lose your man?' He does his most emphatic puff yet. 'And this is to impress me? This happened to us all, Maggie.'

'But...' I struggle, 'Listen, back home, the religious right! They'd actually try and *kill* anyone who said-'

Peter snorts. And I remember that he was crucified in Rome. My head is so very, very heavy that I can feel the discs in my spine grind together clear down between my shoulders. It feels as big as a prize pumpkin. I lie back and rest it on the pillows.

He says, 'Big deal.' He says, 'We all died, Maggie.' He jumps to his feet and begins to pace again, around my sleighbed. I can hear his feet slapping my floorboards back and forth.

He says, 'Do you think any of us wanted to take up this burden? Do you think James wanted to abandon the family business and move to Jerusalem? Do you think we all wanted to leave our homes and travel? To be poor? To see our friends killed before our eyes?'

I don't answer this barrage of rhetorical questions. I don't think I can. I'm staring up at my ceiling, wondering, Can they actually do this to me? Can they make me? Suddenly, I'm all too convinced that they can. And it makes me feel completely powerless. My throat goes dry with what I recognise as terror.

He sits back down and takes up my limp, unresisting hand. He says, 'When you are called, Maggie, you must come. There is no choice in the matter.'

I still can't speak, but my eyes spill over with tears. Peter makes a clucking sound and shakes his head. 'I do not know if you will be called to sacrifice as I was. You may not have to sacrifice any of the things you say. But you will do this work, Maggie. Because you must.'

185

'You're going to force me? It won't even do any good! No one will listen.' My voice is breaking. I whine the last words. A great sob of fear, anger and frustration escapes me.

'Maggie...' he sounds exasperated. 'You will find yourself wanting to do it.'

That's even worse. 'I hate this. And I won't want to do it! I'll never want to do it.' Tears ooze out of my eyes. I feel like I'm choking. 'Unless you guys fuck with my mind some more.' I'd be more forceful if the top of my pumpkin hadn't apparently exploded. The pain in my head is intense, and when I speak it seems to increase. 'What about...bloody,' ow, 'free will, and...'

Then something really weird happens. I start to shake. I hold up my hand in front of my face, and it's dancing as if I've got a nerve disease. I manage to whisper, 'What's happening to me?'

And then Peter is looming over me, at last registering some concern. He blurs as my glasses are removed.

I hear him say, 'I will give you time, Maggie. I will come next week,' which makes me writhe with impotent fury.

And then the blessed darkness takes it all away.

I am sitting on the number 10 bus and I'm not really sure how I got here. It takes me a minute to realise we are bumbling down Gower Street. The dirty stone buildings look unfamiliar to me, even though I see them every other day. Part of me is shouting 'Gower Street, Gower Street' inside my head, but the voice seems far away. You mean I live here? another voice says. This one is closer, it's tones filled with wonder and disgust. I live here, in all this black dust? I breathe that, every day?

I don't remember much about this morning. I look down and find that I am perfectly dressed in a neat grey suit with a long jacket under my overcoat. I even have gloves on and, yes, stockings and shoes. My case is by my side. My bag is slung over my arm. I open it and take out my lipstick compact. Someone has even made me up and done my hair. It just wasn't me.

I listen for more voices inside my head, but they've all gone quiet. The bus lurches around the corner of Tottenham Court Road. It is a Routemaster, my favourite, but it seems filthy. Dirt is ingrained in every crack, every grain of wood, even the upholstery. Next to some shiny chrome stripping is a line of embedded dirt. It comes from London air. It must be toxic.

I nearly miss my stop, looking at the dirt, and then when I get up, have to be reminded by a fat man in a Burberry to take my case with me. I step off at a set of lights on Oxford Street without looking anywhere, really, and a bicycle screeches to a halt inches away from my legs. He shouts at me, but he, too, sounds far away. I just look at him shouting. It doesn't seem like it has anything to do with me.

The wide sidewalk is nearly empty. I pull myself together, or try, when I cross the little narrow road that leads from Soho and remember to look both ways. I am relieved when I am across it, all four feet or so of it, and stand on the corner, working again at pulling myself together.

I've come face to face with that big sheet of mirror again. This time I walk closer, and inspect myself. This body doesn't seem to belong to me. I'm steering it, like you would a rental car, not knowing where the corners are or how it will respond. I steer it to the mirror and look at it for a moment.

There is nothing at all remarkable about the way I look. It's a nice suit someone has hung on the rental body. It's a nice hairdo, too. A bit severe, maybe, but flattering. The makeup is subtle and pinky-brown. Just the sort of thing I might choose. But I wouldn't be doing this, would I? I wouldn't be running to work in a suit at seven o'clock in the morning. I'd be going for bagels or croissants. I'd be watching the *Big Breakfast* or something and running a bath.

I turn to the side. I recognise the eyes as they follow me, but not the arched browlines anymore than I do the aggressively outlined lips. The loud voice suddenly shouts to get a move on, and so I do. The feet seem to know where they are going. I don't have to worry about that.

'Alienation. Denial. Depression,' Finchley is saying. I don't know how I made it through until our appointment. I know I made a date with myself to break down today, but I didn't really think I'd keep it. I'm struggling hard to get some kind of grip.

'Depression? But I don't feel depressed.'

'What do you feel?'

'Well, I've been very busy lately, with this campaign, as I said, and-'

Finchley holds up a hand. 'What do you feel, Maggie? Can you start a sentence with I Feel?"

This kind of thing isn't going to do anything for me, these ridiculous childish games. Of course I can start a sentence with I Feel. Only when I try, I can't. The mouth I'm using makes a few movements, but nothing comes out. I look at Finchley and horror must show in my eyes.

She fumbles in her big bag and brings out a box of tissues, which she slides onto my desk.

'I don't know how I feel,' I say, and then suddenly I do know, because I'm crying quite hard. I am good at doing whatever task is set me. If I'm meant to feel, I'll start feeling. I croak, 'I feel bloody miserable,' into my tissue, which makes Finchley smile.

'Well,' she says, 'there's the Denial shot full of holes. So let's talk about Depression.' And I sit there crying buckets, hoping whoever packed my bag this morning remembered concealer, foundation and mascara.

In the hall, hours later, I bump into Quentin. 'You feeling better about the launch?' he asks me.

I shrug. 'I'm not sure,' I say.

'Well, we never are completely sure, are we?'

He looks at me carefully and I thank God for makeup. 'Your eyes look sore,' he says.

'It's these damn contacts. I think they object to my hours.'

At this, he gives an avuncular chuckle, and pats me again on my shoulder. More mentoring, I recognise. And I try to make the face I'm wearing look grateful.

I am grateful when I'm back in my office. Grateful to be alone for a few moments. I really don't know how I'm getting through this day. I'm having a crisis, according to Finchley. I wish I could remember her real name. I ended up just calling her You. I could look in the file again, but I've looked a hundred times and each time I think, I knew that. I knew that. Of course I did. I just won't tell myself.

I've often wondered what a nervous breakdown feels like. Finchley says they feel different to different people. What I've got is alienation. I have homework to cure it. I take out the post-it note I've written it on. I'm keeping it in the pocket of my suit and it crunches to remind me.

I'm to call my mother. I'm to try to arrange a date with a friend. I'm to try to tell one other person about my visits from Saint Peter. And every hour, on the hour, no matter what I am doing, I'm to think about how I feel. It all looks impossible, and I've only got a day and a half until my next appointment with her. I look at the watch on my wrist. It's five 'till three, but I figure I can get a little ahead if I go ahead and feel now.

I feel remote, still. I feel not much. I feel like the last thing I need is more to do and this little list of tasks is getting on my nerves. I sigh, and then say 'Shit' out loud to an empty office. That's not good. That's not good at all. Well, none of it is, really, is it? I have to face it that I'm not doing so well today. I have to face it that I'm not doing so well at all.

And besides, I'm used to hitting my targets. I always do. It doesn't matter how absurdly difficult they might be, I do the tasks I'm set. I achieve whatever I set out to do or whatever anybody sets out for me. Simon says 'Make some money' and I make loads. Simon says, 'I want a bigger place' and I buy him a three bedroom house with an eighty foot garden in Zone 2. Quentin says, 'I'd like you to take over this launch' and I take over the launch. I do it all. I do anything, and do it well. That's me.

That's me. Whoever I am.

Whoever it is reaches for my contacts book and begins to trace Felicity Powell, last known whereabouts, book publishing. I will see if she wants to have lunch or dinner or something, as if I have the time. I don't have the time to completely go out of my mind, either, I remind myself. And I don't really want psychiatric treatment if I can do this myself, although anti-depressants sound pretty tasty right about now. I begin punching the buttons on my phone.

The receptionist puts me through to a secretary and it takes a moment for me to realise that Fliss has her own secretary. I kind of fumble when I ask to speak to her, which puts the secretary in protective mode. 'Is she expecting your call?'

'No,' I say. 'I'm an old friend, just trying to track her down. It's purely a social call.' I have now completely alarmed the secretary, and she makes me spell my name, even though White isn't usually much of a poser for most folks. Then I get to go on hold.

'Strewth, Maggie! I thought you were dead!' Fliss has been in London even longer than I have, but her Ozzie accent sounds like her boots are still muddy from some *Crocodile Dundee* swamp. If anything, it's stronger than when I first met her. I think she must put it on thicker, just for the locals.

'Not dead, just busy. Sounds like you have been, too. What are you doing there now, running the place?'

'Ah, you had to chat to my pet dragon, did you? She's a great gal, I don't know what I'd do without her.'

I have to take a deep breath before I ask her if she'd like to meet up. I realise I'm a bit frightened that she'll say no. She doesn't say no.

She says, 'What about dinner tomorrow? Tell Simon to learn to open a tin. We'll go someplace posh, my treat. Can my dragon ring you? Her name is Ellice. You should see her, too, a thing of beauty, if not really a joy forever. I know sometime soon she'll be snapped up by some author with a big advance and abandon me. You still at the Blues?'

'Yes,' I manage to work in, and then she's gone.

I'm still sitting there with the phone to my ear, feeling like I'm in a different space/time continuum. The energy Fliss projected, even down the phone, is daunting, and I fight an almost over-whelming urge to call Ellice and tell her that I've just found some-thing in my diary. Instead, I tick off one task on my post-it note.

I still have the phone up to my ear, and I'm on what passes for a roll when the world is grey jelly. So I ring home. It's about 10 in the morning there. The phone rings four times, but the answering machine isn't on. My office is quiet. I just sit there and listen to the ring, the American ring, one long jangling tone. God, that sound, I think. My eyes fill up. And how about freight train whistles, and coyotes in the night? I have to stop thinking about it, I'm going to spoil the makeup again. But I can't bring myself to take that ring away from my ear.

By the tenth ring, I am picturing my mother out at the grocery store on Sixth Street. I imagine her choosing apples, rolling her cart down the wide aisles, chatting with the ladies at the deli counter. So it's a shock when she breathlessly says, 'Hello?'

'Hi, Mom, it's me.'

'What's wrong?'

'Wrong? Nothing's wrong.'

191

'Oh, thank God for that.' There is a small rustling sound as she sinks down onto the kitchen stool. 'I almost missed you, I've been out shovelling snow off the sidewalk.'

God! With her blood pressure, this is suicidal. 'Mom! You know you shouldn't do that!'

'Well, the kid next door is out of town, and I didn't want somebody to fall and break their neck on it. Anyway, it's not such hard work if you catch it early.'

There's a silence. I can hear home somehow, the black clock in the range ticking, the furnace blowing hot air.

'I'm sorry to jump on you about something being wrong,' she finally says, 'but you never call, Sweetie, and so I just assumed something had happened to you or Simon.'

'I never call?' I sound wounded, even to myself.

'Well, no, Princess, you don't. I haven't heard from you for two months.'

That can't be right. That can't be right. 'That can't be,' I finally say.

'It is, you know. I always mark the calendar when you call. It's a red letter day.'

Oh, Jesus. My mother marks the calendar when I call, and I don't call. She marks the fucking calendar when I call. The eyeliner takes another bashing, and I don't need to look at my watch to know how I Feel. I feel guilty. 'God, Mama, I'm so sorry. I feel so bad about that, I can't tell you.'

She laughs, a little tinkling sound, like ice tea stirring in glass. 'Oh, baby,' she says. 'I'm used to it. As soon as you could crawl, you were going in one direction. Away. That's just you.'

I picture my little town in aerial view, the kitchen extension roof where my mother talks on the phone, the bare trees of our neighbourhood. The yards would be squares of white. The streets would be wet, shiny and black, and the brick sidewalks would only show intermittently, where someone as conscientious as my mother had done their duty. I stop when I realise how much doing this hurts.

'I'm going to come home and see you.' I didn't know I was going to say that. I think I'm more surprised than she is.

'You are? When?'

'I don't know. But I'm going to come soon. Maybe for Thanksgiving. Are you cooking this year?'

Mother laughs. 'As if Helen would let me. Before she and your brother were even engaged, that girl was telling me about her family stuffing recipe. I knew my turkey basting days were over, right then.'

'How is Helen's stuffing?'

'Oh, it's alright. Not as good as Stove Top, if you ask me. But Jack sets store by it and so I make all the right noises. It sure would be nice if you could come, though. I still make the cranberries and some of the pies.'

The burnt sugar taste of my mother's pecan pie immediately enters my mouth. 'I'd like to be there with you. I'll see what I can do. And I'll call more often, I promise.'

'Alright, Pumpkin, you do that.'

I clear my throat of tears, and remember what we talk about in Lawrence, Kansas. I say, 'So how much snow did you get?'

'It's still coming down, but they say we'll get up to four inches.'

'Are the schools closed?'

'Naw. Might be tomorrow. I'm glad you aren't on one of those buses. It used to give me palpitations to think about you sliding all around with Junior Biddle behind the wheel. And now you're hopping on and off those big red ones in the middle of all that traffic. It's a good thing I learned to stop worrying about you, Maggie.'

Her voice prattles on, her drawl leaching through my ear like set honey, flooding down my throat into my chest, where it warms me like nothing else ever could. I can't believe I've been doing without this. I can't believe I've been doing without her. How could I? How could I do that?

In between a meeting with Creative to do the final okay on the print run for the shelf wobblies and one with Celia to help her plan for the bi-annual review of a shampoo account, I land at my desk for another five minutes. While I wait for my password to log me into my email, I hear the crinkle of the post-it note in my pocket and pull out my list. It's ten past four, and I've forgotten again.

I Feel... I feel odd. I feel like the only times. I've been alive today are on the telephone to Fliss and to my mother. I feel like the rest of the time I've been walking around this office, dead. And nobody has even noticed.

Chapter Sixteen

You know how it is at Quo Vadis. You walk in and everyone makes sure that you're nobody special. It's a bit daunting when you aren't. I was a little late and Fliss was already at the table, swigging something sparkling from a flute. Fliss actually looks Australian, if you know what I mean, she has that broad, strong-browed face you often see on them. Her dear eyes are a little piggy, but she has a lovely retrousse nose and a gorgeous smile. She always pulls the blokes, who probably never get around to looking at her nose or her eyes or her brows, for that matter. She has enormous breasts, Fliss, and she's a blonde.

She jumped up when she saw me. 'Darling!' she said, and instead of air kissing me, she smacked me right on the lips, holding my chin so I couldn't get away. 'God, I've missed the sight of you! How the fuck are you?'

This kind of thing would pretty much stop traffic in most restaurants in most towns, but in London, and especially in places like here and the Ivy, a strange kind of privacy exists. In a banquette, Robbie Williams is dining with two folks, one wearing a lot of stretchy pink and one in some species of suit. They aren't getting any attention, either. I say, 'Fliss,' and am amazed at how much I put into it. I say, 'I've missed you so much,' and again, realise from the tone in my voice how much I mean it.

'I rang Maureen and told her I was going to see you. She's jealous. We've got to have a girlie night soon.' Fliss reaches into the bucket and wipes the dripping bottle on the provided napkin. The waiter rushes over and takes it away from her. I don't know how Fliss can afford Bollinger, but he's pouring it in my glass.

It tastes fantastic, and I don't know if it's the wine or Fliss or doing my homework or the aubergine walls or what, but all of the sudden, the world gets a bit brighter. It's like the beginning of *Wizard of Oz* when it goes Technicolor. And I take another drink.

Four hours later and the restaurant is emptying. Fliss's just come back from the toilet, where she is spending an increasing amount of time. I have finished the third bottle of wine and we're now onto the 1976 Grahams Malvedos. We're also nibbling on chocolate. I don't know why. We don't need anything else to drink and we certainly don't need anything else to eat. We've both surreptitiously undone our skirt buttons.

'And another thing about this bloody island,' Fliss is saying. 'This whole Camilla backlash is a pile of shit, don't you think? Come on, what's the problem? I'm sure she's got more between her ears than Diana ever did. And she's probably a better goer as well. Okay, she's ugly. She's ugly!' Fliss waves her port glass around in a circle. 'But old Charlie's no pinup, now, is he? And I've read that thing on architecture. He may not be stupid, he may even be a genius by royal standards, but he's not exactly a blinding light of intellectual haumphingness.'

I don't know whether that was her mouth, my ears, or a word I don't know. I try and find out. 'What was that last bit?'

'Doesn't matter. I can talk to you about anything, you know that? Anything at all. You better bloody well see us more often.'

'I will,' I promise. I grope for her hand, but find the chocolates first and pop one into my mouth, pouring some Port in with it so that the acridity of what tannins survive will stop me gagging as my body rejects another bit of sugar.

Fliss's still talking. 'I tell you anything. You can tell me anything. It's great.'

I hear that I can tell Fliss anything and somewhere inside of me a thought is born. It's born sideways and with great pain and difficulty, but it's born, and since I lost the ability to screen my conversation midway through the second bottle of Claret I immediately say, 'I've got something to tell you, Fliss. And I haven't told anybody else. And it's big.'

She leans forward, putting her elbow in her cappuccino, which she has forgotten to drink. She imperiously pushes the coffee aside. 'Tell me,' she says seriously. 'Tell me. I'm your friend.'

I clear my throat. 'Well,' I start.

'Come on,' she says. 'Pitch it.'

I say, 'You know I told you about the tampon being wonky.' She nods. 'And about Simon and his whatsit girl.'

'Fucking his assistant,' Fliss shakes her head. 'They're all bastards, you know. All of them. Even the beautiful Simon.'

She raises her Port glass and we clink. But I'm not going to be distracted now. I'm halfway to crossing off my last bit of homework from Finchley and I'm taking the conversation over like I would a runaway train.

'Yeah, yeah,' I say, 'but listen. Saint Peter starts appearing on my bedside.'

Fliss cocks her head to one side. 'Saint Peter?'

'Yeah. Saint Peter. But he looks like Sean Connery. He wants to hire me. Or Jesus does. It's kind of complicated.'

Fliss's mouth is hanging open in a concentrating kind of way, and I stumble on. 'He's telling me all this stuff about Jesus. Bible stuff. About what really happened. It's incredible, Fliss. You wouldn't believe it. Well you would. I do. Or I think I do. I went to the British Library and read up on loads of it. I think it's probably about right. Or I might be just cracking up. I'm not real sure right now.'

'Go on.' Fliss's eyes have started to narrow. She is getting her business face on, and I don't know why. I remember when we worked together how she could switch it on and off like a tap. Now she's switching it on. Maybe someone important has walked in. But they haven't. The place is getting emptier and emptier.

'Anyway,' I stumble on, 'I'm supposed to put a new spin on the

New Testament. For Jesus. But I only talk to Peter…or Sean…no, Peter I guess.'

'Maggie! That's fantastic. And you haven't come to anyone else?'

The tablecloth is a mess. I dab at some sauce I spilled with my napkin. 'Uh-uh,' I say, shaking my head.

'Do you have an agent for this?'

An agency for finding supernatural work? What? What is the woman talking about? I say, 'Agency?'

And she says, 'Don't. Don't, Maggie. We'll take it. You can get the contract checked out by the Guild.' Fliss is moving all around now, putting her bag on the table and fishing out her phone. She starts pushing numbers. Taxi, I think to myself. She thinks I'm crazy and she's getting a taxi so that she can run away. My hand fumbles to the stem of my glass and with a wrenching swallow I shove another mouthful of Port down my oesophagus.

'Richard?' she shouts into the phone, but there aren't any people left around us to glare at us with British disapproval. 'Yes, I know what bloody time it is. Wake up Gloria. Wake her up, Richard. I've got something hot, really hot, and it won't wait.'

She fumbles in her bag and emerges with a cigarette and a lighter, and uses the combination with one hand. She's so co-ordinated. I can't believe how co-ordinated she is. I don't think I've got the physical co-ordination to take a leak right now, and she's phoning people and lighting cigarettes and moving her bag around and everything. She's so competent.

And then I concentrate for a moment because she's saying something about Saint Peter and Sean Connery into the phone. And then 'modern marriage' and the word 'millennium' and something about pocket Canons and Nick Cave that I don't quite catch. And then she's talking about rock and roll promotions and short stories in the Iowa University press and something about my agency and I realise that she's talking about me.

And then she stands up, pointing her cigarette like a loaded gun at the door.

'Now listen, you two, this is going to be bloody big. And I don't want to miss out like we did with *Flake*.'

She listens for a moment and snorts. 'Yeah,' she says, 'sleep on it. And guess what's going to happen while you sleep? Little, Brown are going to happen while you sleep, that's what. HarperCollins are going to happen. See if you can sleep thinking about that. I sure can't, that's why I'm on the phone to you instead of in a nice warm cab on my way home.'

She listens for a moment longer. 'You want me to put my neck on it on this one? Do you? I'll put my neck on the line with it. No problem. If this doesn't tear it up, you can finally get rid of me, if that's what you want. And sleep.' There's a pause, and Fliss smiles, squinting down at me through smoke from the ciggie she's got clutched in her teeth. 'I've got her right here, right now. She hasn't gone to anybody else. She isn't even agented.'

A pause. 'She's a mate.' A briefer pause. 'But yeah, we might. A bit, anyway.' And then, 'Good, good. Sorry about the hour, but you know how it is. Good. I'll talk to you in the morning. Yeah, yeah, I will. Yeah, I'll get it by next week. Eight-thirty. Yeah.'

I'm listening as closely as I can. But I still don't understand.

'How much have you written?'

'Written?' I look at her.

'Jesus, Maggie, snap out of it. I've just sold the damn thing for you, and I need to know how long I'm going to have to stall the rest of the board.'

'Sold?'

She grabs my face again in her hand and bends over. Her eyes are inches from mine. 'I've just bought your novel about Simon and Saint Peter,' she says, slowly and clearly, as if she's talking to a child.

I don't remember saying goodbye. I don't remember walking out of the restaurant. I do know that I've gone the wrong way. If I was walking the right way, I'd be at Oxford Street right now. I'm not. So, I'm not.

I peer down dark Soho streets. The neon that winks on the odd doorway does nothing to enliven the scene of two-am Soho on a Wednesday night. It only seems to deepen the shadows and filth of the corners. I'm trying to look brisk and in control. I'm also trying not to trip on a bin bag and land on my face. And then I just start turning and turning down streets until I see lights, people, something familiar. And I'm on Greek Street, so I go to Frith Street for a big espresso at Bar Italia, fumbling for money, slurring my speech, bumping into people, and generally being completely useless.

I spill some of it, but manage to get most of it down my neck and then go back to Greek Street and through the Pillars of Hercules to Charing Cross Road. I'm looking for a cab, but it's one of those bloody awful nights when there just aren't any cabs. None at all. Or they've all got their lights off because some other bugger's already bagged them. I can't call our cab service because I don't want them to see me this way. Then a late 38 bus comes trundling down the road and I get on.

God, they go fast this time of night, whizzing by stops. There's nobody upstairs but me and this couple up front who seem to be making love on the bus. I find myself staring, trying to figure out exactly what they are trying to do, and then I look away and watch London zooming by my window. Everything is going so, so fast.

I get off at Dalston Junction. Well, I fall off, actually, and wedge myself in between the wheel and the curb. The bus looks interesting from that angle but I know that I shouldn't be laying there. The conductor seems rather frantic, binging the bell a bit and hopping off to say something to me. He's calling me 'Darling' and being rather persuasive about getting up. I try to, really I do, but he has to haul me to my feet and I rock on the pavement, still unsteady. As soon as he decently can, he's binged again and gone.

Naturally, I check my coat and my bag for signs of wear. My shoes have a bit of a scrape, but nothing that polish won't cure. My coat is fine. That's the good thing about good wool. You can put it through hell and it still looks fine. Look at *Braveheart*.

I find my way around the corner, trying to be brisk. I'm tacking from angle to angle, but I'm doing it in a business-like fashion. My chin is held high and arrogant. I think that this is helpful. I am alone at the bus stop, which in this part of town, at 2:30, is probably a good thing. I try not to think about who might be joining me. At least they moved the prostitutes further down after the new Sainsbury's opened. And I don't look much like a good crack customer.

Another night bus is zooming towards the stop. They all come so quick this time of night. I hold out my hand and it squeezes to a halt. I grab the rails and lever myself in. But I snap my pass open briskly and don't really fall that much into the seat.

Four stops and I'll be home. This is such a relief that I close my eyes.

So much for the espresso. Someone is shaking me awake. I try for alert and brisk, but have to wipe drool off my cheek. I find myself saying, 'Hmmmmm?'

'It's the end of the line. You have to get off now.'

The bus is bright when I open my eyes. My contacts are gummy and my eyes feel like someone's been rubbing sand into them. I collect my bag and go to the door. And stop. It's the middle of fucking nowhere. There's a petrol station, but it's shut. And there's nothing else. Nothing.

'Um,' I say, and turn to the driver, who is waiting behind his little screen. 'Is there a taxi rank somewhere around here?'

He looks at me for a moment, 'What?' he says.

'A taxi, or something?' I ask. He shakes his head. And so I say, 'Or maybe you might tell me where I am?'

He comes out from his little screen and stands a couple of feet away from me. 'Where were you trying to go?'

'Stoke Newington.'

'And you fell asleep.'

I grin. I can't help it. He's so stern and he's only a kid. I shrug. 'And you're pissed.'

I shrug again. 'It was all an accident,' I explain helpfully.

He sighs. He gets off the bus and helps me down. I giggle. I don't know what happened to brisk. I can't manage it anymore, and anyway, there's nobody left to be brisk for. There's nothing here at all.

The driver grins back. He says, 'Okay.' He says, 'You see that lamppost down there?'

I do. Just.

He says, 'I'm going to come along there in a red Fiesta in about five minutes. A red Fiesta. Can you remember that?'

I say, 'A red Fiesta,' proudly, and he rolls his eyes.

'Yes. Now don't get in any other cars. Only the red Fiesta.'

'Red Fiesta,' I say again.

'Right.' And he drives the bus away. I stumble down towards the lamppost. At least I'm not tacking anymore. I say, 'A red Fiesta,' a couple of more times to myself, but there's no need to, really. Not a single car comes by.

It takes a long time, but I wait. In the wasteland opposite the lamppost something moves and then I see it. I would have seen it before, maybe, but my contacts have been clearing slow. It's a fox. A lovely, lovely fox. And it's running across the field, running, running. Wild thing.

'Hey! Lady? Hey, pissed lady!'

It's a red Fiesta. I don't know how long it's been there. I get inside. He asks me where I'm going and I tell him, 'It's on your route, my house. You go right past my house.'

He smiles as he drives me. He's got a shaved head which is just a little stubbly. I like it. He's got little lines that go from his lips to his nose when he smiles. I touch them.

'You've got little lines, here,' I say. 'They're nice.'

He slides his eyes over onto mine. 'How did you get so pissed?'

'I went out for dinner. With an Australian.'

He nods thoughtfully. He's lovely. I rub my hand over his head. I find I'm making a little purring sound. 'Nice,' I say again. 'And you're driving me home. That's so nice. I was absolutely fucked out there, wasn't I? I was miles out, wasn't I?'

'Northumberland Park. It's not really miles out.'

I lower my chin truculently. 'No taxis,' I argue.

'No.'

'Then it's miles out, isn't it?'

We've come to Stamford Hill. Again, I am amazed by how quick everything is moving, how empty everything is and how easy.

'You on the one way system?'

'Yep.'

He makes a turn. And another. He keeps looking over at me and finally he says, 'Do you know where you are?'

'Yep.'

'Will you tell me when we get close?'

'We're close.'

He pulls over.

I smile at him. 'You're so nice,' I tell him. 'You saved my life.'

'You're just pissed.'

'I'm not that pissed,' I smile at him. I know exactly what I'm doing. I want to feel those little lines again. I want to lick them. I want to sit on them, actually.

'You're married.'

This seems completely tangential. I look down at my hand and see my ring. 'Yep.' I say again.

He seems to struggle with himself a little and then he is kissing me and then he is saying things like, 'Oh' and 'God' because I am loving it, and I am pulling him over the gear shift to get him closer and I am teasing his tongue into my mouth so that I can suck it hard, suck it almost out by the root. And he says, 'Jesus.' And then I stop because I'm remembering something about Fliss and a phone call. He's fumbling with my blouse buttons and I say, 'Oh, hell,' as I remember.

Then I open up the car door and throw up on the pavement. It isn't nice, but I don't get any in the car. Still, it ends that little romantic interlude. I mumble as I stumble into the doorjamb and thrust impotently at the lock with my key something about not taking the 76 bus again any time soon. When I finally gain entry to my home, I take my contacts out of my eyes and balance them carefully on top of the hall radiator. Then I fall onto the rug in front of the dead fireplace and into an unconsciousness the polite would refer to as sleep.

Chapter Seventen

'Maggie,' someone is shaking me. 'Maggie.'

I moan. 'Fuck off, Peter. Haven't you got me in enough trouble?'

Then there is a silence, which is somehow louder that the noise and the shaking was. I open my eyes but I can't see anything but blur. It's a light grey blur, though, it must be morning. My shoulder and my hip hurt like hell. I roll over onto my back, thinking this must be from sleeping on the floor, but then I remember how interesting the bus looked from the gutter.

The roaring silence is coming from a Simon-shaped bit of blur. He's crouched down on his knees not far away. I crawl over and lay my head in his lap. 'I fell down,' I say. 'And it hurts.'

Simon is frozen underneath me. I can feel him looking at me. 'Who's Peter, Maggie?'

I know what he's thinking, and I try and reassure him. 'No, no,' I say, 'Saint Peter,' and then I think I should have shut up, but it's too late.

I think he's communicating with his facial expression, but of course I'm not getting it. I say, 'I can't see anything, Simon.'

'Who is Peter?'

I sit up. Everything hurts. I think I might throw up again. 'Saint Peter,' I say. 'Saint Peter.'

'I don't care how nice he is, who the fuck is he, and why are you sleeping on the floor, drunk out of your mind?'

'I went out with Fliss. I forgot how much she can drink.'

'Who's Peter, Maggie?'

'Saint Peter,' I say again, and then realise from the noises he makes I'm not getting very far with my explanation. 'Saint Peter has been coming to see me upstairs in our bedroom.'

'Saint Peter.' Simon's voice has no expression.

'Yes.'

'Saint Peter?'

'Yes. Saint Peter. The apostle.' I shrug. 'I don't know why. I mean I know why, but I don't know why he picked me. Well, he's told me, but I just don't believe him, I guess.'

'You don't really believe Saint Peter.'

'Well,' I think about this for a moment. 'I believe that he believes what he says is true. I don't think he's lying to me or anything.'

The Simon blur shakes what must be its head slowly from side to side.

I say, 'Could you possibly get me a glass of water? Or a bucket of it or something?'

The blur detaches itself from the rug and goes past me. I hear things happening in the kitchen, complicated things having to do with taps and opening cupboards. Simon comes back and hands me a pint glass, and I grab his other hand, as well.

'Sit here,' I beg, 'So I can see you.' And he does. He looks lovely in his dressing gown. All warm.

God, the water is fantastic. I'm going to take a bath after this, I tell myself. A really deep bath. 'What time is it?' I ask.

'It's only five. I couldn't sleep. I was so worried.'

'You knew I went out with Fliss.'

'I kind of thought you'd be home at some point.'

'Sorry. I got lost.'

'Lost?'

'I fell asleep on the bus.' I suddenly remember snogging the bus driver and shut abruptly up.

Simon is looking at me funny.

'What?' I mean I know I must look like hell, but…

'Saint Peter is appearing in our bedroom?'

'Forget I told you.'

206

'As if!' Simon looks at me that way again. 'And what do I do during these visitations?'

'You usually sleep. I don't know if he makes sure you sleep through it or what. But you never wake up, even when he sits on the bed.'

'He sits on the bed?'

'Yeah, sometimes he even has his feet right by you, but you never wake up or anything. And he looks like Sean Connery.'

'Like Sean Connery.'

I shrug, 'Yeah.'

'Is this the research you were doing? And all that going to Mass and everything?'

I nod, drinking some more water. God, water. I'm never going to drink anything but water again. I'm going to drink those eight pints or twenty gallons or whatever it is you're supposed to drink every day. I am. I might do a year's worth of catching up right now.

'You think Saint Peter is appearing to you in our bedroom every night.'

'Every weeknight,' I correct. 'And he's not coming at all this week. Just Monday. We quarrelled.'

'Saint Peter was here on Monday night.'

'Yes. Yes, Simon. Why are you repeating everything I say?'

'I'm repeating everything you say?'

'Yes, you did it just then.' I'm very cold. I start to reach for the throw on the sofa, but Simon stops me. He says, 'Take off your clothes first, you've got sick all down you.'

Gross. I do, too. I go to the corner of the room and disrobe. My stockings are black with dirt and little bits of gravel still stick in my leg. I brush them away. There's a big purple bruise on my hip. Simon gasps. 'What did you do to your shoulder?', so I know there's one there as well. I get the throw and it's heavenly. Simon is crouched now by the fireplace, holding in the ignition button to light the fire.

'I told you. I fell down trying to get on a bus. No, off a bus. Dalston Junction.' It was all coming back.

'When were you at Dalston Junction?'

'About two or so.'

'Jesus, Maggie!' Simon grabs my arms and shakes me slightly. 'That is so fucking stupid.' And he doesn't even know I ended up in Northumberland Park. 'You could be hurt, wandering around drunk. Some idiot could take advantage of you.'

And I know I should be looking ashamed of myself. In fact, thinking about the bus driver, I should be feeling pretty ashamed of myself. But all I can think of is how much he loves me. He really does love me, or he wouldn't be so worried.

'You love me,' I say, stupidly.

'Oh, Jesus, Maggie.' And Simon starts to cry.

It was alright later. While I was in the bath, I told him about Finchley. I told him I knew I was losing it, but that I was working on it. But then he asked me if I really thought Saint Peter was coming to visit me, and I didn't know what to say. I dunked my head under the water to get it wet for a shampoo and just stayed there, holding my breath, for as long as I could.

When I came up, he was still waiting. And so I said, 'I don't know.'

He took it pretty well. Considering.

I'm on the train to Liverpool Street station. I'm avoiding the buses for awhile. I especially don't want to stand at the bus stop on my street. It's ten past eight. I Feel time. I feel sick. I feel sore. I feel ashamed of myself. But I also feel very much alive.

I stay on the Central Line to Oxford Circus solely because I don't want to look at myself in that big mirror again, although by this time they should be covering it up with the bag stands. Down the sneaky back alleyways I go, clickety-click, avoiding the morning crowds. It's nearly 8:30. I can't remember the last time I got in this late. Clickety-click. Clickety-click. As I go, I realise something. My feet hurt like hell.

On Noel Street I pull up in a doorway and look down, afraid I've got on odd shoes or that they're on the wrong feet or that I've worn evening sandals or something by mistake. But there's nothing wrong with them. They're court shoes from Russell and Bromley. They're the same shoes I've been wearing once every two or three days for a year. I take off again. Clickety-click, clickety-click. And stop again. Ouch. There's nothing inside jabbing me or anything, they just feel so tight. And the heel hurts my heel. And the ball of the sole is so thin that I can feel the pavement. I can't believe I've been wearing these all this time. They're horrible.

Celia's in my office with the latest fax from Claridges on the launch timings and menus when the phone rings and a voice says, 'Mrs White? Could you hold for Miss Powell, please?'

'Yes,' I say, and then tell Celia that I'm sorry, but I'm going to have to take this one. I expect her to gather her things and go, but she doesn't, she just nods absently and looks at something tricky with her pencil in the corner of her mouth.

'God,' Fliss says. 'Mags? Do you feel as wretched as I do?'

I want to ask Celia to go, but I don't know how to do it. I say, 'Well, I'm with someone at the moment, but you could say that I feel even more strongly about that than you do.'

Fliss clears her throat, and I start to remember all the cigarettes she consumed last night. 'Look, Maggie darling, this novel. How much have you written on it?'

I really don't know what to say. Luckily, with Fliss, there's hardly ever a chance to say anything. She only waits a millisecond for an answer.

'It's just that after my inspired phone call last night, I've got to produce something fairly terrific, you know what I mean. I mean, how's it looking? I've always liked your stuff, but this is my job on the line. So? How's it coming?'

'Well…' I say. I mean, now's the time, really, to tell her that it's all a misunderstanding, right? But she sounds nothing like the woman who used her mobile like a six-shooter last night. She sounds like a scared little girl. And this is my mate Fliss. We went through hell on a grocery title together. I don't want to let her down. I search for the words to tell her it's all a mistake, but nothing is coming out.

Fliss groans. 'Oh, for fuck's sake, Maggie, don't tell me you haven't started it yet.'

My jaw is wired shut. Celia must even feel the tension, because she suddenly looks up and stares at my face intently.

And then my mouth starts to move without me. 'Oh, I've done a bit of it,' I find myself saying. I'm using this very calm, soothing type of tone. It might work on Fliss, but it's doing nothing for me. 'I've done a lot of research, and I've made a lot of notes. How much do you need to see and when?'

'Could you give me couple of chapters by next week?'

How long is a chapter? Six, eight, twenty pages? I swallow hard. 'That shouldn't be too much of a problem,' the extremely rational voice says for me. 'But it might be the end of next week,' I tack on myself.

'That's fine, darling!' Fliss's voice sings down the receiver with relief. 'The end is no problem at all.' I hear her stretch. 'It's going to be great working with you. I mean, not only will I get to see your sunny little face, but I'll also get to work with someone professional. You should see the bozo I've got waiting for me out with Ellice right now. God, he's a wanker of the first division.'

Ordinarily, this would make me smile, but right now I've just been hit by a car. Or at least that's how it feels. So I tell her that I'm in a meeting, actually, and she shouts a bit more bonhomie at me and rings off.

Celia is still worrying the end of the pencil. She says, 'What did you just commit to by the end of next week?'

'Oh,' I say, running my hand through my hair and noticing great strands of it falling onto the carpet. 'Another client.'

And what is Saint Peter going to think about it, anyway? I forget Celia is there, and groan.

'Maggie, you're getting as bad as Quentin! Don't you even know the word No?'

I'm lucky to have people under me like Celia and Henry, who worry about me and want to protect me. I look at her. Her little pekinese nose is smudged from toner, and looks even more pekinese than normal. And her glossy little head has new careful streaks of colour. I say, 'Some clients you can't say no to.' And she grimaces in sympathy.

And then we dither some more about Earl Grey tea.

It's when I eat that I notice I'm on the edges of death. At two-thirty, after wolfing two boxes of sushi from Ninya's, I close my door so no one can hear my moaning. I drink another four little bottles of fizzy water and then run to the toilet twice to wee. By three, I have fresh lipstick on and I haven't vomited, so don't do too badly in the final meeting with Creative. Life is sweeter at four. I'm looking at a photocopy of the hotel's latest fax. Celia's doing all the real work. I'm just writing out a list of what clothes to bring when Finchley walks in, saying, 'Anya told me to come on back.'

I completely forgot. I push my desk into some kind of order and stand up, ask her if she'd like some coffee.

'Melanie's bringing me something.'

'Good. Good.'

We sit down and I open the bottom drawer and twitch the shrink folder out from where I keep it on top of Mount Stocking, open it and say, 'You must have met just about everybody now.'

'I think so.'

She seems vaguely threatening to me today and I don't really know why until I realise that she's wearing quite a sharp little suit instead of her usual flowing fabrics.

'You look smart,' I say.

She grins. 'Don't be fooled. I had an interview in the City.'

'How did it go?'

She shakes her head. 'I don't know why I went, really. Tempted by money, I imagine.' Finchley raises her slim little hips and tugs down the hem of her skirt. 'I hate wearing this sort of thing,' she says. 'I can't imagine doing it all the time. This waistband is cutting into me and I know I haven't gained any weight since I bought it last week.'

Melanie appears, glides in with a bottle of mineral water and a glass, smiles at us both and withdraws, shutting the door behind her.

I am suddenly aware of my own waistband. 'It's the shoes that are the worst,' I say. I look at her feet in sensible loafers and swing out one of my Russell and Bromley specials to prop it on the waste bin. 'They don't look like instruments of torture, but they are. I can feel every pebble of this city, every grain of sand on every pavement through these soles.' She raises her eyebrows. 'I only realised it this morning. I've been wearing them for over a year.'

'And they hurt you.'

'Terribly.' She pulls out her little notebook and I realise my session has started.

'Is it just the soles?'

'No, they pinch as well.'

'Hmmmm.'

I'm still hung-over, so I'm testy. I say, 'Don't hem at me. It makes me feel like a car no one can fix.'

Finchley gives a wry smile. 'Fix is a very American word.'

'A car past mending, then.'

'What's wrong with sounding American?'

'You sound stupid when you use American words.'

'I do?'

'I meant one does.'

Finchley cocks her head to one side and smiles at me again. 'Americans all sound stupid?'

I think about this for a moment. 'No, of course not.'

'Do you think being American puts you at a disadvantage in your work?'

'In just about everything. You guys aren't particularly kind to foreigners, you know.'

'Who has been unkind to you?'

'Oh, it's nothing I could prove in a court of law. Everybody is terribly nice on the outside. But you can feel the condescension.'

'Anyone in particular?'

'Yes. Anyone middle class, pretty much.' I think about Simon's mates. Bets. Katie. Phil. Amanda. They do a lot of eyerolling not quite behind my back whenever I open my mouth.

'What about Quentin?'

'He wasn't thrilled when I was assigned to him, but he's got over it.'

'So you feel there is a prejudice against Americans, but that if you work hard, you can "earn", 'Finchley makes little quotation marks with her fingers, 'to be treated fairly.'

'If given half a chance.'

'Hmmmm.'

'You're doing it again.'

'Sorry.'

'Are you comfortable in your office?'

I look around for a moment. It's nice and clean, that's for sure. And I work pretty hard to put files away when I've finished working on something, so it always looks tidy. I inherited the Georgia O'Keefe print, but I like it well enough. And the plant people do

213

wonders keeping that ficus going strong. I've always killed them at home.

'It's alright.'

'That's not what I'm asking. Are you comfortable in it? When you get here, do you feel safe?'

'Safe? In this agency?' I snort. 'It's like swimming in a shark tank.'

She makes a 'go on' motion.

'Where should I start? Everyone below me wants my job. Everyone above me wants to get rid of me so that they can add my salary to their own. The only people that really want me to keep going are the ones I report to, because they don't want to have to do my work.'

'It sounds stressful.'

'Of course it's stressful! You don't get into my salary range without stress.'

'Is that why you do it? For the money?'

'Yes.' I think a minute. 'No.' I think again. 'I don't know.'

'Are you good at your job?'

I take a deep breath. No, is the first answer that springs to mind. I think about Henry and how well he's done. He's good at his job. I'm just good at working my ass off. 'Not naturally,' I say. 'It's not really me. But I manage to do a good job anyway.'

'How?'

'Working my ass off.'

'Do you enjoy that?'

'Are you outta your mind? Of course not.'

I start to feel a little panic of horror. Finchley watches as it dawns on my face. She gives me a little reassuring smile, and asks, 'What are you feeling, right now?'

'Panic.' And I'm not overstating the case. I'm starting to sweat and I feel my heart racing.

'Do you want to take a break?'

214

I shake my head, no.

She starts to come over to me and then realises in her sharp suit she won't be able to kneel on the carpet, so she goes back and tugs her visitor's chair around my desk. She takes my hand and holds it tightly. Her little dry hand feels terribly reassuring in mine.

I'm looking down at my feet, my feet that hurt so much.

'Why did you start your career here?'

I swallow. 'Simon.'

'Simon got you the job?'

I shake my head again. 'No. He wanted me to get a steady job. He wanted a bigger place to live. He wanted to start saving.'

'He wanted more money.'

I nod.

'What were you doing before?'

'I really can't talk about this.'

'Why?'

'It hurts.' And it does. I can't believe how much.

'Do you think it won't hurt if you don't talk about it?'

And when she puts it like that, I feel pretty stupid. 'I guess not.'

'Do you think it won't hurt if you don't think about it?'

I haven't actually cried, but my nose is running. I let go of Finchley's hand to fish a tissue out of the drawer and blow. 'I think that's been my strategy.'

'And how is it working?'

We look at each other for a moment. I feel like one of those tower blocks they're bringing down all over the place. They blow out the foundations and the whole thing comes crashing. Finchley, though, seems terribly amused. Behind the sympathy in her eyes is a little twinkling light.

I shrug. 'Well, maybe not so well.'

She starts to giggle then, apologising. She needn't worry about it. I join in. I might be completely around the twist, but at least I haven't lost my sense of humour.

Simon rings not long after she's left. I'm sitting there looking at a post-it note. Keep feeling EVERYTHING is number one. Keep in touch with Mom. I told Finchley I was seeing Fliss in a couple of weeks, but I didn't tell her why. So Finchley thinks I'm rebuilding my relationship with my mate, when really I'm in deep shit and probably about to render Fliss jobless. I would have corrected her, but the hour seemed to go so fast. I miss what Simon is saying.

'Sorry, darling, what was that?'

There is a pause on the end of the line. I can almost hear him thinking. 'What did you hear up till?' he asks.

I stammer.

'I'll start again, it's okay.' He takes a deep breath. 'The Waterloo and City line is down and I'm going to come home by way of Tottenham Court Road. Shall we meet up?'

Wow. 'Yes!'

'Do you want to meet in a pub or outside the station?'

'Outside the station, if you don't mind. I don't think I'm ever going to touch alcohol again.' And then it hits me. 'You don't want to have a big talk do you? You aren't leaving me, are you?'

I hear that same pain in his voice that I caught this morning. 'No. I'm not. I don't think I ever am, Maggie, so just stop worrying about that, okay? You've…'

'I've what?'

'I was going to say that you've got enough to deal with.'

'Don't stay with me because you think I'm loony, Simon. I couldn't stand that.'

Simon's laugh comes down the line, as warm and brown as his chocolate eyes. 'Don't be an idiot, woman. What time shall we meet?'

I still feel like hell, and this launch is so almost ready that I don't think I'll be able to tell when to stop. 'Early?' I say.

So at six-thirty I pack up for the night and meet at the coat cupboard with all the sane people who always go home around that time. One of them is Henry, who goes to fish out my coat and can't find it. 'It's in the cleaner's,' I say, and shrug into my mac.

'It's getting nippy,' he observes.

'I'll be okay.'

He looks at me searchingly, but I'm not about to tell him I threw up on it last night, am I? That boy misses nothing. At times like these I can practically feel him measuring my office for a new carpet.

I forget about everything when I see Simon. It strikes me that I don't really care if he thinks I've gone round the twist, if he is going to be this nice to me. On the train, snuggling up on the seat together, I say, 'I've got to work on another project this weekend.'

He looks at me carefully. 'Who's this for?'

And when I say, 'Fliss,' I can feel him collapse back into comfort. 'Why, who did you think?'

He avoids answering. 'What are you doing for Fliss?'

'Writing a novel.'

'What? That's brilliant, Maggie!'

He's too loud and all the *Evening Standards* rattle. 'Shhhhhhh.'

'That's brilliant,' he repeats, quieter.

'If I can do it.'

'You can do it. Does she think she can get her company interested?'

'She's already bought it. It was a complete misunderstanding, if you really want to know.'

We're only at Bethnal Green, so I perch up on the edge of the seat, so that I can face him. 'I was trying to tell her about Peter.' I put rather a lot of emphasis on the last word and Simon nods knowingly. 'And she thought it was a novel I was trying to sell her.'

'So? Do it, Maggie. It's perfect, can't you see?'

I know he doesn't understand, or he wouldn't be so supportive.

217

I say, 'I told her everything that had been going on in my life, Simon. Even about what you and I have been going through. You know?'

He shrugs that concern away. He won't be shrugging when he sees the intimate details of his life for sale at WH Smith, I think. He says, 'I think you can do it. It's the perfect solution. We can sell the house, move into flat number two.' He pulls me to him to whisper, 'Make babies,' in my ear and then shoves me away enough to look at my face. 'And you'll still have something to do. Something you like doing. Perfect.'

This man, so shy that he can't say 'make babies' in a railway carriage in an undertone, thinks that me writing an autobiographical novel is a good idea. It makes me Feel angry, but I don't know why.

I try again. 'It'll have all sorts of things in it. Things that happened between us. You know?'

He just shrugs again. 'Perfect,' he keeps saying. 'Perfect.' And then he starts telling me that he'll do the shopping this weekend, that all I'll have to do is write in the study. He'll cook, or he'll get in takeaways. He keeps telling me I can do it, until it's our stop.

There's a hell of a concrete staircase at Rectory Road. He can't keep talking and run up it at the same time. I find myself feeling terribly grateful to the thing for shutting him up.

Chapter Eighteen

'There's nothing wrong, Mama.' I'm in the study. I feel locked in there with Simon hovering helpfully around the place. I came out to make myself some ice tea and he pounced on me, got my order, and sent me back in. I can't bring myself to tell him that although I've been in here four hours I haven't written a word.

Well, that's not true. I've written loads. I've just deleted them again immediately. How do you start a novel? How am I supposed to introduce myself and my situation? You can't talk directly to the reader, like you would a friend. You can't be completely honest, can you? You've got to sound a bit detached and a bit, I don't know… I think I'm meant to sound a bit hip and aware. Jesus.

I came to that realisation about three hours ago. Since then, I've been drumming on the desk and looking out the window. It was when I started thinking about shinning down the drainpipe that I called my mother.

'There's nothing wrong. I just miss hearing you. It wasn't till I rang you last week that I realised how much I miss you.'

'Well! Isn't that nice?' My mother rustles onto the kitchen stool. 'That's just the nicest thing anybody's said to me in a long time.'

This is no doubt a complete lie. People say nice things to my mother all the time. They just can't help themselves.

'How are you? How much snow did you get?'

She blows 'pooh' down the receiver. 'It was nothing. Hardly two inches. People get so excited over that first one, they act like they never saw it before.'

'Were you okay after shovelling?'

'It wasn't really shovelling, Maggie. I wouldn't do that, you know. I was just kind of pushing it around. I only used the shovel because it was too wet to use the broom.'

Ah, the different types of snow. I know the kind she means, wet and heavy, freezing solid on the top overnight. When you walk on it, the crust breaks jagged and you sink down to the ground through the hole. 'I wasn't mad at you about it,' I say. 'I just wondered.'

'Yes, dear, I was fine. What's the weather like there?'

'I don't know. Simon won't let me out of the study.'

'What?'

'I said I haven't been out today. I've been working inside.'

'Isn't it Saturday over there, too?'

I wish I'd learn to shut up. 'Yes. I'm just doing something extra.'

'Something extra? Sweetie, you work way too hard as it is. Last time I came over there, I hardly saw you!'

I don't want her to know that I took so much time off my normal schedule for her visit that I was behind for a month afterwards, so I don't protest. There seems to be so much I can't say to her. I love listening to her, though, love the sound of her voice in my ear. I even like listening to her breathe. This line isn't as good as the one I got from work. I can't hear the range clock ticking. But just thinking about not hearing it puts me in that kitchen, inside the white walls by the turquoise Formica counter.

I need something to keep the conversation going without any input from me. I say, 'How's my brother?'

And then I just sit and listen to my mother talk, letting it wash over me like a wave. Everything she says contains detail; people, places, brand names. It acts like an anchor, securing me in the free flow of her associations. Every once in a while I have to interrupt to ask for a definition of something new. You'd be amazed at the things consumers take for granted back home. I am.

I finally hang up with another promise for Thanksgiving, thinking I must ask Simon about it tonight. This makes me think of talking to Simon, which makes me think about deciding whether or not to move, which makes me think about the novel, and how Simon assumes I'll be leaving the agency to write it.

Then I think about the launch, the tampon, the bus conversation. My hand is still on the telephone. I could call Fliss now, and explain everything. What do I want? What do I really want to do?

And then I hear Sean Connery's voice saying, The Master has called and you will follow. Perhaps I really don't have a choice. I wait to Feel anger, but it doesn't come. Perhaps Jesus has found a way. Perhaps I really do want to do this. Perhaps the best thing for me in this case is just to go with the flow. And that sounds ridiculous, even in my own head.

The screen saver is irritating me, stupid little rolling hedgehogs Simon downloaded from somewhere or another. I push a key to click it off. And then heave myself upright in front of the screen. I need to start this, if I'm going to have any choices at all. I need to start this thing.

How can I explain it to anyone? How can I explain what's happened to me? I was just going to work, minding my own business. I prayed because I thought I was going to die. And then Saint Peter came. Or is it that my life is so insane and I have put myself under such pressure that I hallucinated Saint Peter? And what about my marriage? And what about the tampon? I'm never going to be able to get all this in any recognisable form.

I move the cursor to the right and then back to the left, poking at the arrow keys with one finger. I can't even remember how I ended up on Euston Road that morning. There are so many ways I get to work. And so I punch in, 'There are five or six ways that get me to work in the morning, but none of them actually get me there on time.'

Lame. But it will have to do. *Blind Date* is on tonight, and I'm not missing it. I briefly gnaw on my knuckle. 'My general rule is to hop on the first thing that's moving and hope for the best.' And that's what I do here, too. I just keep hopping on every passing thought, putting one sentence after another, trying to tell the tale. I wonder if the reader will know that I'm telling it to myself, as well? If there is a reader. If I don't lose my mate her job.

Two hours later I shout down the staircase. 'Can I come down yet? I've done fifteen hundred words.'

Simon appears and beams up at me. 'You can even have a biscuit.'

I come halfway down and sit on the stairs, like cat does. Cat herself, I can see, is asleep in her radiator hammock. 'Is that as far as you're going?' Simon asks. 'Or do you want me to carry you the rest of the way?'

I look at him all happy with his life all solved. He gets this way sometimes. He thinks he has figured things out, that everything will now be all right, that he will never have to worry about anything ever again. But I know he hasn't thought this through. I know he will be mortified if this goes through to publication. Like this flat he wants to buy. It's miles away from his mates. Socialising is going to be a bit tricky. And then I wonder why we haven't seen his mates in a month or so.

I say, 'We haven't seen Phil or anybody for awhile.'

He shrugs. 'I know.'

He turns away to see to the teapot, but I'm still watching him. 'Is there any reason for that?'

'Not really.'

'Did they know about Sandy?'

He goes to push back his hair, but he's had it cut and there isn't much of it to push. So he has to turn around and look at me. 'Yeah. Yeah, they did.'

'So now?'

'So... I don't know, Maggie. I just don't... I mean, they're from college days, you know. Nice people and all, but...'

I think about what I told Finchley about them and feel a bit

222

unfair, like I've betrayed Simon. So I don't say anything. I just sit there.

Simon's looking at me, so finally I kind of nod. 'Okay.' I get up and come down the rest of the stairs. 'It's going to be harder to get together with them if we move.'

'Yeah, well.' The kettle whistles, and Simon starts to make tea. He does it intently, as if it was a chemistry experiment. It's always like that. I half expect him one day to pull a little notebook out of the cutlery drawer and make some calculations.

Finally, he puts out cups and saucers, a milk jug, a sugar bowl (even though neither of us take sugar), teaspoons and biscuits.

Biscuits? 'Where did these come from?'

'Sainsbury's.'

'You didn't even get a list!'

'I can count toilet rolls, Maggie. I got us some more bin liners, we were out.'

I realise my mouth is hanging open and I close it. I try to act calm. I say, 'I know. Ravinder left me a note yesterday.'

'I got a bunch of those oven things.'

'What oven things?'

'You know. Curries and things. Ready meals. I thought you might be a bit busy next week with the launch and the deadline and everything.'

It's like I've never seen him before. I stare at him as he nonchalantly munches a bourbon cream. I say, 'Wha-?'

He grins. 'I think it's about time I started pulling my weight. Don't you?'

I should be feeling happy about this. That's what I keep telling myself. But I just stare at him.

He can't stop smiling. He says, 'I don't think I realised until Thursday morning how stressed out you are. And now, with the novel to do...' He shrugs again. He says, 'Stop staring at me.'

'Sorry.' I look into my tea-cup and pour in some milk. He's

taking all this awfully well, I think. He's being pretty damn wonderful. But I've got a problem with that. It's not making me happy. And I don't know why.

'So, have you decided on moving?' he asks, and the penny drops. Now I know what the problem is. I can see it all, now. He's been buttering me up so that I'll sell the house and he can buy his nice little flat before he dumps me for Sandy. He's just keeping me sweet until he can get his hands on my money.

I lean over the table and hiss at him. 'So! That's what all this is about!'

'What? What are you talking about?'

'You just want to get rid of me, don't you? You just want to get the money out of this house so that you can dump me! Now that you know I'm crazy, you don't want me anymore.' I gesture wildly and knock the handle of my cup. It spins across the table, spilling in slow motion.

From the look on his face I know that I'm wrong. Even as I'm talking I can tell that I'm wrong, that he's just been trying really hard to please me and make things work. I know this, know it in my heart. And I know I'm ruining everything. I just can't stop. I really hate him right now, and I want to hurt him. And this is how I'm doing it. Simon looks as though I've slapped him.

I start to cry. It's like I'm watching a scene in a play. I know it's me crying and making the wild accusations, but it's also me watching it happen, more than that, planning it. Part of me rehearses the lines before I sob, 'You don't really love me, do you? Do you? And now I'm crazy. And nobody else will have me…'

'What's wrong, Maggie? God, what's wrong?'

He's kneeling on the floor now, holding me around my waist. And suddenly I slam back into one person. It hurts like hell. I cry as if every bone in my body is being broken.

'That's not true. You know that's not true. Don't you? Don't you?' My face is buried in his neck, but he shakes me a little as he asks and I nod into it.

'I know,' I whimper. 'I know. I'm sorry.' I try to be honest with him, but all I feel like I can say is, 'I'm so scared, Simon.'

He hasn't tried to lift me since the day we got married, but he does it now, somehow, and carries me into the living room, laying me down on the rug in front of the fire and shoving cushions under my head.

'This is all my fault,' he says.

'Oh for fuck's sake,' I wail. 'Can't this, just for a moment, be about me?'

He lays down next to me and strokes my arm and then my forehead. 'Sorry,' he says. 'I just…sorry.'

I feel hot and I sit up to wrench off my jumper. Even my vest is sweaty, clammy on my skin. I'm panting, I notice. This is it. This is the big breakdown. What would Finchley tell me? She'd ask me, What do you Feel, Maggie? So, what do I Feel? I don't know.

'What's happening to me is not just about you, Simon,' I say. The words come out pointy and he moves a little away. 'I don't know what's happening to me. I think it might really be Saint Peter, you know? I think it might be. I really do.'

He is silent, watching my face for clues on how he might somehow deal with this. I can't help him. I can't deal with it either.

'I mean, he's told me things, Simon. He's told me things that nobody else should know. Really.'

'What kind of things?'

'About Jesus. About the crucifixion. About Judas. About all kinds of things.'

'Couldn't that just be your imagination?'

I strip off the vest. I just can't stand it next to my skin. So now I'm having this conversation in jeans and a bra. It's not how I pictured it. If I ever did picture it. 'What, like I'm a Biblical scholar?

Like I know a heck of a lot about ancient Palestine societies? How could I make this up?'

He just looks at me blankly.

'Nobody even thinks that this might be Saint Peter visiting me. Nobody! Finchley thinks, at least I think she thinks, that this is some kind of subconscious expression of my emotions. Fliss thinks it's a great idea for a novel. You think I've lost it.'

'No, I don't. Really, Maggie.'

'Bullshit, Simon. You're treating me like cut glass.'

Now he's angry. He takes me by my shoulders and looks deep in my eyes. 'Perhaps that's how I think I should treat you. Perhaps that's how I've always thought I should treat you.' He looks at his fingers digging into my flesh and suddenly lets me go.

'This is about me, too, Maggie, you know?' He grabs me again, but softer. 'I was inches away from losing the best thing that ever happened to me.' He kisses me with such passion that my thigh muscles go weak and I collapse down to sit on my feet. He follows me, leaning over me as though he has to have proximity in order to communicate what he's saying.

'It doesn't matter to me if we live here or in Streatham. It doesn't matter to me if you're a consultant or an account handler or a secretary or a novelist. It doesn't matter to me if you're the new-,' he chokes on a word and chews the air for a few seconds before he finds a substitute, '- the new mouthpiece of ... Yahweh.' He shakes his head as if he can sling this possibility out of his mind by sheer force. He says, 'Whatever.'

He says, 'Look,' and gives me a little shake, as if I'm not paying attention, as if I'm not hanging on his every word. 'All that matters is us. Just us. You and me. That's everything to me, and I know it is to you. Everything else is just not really real, you know? Not really important. The rest is just posturing and bullshit and things,' he lets go to waggle his hands in the air, 'completely out of our control. Right here, this is what matters.'

Somewhere during that speech I started to cry again, and now it's really getting messy. Simon jumps to his feet when he finishes and comes back with kitchen towel. Kitchen towel! We haven't had any for six months. He clumsily mops at my face and sticks a bit in my eye. I try not to let him see me wince. He clamps it around my nose. 'Blow,' he says, and I do.

And then he goes away and comes back with a fresh cup of tea, and says, 'Now eat your biscuit, will you?'

And I think, Hell, why not. I think, keep going with the flow. I think, drink your tea, sell your house. So I say, 'I'll call the estate agent on Wednesday, after the launch. We're moving.'

'Are you sure?'

What a stupid question. 'I'm not sure about anything anymore, Simon.' I just can't keep thinking about everything. I tell him, 'I did all that being sure stuff, didn't I? Do I have to keep on being dynamic and together and sure about things forever? Can't I stop all that, now?'

Just the thought makes me want to lie down. Simon pulls my head onto his lap and sticks the biscuit in my mouth. 'Just chew, okay? We'll start with just chewing, the two of us, and see where we get with that.' His eyes seem so warm.

I like bourbon creams. They're my favourites. I start chewing.

After *Blind Date* I feel tired. I'm falling asleep on the sofa over a glass of New Zealand Sauvignon Blanc that I know I can't finish. And then I remember and say, 'Can you get ten days off work at the end of next month?'

'Ten? Why ten?'

'Do you want to go home with me? It's Thanksgiving.'

Simon strokes my head again. 'That sounds great. I'll ask Mick and tell you Monday night.'

'I won't be here Monday night. I'll be at Claridges.'

'I'll use a telephone. Unless you want me to come by, and put that big bed to use?'

I smile at him. 'I'll be too tired,' I confess.

'Don't you like that wine?'

I look at my glass. 'Alcohol still tastes like poison to me.'

'Not like Mom's pecan pie, eh?'

'Oh, don't!' Although I've just eaten, I suddenly feel tragically empty. I clutch my stomach and roll into a ball.

'How about her cranberries? And those drop scone things?'

I cover up my ears, pleading, 'Stop, stop.' It sounds nice, covering my ears. It reminds me of the sea. The next thing I know Simon's shaking me. I've fallen asleep in my ball. My neck hurts.

He says, 'Time little novelists were in bed.'

Which doesn't make sense to me until I've climbed the stairs and toothbrushed myself half awake again. 'I might not be able to do it,' I remind him.

'Okay,' he says. 'But I'll bet you a fiver you will.'

And I'm too sleepy to argue about it.

Chapter Nineteen

It's a cab job over to Claridges, since I'm dragging a hanging suitcase, a cosmetic case, my bag, my briefcase and a Paperchase bag full of promo material. Lamplit London in the fine, steady rain turns rather painterly. Streets and bare trees shine pure lamp-black, and the crumbling Georgian terraces we are whizzing past seem freshly blocked out, the broken pavements blurred with reflection, the chipped facades a kind of impasto in the mist.

Or maybe it's just that I'm wearing my glasses. My contact lens people biked over temporary replacements for the ones I fried on top of my hall radiator, but they don't correct my astigmatism. The temporary ones are a bit uncomfortable, so I'll wait until the last minute to switch over. I'm wearing jeans, one of Simon's shirts, a blazer, my mac, and a pair of Bally loafers. My hair is scraped back in a ponytail. It needs cutting, I realise, if I can do that. Usually when it needs cutting it drives me crazy. It isn't. That must be because I've lost so much of it.

It's a little after six in the morning, and already Grays Inn Road is a nightmare, jammed with traffic and the empty shells of buses. My driver turns his neck halfway around and talks to me out the side of his face, watching me in the rear view mirror. 'Where are you from, in the States?' he asks me.

Nobody has asked me that for ages. 'Outside of Kansas City,' I say. 'It's a little town.'

'Kansas?' I nod. He muses. 'Wheat and cattle, right?'

I'm sure my smile must half split my face. 'And oil,' I add, and then say, 'Most people don't know anything about my state.'

He grins in a self-satisfied way. 'It's right in the middle, isn't it? It's Texas, then Oklahoma, then Kansas.' I nod again, grinning back.

We inch forward a bit, but then the lights change. 'You ever go?' I ask him. 'To America, I mean?'

He shrugs, 'A bit. Florida, of course, for the kids. New York, San Francisco, Los Angeles.' If possible, he looks even more self-satisfied as I register astonishment at his travel record. 'Tell you what, though, I'd like to see Yellowstone. You ever been there?'

'I worked there for three years!' I scoot forward, balancing on the edge of the seat. 'I spent three summers there, waiting tables in a hotel. It's brilliant.'

'How long do you need to see most of it?'

'It's two point five million acres. Hardly anyone has seen most of it. I certainly haven't.'

His eyes are intent on mine.

'But you can have a really great time for as long as you're there.' I grow enthusiastic, 'Especially if you get out of the car and walk a little bit. You don't have to go very far to get completely away from people and see more animals and plants and things.' For some reason, thinking about moose and bears makes my chest constrict, and I find that tears have come into my eyes. I look at the cabbie, and he's still watching me carefully.

He says, 'What are you doing here, when you could be there?'

And, though it's a lie, I just point to my wedding ring, as if Simon made me come. The cabbie's eyes seem to accept it, though. And then we're past the bottleneck, and I don't have to talk about it anymore.

I don't know what I would have done without Celia. She arrived, looking similarly casual, with her own hanging suitcase, seconds after I landed in the suite, and immediately started tugging tables around and arranging lighting. As soon as a cleaner had cleared a surface, she plunked a brand illustration on it – a table tent made out of the magazine inserts or one of her other ideas. She's even mounted a shelf wobbly on the towel rack over the toilet, so that male guests can muse upon it as they tinkle.

And now, midway through lunch number two, she is still sparkling, reminding me subtly of things I ought to remember to say. There's so much of it, so much to hammer home to the gerbil-like skulls of these journalists. I wet my lips with my wineglass and then pour for everyone else. I notice Celia's actually drunk about half a glass of Chablis. I hope she doesn't start flagging towards dinner, but then I look at how perky and excited she is and know she won't. I lean forward and clear my throat and they all get quiet.

I say, 'Finding the right applicator took quite some time. You see…'

And Celia's bright eyes are shining, as if she actually gave a shit. You know, I think she actually might.

Hours later, we have our feet up and we aren't wetting or sipping the Chablis anymore, but taking nice big swigs of the stuff. I think I'm drinking it because I think I should. It's lovely wine, but it doesn't taste nice to me. When I realise this, I sling my glass onto a nearby table.

The room service staff are cleaning away the last traces of the canape buffet. They even come in and hoover around us. This is fairly easy, since we are motionless in our chairs, except for Celia's continued swigging.

After they turn the thing off, I ask. 'Are you sure about going home? You can share the bed with me, if you want.'

Celia shakes her head. 'No. It's okay. I'm only in Clerkenwell.'

I raise my eyebrows at her. 'Clerkenwell? Wow!'

She shakes her head again. She does that a lot. I wonder if she knows how shiny her hair is and how cute she looks when she does it, or if it's just her pert Peke nature. 'I moved there ages ago when it wasn't wow at all,' she says. 'I don't even want to know what my

231

flat is worth these days. If I find out, I'll be too tempted to sell it, and I don't want to move.'

This makes me smile. 'So, you've decided not to tell yourself?'

'Well... I guess I really do know, but I've decided not to realise. It's a bit like not wanting to hear the results before *Match of the Day*. You know, really, but you just don't admit it.'

This makes me feel uncomfortable, and then I immediately shy away from wondering why. I notice this, and it kes me grin. 'I think I'm that way about almost everything,' I iy, and we both laugh.

I tell her, 'You were really good today.'

She is now a shy Pekinese, looking up at me from lowered lashes. 'Oh, I don't know.'

'Well, I do.' I unfold myself and stand up, yawning. 'Now go away and sleep, so that you can be wonderful again in the morning.'

And she trips out the door. She still has energy. It's only nine o'clock and I feel like I've been boiled in the bag. I take a nice, long shower and during it the phone rings. I know who it is. When I get out, I slide into bed and ring Simon back.

When he answers, before he can speak, I say, 'I'm in the big bed.'

And he says, 'Keep talking, I usually have to pay for this kind of thing.'

I can hear him grin down the line.

'How grim was it?'

'Oh,' I try to think about the day, and find it gone. 'I don't know. I just sat there and tried not to notice it was happening.' I say this before I think it, and then I know that it's true, that that's what I do with most of my working life.

'How was Celia?'

'Great. Very enthusiastic.'

'So you could just stuff yourself silly?'

'I've eaten tons, Simon. I didn't really mean to, but you have to set the pace. I had to have them all trough, listen and leave. Bing, bang, boom. Now I feel like I might explode.'

'So this is a beached whale sex line?'

I giggle at him, and while I do, he says, 'We're going home for Thanksgiving. I got the time off.' For some reason, this makes my eyes fill with tears.

I say, 'I'll book the tickets,' but he says, 'I've already done it. And I called your mum and made sure of the dates. You just have to heave your tremendous bulk to Heathrow on the twenty-fourth.'

'You're doing everything these days.'

'It's the new proactive Simon.'

'I like him. But then, I liked the old one.'

'I didn't. He was okay, but he was crap to his wife.'

The tears are now trickling down my cheeks, and I sniff.

'You aren't crying again, are you?'

'I can't help it.'

'Don't forget to blow your nose. Or else you'll breath through your mouth all night and wake up looking like an extra in *Deliverance*.'

'You're mad,' I say to him, and then there's a longish pause. I sniff again. 'Oh, no, that's me, isn't it?' I finally say, and then he sighs with some kind of relief and we laugh at each other. I picture our voices mingling somewhere near Angel Station. At the top of Pentonville Road, we are laughing together.

When we stop he says, 'Hooo,' and we giggle again. And then he says, 'Say goodnight, Maggie darling.'

So I say, 'Goodnight, Maggie darling,' and put down the phone.

I look at it for a while then, wondering if I'm okay with all this, if I'm alright with being Simon's mad wife that he needs to take better care of. I can't decide. I suppose I could try and Feel about it, but I'm really too tired to start Feeling. Instead, I look at the phone until my eyes start to dip shut and then click off the elegant little light with its elegant little shade and drop into the supreme softness of a crisp, empty bed.

'Maggie,' someone says. 'Maggie.' Have I overslept? I slam on my glasses, but the place is dark as a tomb. I fumble with the elegant little light and finally get it switched on. By this time, my heart is in my mouth with fear.

Which means I'm actually grateful when I see Sean Connery dressed as Saint Peter, standing by the bed.

He says, 'It has been a week since our last visit.'

I didn't think he'd come to me here.

'I didn't think you could come to me here.'

He shrugs. 'It's not that much of a problem.'

He looks shabby in the gold and white of the bedroom. 'Sit down,' I say, and, although there is an empty easy chair two feet away, he sits on the bed with me. He is hesitant in this place, looking around at the gold leaf on the walls and the chandelier, fingering the brocade of the bedcovering. It makes me smile.

'Posh, isn't it?'

He nods absently.

'What's wrong?'

'You still do not want to proceed, do you?'

I've been doing my best not to think about it. I didn't even go to Mass on Sunday. I just lie there, watching him read my face. I know he doesn't need to be told.

Peter goes to the window and pushes back the curtain instead of using the pulley. I don't correct him, even though he really has to give it a good push and I lie there worrying about damaging the mechanism.

'I think then, that our time together is at an end.'

I am astonished by how much this hurts. I say, 'I don't want you to go.'

234

He shrugs, staring down at the loading dock.

I get out of bed and start fumbling around for the dressing gown. Peter takes one look at my naked body and turns himself resolutely back to the window.

'What, I have to make an absolute ass out of myself? Or else you'll dump me? That's just not fair.'

'Fair?' Peter snorts, 'What do you understand about true justice?'

I sink into the easy chair. Peter is looking at me, but I'm seeing him with my far away eyes. He says, 'Things are much larger than you think, Maggie. And what you like or do not like is of very little importance.'

'What about what you like?'

He comes and sits down at my feet on the thick carpet. 'Are you still hungry for praise, Maggie? Even now you and your man have no more troubles?'

I blush. 'It's not that,' I say, and then realise that I don't know why I so enjoy Peter's company.

He laughs, one short burst. 'I, too, like visiting you. But we did not achieve what the Master asked of us. And so, I must go.' Although he's smiling up into my face, his eyes still bear that heavy burden.

When I see it, I Feel guilty. 'I'm sorry,' I say. 'I wanted to help you, but…' I think for a moment. 'When you did your work, you could just go and sit somewhere and talk to people. You can't do that anymore. Now you have to get on television and radio. And that costs money. You need to convince people who have money that what you are saying is important and that you are the right person to say it. Otherwise they won't even let you speak. I'm just not the right person. And I don't even know anyone who is.'

He nods thoughtfully. 'And yet the Master sent me to you. To Maggie.'

'I don't know why.'

His eyes narrow as he looks off into the middle distance, through a mahogany side table. 'I think,' he says slowly. 'I think it is something…' His eyes snap back to mine. 'You are the first person who ever thought of my problems in this. Who did not say that this was bad or that was bad or ask how the Master could do something…'

I understand what he's getting at, but I have to admit, 'Well, some of the stunts you pulled were a bit dodgy. I just didn't want to say. Like telling people Jesus went to heaven when he was actually going up a mountain, or-'

'It was a very high mountain,' Peter interrupts and then gives one of his eloquent shrugs. 'The sheep had to be told something.'

'Sheep?'

'I mean the people who-'

'I know what you mean. It just bothers me.' And it does bother me. I get up and walk away from the chair. Peter twists to watch me pace around the big bed. 'Nixon used to say that. Sheep.'

He doesn't ask who Nixon was. He probably met him.

And I don't know why I should be getting all righteous when all day long I've been trumpeting on about the tampon consumer and what she wants. As if I know. I let myself sit down on the bed.

Peter gets up to sit with me and we both lie back and stare at the ceiling. It's got some fantastic decorative plasterwork, so it's not boring. He says, 'You know, I think this word sheep might be important.'

I pooch up on my elbow to look down at his face. 'What, you mean you got one of your 'aha' moments?'

He nods.

I lay back down to stare at the plasterwork.

Finally I say, 'Sheep is really bad. We can't go around assuming people are weak sheep that need to be led. Or even misled. That's Hitler territory, Peter.'

I pooch back up to see him deepening the furrows on his brow. Finally he meets my eye. He gives me a brief nod.

'And yet we do it all the time. I do it every day.' I push myself back to my feet. I want to move. I start pacing around the bed again, from one set of pillows to the other in a horseshoe shape. I'm talking slowly, as if my brain is idling with the clutch in. 'I mean, I know this tampon campaign might be completely... I mean, women have a perfect right to use whatever tampon they damn well want. If they find that the lengthway ones work okay for them... And they must, a lot of them must, because the company that makes them is doing fine with the product.'

Around and around the bed I walk. 'And all this bullshit that it's only because of poor education and that those women would be using widthways tampons if only they weren't so clueless is a load of bollocks. And anyway, some women still like pads. Pads!'

I stop, and look at Peter who drags himself up to sit. I say, 'Do you know what that means?'

He does his gulping thing and asks, 'Must we talk about this?'

I sigh at him. 'It's not about the blood, Rock. It's about us, you and me, thinking we know better than the consumer,' I amend this, 'than other people.'

His face is screwed up with effort , but he shakes his head. 'But Maggie, I *do* know better.'

'Do you? Do I?'

We stare at each other for a moment. He's still not getting it. He says, 'Yes, of course. All of these things I have told you. They are the truth, and the sheep-'

'Will you stop it with the sheep business?'

Peter raises his hands at me, as though I've gagged him.

'What?' I say, 'You can't talk to me unless I believe that consumers are ignorant?'

He blows out his lips. 'But they are ignorant. Ignorance only means they do not know!'

I lean over him. 'What don't they know, Peter? All that stuff you told me, I found most of it in the British Library. And Waterstones! Waterstones had *Jesus Lived In India* on a freakin' table stack.'

'They don't know that the Master really did die and come back to life.'

'Are you sure about that? Somebody, I can't remember who, talks about the Swoon Theory. They might not know exactly how it happened, but they know it did. Or at least might have.'

Something starts to dawn on Peter's face. He reaches up and grabs a lapel of my dressing gown.

My words speed up as my brain suddenly switches into gear, 'And anyway, you told me that wasn't what you wanted to get across to people. You told me you wanted to save the Master's words. Isn't that right?'

The dawn darkens again, but his grip on my lapel tightens, as if he could pull his 'aha' out of me by sheer force. 'But, Maggie, I know that things in your Bible are wrong!' His face is screwed up like a ball of paper.

'And you, Peter, know what's right?'

'Yes, of course.'

'Are you totally sure?'

Our eyes are locked. Time stops. Although we aren't speaking, there is a tiny flame of understanding we are batting back and forth between us like a tennis ball. I feel something opening up in my head, releasing the pressure. And just by watching the muscles around his eyes I know we are working towards a major 'aha'. If we can only get there.

'No,' he finally says.

'No. Of course not.' I Feel smart for the first time in months. I Feel like I know what I'm doing. I'm getting terribly excited. 'Didn't you say that I couldn't know anything about true justice?'

Peter nods, slowly at first, but then so vigorously I'm afraid he'll hurt something. He's shaking me by my lapels now, and he's so excited I think he's about to burst.

'Do you understand all about true justice? What is it, Karma? Do you understand all about Karma?'

'Of course not. Not even the Master understands everything.'

'So, if you can't figure out what is "True Justice"', air quote, 'how do you know what is the "Truth"?' air quote.

Saint Peter lets go of my lapels and turns his face to the ceiling. A smile wraps it from ear to ear. He cups his hands and holds them up as if he is collecting rain.

He says, 'That is why I keep making it worse. I kept trying to say what is true. The Master's words are buried under layers of what I think is true, what Saul thought was true.'

'What every bugger after you thought was true.'

'Yes, of course!' Peter jumps to his feet and seizes me. 'Yes! Maggie! This is what the Master was trying to say to me! Why he kept sending me to you! How can you put it right? he kept asking me. How can you reveal the truth? Over and over he asks me this… And you can not! That is the answer! You can not, because you can only ever reveal *your* truth! The real truth can only reveal itself!'

He holds me close and begins jumping with me, bounding around the room. Then, wearied of my incompetence, he leaves me to dance on his own, leaping from foot to foot and uttering little cries of triumph in that throat-gargling language he usually reserves for cursing.

I sink down onto the chair. 'You can't mediate other people's experiences. You can't tell people what to think. It fucks everything up. It makes everything more difficult for them, for you-'

'Especially for you.' Peter puts in from where he is dancing by the wardrobe. 'Do you know how long it has taken me to learn this? And how much pain I have caused? And worse, felt myself?'

'And for the product,' I say. 'You also fuck things up for the product.'

'Which is the words.'

'Or the tampon. Or whatever.'

Peter stops dancing quite suddenly.

'Whoever wants to find out something, will find out. Whatever we have to say will make some people more interested, but will make other people not interested. All we can do is give out the information that something exists. Everything else is... well, it's actually harmful, Peter.'

'Yes. This is true.'

Peter comes to stand over me. 'This is all truth, Maggie. I feel it, here.' He slams one massive palm across his chest.

I feel it there, too.

'I am filled with the Spirit!'

'Don't start speaking in tongues or snake handling or anything. The management will object.'

I'm getting that far away feeling again. I stare out to the far wall, through Peter, who sinks back down in front of my chair. 'What will you do, Maggie?'

'Hmmm?'

He tugs at the hem of the dressing gown. 'Maggie? What will you do? To earn your bread? You will not be able to go on in this way, will you?'

So that's what's bothering me. I have to start talking to myself. Perhaps I get this far away feeling when I have something to say and no one upstairs is listening. With what Peter says in his Connery growl, I seem to zoom back into my body. You can almost hear the click.

'I guess not,' I say. My eyes focus on the leather of his face, the warmth of his famous eyes. I think about telling Quentin what I've just told Peter and my mouth goes dry. 'At least not at the Blues.'

'What will you do, Maggie?' He takes one of my hands and warms it between his own rough paws. 'You are cold. Get into bed.'

240

I take off my dressing gown without a second thought, and slide between the sheets. Peter sits by my side. 'Your man, can he take care of you?'

I sigh. 'Not as well.' It makes me sick with fear to think of Simon in control of all our outgoings. Imagining him going through my Visa bill makes me want to puke.

Peter shrugs. 'This is not so bad, is it?'

'I'm afraid that he won't treat me well.'

And then I remember. 'I'm supposed to be writing a book. For money. Maybe that will help.'

'A book? What kind of a book?'

'A novel.' He doesn't look any wiser. 'A story book. A story that doesn't even claim to be the truth. It's about you.'

He chews on this for a while, and then his face breaks out in another of his blinding smiles. 'I told you Maggie! I told you! This is something you want to do, no?'

I stare at him for a moment and then say, 'Oh, shit,' which makes him laugh.

'Strand upon strand, the Master's mind,' he says, hooting with laughter. 'You will never best him, Maggie, so do not even try.' He scrapes the side of my face with his calluses, patting it what he must think of as gently.

I can't stop looking into his eyes, and I finally realise why. The eternity of sorrow is missing. 'You're happy.'

'I am at rest,' he says. 'I am filled with the Spirit once more. With you... You see, Maggie, the Master has found a way to make me see my arrogance.' His smile turns into a rueful grin. 'Again.'

'Again?'

'This is a lesson I will need eternity to learn, I think. And even then, I am not so sure that I will attain it.'

He sits there, smiling at me with his LA dental work. His borrowed face is alight. He's holding my hand in what has become a familiar shock of rough skin. And then I am crying.

241

He scoops me up out of the covers and holds me, naked, tight to his chest, stroking my hair. Just from the way he touches me, I know that my body no longer arouses him. But this doesn't bother me at all, in fact, I love being here, cradled in those strong arms.

'I don't want you to go.'

'I know. I know. I feel it, as well.'

'Then why aren't you more sad?'

The barrel chest moves against me and his huge guffaw booms across the room. I am peeved at this, and ineffectively push at the huge shoulders. He grins as he uses the sheet to dry my face, carefully swiping under my lenses. 'You believe in death,' he says. 'I know I will see you many times again. You only grieve because you see things so small.'

'Small?'

'Small, like a young child. His mother goes into the other room, or to the neighbour's house to borrow salt. But all he knows is that his mother is gone. He cries as if he will never see her again. Even as you comfort him, you laugh.'

'And you see things big.'

He smiles at my truculence. 'Bigger. Even the Master still learns.'

I flop back onto the pillows, and Peter covers me up. I tell him, 'I think I could have gone several lifetimes without hearing that.'

His smile widens. 'Why?'

'Well…' I struggle. 'I thought you got somewhere eventually. With all this growing and trying to do the right thing, and everything.'

'You do get somewhere.'

'But it never ends!'

'It ends.'

'But when?'

I know he can't tell me. Perhaps he doesn't even know.

It's funny, all this time, I've only intermittently realised what

242

I'm dealing with, who I'm talking to. And now, I recall that no matter whose body he's borrowed, I'm talking to one of the most enlightened beings that ever graced the planet. I've been able to hear things that most people would die to hear. Things most people do have to die to hear. I say, 'You know, I feel really lucky.'

'Lucky?'

'To have known you so well. To have...' My chin collapses and I start to cry again. 'To have spent so much time with you.'

'You're always with me. You just didn't know it before.'

'I guess.' I sit up a bit. I can't believe I have to say goodbye to him. He looks just like he always has, but happier. Maybe happier is the wrong word – calmer might be better. It's hard to explain. If you've ever seen the Dalai Lama or somebody like that, you might understand what I'm talking about. He just looked more whatever we try to be than he had before. And he looked more like Saint Peter. As if Sean Connery had suddenly found some key to his portrayal. As if he was going for another Oscar.

Otherwise, it was just the same. Still the same movie star, with the same twinkle in his eye. Even the same robe whatsit, with the same leather thong around his neck. I never found out what was on the thong, I think to myself, so I grab it and pull up an oxidised copper pendant. It's in the shape of that little fish thing that people put on their cars.

'This is seriously naff, Peter. You can't go around wearing this anymore. It's awful.'

He tucks it back in the slit, frowning. 'It was many years ago, Maggie. And important to me.'

'I wish I could see what you really looked like.'

'That would be dangerous. I was much more handsome than this. You would not be able to control your lust.' He grins at me and I find myself blushing. I'm not looking at him anymore, but I can feel his eyes on me. He reaches over to me with both hands and gently unhooks my glasses, laying them carefully in the case, which he shuts with a soft snap. Then he stands up and peers at the elegant little lamp for a moment, before competently switching it off.

Saint Peter gets into the bed with me, under the covers. I turn to face him and we lay together on our sides, our arms around each other. He holds me close. I smell him, the water of Kinneret and the salt of his sweat. Then he pushes me gently onto my back and kisses my eyes, one after another. I hold them shut, the tears leaking out the sides. There is a small, low sound, like wind through a pine tree. And then I am alone.

I switch on the light, and grab my glasses back out of their case. Frantically, I start searching the bed and the carpet. I'm looking for anything, for a hair, a thread, a flake of skin. But what I find is all my own. I keep having to wipe my eyes clear to look and my glasses are steaming up. Suddenly, I realise that there isn't going to be anything left for me to keep, that all I had of him is gone, and this goes into my chest like a knife.

I roll into a ball on the bed and choke on the meaningless syllables of grief. I think I might die from this. I pull my knees tighter and tighter into my chest, as if I could make myself so small that I would disappear too.

I never said goodbye.

Chapter Twenty

'Why aren't you dressed?'

The voice is far away. If I keep my eyes closed, it might stay that way.

'Maggie, my God! What's wrong?'

It was Celia's voice. She is shaking my shoulder. 'Maggie? Maggie! Can you hear me?'

There is a scrabbling sound and then, 'Is that Reception? We need a doctor. I said, we need-'

I've reached out and broken the connection. 'No we don't.'

'Maggie! We've only got half an hour to go and you look like...What did you do when I left last night? You said you were going straight to bed!'

I've slept in my glasses and they're smeared. Still, I can see Celia. 'That's a lovely skirt,' I say, and it is, a nice long floaty one that goes very well with her jacket.

'Maggie, *Marie Claire* are here in-' she glances at her watch, 'Fuck! Twenty minutes. Maggie, you have to get ready.'

For an answer, I just shake my head at her. 'No,' is all I can come up with to say.

She flings the dressing gown at me and starts rummaging in the closet. 'Quick shower now,' she says. 'Don't bother with your hair, a brush and some clips will have to do. You do have some clips with you, don't you?'

She's starting to perspire. She's going to ruin her makeup if she does that. 'Sit down,' I say, and there is such authority in my voice that she does it, immediately.

'You don't need me. I'm going home.'

'Maggie! Please? Tell me what's going on?'

She looks so sweet sat there. She's such a nice girl. Why do I always make fun of her, saying she's a Pekinese? She's lovely, just lovely. And I'm worrying her. 'I lost my best friend last night,' I say.

Her mouth drops open, 'What?' she says, 'Dead?'

Two thousand years, more or less, I think, but only nod. Even without saying his name, the pain has sharpened. I close my eyes, afraid I won't be able to do what I need to do this morning.

'Oh, God, Maggie. We'll cancel everything.'

I get up and into the dressing gown. She's so upset, she forgets to not watch and keeps looking at me naked, as if she wasn't English at all. 'No,' I manage to say. 'You'll be fine.'

I get out the clothes I came in and start struggling into them, not bothering with knickers and bras and things. I manage to brush my hair into the ponytail again without looking at my face in the mirror. I can only imagine how bruised my eyes must be, how white and drawn my face. 'Can you bike my clothes over to me this afternoon?' I ask.

Celia still has her mouth open. 'On my own?'

And somehow I find the energy to go over and sit back down on the bed and take her hand. I say to her, right from my heart, 'You are much better at this than I will ever be. Don't think twice about it. You'll be fine.'

And then I stumble across the room and get my mac and my bag. There's just room in my bag for my contact things and make-up. Celia's sitting like she's been stuffed and mounted. 'You will send my gear, won't you?' I ask.

And this seems to snap her out of it. 'I manage on my own and then I send you your things this afternoon by courier,' she parrots.

I turn to go, and then stop and go back. I stand in front of her until she meets my eye. 'I'm sorry,' I say.

But she's better now. She says, 'No, I'm sorry, Maggie. It must be a terrible shock. Go on. Just go ahead.'

I can't stop myself from hugging her, and she doesn't pull away too much. I think she even kind of likes it.

246

She's still a bit stunned and the room looks like hell, so I pull the door to behind me. As the catch clicks on the latch, I whisper, 'Goodbye.'

The room service staff are already busying themselves around the table in the other room. They don't even look up as I wade through the thick carpet and let myself out. I wonder, as I walk down the hallway, if I'll ever be in a place like this again. The lift doors open and the *Marie Claire* people come out. They walk right past me without even seeing me. They don't so much not recognise me as their mate from the Blues agency as not even recognise me as one of their own species. It's already over. So I get into the gilded car and ask for reception.

The cab driver had objected to my neighbourhood in a peculiar, non-verbal way ever since I climbed in the back at Claridges. He shot off as soon as the notes touched his hand, before the last syllable of 'Keep the change' had even left my lips. But I stand there, watching him fondly, or at least the cab fondly, as it trundles down my street. Black cab rides are something else to say goodbye to, I suppose. At last I notice that it's turned quite cold, and I start fumbling for my keys.

Cat is upstairs on the bed, so soundly asleep that she doesn't even hear me come up the metal stairs and into the room. I clear my throat and she jumps lying down, actually lifts a couple of inches off the duvet by just tensing her muscles. Before she can leap to her feet, she's clocked that it's only me, and collapses back horizontal.

'That looks nice,' I say, and I shed all my clothing in a heap at the head of the bed and crawl into my sheets.

'Hey, Tiger.' Simon is sitting on the bed where Peter always used to sit. I can see him because I fell asleep in my glasses again.

God, I'm glad to see him. I wriggle down so that I can put my head on his lap. He pulls out my hair elastic for me, and combs through my hair with his fingers. 'Who died, Sweetie?' he asks.

'I think I did.'

My husband tilts my chin up so that he can look into my face. My misery is reflected in the compassion it generates in his. 'Quentin rang me to see what was going on. I had to say I didn't know.'

'Sorry. What time is it?'

'About two o'clock. You didn't answer any of the phones, so I came home to see if you were here.'

'I'm here.'

'Yeah. Good.' Cat stretches, yawns, and then walks across me to get down off the bed. I can hear her pad over to the door and then the ringing sound her claws make on the spiral staircase.

'Do you want to talk about it?'

I nod, and push myself up to lay down on the pillows properly. 'Peter had to go last night. I'm never going to see him again.'

'Saint Peter.'

I nod again. 'But we had this long talk.' I sniff.' Simon, I just can't do my job anymore. Not at all. Not even one more day of it.'

I see him swallow, thinking of all that lovely nicker, but he gets hold of himself and says, 'Okay. You don't really have to, do you?'

'I should, I guess. But I can't.'

'Can you tell me why?'

'I can't keep telling people what to do. Remember when I was talking about being sure? And how sick of it I am?'

He's looking at me intently. Finally he says, 'Yes. I remember.'

'I just can't, Simon. And the shoes hurt my feet. And Finchley's right about the waistbands on those damn suits. And I just hate it, Simon. I just hate all of it.'

'I know.'

'You know?'

He smiles at me. 'Of course. Why do you think we're moving?'

'I thought that was all about babies.'

'Let's just stick with one thing at a time, okay?'

He looks a bit harried, and at last I really think about what it must have been like to get a phone call like that, from Quentin, telling him that I'd completely lost it, that someone was dead and I was in a bad way. So I say, 'I hope you didn't have meetings or anything. I'm really sorry. I should have rung.'

'It's okay.'

He stands up and takes off his cashmere overcoat and his Paul Smith jacket and dumps them on the floor next to my stuff. Then he kicks off his shoes. 'Are you hungry? Do you want a pizza?'

And thirty minutes later we are laying there together, eating pizza in bed, drinking some delicious new Greek wine, listening to the afternoon play on Radio Four. It's funny, this whole thing. I still hurt, but I don't feel upset at all. And Simon finally says, 'Sweetie, I wouldn't feel so guilty if I were you about interrupting my work day. I wish we could do this every week.'

I didn't know that I could still laugh. But I can. And I can still kiss and do a lot of other things. Simon showed me.

I'm dressed now. In thirty minutes, I'm going to leave the house. We need bread and I'm going to catch a matinee at the Dalston Rio. I'm also going to get some more cleaning supplies. I don't know how Ravinder manages with that one crap duster. I'm going to get a feather thing or something. The light shades are in an appalling state. I think I'll go by Woolworths, as well, and see if I can get gardening gloves in the off season. My Isotoners are getting chewed to bits with all the pruning.

The first people come to see the house on Friday. There's a few things I want to get done before then. Washing powder, too. I need more washing powder. My dressing gown has real problems after I lived in it for three days.

What can I say? I told Simon I didn't want to do anything for a while that I didn't want to do. I've been lying down most of the time, but every so often I get up and do a little on Fliss's chapters. I'm on Chapter Five already. Somehow writing about me and Peter is nice. Simon's biking the whole thing around to her today. If she doesn't like it, I'm sure I can find somebody else. It's hard to tell, but I think it might be pretty good.

It feels weird to be wearing clothes again. I nearly put on a blazer when I got out of the bath, but instead a polar fleece convinced me to slide it on. My walking shoes are almost more comfortable than going barefoot, and certainly warmer than the wellies I've been wearing in the garden. I wonder what the neighbours thought of me out there in my dressing gown and wellies.

The kitchen is yellow with sunlight. Little dustmotes dance above the scrubbed pine table. Cat dozes in her freshly-washed radiator hammock. She tries to keep awake, but it catches up with her eventually. She needs sixteen hours of sleep a day, I heard it on *Pet Rescue*. She finds following me around exhausting, I can tell, even though I've mostly been moving from one soft place to lie to another.

My mint tea is nearly cool enough to drink. In a moment, I'll drink it.

Chapter Twenty-one

I'm talking to Finchley on the phone.

'I don't need to talk to your psychiatrist mate. I don't need a sick note. I've put in my notice.'

There is a long pause.

'I know it sounds like I've gone crazy, I know it does. But really, I think I've just gone sane.'

'Can you come and see me, Maggie?'

'Why? Do I have to prove it to you or something?' I listen for a moment to Finchley's agitated breathing. 'Look, I'm sorry if this fucks you up with the Blues.'

'That's not a problem.'

'Good.'

There's a long silence.

Finally I say, 'You really helped me get here, actually.'

And she says, 'I don't know that I'm terribly proud of that, Maggie.'

'Why?'

'Well...' she thinks for a moment, about how to put this in therapist speak, I guess. 'Usually if someone loses their livelihood during a crisis, it's a pretty clear indication that things are not going well.'

I forgot. I never told her. 'I wouldn't worry about that so much,' I struggle to remember her name, but it's just not there. 'I got a check last week from Camburet Publishing. I've sold a novel. I'm writing it now.'

'I see.'

'So it's not like I'm really destitute or anything.'

'No.' She's still not happy.

'I don't get any, like, congratulations or anything?'

'Sorry. Congratulations.'

'I can tell you aren't happy with that, either. Why don't you just tell me what you're worried about?'

'I'd like to be having this conversation in person, Maggie.'

'But we aren't, are we?'

She breathes for a few moments, so I keep going, 'I mean, I'll come to Finchley if you want, but we might as well finish this one we got started on, don't you think?'

She sighs. It's like a virus, this sighing thing. Even Simon's started. 'Well, even if you are changing jobs, the way you are going about it is highly irregular. Quentin is quite upset.'

'I'm going to ring him today.'

'Okay.'

There's something else. I can tell. 'There's something else.'

'I'm just a little concerned that your relationship with Felicity has immediately turned into a professional one. I fear that you still aren't making any support for yourself.'

'I'm going home for Thanksgiving.'

I can hear her exhale with relief. 'Good. That's good.'

'I'll look people up while I'm there. Old friends, you know. American ones that I can understand.'

You can hear someone smile on the telephone sometimes. I hear it now.

We sit for a few seconds in silence.

'I really haven't gone nuts. I'd tell you if I had. Really, I would.'

'I'm going to give you my number, just in case. And my address. Why don't you come to see me when you come back from America?'

'Just for a top up?'

'Something like that. That puts us into December, doesn't it? I can do the evening of the fourth.'

'I don't have my diary with me,' I say, 'but since it's absolutely empty, anyway, that should be fine.'

'How do you feel about it being empty?'

'Don't start. Save it for December.'

She can't help but giggle down the line, and I add, 'I only want to see you because you laugh at my jokes.'

'I think I'm just relieved. And you will call Quentin?'

'As soon as I put the phone down.'

But as soon as I put the phone down I hear the swish of post, which wakes up Cat. She knows that I always run down to check it and she also knows that this brings me into closer proximity to her bowls and that if she looks pitiful enough, she might get a few more crunchies. She waits for me with her ears all up and eager, so I go on down the staircase for the post, just to make her happy.

When I see the foil mailshot envelope in that particular shade of lilac, it knocks my feet out from under me and I sit down on the tiles under the coat rack. It looks quite nice, really, quite tasteful. I got a washing powder sample through a couple of days ago. I don't know who had the account, but it was in orange printed black foil and it looked positively toxic.

I crinkle it for a moment in my hands. The printing is slightly darker purple, it says, 'Something New From The Brand Name.' Discreet. Roberto worked like several dogs to get just the right shade. The first five didn't show up at all. The next four or five were too brash. He said he felt like Goldilocks and that the printers were talking to Mafia hitmen before he found the right colour. I pull it open.

It's a pack of four, and the pack is slightly higher grade card than the brand usually use, just to make that impact of quality and investment. There's a shiny leaflet to go with, and a coupon. No car to win, nothing in your face. Everything is in tones of the same lilac and purple, with just a small flash of colour on the boxes to indicate the absorbency levels of the tampons. It's a class job, no doubt about it. And I'm proud of it.

And then I see the slogan, 'Now The Brand Name gives you control.' Gives you control. As if the consumer had never had it before. I groan. And 'gives you'! As if it's some kind of a treat the brand name is allowing you to have. On something you actually insert into your body! It's terrible. It's just terrible.

Cat has given up on leading me to her bowls. She comes and noses at what's in my hand. 'Don't, darling,' I tell her. 'It's rubbish.'

'Hiya! Melanie?'

'Jesus, Maggie!' she drops her voice down a volume notch. 'Quentin's going spare.'

'Is the post in yet?'

'Not yet. I've rung the Post Office, but they say they're training new staff in W1 and-'

'They're always training new staff in W1,' I say irritably. This means I'm going to have to break the news myself.

'Look, he's in, Maggie. I really think you ought to-'

'Okay, kid. Put me through. And thanks.'

'Are you okay?'

'I am now. I might not be after I talk to Quentin.'

This makes her giggle. 'I'm putting you through now.'

There's an extremely brief pause.

'Maggie? Thank fuck!'

'Quentin, I'm really sorry -'

'It's alright. These things happen. I was sorry to hear about your mate.'

'Quentin, I-'

'I'm so glad you've rung. What's that dildo at Safeways called?'

'Ken Barrister?'

'That's him. He's being a bloody nuisance about-'

'Somebody just needs to go and see him and show him how the shelf wobblies work. Every time we have any innovations on the design, he gets a bit frightened. Celia or even Roberto can do it.'

'I'm not going to send Roberto to a supermarket. He'll alienate them forever.'

'Celia, then.'

'Will you just ring him? I've got his number here. I tried to talk to him, but to tell you the truth, Maggie, I just wanted to thump the little pipsqueak.'

I sigh. See? I've only been speaking to him for a couple of minutes and I'm sighing again. 'Look, Quentin, I understand that the post is late.'

He's a bright man. There's only a brief pause while he figures it out.

'No!'

'I'm sorry, but-'

'Shit.'

'And I'm owed about eight weeks holiday, so-'

'Fuck.'

I stop talking and listen to him fume.

'I'm not going to accept it.'

'Quentin, you've got to hear this, I'm-'

'No, Maggie.'

'But-'

'Monday morning, I want you at your desk. Nine o'clock. We'll talk about it then.'

'Quentin, I've resigned!'

'Not yet, you haven't. And you won't be, if I have anything to say about it. How's the post up your way? Did yesterday's arrive yet?'

'Yes. But, Quentin, I-'

'You might want to have a quick dekko at this week's *Marketing*. See you Monday.'

'I'm not coming...' I put the phone down when I hear the buzz. Well, that went well, didn't it?

It takes me a two-hour nap to recover from the phone calls. Actually going into the office on Monday will probably wipe me out for the week. I groan again, thinking about my telephone conversation with Quentin, and that wakes up Cat, who goes downstairs for a nibble. Cat's got the whole life thing taped. She's my guru. I go down for a nibble, too.

On the way to the kitchen, I look down the hall and see the post still at the door. I pick it up and take it with me through the living room to put it on the table where we always keep it. *Marketing* magazine is still in its plastic wrapper. I select an apple and polish it on my sweats, looking at the wrapper for a moment, and then sit down and rip into it. PETA's never gonna get away with those images on billboards, I think to myself, and then I turn the page and see my product pack staring at me.

Brand Name spend £1.4m with Blues. In the copy it talks about big-spend below the line and that the whole thing is PR led. My name is mentioned. The words 'bold' and 'easy on consumer sensibilities' feature.

I throw my apple, half-eaten, in the bin and go to run myself a bath.

Half an hour later, I'm washed and dressed, drinking ice tea at the kitchen table. When Ravinder's key goes in the door, it's a loud, shocking sound. I clear my throat. 'Ravinder? Don't freak out – I'm home.'

She bustles through the living room with all of her bags, which she drops onto the kitchen counter. 'Miss? You sick?'

I shake my head. 'No. I left my job.'

'You left? What happened?'

'Do you want a cup of tea?'

She looks around for a moment, struck by something, and then wanders into the living room. I can hear the light go on in the downstairs bath. 'It is all clean!' she says, accusingly.

I can't look at her properly, so concentrate on the tops of her shoes, which are cut to look a bit like sandals, with little holes around the toes. Her black stockings make pouches around these. I say, 'I'm sorry. I just was bored and so...'

She's still inspecting. 'You did good job! Maybe you don't want me, now.'

'God, no! I still want you.' I finally manage to look at her face. I Feel guilty again, I guess. Guilty for having a cleaner to begin with and now guilty for doing her job for her and making her feel useless. 'It's just that sometimes I'll be doing a lot of it myself.'

'Look, Miss, I'm sorry, but I can't work this way. I have to earn so much money a week. If sometimes you need me and sometimes you don't, then I must get another job for when you don't, and-'

'I'll still pay you.'

'Oh!' She takes off one glove, a man's glove, too heavy for her little hand, weighs it. 'Oh!' she says again.

'Look, sit down, will you? And have a cup of tea? I've even done the ironing and the toilets and everything. Honestly, there's nothing to do at all.'

She giggles. 'What will your husband think?'

I shrug. 'I think if we just don't tell him, that will be best.'

She giggles again, like a little girl, and hides her teeth with the glove.

'How do you like your tea?'

'I make. I make. You sit down now.'

And I do.

Ravinder takes off her coat and hangs it on the apron hook, and a little mystery is solved for me, the mystery of why the apron hook is always falling off. It is strange watching someone in my kitchen, someone competent with the little milk pan and confident of the contents of my refrigerator and cupboard. Ravinder's headscarf slides down the back of her head while she bustles about, revealing hennaed grey streaks in her hair.

257

Ravinder's a bit of a mystery herself. Her English is pretty good, yet her appearance is stamped by poverty. I wonder if that's why she can't get another job. She can read and write English, not terribly well, but well enough to do something better than clean houses. Maybe she's raising her kids on her own, and this kind of work lets her be there when they're in school, and home when they're not. I don't know.

And I'm never going to know, because I can't bring myself to invade her privacy enough to ask. But I can sit here and think about it, imagining all kinds of scenarios, why her husband left her. In one he is a horrible rat who makes loads of money importing drugs and never sees his kids, having abandoned Ravinder for a succession of blonde nymphets. In another, he fought bravely during something or other and died, leaving her with only his children and his memory.

I do this sort of thing all the time. I guess I have finally found what I'm hopefully going to be good at. A journalist would have just asked, and a really skilled PR person that wanted to know would just wheedle the conversation around. I'm through with wheedling. Even the thought makes me feel tired. I slump down in my chair.

Ravinder has just spiced the milk with cardamom and something else she rummaged out of my cupboard. Now she's putting sugar and the tea bags in. I say, 'That looks fantastic.'

'You want?'

I shake my head. 'No thanks, I'll stick with this.' I whirl the ice around in my glass.

'You drink cold drinks when it is cold?'

I shrug. 'I just like it.'

She gets a mug out of my cupboard and strains the mixture into it. The pan hisses when she pours. When she comes to sit down, she smiles with embarrassment, fiddling with her head-scarf.

'Isn't it funny how everybody drinks tea differently? I mean, English people think that only they can make tea properly.'

'I work for one lady who is very fussy.'

'She has you making her cups of tea?'

'Oh, my yes! I go every morning. I clean around, make tea and toast, make clothes clean.'

'Wow! A daily!'

She smiles modestly. 'It's only one or two hours every morning. But it is early, you know, nine o'clock. It is steady. I have been going there six years now.'

I shake my head. I can't imagine the luxury of having someone tidy up every morning and bring me breakfast in bed. I'd die of shame. 'Doesn't she do any of her housework?'

'Oh, yes! She does cooking. She does washing up. Well, she has dishwasher. She does not do the pots. I do pots. And she does…' Ravinder tries to be charitable, describing one white lady customer to another, '…she does flowers and other things. You know. Puts books away.'

I nod, all the time thinking 'lazy cow.'

'Does she work?'

'I think maybe a little.'

Bloated bourgeois. But I don't know. She may be on the game for all I know, exhausted by all of her Johns the night before. Or she may be doing loads of charity functions. Talking on the phone and filling out invitations wouldn't look much like real work to Ravinder. I shouldn't be sitting here judging some poor woman I've never even met.

I try and change the subject. 'You must see some strange things.'

She nods. 'Oh, yes, many.'

'What's the strangest thing that has ever happened to you?'

She thinks. She says, 'You know when summertime? You know when all that sand was in your bedroom? All that sand around

259

your bed! I never know why. Much, much sand. And I never do know why. Why was all that sand there?'

And I just look at her, my mouth open. I say, 'I really don't know, you know.'

And she says, 'Maybe your husband tells you.'

I nod. A few minutes later, I get some money out of my bag for her and send her on her way. I can't remember what we talked about before that.

Upstairs, I go straight to the study and rummage in my growing library of reference books for the Lonely Planet guide to Israel and the Palestinian Territories. Lake Kinneret, or what we call the Sea of Gallilee, isn't a sea at all. It's a freshwater lake, with a 'packed mud' bed. Beaches must have sand trucked in, because those that don't are described as 'stony'. I doubt if Capernaum had sand trucked in to make it appealing to the tourist trade in 10 BC. I doubt that very much.

I wander into the bedroom with my finger still keeping my place in the guidebook. 'Sand?' I say to myself. I sit down on the edge of the bed and think about it for awhile. I think I assumed that Peter had tracked it in, but he couldn't have, could he? And now I know he also doesn't leave things behind.

I just don't get it. I look at the bedside clock and yelp. I'm late for the pub.

Chapter Twenty-two

I've flown down the street, but Simon's already got them in and got us a table. It's towards the back, but not in the horrible no-smoking conservatory part. When we first moved here, we used to sit in the front bit, since it was livelier, and we thought we would meet people that way. But just because many races were represented in the same space, didn't mean that they actually talked to each other. When we figured that out, we decided to retreat from the noise of shouted conversation towards the back bit, where all the white people sit and it's quieter.

Simon's got this huge round table. We'll probably share it with somebody as the place fills up. He's looking at some work stuff when I come in, which he shoves hastily away. He's been so happy since Camburet signed me that I suspect he hasn't even used the soles of his shoes. Before he even kisses me, he says, 'I biked that package off to Fliss. And I rang her, and it got there.'

I kiss him and thank him.

He says, 'Why do you have that book with you? Am I too boring to talk to anymore?'

I look down, and the Lonely Planet guide is still clamped around my finger. I must have left the house with it. I lay it on the table and have a drink of my pint.

'It's called Honeypot.'

Intellectually, I can tell that the beer is very good. It just doesn't grab me for some reason. Ordinarily, I fall upon my Friday pints somewhat in the manner of a lioness on a zebra, but after my first sip, I just let it sit there. I'm thinking, or trying to.

'What's up?'

Simon's voice is coming from far away. That means I'm not

telling myself something. Unfortunately, knowing this doesn't help me figure out what it is.

'Do you know anything about sand in the bedroom?' I ask him absently, and then watch as he turns red and away.

'Simon?'

He chokes out, 'What do you think of the beer?'

But I'm not going to be put off. 'What do you know about the sand?'

'Oh, shit.' Simon buries his face in his hands.

I just wait. When he finally looks at me, it's like he'd hoped that I'd disappeared. I say, 'Still here, darling.'

He takes a drink which turns into a half-pint gulp. And then he wipes his lips with the back of his hand and says, 'It was from Sussex.'

I raise my eyebrows.

He says, 'I went to Sussex and got sand in my clothes.'

'How did you get sand in your clothes?'

He closes his eyes. 'I was on a beach.'

'With Sandy.'

He nods.

'How aptly named she is.'

'Don't, Maggie.'

'Okay.' We look at each other some more. 'So, you had sand in your clothes. And shoes?'

He nods.

'Why wasn't the sand by the closet or in the laundry basket? Why was it around the bed?'

'Because I got undressed in the bedroom.'

And suddenly I know what I didn't want to tell myself. 'You slept with Sandy in our bed.'

He closes his eyes and nods.

'You slept with Sandy in our bed?'

He nods again.

262

I stop myself from saying it a third time. I try and Feel, rather desperately. But there's nothing there. I've gone all cold and remote again. Is this what our marriage is going to be like for the next few years? Am I going to keep finding things out, one after the other?

'What else should I know, Simon?'

'I need another drink.'

'Have mine.' I slide my pint across the table. 'I don't want to find this shit out in dribs and drabs. What else should I know?"

'Do we have to do this, Maggie?'

I recognise how passionless my voice sounds. I'm pleased to be handling this so rationally. 'Yes.'

'There's not much else to tell.'

'Well, tell me the not much else.'

Simon slides off his tie and undoes the top two buttons of his shirt. 'I brought her to some parties and things.'

'Sandy.'

'Yes. Look, I'm telling you, okay?'

'What parties?'

'You know. Phil's birthday. Katie's sister came into town from Sydney. Things like that.'

'For how long?'

'Katie's sister?'

'No. How long did you take Sandy to your mates' parties?'

'A couple of months.'

'A couple of months?' My voice screeches on this last word. A couple who had been bringing their drinks over to our table abruptly veer away. Perhaps I'm not in such good control. I take a deep breath, or at least my body does.

'Were you that sure you were going to leave me?'

Simon finishes my pint. He shrugs.

'So everyone knew before I did.'

He starts to say, 'I'm really sorry about-' but stops when I hold up my hand.

263

'Did you use condoms?'

'Of course.'

We look at each other for a moment. 'And this is why you're avoiding Katie and all that group?'

He swallows. 'Well, they're a bit angry at me. They really took to Sandy.'

'What?'

He shrugs. He tries, 'I...' and then 'It...', but neith of them work.

I get up and go to the bar. It's Friday evening, and it's the kind of pub that roars on Friday evening. There are labourers still in their work clothes. There are the polyester suits of whatever losers have offices in this part of town. There are masses of young folks, all leather and feathers and facial piercings, getting a buzz on before they hit the higher prices of the West End. I stand there forever, waiting.

Of course, since I'm in my daze, it doesn't really bother me. Why aren't I angry? Maybe it's just because I've already decided that I want to keep him. Maybe I don't want to cause a scene for him, here in his local. I guess this dump is his local. You don't want to cause a scene in your Englishman's local. He'll never forgive you.

Forgive me? I'm worried about Simon forgiving me?

Or maybe I've pretty much known something like this all along, but just didn't tell myself. Maybe it's good that we're getting it all out. Our relationship has been wounded badly, and we've allowed it to skin over, but there was still infection underneath.

Draining pus isn't a very nice metaphor for a conversation, but it isn't a very nice conversation, either. Even now, I can't Feel. Maybe I'm glad it's finally happening. That's what I try and tell myself.

I finally order a pint of Honeypot and a Coke, get it, pay, and go back to the table. I half expect Simon to have fled, but he's still there.

'Here.'

'Thanks.'

We look at each other for awhile. And I say, 'Let me get this straight. Your friends are angry at you because they preferred Sandy.'

He nods without moving his head more than an eighth of an inch. He's starting to look truculent.

'And that's why we haven't been seeing them.'

He does it again. I shove his pint towards him. 'Here,' I say again.

Simon excuses himself to the toilet, and I sit there, trying to Feel. I'm not getting anywhere with it.

I take a sip of my Coke and it tastes so nice to me. I don't usually drink that much caffeine, but here lately I really enjoy a glass of tea or a Coke a couple of times a day. Something niggles me about this. I look at my glass and decide I'd better make this my last one for awhile. I don't know why. Something else I guess I'm not telling myself.

When my husband comes back from the Men's, he's washed his face and dried it with toilet paper. He has microscopic white balls of paper caught in his five o'clock shadow which give him a fuzzy, undetermined look. I resist trying to pick them out. I say, 'Speaking of people who don't like me, maybe we ought to go up and see your folks before we go to the States. If we get some offers on the house.'

Simon looks at me as if I were a stranger. 'Is that all you're going to say?'

I shrug. 'What else can I say?'

'Aren't you angry?'

'I'm not pleased about it, no. But then, I never liked your mates anyway.'

265

'Maggie!'

'Sorry. They've always been bastards to me, Simon, you just never could see it.'

'You never said.'

'I didn't want to, I don't know…' We look at each other some more. Now that he's back, he's not sitting so low in his chair.

So what if I don't Feel angry? What am I supposed to do, wail and gnash my teeth? Burn the bed? It's been, what, three months since he slept in it with her? What can I do about it now? I already knew I'd been betrayed. Betrayal brings me back to his mates.

I say, 'Look, they never liked me. And I didn't want to make things hard for you, so I just took it.'

'I'm sorry.' Simon sighs, exhaling forever, like they try and get you to do in yoga. 'I'm sorry about all of it. I've been such an arse.'

'Well,' I shrug. My remote self decides that I'm handling this terribly well. 'Thanks for telling me, anyway. Is there anything else?'

'That's it. I swear.'

Now I swallow, now tears come into my eyes. From where? Where is it hurting? 'Because if you lied to me now, Simon…'

'I'm not going to. I'm not going to lie any more.' Simon drinks a bit, looking back off to the Men's, as if he's left part of himself there. 'I think I was lying to myself more than to you. Really.'

'I don't care about that. That's your problem.'

He looks at me like I've slapped him, but I'm not going to nursemaid him through his guilt. I sigh. I look at my hand. It seems so far away, my hand. It seems difficult to wrap it around my glass.

I manage to take another drink of my Coke, and he says, 'You're right. You've got enough to deal with.' I kind of hear this, but not really. I'm not really hearing much.

'What time is the curry for?'

He glances at his watch. 'Not for another ten minutes.'

He manages to look in my eyes. Whatever he sees there isn't encouraging. His drop to the table. 'What are you drinking?'

'Coke.' He looks at me, and I shrug. 'I don't know. It's what I wanted.'

'Don't you like the Honeypot?'

'It's good. I don't know. Ever since that night with Fliss, alcohol just...'

He looks at me speculatively, but doesn't say anything.

'I don't know. It just doesn't taste good. I'm not going to drink something if I don't like it.'

'No, of course not.' He has another swig. 'About this trip up north...'

I watch him as he talks about his meeting schedule and I realise that he is fine. Simon is absolutely fine. He's just had to tell me the most awful things, but since I haven't got too upset, he doesn't worry about it anymore. He's so fucking simple. If it doesn't hurt, there's no pain involved.

His mates, the bastards, preferred Sandy? Well, they would, wouldn't they? Honestly. I haven't told you much about them, but they are the most stuck up bits of... Oh, what's the use thinking this way? They probably had their reasons not to like me. Just like Simon had his reasons to fuck his secretary and start preferring her company to mine at parties.

'Maggie?'

I find that I'm still smiling attentively, but that my eyes have glazed over. 'Hmmm?' I ask.

'Nevermind. Let's go get the curry.'

We leave the pub and walk to the restaurant. I wait outside while Simon picks up the brown paper bag with the little brown paper loop handles. He's still got his case, so I take this from him and slide the Lonely Planet inside. He reaches out to hold my free hand. He's talking, but I can't hear what he's saying. I can't follow it at all.

There's a strange sound in my head that I'm listening to, a kind of whirring sound. It's how I imagine a plague of locusts would sound in the distance, coming closer. And this one's coming closer, too, well, getting louder anyway. I know it's inside, not outside, but I can't quite place it.

We stumble down the broken brick pavement of Leswin Road, down our street, and into the house. I go into the kitchen and wash my hands at the sink before getting the little wicker trays out and lining them with cloths, putting napkins on them, pulling knifes and forks out of a drawer. I check the level in the water filter jug and add a bit more, just in case the balti is too hot like it sometimes is, and then pour two glasses of water. I get the bowls from our everyday wedding set out of the cupboard and the matching little bread and butter plates. I get big spoons and the yoghurt from the fridge and start spooning curry into both bowls and yoghurt on top of my curry.

Simon comes back down the stairs in sweats, picks up his tray and his water and flops onto the sofa, swiping the remote from the coffee table and pushing 4, for *Friends* or *Frasier*. Something mindless.

It's wasted on me. The whirring noise is now so loud that I can't hear the television. I look at my food and it seems like a completely foreign substance to me, but something that is precious to something else, or someone else that I am, or will be later. Right now, though, I am something that doesn't eat.

This is strange. This whole thing is strange. I take my tray back into the kitchen and look at it for a moment after I set it back on the counter. And then I look at Simon, really look at him. He's all snug on the sofa, dabbing away with his chipatis at his curry, engrossed in whatever crap he's chosen. And suddenly I hear that click again, that very loud click, that signals I am back in my body. With it comes a rage I thought I left behind in childhood.

Oh, I think, it's blood. That whirring sound. It's my blood that's been pounding in my ears. And then I stop thinking at all. I just start doing things.

A tiny little bit of me is left to watch, but although it is screaming that I must calm down, it can't stop the rest of me picking up Simon's bowl and shoving it in his face. I hear myself screaming as I slam it once, twice, three times into the front of his skull. I'm sure he's saying something, because when the bowl breaks, his lips are moving, but by then I'm hitting him so many places it's difficult to concentrate on anything else.

The whirring sound finally clears and I find that I am shouting, 'my bed' over and over. The bowl is in pieces on the rug and Simon's got his head between his knees, and his hands over his head, like they tell you to do in case the airplane crashes, so I go to the side of him closest to the window, where the arm of the sofa doesn't get in the way of me kicking at his ribs.

He's lucky I'm wearing trainers. I almost wore riding boots with these jeans, but the legs wouldn't come down over the tops. I really should get a pair of more flared ones. I saw some at Gap that would work. When I think this, I can't keep kicking anymore, and I stop.

I'm sweaty and my hair is in my eyes. My hands hurt pretty badly, and my husband is curled up like a woodlouse. Not all the red stuff on his trousers is curry.

I thought I'd handled this so well.

My legs collapse and I sit at his feet.

He hasn't moved much since I stopped.

'Simon?'

He's breathing at least, pretty fast, but still a good sign, surely.

What do you say when you've just tried to kill someone?

'I'm sorry, Niles, something just came over me...' The remote is still on the coffee table and I switch off the television, and Kelsey Grammer's whining voice.

269

Something just came over me? It was like something just inhabited me. If I believed in Satan I'd say I'd been possessed. It felt like being possessed.

I've never hit anyone in my life. Except my brother. We used to beat the shit out of each other. And Johnny Barkley in the third grade. Oh, and in high school, Susan Bulmer and I had a big fight over something she said about my softball skills. And once I lost it with this guy in a mosh pit. He was an asshole.

That's quite a few, actually, isn't it? I guess I've hit enough people. I guess this isn't completely without precedent.

'Simon?'

'Are you quite finished?' he says icily, and this frightens me to my spine.

'I'm sorry,' I say, 'I don't know what came over me.'

He looks up and he's got a cut over one eye and his nose is bleeding. I run to the kitchen and come back with a huge banner of kitchen towel. He glares at me, but lets me wipe the food off his face so that I can see how bad it is. It's bad. I'm pretty sure I broke his nose.

'You're going to have to go to Casualty,' I tell him. 'I'll ring for a taxi.'

Simon yanks the towelling out of my hands, and begins to clean himself up. I got remarkably little on the sofa. 'I can't go into A&E and tell them my wife's just done me over.'

At last our eyes meet. I expected his to be colder. He looks at me grimly while he runs his hand down his left side.

'How are your ribs?'

'Okay. Feel like I've been in a bit of a scrum, that's all.' He sighs. 'Get some more towelling so that I can stand up without completely staining the sofa.'

I do this, and help clean him off. He walks into the laundry room first and drops his sweats on the floor and then goes naked into the downstairs bathroom and contemplates himself in the

270

mirror before he starts to wash. I fly upstairs for some antiseptic and when I come down, he's already towelling off.

'It's my nose mainly,' he says to himself more than to me, 'I think I'll probably take a few stitches as well.'

'God, Simon. I'm so sorry.' And I am, I'm shaking as I hand him the antiseptic cream and rummage for some plasters I keep down there for guests. 'I couldn't hear. It was like someone else had taken over my body.'

'Are you completely cracked, Maggie? You realise I could have you put away for something like this?'

Again, he's talking cold, but his eyes are still warm. I'm just holding his eyes with mine, trying not to stray to his injuries. This is it, part of me is shrieking, This is it. You've fucked up now, you crazy cow.

My mouth has gone dry, and I guess I'm trying to explain when I say, 'I got really angry.'

'You didn't seem that angry when I told you.'

I know, I know. I don't understand it myself. I say, 'I…It…' I'm still shaking, and I think I might be sick. 'I don't know. It really just came over me. It happened slow.'

'So, are you leaving *me*?' he asks, warm eyes still holding steady.

What? What is he talking about?

'Are you leaving me? That's the question, Simon.'

'No,' he says. 'I'm not. I deserved it.'

And then I start to cry and say, 'Jesus. Nobody deserves that, Simon.' My legs give out again and I'm sitting on the tub. 'I'm so, so very sorry. I don't seem to tell myself what I'm feeling. I just tried to be calm in the pub. I didn't want to show you up, I guess. I think I'm always trying to be what you want me to be – what everybody wants me to be. Sometimes I don't even tell myself how…'

'How you feel. I know.'

I nod, staring at the black and white tiles.

271

Simon sighs. 'I'm rather glad you got this over with, I suppose.'

'You're glad?' And now, I can look at him again. He starts to smile at me, but it wrinkles his forehead and comes out as a wince.

'Well, I was fairly sure you'd try to kill me.'

'I was trying to be reasonable, really I was.'

'I guess I should be thankful about your choice of weapon. I don't think anyone's ever been soupbowled to death.'

'Look, you've got to get to Casualty. I really do think I broke your nose.'

Simon sinks down onto the toilet and closes his eyes. 'This whole few months has been so humiliating.'

'I'm sorry.'

'The affair was embarrassing enough. Really, Maggie - how could anyone think I'd leave a woman like you for Sandy? I was just being pathetic, trying to get your attention.'

'Don't say that.'

'It's true. None of this has anything to do with anyone else, not Sandy, not the Blues, not even Saint bloody Peter. It's just you and me, you and me. It's all about us. Who's on top. Who's in control.'

His forehead is bleeding again, and I go and lean over him to unroll some toilet paper, which I make into a pad and hold against the wound, until he takes over holding it for me. I say, 'Well, I'm not in control, that's obvious. I'm completely out of control.'

Simon snorts. 'You? How do you think all this has made me look at work?' He gets up and examines his nose again in the mirror. 'But that's not what I'm talking about. I'm talking about who's controlling this marriage, you know?

'It's always one of us controlling and the other one trying to fit in. It was me controlling it until you got that big lolly job. Then it was you controlling until I started up with Sandy. And then I got back in the saddle for awhile. And now…'

'And now, what?'

'I don't know. Like you said, you can't even control yourself.

272

But if we base it on money, you're still top, with that whacking great signing fee.'

'It's not that big.'

'It's big enough.' He turns back to me. 'It's nearly my basic salary for two years, Princess.'

My chin trembles. 'It's all a mistake. I'm not going to be able to do it, you know. Fliss's sent me these comments and I don't even know what she means.'

'You'll do it. And it'll probably be a bestseller.' He sits back down on the toilet. 'Shouldn't I get to wear the pants, at least for a little while?'

He's naked, still, and that doesn't help him. 'Can't we talk about this on the way to the hospital? You must be freezing.'

But he's still talking. 'And now you've duffed me up. Wonderful. I feel such a man.'

'Tell them it fell out of the cupboard on you. From a great height.'

'At least I didn't hit you back. I would have had to top myself if I'd done that.'

'I won't do it again, Simon. I've only lost it like that maybe five times in my life, mostly with Jack.'

'Your poor sodding brother. And when's the last time you talked to him? Did you know he offered to pick us up from the airport?'

'No.' My little brother. He's always hated me. I've learned just to ignore him.

'I'm going to buy that boy so much beer when I see him again. Poor kid.'

'Simon, he hates me.'

'And can you blame him? Did you ever think what it was like for him, growing up behind superwoman? Having your teachers?'

'I'm not superwoman!' It's no news that Jack's always resented

273

me. What's news is that Simon has, as well. 'What am I supposed to do for you guys to like me, act stupid?'

'Oh, thanks, babe.'

The tub is dry, so it doesn't matter if instead of just sitting on the edge, I slide down to the bottom. I lay there and stare up at the plaster of the ceiling. The people that came today to see the house loved the flat ceilings, I could tell. They kept saying how clean everything looked. Something else I do too well, probably. I've always tried so damn hard to do well. Why did I bother? Nobody loves anybody for doing too well.

'It's not easy for me, you know. It's not like it comes easy. Look at that whole PR thing. I worked my ass off for that money.'

'I know.'

Simon stands over me at the head of the tub. I can see his face upside down, see his nose starting to swell. 'I'm going to Casualty,' he says.

'Good.'

'Call the cab.'

I haul myself up. 'I'm really sorry,' I say again.

'I deserved it.'

'Stop saying that!'

'Okay.'

'And go put some clothes on.'

'I was going to.'

'Good.'

There's no way to kiss him on his face, so I kiss him on his shoulder. 'I'm so sorry. For everything.'

'It's not your fault.'

'Beating you up isn't my fault?'

'I meant being better at everything.'

'Oh, God.' I cover up my eyes with my hands, and can hear Simon start up the stairs.

'Call the fucking taxi, will you?' he shouts down, and he sounds almost joyous as he shouts it, singing it down to me, as if we've solved something, as if we've made anything any better.

Chapter Twenty-three

If you are going to go A&E in central London, you might want to make sure that you don't do it on a weekend evening. They check Simon into the system and give him a better pad for his head than the soaking toilet paper and then we sit in reception, where every third person seems to be either loony or drunk or both.

It strikes me how many Celtic accents there are in here. None Welsh, though. Just Glaswegian, Highland, and various Irish tones, all blending in a cacophony of misery and rage. One older man against the wall near us is rocking himself and muttering in a Belfast accent.

There's a lad here with a big bottle under his jacket. He's handcuffed to a policeman. Every few minutes, they both disappear into the toilets together, and once when they come out I see that the big bottle is full of urine. I have no idea what that's all about.

They call out Simon's name, but it turns out to be Light, not White, and a mother and son shuffle hurriedly by someone puking on the floor.

The noise level drops as everyone listens to the puking, rating it, no doubt, out of ten. And so we can hear the Belfast guy, and what he's muttering is, 'I've seen Mary, so I have. The mother of God, she came to me, she said, "Jimmy, you're not so bad." She said, "Jimmy," she did...' Then the noise level perks back up, discussing the puking, I guess, and we can't hear him any more.

Simon, drawn and white, changes the hand that holds the pad and says, 'If you'd like to go talk to your mate over there, and compare notes, I'll watch your coat.'

I'd really like to hit him again, but instead I say, 'I wonder what the poor soul's wife did to him?'

I enjoy watching Simon flinch at that. 'Don't even think you've got the upper hand now, Simon. Don't even think about starting all that up again.'

'All what?'

'All that who's on top shit.'

To look me in the face, Simon has to bend his arm and look under it. He does this.

I continue, 'You aren't so great, Simon. You really fucked up, too, you know. And I'm not so great, and I've really fucked up. We're even.'

'I didn't hit you.'

'I didn't sleep with Quentin.'

Simon really does look like hell, but he takes this in. 'What, forever?' he says.

'What do you mean, forever?'

'Do you think we can keep it up forever?'

'Keep what up?'

For an answer, he blows out his lips. He changes arms so that he can see me better and I notice that the pad is nearly soaked through. I've heard head wounds bleed heavily, but I don't think I'd ever really seen one before. Simon says, 'Neutrality, I suppose.'

'Yes,' I say. 'I'm not better than you. You're not better than me. If we're going to keep going, then all that shit has to go right out the window.'

'Mr White? Simon White?'

And thank fuck for that. A personage in dark blue leads us to a little cubicle made of what looks like old sheets, where Simon is instructed to take off his clothes and put on a gown and told that a doctor will see him shortly. I help him do this, holding the pad while he takes off his jumper and taking off his trousers myself. I mean, I've done it often enough.

Then the idiot gestures at the bed and says, 'You take it. I can sit in the chair.'

He's actually wavering a bit on his feet.

I say, 'Lie down, crazy man.'

He does, and gives a little sigh. He says, 'You're right.'

'Well, you look a bit tired.' I arrange self and clothing on and in the plastic chair.

'I mean about giving up the who's on top game.'

'It just shouldn't be about that.'

'I know.' He only has the dirty ceiling tiles to look at, and he chews on his lip as if he really needed another facial injury. He says, 'I think playing it makes me feel a bit better. Makes me feel like you're with me more.'

'I'm with you.'

He shakes his head impatiently and then immediately regrets it and starts to wince, remembers about his forehead, and sighs. 'Oh, fuck,' he says, 'I can't talk properly here.'

'Let's leave it then.'

'No.' He takes in air and says, 'I never thought I'd really pull you, you know? This American woman, so bright…'

'Simon, surely you've noticed how beautiful you are.'

'It's not the same. I mean, why me, Maggie? I've never under-stood that. Why do you want me? Those men at our wedding? Dentists, doctors. You could have had it so easy. Then none of this would have happened.'

'Money? Are we talking about money?'

'It's not just money. It's social, as well.'

'So, we're talking money and class?'

English people always wince when you bring up Class. I should have remembered this and saved Simon more pain in his forehead wound. I say, 'That's not what I wanted. I always wanted some-thing different, something interesting. You've always been inter-esting to me.'

He nods a bit, as if he's thinking something through. I'm a bit afraid of what this might be, so I flounder on. 'And anyway, what about you? You could have had somebody else, anybody else.

Somebody who fit into your circle. Somebody your parents liked. Somebody like Sandy, I guess.'

'Don't.'

'I'm not.' I touch his arm. 'Really, I'm not. I meant it. I certainly don't fit in.'

He sighs. He says, 'I didn't want anybody else. I still don't.'

It hits me then, what we're actually saying to each other. Is it possible to hold yourself in tight somewhere for ten years? I don't know. All I know is that I feel something, somewhere relax. I say, 'Well, then.'

'Well, what?'

'Well. Let's just listen to that for a moment, okay? Let's just listen to the fact that we want each other. Maybe we just need to Feel that, inside.' I point to somewhere three inches above my navel. I don't know if I'm actually communicating or not. I don't know that it's something you can communicate. I watch him carefully to see if I've made any sense to him.

'We do?' He lays there for a moment, and then transfers hands again. It's hard to read his face with that thing over half of it, and his nose swollen to about twice its usual size. Slowly, he says. 'Yes. I think I see what you mean.'

And then the curtain is whipped aside. 'Mr White? I just need to take your blood pressure.' It's someone else in blue. I can't keep track of the ranks of the various nursing staff. Some are in white, some are in light blue, some are in dark blue and some are in scrubs. God only knows what species the dark blue are, but that's who we've been mostly seeing.

She has a clipboard with her, and scribbles down the blood pressure before slapping a thermometer in Simon's mouth. Simon looks at me kind of through her, as she messes about with his pad and looks at his nose a bit. I don't think I've ever seen him look at me that way before, or at least not since we first met. It hits me again, and again, and again, that he loves me. It's like being in a

279

rough sea, and letting the waves toss you about. Why do we keep on forgetting this? We mustn't forget it any more.

'Now, Mr White. Can you tell me again how you received these injuries?'

'A soupbowl fell out of the cupboard.'

The nurse looks down at my hands, so I do as well. They've swollen a bit, and have that shiny look that precedes bruising all around the knuckles. Simon is the last one to follow our eyes.

She says, 'A soupbowl?'

Simon clears his throat. 'It was stoneware,' he says, and he's gone up a couple of notches in his accent. His intonation's turned into pure Bertie Wooster. 'Big, heavy thing. Silly really, keeping them up top like that.'

'Hmmmm.' She looks at me and then at Simon, carefully. And then says, 'We've put out a call for the doctor. She should be with us quite soon.'

'Good, good,' Simon says brightly.

When I try to talk, I discover I have to clear my throat first, and then I say, 'Could we have another pad? That one's about soaked through,' and get another careful look.

'Certainly,' is all she says to me. I've never felt so awful in my entire life.

Chapter Twenty-four

Without visits from Peter, and without drinking anything, I keep waking up terribly early. Monday morning I'm up around 5:00. Cat and I go downstairs and have something to eat and then I run a bath. I haven't had a shower since I left the Blues. I like baths. After she eats and goes outside for a moment, Cat comes in and curls up on my dressing gown while I soak. When I dunk under to wet my hair for a shampoo, though, she leaves. I'm sure she thinks immersing yourself in water voluntarily is behaviour too bizarre to tolerate.

Upstairs, Simon's alarm has just gone off and he's sitting on the toilet. I stand in the dressing room for a few moments and finally shout through the door. 'Do you think I really have to dress properly?'

'Do you want to go back?'

'No.'

'Then wear what you want. Unless you've got something else on today.'

'Naw. I'm only seeing Fliss.'

'Why not be comfortable, then?' I hear a flush and he opens the door. I keep forgetting how terrible he looks. He's got two black eyes, a seven stitch gash on his forehead and one of those little silver braces on his nose.

I cuddle his cheek with my hand. 'Ah, babe,' I say. 'I'm so sorry.'

He shakes my hand off. 'Stop it. We said we were even, right?'

'I know, but you look…' I trail off. You look terrible, probably isn't the most tactful thing to say. 'What are you going to tell them at work?'

'Soupbowl. Great height.'

'Well, at least it's more original than walking into a door.'

This makes him smile. 'Wear whatever you feel like wearing. Wear something comfortable.'

'Thanks.' I have to be careful when I kiss him not to knock his nose.

I get onto the 7:15 train and manage to find a seat between two pinstriped City gents behind pink newspapers. When I go to sit down, they both glance at me with disapproval and give identical rattles to their papers before settling back down. It's like being a book between two hostile bookends.

What I felt like wearing was my new flared jeans I bought at Gap yesterday. I know it seems a bit sick, but I kept thinking about them. After I'd chatted to the fourth couple coming to view the house, I got a minicab to town and bought them. I thought they looked groovy over my new Merrill hiking/climbing booties. I thought those, in black suede, looked terribly sophisticated with my black cashmere turtleneck. I thought that made my breasts look bigger. I thought I looked fine, actually, with my hair in clips and just a bit of a stain on my lips. I did until I got on this train, anyway.

Now I'm not so sure.

When I get into Liverpool Street station, I'm even less sure. The choreography doesn't seem to be working for me. People aren't letting me make my usual diagonal sweep into the ticket barriers. Suit after suit after suit just sweeps by me, even though I'm obviously trying to move over there. I end up perfectly stationary at one point, and then I have to kind of hop between people, one by one, to make it to the barrier.

It doesn't stop once I'm there. There's a serpentine of black and navy sliding their cards through the slots. Usually, they make room for me, but they don't today. I wait politely for a moment and finally just shoulder my way in, muttering 'Excuse me.' The person behind me clicks their tongue against their teeth.

It's not like that in the West End. I'm not shouldered out of the Tottenham Court Road escalator queue or anything. I'm dressed just like a Creative, I suppose. Or someone in retail, or something.

Still, at the office I feel like an intruder. The lights aren't on in reception. I swipe my card to go through the door. Now I'm a burglar, rummaging in the filing room for boxes. Silent in my rubber soles I pass the boardroom, where light spills out underneath the door. I still wonder who goes to buy the pastries. I'll bet it's Martin. He has such a nice face.

In my office, I close the door and switch on my light. I still feel like an intruder, even now, even in here. I think I always did. I never felt like I really belonged here. I always felt like I was busking it, just getting through one day after another.

The boxes are so complicated to construct that there's a little diagram telling you how to manage it. When they're done, though, they're terribly sturdy. Will I need one or two? If it's two, I might as well do the other one now, while I remember how.

I look around the office for what I'll be taking with me. There's a picture of Simon. It's a black and white one of him in the middle of a stream, casting. All you can see is his handsome face, the collar of his moleskin shirt, and white water in the back ground. Simon as fisherman.

The doctor said he shouldn't have a scar.

The silver frame isn't large. It would fit in the nylon satchel I've slung around me. I look for what else to put in the box. The desk set was here when I moved in, as was the Georgia O'Keefe print. Files? My contact book, of course, but that will fit in my satchel as well. I sit down at my desk and switch on my computer. When NT loads, my email notifier is silent. Someone must have been answering them for me.

I open my top drawer. There's a box of the pens I like that Anya always orders for me. I look at them for a moment, but decide just to tear off the label so that I can order some for myself. I open the next drawer, files. Those will go to Quentin. On the other side, there's product. Deodorants, body sprays, tampons, toothpaste. The tissues that Finchley brought me. And then down at the bottom, there's the shrink file on top of the stocking mountain.

Should I take my stockings? Surely I'll want to wear them again at some point. Or will I? I look down at my legs in my lovely new jeans. I slide the drawer closed.

I'm playing on the internet when the phone rings. I'm on the website of the *Lawrence Journal World*, my hometown newspaper. They have a camera pointed at the main street of Lawrence and if you click on it, it takes a picture every three seconds. I'm watching the taillights of one lone car jerking down towards the bridge over the Kaw River. It's 2:07 am there. Finally, I pick up the telephone.

'Maggie White.'

'I've been waiting for you.'

It's Quentin. 'You're out of board, then?'

He doesn't answer.

'I'll come down.'

His door's open, so I just walk inside and slide it closed. He's in full power mode, he doesn't get up or smile or anything. He's playing with a pencil and he keeps playing with it as I shut the door and stand there. Finally, I decide that this is silly and sit down. I'm not going to say anything if he isn't. He's the one that wanted me here, after all.

'Two weeks.' That's the first thing he says.

I haven't the faintest idea what he's talking about.

'Compassionate leave is usually only a few days. You've been out two weeks.'

I now know his choice of control ploy. I suppose I'm supposed to argue my case now, go into trying to please the boss mode and suddenly find myself re-employed. It makes me smile. It also makes me feel tired. 'That doesn't really matter, now, does it?'

'Don't be silly, Maggie.'

I hate this. I'm not going to show it, though, I'm just going to keep smiling at him. You know, it's no great wonder that I got so good at playing these mind games that I started even fooling myself. Mind your appearance and repress anything inconvenient. The company culture. Hell, the industry culture. Hell, the whole societal culture. It's London. I catch myself inhaling for a sigh. I'm not going to start sighing again. God!

'You don't want to lose your job.'

'Oh yes I do, Quentin. Really.'

'Did you see *Marketing*?'

It's like we aren't even speaking the same language.

'It doesn't matter. And anyway, wait until this weekend's sales results are in to break out the champagne.'

He takes some time to reconsider his approach. 'You aren't the first,' he says, and then explains. 'You aren't the first one to lose it during a product launch.'

I just look at him.

'You should have seen Rob midway through Red Steer. He wouldn't leave his bathroom for two days. Margaret had to slide food under the door.' Quentin holds the pencil horizontal and squints at it. 'Flat things. Ryvita. Kraft singles.'

He puts the pencil down and leans over the desk. 'Jenny told me that you'd been going through quite a lot.'

'Jenny?'

'Jenny Levine.'

I look at him blankly.

'The psychologist you hired?'

So that's Finchley's name! Jenny Levine! 'Ah!' I say, and nod a bit.

'Celia did a fine job, taking over from you.'

'I knew she would.'

'So there's no harm done.'

'She's much better at that sort of thing than I am.'

'She even got us through that sticky patch with Safeways.'

I nod.

'In fact, she's done such a good job...'

He picks up the pencil again. 'We've been talking about you, Maggie, your strengths and weaknesses.'

Like I need to hear this? 'Quentin, I've resigned.'

He holds up one hand. 'And where we think you really shine is on project management.'

That's probably true. It's the people side I hate the most. But that's hardly relevant now. 'Quentin, look at me!' I nearly shout. 'Look!' I stand up so that he can get the full eyeful of my groovy new jeans and suede booties. 'Do I look like I'm interested in continuing my career in PR?'

But he just smiles at me.

'Do you remember that website you did for *Teen Sparkle*? Those CD-Rom packs you did on *Look* and *Sugar*?'

I nod. Of course I remember. 'Well, we're starting a new media side. I know you suggested it then, but...' Quentin smiles at me. 'We've been spending a hell of a lot with Razorfish. We'd save tons by bringing it in-house. Roberto knows quite a few geeks with web experience...' he leans forward. 'We think it's probably time.'

I suddenly see where this is going.

'Now you did such a good job working with Creative on the tampon. Fine work, Maggie, really. And Sam was really impressed that you didn't cry on Advertising's shoulder like PR usually do.'

I'd like to say something right now. I'd like to say, Thank you Quentin and good night. I'd like to run out the fucking door. But instead I find myself sitting down.

'And so the board thought that you'd be the perfect person to head up New Media. I mean, you can talk to techies, can't you? All those Hmsomething writers?'

'HTML.'

'See? You know all the lingo.'

I'm kicking myself for opening my mouth.

'Jenny says that you would be a prime candidate to work mainly from home, and what we were thinking was that you could just come in one day a week, say Monday. You could report to the board, meet with the geeks and Creative, or whatever. And then the rest of the week, you could just beaver away from your study or your kitchen or wherever. I mean it will all be,' he does air quotes around, ' "on line" anyway, won't it?' Quentin leans back in his chair and beams at me.

'Quentin, I've put in my notice.'

'You say that, but I never got it.'

Surely even the post in W1 can't be that crap. 'What do you mean, you didn't get it?'

In answer, he just smiles some more.

I jump up and start pacing in front of Quentin's sofa.

'You're interested, I can tell.'

And damn it, I am. Oh, damn it all to hell.

I sink back into the chair and rest my head on my knees. 'It's not just that, Quentin.'

'I can hardly hear you.'

I sit up properly. 'Sorry.' Get a grip, Maggie, get a grip here, girl.

I suddenly think of Peter, dancing around the suite in Claridges. I need to be honest with Quentin. I need to be honest with myself. I've got to stop this posturing. Simon's right, it's all bullshit.

Quentin's waiting.

I sigh, long and loud. 'I had this conversation with my friend the night he...' I swallow, 'the night I lost him.'

The confidence Quentin has shown throughout this meeting suddenly dissipates.

'We talked about, oh lots of things.' Jesus, heaven, Saint Paul. 'And one of the things was PR.' I jump up to pace again. 'And I'm just not suited to it, Quentin. In a way, I think it's a bit wrong, to be honest. Pitching, slanting, spinning. All that trying to make people think a certain way. I think, in a way what we do is actually harmful.'

I finally look at him, expecting, I don't know, shock or something. But he's just nodding.

'Harmful not just to the punters, but to us, and to the product, too.'

There's no stunned incomprehension on my boss's face, he just nods again.

'So,' he says, 'how are people going to find out about something new. Say, the tampon?'

'They'll see it on the shelves.'

'Will they? Without display?'

I think about my trips to Sainsbury's. I don't think I even look where I'm going, I just buy the same things over and over. 'Maybe not.'

He waits for a moment. 'Well, okay,' I finally say, 'But if people need information, why can't we just give them straight information? Why is it always so...' I hunt for a better word, but '...cynical?' is the best I can come up with.

'Where are they going to get this information, this wonderful naïve information?' Quentin asks, putting his fingertips together. 'A newspaper? Which newspaper?'

I get it. He sees that I get it, and continues. 'The second you start making choices like that, you start spinning. It's inevitable.'

My head's starting to hurt.

'Fine. Start spinning. Spin away. Just do it without me!'

He smiles at me. 'And what are you going to do? Try and live

288

on Simon's salary? Why the hell did he go into wine, anyway? That's a rich boy's game, you can't make any money in it.'

'Leave Simon out of this.'

Quentin makes an apology motion with his beautifully tailored shoulders. I sit back down. 'None of this matters anyway,' I say. 'I'm out of this business. I'm writing a book.'

'A book? What, a novel?'

I nod.

'You're writing a novel to get out of Marketing?' Quentin laughs at me.

'What? What's so funny about that?'

'Maggie, there's nobody in the world as much at the mercy of marketing as a novelist.'

'Nonsense.'

He grins at me. 'You just wait. You've just been spinning products to fit the market. Now you're going to have to *produce* to fit the market.'

'No, I'm not. I've already sold it.'

'Did you now? And what suggestions did your publisher make?'

I don't know. I don't really understand them. I look at him for a moment, and he smiles at me. There's a great deal of kindness in his eyes.

'Maggie, you can't run away from the way the world works. Even if you do find it distasteful.'

I Feel a lot smaller than I did when I came in.

'Take another week off to think about it. It's okay, you're owed quite a lot of holiday. I think I read that somewhere.' His turquoise eyes twinkle at me.

He read it in my letter of resignation. The one he said he didn't get.

'I'm going home for Thanksgiving. I won't be back until December first.'

He shrugs. 'Okay. I'll stall the board.'

He stands up and sticks out his hand. 'Come in then and we'll get started on the New Media department. You'd better give me your home fax number and your email there. I'll get some new cards printed up.'

'I-'

'It's perfect for you.'

I put my hand in his. 'I'm not promising anything.'

He grins. 'Of course not.' He shakes my hand once, and lets it go. At the door, I have a thought and turn around again. Quentin already has one hand on the telephone, but he drops it. 'Yes?' he asks me.

'What's happening to my job?'

'Henry is becoming you. Celia is becoming Henry.'

'Who's becoming Celia?'

'We don't know. Carol had a friend, but it fell through. I'm going to have to get onto the agency.'

I walk back to his desk. 'What about Anya?'

'Anya?'

'Sure,' I say. 'Melanie could do her job, and anybody could do Mel's. Anya's got a degree, you know.'

'Does she?'

'Philosophy. Leeds.'

Quentin says, 'Hmmm.'

'She trains all the new handlers.'

'Does she?'

'She trained me. And helped Henry no end. Ask him.'

'Good Lord.' He shakes his head. 'I had no idea.' I watch him run all the information through his brain. 'Maggie, that's a smashing idea.'

'Really?' I hear delight in my voice.

'Absolutely super. Would have never thought of it.' He smiles at me again. 'You know that saves us thousands on recruiting?'

This is the only thing that's made me happy since my bath. 'I'm sure you won't regret it.' I say.

'Anya,' he says again, wonderingly. 'Never have thought it. Smashing.'

I finally make it out the door, calling back, 'See you, Quentin.'

I go back to my office and slide Simon's photo and my contact book into my satchel, and then pop on my fleece and sling the satchel over my shoulders. I expect to be mobbed, but when I walk down the shantung hallway, it's empty. I run my finger down it and feel it bump and catch.

Will I be coming back here? I ask myself, but I'm not answering.

At reception I find Carol sitting at the switchboard.

'What are you doing here?' I ask her and she grimaces.

'I know how to work the thing. Quentin wanted Anya and Melanie in his office right away. God knows why. Anyway, somebody had to take over the phones.'

This makes me smile.

'How are you doing, Maggie?'

My smile immediately fades. 'I don't really know,' I say truthfully.

Carol starts to put out her hand to pat me but then the switchboard rings, and she uses it to pick up the receiver. I push the button for the lift. Four lights come on the switchboard, one after the other, and start blinking as Carol tries to put the first caller through. She says, 'Oh, bugger.' The lift arrives.

I step in and turn around. And then the doors close it all away.

Fliss is now fifteen minutes late for our meeting. Ellice stops typing for a moment to ask me if I want anything else to drink. I've already hammered down a Coke, and feel that strange caffeine guilt again and so say, 'No, thank you.' I was dying for that Coke. I should have eaten breakfast, I knew I was in meetings all morning, but somehow I just wasn't hungry. Even the thought of toast made me feel ill. Nerves, I guess.

'She's still talking to New York.'

'It's okay.'

Ellice really is extraordinarily lovely. She's Asian, though I can't tell which country, China, Japan, Taiwan, something like that. She has gorgeous glossy black hair done up into a kind of cone shape and pores so fine her face looks like it's been cast and fired. I honestly don't think I've ever seen anyone, even back home, so well groomed. Probably Japanese, I decide.

A man in his shirtsleeves and braces comes out of an adjoining door and talks to her briefly, giving her some more typing. She's not just Fliss's. Fliss shares her with two other people. It's typical of Fliss to give the impression that she doesn't.

A buzzer sounds on her desk. 'You can go in, now, Mrs White.'

Fliss's scribbling something frantically when I go in the door, so I just plunk myself down in a chair. Finally, she slams the pen down on her desk. 'Let me look at you. God, you look a lot happier.'

'Do I?' That's nice, considering I've just been hit by a truck. Or at least that's how I Feel.

'And how's the beautiful Simon?'

'Not so beautiful.' Fliss looks a question at me. 'He's got a broken nose and a cut on his head. Two black eyes.' She's got a fantastic view. I trail off, looking towards the Post Office Tower, which shadows where the Blues have their office.

'How did that happen?'

'I hit him.'

'What?' Fliss laughs delightedly, long and hard. When she gets her breath back, she says, 'Over this little tramp?'

I nod.

'Good on ya! He won't do that again in a hurry, will he?'

She thinks for a second. 'It's, uh, not going to damage his looks permanently, is it?'

292

'He might have a bit of a bump on his nose, but the wound isn't suppose to scar.'

'Fine. That's what our boy's good for, isn't it?'

I find myself angry. 'I'm afraid I don't agree with you there,' I say coldly.

She grins. 'Back in love, eh? Fair enough.'

Do I need this? Do I really need this?

'You know that's good for the book. Put it in. Everybody likes a happy ending.'

I say, 'About the book. I don't really-'

Fliss pulls out a copy of the sheets that I'm hauling out of my satchel. 'I know it can be awkward to get used to thinking of your stuff this way,' she says. 'So let's go through them one by one.'

She purses her lips for a second, and then says, 'Ah, tone.' Which leaves me no wiser. This must show on my face, because she continues, 'It's too even. It's a bit boring. You need to break up the tone, the pace. You know what I mean?'

I look at her dumbly. It's pretty obvious I don't.

Fliss asks, 'How'd they take the news at the Blues?'

'Don't.'

'Don't what?'

'Fliss, what do you mean, Tone?'

'It's your character, what do you call her?'

'Mimi.'

'Cute. You've got Mimi just walking around like an automaton. She does this, she does that. She's narrating, but where's her interior life?'

'She doesn't let herself have one yet. It's going to come.'

'Right.' Fliss swivels about a bit. 'When?'

'It happens gradually.'

'Don't make it happen too damn gradually or every bugger's going to go to sleep.'

'When Peter starts to visit, she starts realising that she's unhappy. That's when it all really opens up.'

'Okay. I'll wait to see on that one. About Peter…'

'Yes?'

Fliss makes this screwed up little face and waggles her head a bit. 'I don't know.'

'What do you mean, you don't know?'

'The whole Sean Connery angle is good, but does he have to be Saint Peter?'

My mouth drops open. 'Yeah,' I say, and I can hear the outrage in my voice. 'Yeah, of course he does. That's the whole point.'

'Well…' she thinks a second. 'Do you think we could see them fuck, then?'

I can't seem to close my mouth. I just stare at her.

'And cut all that stuff about Jesus. Who wants to read that?'

'I can't do that.'

She was about to say something else, and now she stops and just looks at me.

'What did you say?'

'I said I can't do that.'

I wish I'd asked for some mineral water. My mouth is dry and my stomach is doing flips. But from the look on Fliss's face, I don't think that now is a good time to mention it.

She comes around her desk and leans against it, looking down at me. Is everyone going to play these ancient power games with me today?

'Maggie,' she growls, 'Darling.' She sounds like she's auditioning for the part of Cruella De Vil.

I wait.

'Neither one of us harbours any kind of illusion that you know the first thing about writing a novel, do we?'

I shake my head no, slowly. How much smaller am I going to

294

be made to feel today? I'm down to the size of a dust particle already.

'So if I tell you that it's probably a good idea for...what is the character's name?'

'Mimi.' I'm starting to hate the name already.

'Cute. For Mimi and Sean Connery to fuck, then you should go away and write it that way, shouldn't you?'

I sigh. Damn it.

Fliss continues while walking around her office, 'And as far as the Jesus stuff...I mean, really. I can't even bring myself to wade through all that. I just skip it.'

'I can't change that, either.'

Fliss takes a deep breath. She's got her back to me, and I find myself feeling grateful for this. 'Maggie?'

Well, what am I supposed to do? I'm only really writing this because... Why am I writing the damn thing, anyway? To save Fliss's job? I'm not doing this for Fliss anymore. I'm doing it for Peter. And Jesus, I suppose, whether I meant to be or not. And I'm not going to write a pack of lies about Peter. I just can't. And I don't want to leave anything out that he told me.

'I can't, Fliss. I'm sorry. I just can't change those things. Anything else, but not those things.'

Fliss sinks down behind her desk. 'Just once,' she says. 'Just once I thought I was going to work with somebody who had half a brain.'

Poor girl. I've got to stop this posturing bullshit. I've got to start levelling with people. I take a deep breath. I say, 'This is really all the result of a terrible misunderstanding.'

Fliss looks at me blankly. 'That night at Quo, I wasn't really pitching a book. I was trying to tell you something.'

She closes her eyes. 'I have a feeling I don't want to hear this.'

I get up and come to sit on her desk. I take her limp hand in mine. 'You have to, Sweetie, it lets you off the hook. You see, Saint

295

Peter really was appearing to me in my bedroom. Everything I've written is absolutely true. And I never could think of a campaign to help him, until you thought it would make a novel. And so, I can't change much, you see? I mean, I can write it better, but I can't change tons of it, really.'

Her eyes are still closed. I take her hand and shake it about a bit by the wrist.

'Fliss? Do you understand?'

She lays her face in my lap.

I've never seen her silent for so long. I never thought she ever stopped talking for that long. I've been in hotels with her and I know that she even talks in her sleep.

I'd pat her head but her hair's all done up and I don't want to ruin it.

She says, 'I understand. I understand that you're even more fucked up than I thought. Maybe even more fucked up than I am.'

'Well, I'll give the advance back. I'll publish it with someone smaller or something. Or maybe even publish it myself.'

She pushes away from me to lean back in her chair. She still hasn't opened her eyes.

'And then we'll both be okay, see?'

Her voice, when she finally speaks, is low, and prefaced by a groan. 'You don't know anything about this sector, do you? Why did I think you did?'

She jumps to her feet and goes to look out her view again. 'Why did I think you did? I was just so eager...I just wanted to work with somebody I could trust. Trust!' She spins around to lean on the glass and faces me. She looks terrible.

'We don't buy novels because we *like* them, Maggie,' she says, swallowing. 'We buy them because we think we can sell a lot of them. We allocate a budget for marketing, depending on how many units we think we can move. The three of us work very closely with our head of Marketing. If he says go, we go. If he says no, we don't.'

I feel silly sitting on her desk with her not there. I go back to my chair.

'You understand that, don't you?'

I shrug. 'Sure. I get it.'

She swallows and closes her eyes again. 'Do you have any idea of our plans for this novel?'

'No.'

'Simultaneous printing and release in London and New York. A promotional tour for you that make the Rolling Stones look like homebodies. I'm not even going to tell you the budget. If I told you the budget you'd be so terrified you'd never be able to write another word.' She kind of rolls around until her face is against the glass.

She says, 'Maggie, this isn't all your fault. I know that. But if you don't produce the kind of novel I sold to the board...'

So. It seems Quentin knew what he was talking about. I say, 'Oh, shit,' and fold myself over again, resting my head on my knees. It's a good thing I skipped the toast. I nearly want to throw up my Coke.

I hear Fliss move around a bit and finally her chair creaks and she makes that little sound people make when they're tired and get to sit down. She says, 'It's not your fault, really it's not. If I hadn't been doing so much coke at Quo that night... And then if I could have only admitted that I'd just been silly again...'

Cocaine? So that's why she was so together and able that night while I was a blithering wreck.

I sit back up and we look at each other for a few minutes. I say, 'I should have told you straight away, but I didn't want to get you sacked.'

She barks a short, dry laugh. 'Don't reckon I need any help in that department.'

'Well how did you sell it in? What did you say it was going to be?'

'Oh, hell, Maggie, I can hardly remember. The meeting was at 8:30 the next morning. I think I only got through it at all because I was so shit scared. I was jacked up on fear.'

'Jesus, Fliss.'

She's actually shaking. 'I don't know,' she says, 'I said it was a great start of the century novel. That it had everything, right? Religion and war of the sexes and everything. I said it was hysterically funny. I think I said it was clit lit with a twist. I don't know, I don't know.' She wraps her arms around herself tightly. 'Maybe I should go back to Melbourne, get a job in a biscuit factory, make a few babies with some strapping footballer…'

I think for a moment, and tell her, 'I can do that.'

'Pack biscuits?'

'Look, the stuff I sent you is funny, isn't it?'

'God, yeah. That's not the problem.' Hope starts to dawn in her eyes. Poor little piggy eyes, all swollen with the effort of not crying.

'We're two bright women. Surely we can manage to do both, can't we? Can't we kind of slide in the religious stuff?'

Fliss looks at me for a few moments. 'Are you sure you wouldn't rather come with me to the biscuit factory?'

'Don't tempt me.'

'Why are you even doing this?'

I don't know. I say, 'Well, you and Peter, I guess. And I think I might be good at it, really.'

She nods for a little while. At last she says, 'It's not going to be easy. You've got a lot to learn. And you'll have to do what I tell you.' She gives a little sniff and wipes her nose on the back of her hand. 'Despite the fact that I'm losing it, I am damn good at this.'

'But I'm doing it for Peter, too, so…'

She closes her eyes again. 'I can't really listen to that, Maggie.

You've been talking to Saint Peter? Strewth! There's a limit, you know?'

I sit there. I think I'm even more unhappy than when I came in.

Fliss opens her eyes and takes this in. She does her best to be kind to me, saying, 'I mean, if you want something a certain way, we'll just have to call it artistic differences, okay? I'm not going to let you tell me you've got some hotline to heaven. You'll win some, you'll lose some. It'll be like working with any other halfwit author.'

I try and swallow, but my throat is so dry. 'Could I have some mineral water?'

'Not until you promise me, *promise* me, to do everything you possibly can the exact way I say.'

We look at each other some more. There's nothing else I can do. I promise.

I get on the 73 bus in a bit of a daze.

If I start thinking, I'm going to go to sleep and end up in Tottenham. I just can't do it anymore, think and worry and things. I just can't.

My head feels heavy on my neck and I lean it against the window. The glass is cold enough to feel through my hair.

I wish Peter was here. I can't remember any more what it was we decided. And it seemed so important at the time.

Chapter Twenty-five

I do not honestly know, so I cannot tell you, how I came to be here. I got off the 73 on the corner, but instead of walking home I walked the other way, down Church Street, and then turned. I don't know why or how I even remembered that they were leaving the Lady Chapel door open.

I'm not really praying or anything. I'm just kneeling here, looking at the chipped plaster statue of Mary and the candles of the believers.

Well, where else could I go? I have a friend who lived near here, a delightful Scots girl with honey coloured hair. I haven't seen her in ages. Her husband buys her amber, big chunky pieces with flies and things inside. And that's exactly how I feel, fossilised inside something. I can't even move to struggle.

Everything in my life seems controlled by the marketplace. Even my home is for sale. I can't leave anything lying around. I can't cook anything smelly. I can't relax, basically.

The marketplace.

It's nearly ruined my marriage.

What's Simon going to think, anyway? I have two choices, Honey, I can either head a new department for one of the world's largest advertising agencies or I can try and become a bestselling author. Hell, my advance made him feel small. And that's peanuts. I didn't even ask Quentin what they were thinking of paying me. I don't think I wanted to know.

Maybe we just won't come back from Lawrence. Maybe we'll just sell the house and find a little place in the country. Build a log cabin from a kit. And what? Pack biscuits?

Yeah, work at the plastics factory. Me and Simon, side by side, same wage, same hours. And what if the factory shuts down? Due to, I don't know, pressure from environmentalists? It's not like jobs are easy to come by in my hometown.

I'd still be subject to market forces. I just wouldn't stand a hope in hell of controlling them.

Like I control them now?

Shit. I lean my head against the wood of the kneeler.

Why are those two jobs my only choices, anyway? Why do I need to keep going like this, trying to control things? So I'm a stuck bug. Can't I just be a stuck bug? Must I keep on trying to rule my bit of amber? Must I continue trying to be the best stuck bug there's ever been?

What attracts me about this new media job anyway? Why do I want it? Do I think I'll get more respect at Liverpool Street station? That I'll be able to go clickety-click again? Like I really enjoyed that?

When did I ever enjoy what I did for a living? Simon actually likes what he does. I used to try and get him to change jobs. I even set up interviews at big agencies. But he always flubbed them. He didn't want to move out of his little in-house gig. And Peter liked what he did, too. His face used to light up when he talked about fishing.

Peter. I want to talk to Peter.

I wonder if I can. Peter? Can you hear me, Peter?

Nothing.

I hear myself groan. Am I going nuts again, or what? But then, look at all these candles. All of these people can't be insane. But then they don't all know what I know about Jesus and Mary. But what about God? The rest of the holy trinity? It strikes me that I know very little about that side of things. If you pray, does something hear you? I don't mean Peter or Jesus. I mean something powerful, that can actually make things happen.

It's not like I've got any other ideas.

Please, God. Please let Peter come to me.

I start to cry when nothing happens.

I cry so easy these days. I don't think I'm really crying because nothing's happened. I'm really crying because I feel so damn pitiful kneeling there and trying.

'Mrs White?'

I jump a couple of feet kneeling.

'It is Mrs White, isn't it?'

It's the nice priest. I wipe my face on my polar fleece and gulp a hello.

'Are you alright?'

I'm having trouble speaking, but I get to my feet and nod. I'll just go, I think. I'll just go now, back to my showplace. I can cry there, as long as I don't smudge anything.

'Would you like a cup of tea?'

With my new caffeine addiction, this sounds heavenly. I nod again before I even think about it, before I can even think that I've already had a Coke today.

I'm thinking about it as I follow Father out the door and up the stairs to his flat above the church hall. I'm thinking of asking myself what the hell I'm doing. Once I'm there, he kind of motions for me to have a seat in his living room while he goes into the little kitchen.

I'm shocked by how horrible his furniture is. And those curtains! Well, at least they're clean. He comes back out with a melamine cup and saucer. The cup's got a burnt orange rose screenprinted on the side. He's also got an industrial sized tin of biscuits.

He says, 'I went ahead with the milk. Do you need sugar?'

And I shake my head no. I don't know why I can't talk, but I can't. The tea is of the same crap standard. The UHT milk (you can always tell) can't disguise the oily film of tannin on the top. It still tastes heavenly to me.

'Oh,' I finally say, after swallowing about half the cup. 'That's great. Thank you.'

Father sits there, his keen blue eyes missing nothing, but biding his time. He runs his hand through his thick brown hair and when he brings it down I can see him restrain himself from checking his watch.

I say, 'You must be busy.'

'No,' he says. 'It's a bad habit. Ever since I took over my first parish. I'm trying to stop it, it must make people very uncomfortable. I've got nothing for a few hours.' Is he Irish? It's such a slight accent in some people, and often sounds American to me at first. I can't concentrate enough to tell.

'But you must have private things to do.'

'Mrs White.' He clears his throat and finally meets my eye. 'Right now, this is my work. I have a feeling you need to talk to me.'

The tears instantly spill out again. You bastard, I say to God. This is your doing. You sent him, instead.

I didn't want him. I wanted Peter. You can't fob me off with some stupid priest.

Father is sitting there, patient. He's no doubt lying through his teeth. He's probably got twenty places he needs to be. He's just trying to do his work, which must include mollycoddling middle class parishioners he finds crying in the chapel.

His work. He works. I wipe my eyes with my sleeve again. I say, 'I'm sorry. I'm having a bit of trouble with my work.'

Father nods encouragingly. Oh, hell. I might as well give it a shot. On the off chance that God knows what he's doing.

I try to laugh, but it comes out a bit choked. 'I don't know if you're the best person to talk to about this. Do you ever feel trapped by market forces?'

'Market forces?'

'Yes. Do you ever have to…kind of tailor what you really should do? So that you don't scare off the punters? Is there ever any tension for you there?'

Father takes a sharp intake of breath. 'I don't know that I should discuss parish politics with you, Mrs White.'

But now that I've started, I find it difficult to stop. 'I don't want to know specifics, Father. I just wondered.'

He nods. 'Well, then. Of course. Of course. I don't know any parish priest who doesn't have this, how did you put it? Tension.'

'Does it make it difficult for you to do what you think is right?'

'Sometimes it makes it nearly impossible.' He grins at me, and the burden in my heart is perceptibly lightened, just because I know it's shared. He opens the biscuit tin and selects something with a dot of improbably coloured jam on top. 'Why?' he asks before he bites, 'is that the sort of conflict that's bothering you?'

I let him swallow before I tell him. I don't want him to choke. And then I say, 'I'm writing a novel.'

He nods.

'About Saint Peter. And for Saint Peter. Well, he liked the idea, anyway.'

He catches himself mid nod. He just kind of looks a question at me.

'It's a long story.'

'It must be.' He eats the rest of his biscuit quite calmly. 'So, where's your market forces problem?' He seems to like saying "market forces".

'You don't think I'm mad?'

He motions to his dog collar. 'You expect me to tell you that it's impossible to communicate with saints?'

When he puts it that way, I feel silly for asking. 'Well, I thought I'd just be able to tell people all the things Peter said to me, you know? In a novel, I wouldn't have to prove anything and I wouldn't get into trouble with you guys.'

Father is nodding. He doesn't seem offended by the reference to the church. 'But?' he prods gently.

'But I'm probably going to have to cut a lot of it out. The publisher said that people wouldn't be interested.'

He waggles the tin at me again, and in a moment of weakness I choose something that looks like a chocolate biscuit. When I bite into it, I nearly gag. All the food colouring in the world can't hide the taste of lard and cheap beet sugar. It hits my empty stomach like a superball thrown from the roof of the Empire State Building and bounces up against the back of my teeth. I choke it back down with nothing but willpower.

Father leans back in his chair. 'Do you think this publisher chappie knows what he's talking about?' I can't believe I had a problem telling whether or not he was Irish.

I nod, and Father scratches the back of his head. 'It's not an easy one, that,' he says.

I knew this was going to be useless. I don't know why I bothered. But he thinks for a moment and says, 'Cardinal Hume said, and I can't remember it exactly, but something about it not being a good idea to water down the message.'

I must look blank, because Father rolls on to explain. 'It's like if you're having a party and you want everyone to have a really good time, but you've only got enough money for so much whisky. If you serve the whisky straight, only a few people will get drunk. But if you water it down to go around, then nobody will.'

Light dawns. 'The Cardinal said nothing about whisky, mind, that's my own example, and it might not be the best. But you know what I mean.'

'But you can do that, can't you? You can afford to do that, in the church. You've got such a massive following, and so much money...' Father gives me a look, and I shrug apologetically. I mean, I know he doesn't have much, look at the way he lives, but the Vatican could sell a painting or two and insure that every priest in the British Isles lived well for the rest of their days. I say, 'Well, the Roman Catholic Church isn't poor, Father,' and he seems to give me that.

'You're already powerful. People already listen to what the Pope has to say.'

He eats another biscuit and offers one to me, but the first one's still bouncing up and down my oesophagus and I wave the box away. 'I'm not in that position. If I don't please the publisher, please their marketing department, really, nobody is going to read the thing at all.'

He scratches his head again. 'It's a tough situation. And your man at the publishing company, you say he knows his business?'

I have every confidence in Fliss, even if she is going crazy. I nod, miserably.

He says, 'It's a lot like sermons, you know,' and settles himself into the chair a bit more. 'In the old days, we had a lot more time. Read some of those old sermons, and they must have lasted hours! Can you imagine? When I write a sermon, I think about the kiddies sitting there, you know, used to their computer games and their pop videos. I could explain most of the things I talk about a great deal more, but I try and distil it down to fit their attention span. Do you understand?'

'Yes, but-'

'I know you're going to ask about the important things that get left out, aren't you?'

He's a lot smarter than I thought. I nod.

'Well, you have to trust people to find things out for themselves. I mean, literacy rates are a lot higher in our population than they were for, say, Saint Augustine. And we've got the internet and everything now. It's a lot easier for people find out about things.'

I say, 'Hmmm,' and then, 'that's true.'

I feel like something's come off my shoulders. And Father says, 'Any little bit you work in is going to be more than they would have had, isn't it? You can only do what you can, Mrs White.'

'Maggie.'

'Maggie.' He smiles at me.

He must be relieved that I wasn't crying about Simon beating me. And then I remember how I beat Simon, and my chin collapses. I fight snuffling again.

'Maggie?'

'Sorry. It's not that, you were really helpful.' I take a deep breath. 'I don't suppose you could do me a quick confession?'

He looks at his watch. 'Plenty of time,' he says. And we go back down the stairs.

I get four Our Fathers and five Hail Marys. That doesn't seem like a heck of a lot for beating your husband. I wonder if it was mitigated by the circumstances. I'm kneeling in the main part of the church, now, and I can hear Father unlocking the doors at the back. It must be, what, three-thirty, four? There's probably a school activity here later, choir or something. I have no idea.

It's not like I don't know the words, but I'm finding it hard to get going. I've knelt more today than I think I have in the past twenty years of my life, but my knees don't particularly hurt. My back does, in the lumbar, but not my knees. But then, my lumbar's been aching a lot lately.

It makes me feel queasy again to look at the cross. I can't help but think of the spikes going in, the sound they must have made. How could he have done that? He must have made a mega-jump of the faith. In the soldier, in Joseph of Armithea and the Essenes. In everybody. And, I guess, everything. Jesus must have had so much faith in everything to be able to do that. In God, I guess, if God is just everything, just the way things work.

And maybe that's what I need to do. I've got to stop looking back. I've got to stop spending so much time worrying. I worry what other people think. I worry about the way people treat me at Liver-Bloody-pool Street station. I worry about everything. It's not like it helps anything.

And say everything falls to shit. Just say. Say I try and write this novel and it sucks and Fliss loses her job and it all falls on my head. Well, so what? We were both thinking a bit fondly of the biscuit factory, anyway.

I smile, and something strange happens to me. I stop breathing. At least I stop being aware of the sound of it, which had seemed to echo through the empty church. Suddenly, I feel both very small and very large at the same time. Coursing through me is this immense feeling. Gratitude. I am so grateful, just to be here, just to have everything, Simon, my mother, even Jack. Maybe even especially Jack.

I close my eyes, which fill with tears but don't spill over. That warmth I used to feel from Peter is pouring over my whole body. This has never happened to me before. Although the church is dark on a grey November afternoon, and I have my eyes closed, the warmth seems to make a yellow glow behind my lids.

The light. Holy shit. I think I'm actually seeing The Light.

Chapter Twenty-six

Can you remember how you felt after your first orgasm? Elated and a bit ashamed at the same time? Most of all, eager to do it again?

That's pretty much how I feel walking home. I even have the same wobbly knees. I take the shortcut opposite the fire station. It cuts through a neighbourhood and ends up in a guinnel that runs past a little park behind Stoke Newington High Street. I don't want to run into anyone and have to talk.

I think about sitting down in the park for a few minutes, but I want to get home. Get home to try and see if I can do it again. That warmth was such an amazing feeling. I'm walking down Leswin Road when I decide I can't wait any longer and lean against someone's garden wall to try.

You just have to forget about the logic of it all. You close your eyes and kind of open yourself up. I don't really say any words or anything. I don't really know who does it or how it works. I only know how incredibly powerful it feels. It feels like it's coming from something a lot larger than I am, something with endlessly renewable energy, something that has been waiting for me to use it for a longer time than I can imagine.

When my mobile starts to ring, it takes me a second to register the sound. And then I'm back in the November twilight on the broken pavements of Leswin Road, scrabbling in my satchel for my phone.

'Sis?'

Why is Jack ringing me?

'Sis, is that you?'

'Yeah. Sorry, Jack.' My voice sounds too calm, almost flat. I don't want to hurt his feelings, so I say with more energy, 'I was just thinking about you.'

It's a terrible connection. We have to practically shout.

'Maggie, are you somewhere where you can sit down?'

I lean back against the wall. Something cold starts to grow in my chest. 'I'm ready,' I shout. 'What is it?'

'It's Mom. She's okay, she really is. But she's going in for heart surgery tomorrow. Bypass.'

'Bypass?'

'It's not an easy surgery, Maggie. She's having five done.'

I find myself consciously breathing, reminding myself to inhale and exhale. Jack carries on. 'I've talked to Simon already and he told me to call you and tell you while he changes your flights. She doesn't go in the operating room until five in the afternoon.'

'Five,' I echo.

'It's at Saint Lukes. You know, on the Plaza, in K.C.'

'Saint Lukes.'

'Sis, are you alright?'

Am I? Yeah. I am. I am, actually. 'I'm okay. You say Simon's doing the flights and things?'

'Yeah. He said to go on and pack for both of you. He's going to call you. Are you at home?'

I find my legs have started walking without me. 'I'm almost home. I'm about four minutes away.'

I think about Jack for a moment. 'Are you okay?'

There's a bit of a pause. He says, 'I'm scared shitless. But the surgeon seems like he knows what he's doing. They're supposed to be the best, Saint Lukes. They've got that big new Cardiac wing.'

'How's Mom?'

'Oh, you know Mom. All she's worried about is being sick for your visit. I don't think she's really thought about it yet. It's just an inconvenience to her.'

'She's not scared?'

'She's more like irritated right now.'

I put my key in my lock, smiling at what Jack has said. And

when I smile, an echo of the light seems to warm the cold places in my chest where the fear has lodged.

'You just made me smile,' I tell Jack, and hear him sob, one of those tearing sobs that men give when they never cry.

'Come home, Sis,' he says.

'I'll be there. I'll be there as fast as I can.'

'I know.'

'I wish I was there right now.'

'I know. She just looks so dang little lying in that bed.' I hear my brother sniff.

'Is Helen there?'

'She's taking care of Patrick and the baby.'

'I'll be there super fast. Simon's great at these things. You just wait. Are you being brave for Mom?'

'Oh, sure.'

'You keep on doing that. When I get there, I'll be brave for awhile and you can go fall apart.'

'I'm going to look forward to that.' There's a long pause.

'Thanks, Jack. I'm so glad you're there.'

He says, 'Get your ass home,' and severs the connection.

Cat takes one look at me and doesn't bother running to her bowls. What they know in body language would probably fill twenty telephone directories. I go straight up the stairs and get the two little wheelie carry-ons down from the tops of our wardrobes in the dressing room and put them on the bed, unzipping them. Connections will probably be tight, and we don't want to be waiting around for luggage.

I'm running in with my first armload of Simon's shirts, socks and underwear when the telephone rings. I answer it by saying, 'Jack got ahold of me. I'm already packing.'

And Simon says, 'Can you be ready in twenty minutes? I've got a cab coming for you.'

'Sure.'

There's a brief pause. 'What about the catsitter?'

'I biked him my keys. If you feed her now, he'll come tomorrow morning. He'll do all the plants, as well, so don't worry about anything. Is there anything else that you can think of?'

'No. I can ring Fliss when we get there.'

'Put the novel on diskette. You can work on it at Jack's.'

'I'm not going to worry about shit like that.'

'Maggie, you may be there awhile.' I don't know exactly what he means, but this is chilling. 'Okay,' I say. 'I'll do it.'

'See you at the airport. It's American Airlines. It's Gatwick, not Heathrow. They had the first jet out.'

'I love you.'

'She'll be okay. Pack.'

So I do, putting the phone down and running back into the dressing room. Simon's hiking boots, two jumpers, cords, jeans, fleece. I grab his sponge bag and open it up. It looks fairly comprehensive. We can always buy things like that. Oh, hell, passports. I tear up the office for a moment before I remember where we put them. I stick them in my back pockets.

Now me. Makeup. Glasses. Tampons? Is it that time yet? Or is it even later? I shake my head a bit to clear it and reach for my contact stuff. Then clothes. Knickers and bras. Cargo pants. Jeans. Another jumper. These booties will do. Socks.

That's the optimistic packing. Now for the other stuff. I get my black Joseph jacket out of the wardrobe and a dark grey skirt. Black court shoes. Black stockings. I look at what's in Simon's wardrobe and determine that he's already wearing a dark grey suit, so all I get for him is a white shirt and a black tie. I swallow a bit, standing there with the funeral gear in my arms, but I don't have time to cry.

And I don't really want to. I open up my novel and save it to diskette, then run up and down the spiral staircase with the carry-ons. Cat is sitting on the sofa, aware that something extraordinary is happening, tactfully leaving me to my work. I tickle her under her chin.

I say, 'It's going to be alright.'

She looks up at me, trying to figure out what's going on. She's concentrating so hard on this that she's contracting her forehead. I'm sure there's a wrinkle there under her fur. I'm putting fresh water and crunchies in her bowls when I hear the taxi pip, and I fling my satchel around me and carry the luggage out the door. As I turn the mortise in the lock I wonder when I'll be coming back, or if I ever will.

'We've got to run. They'll check us in properly at the gate. You've got the passports?' Simon throws four tenners at the driver, one after another, and then snatches one of the bags. 'Come on.'

As I run after him I grab his passport out of my back pocket. 'Here', I say, and he takes it like we're in an Olympic relay team. He puts it between his teeth and passes my ticket back to me.

'Up this escalator,' he pants around his passport. We run up and then dart behind Tie Rack. Now I can see Departures. We sprint down, and luckily there's no queue, we just show our passports and tickets and get through. Someone at Security sees us running and waves us in. I unsling bag and push my carry-on through. I don't beep.

Simon does, though, so I collect his carry-on and leave him to sort it out. It's his watch, I think, as I run down to where the transport takes you out to the gate. It always beeps. There's one waiting, it says it's leaving in one minute. I push both bags on and stand in the doorway. Where is he? What can be taking him so long? At last, I see him running down, just as the doors start to close. I jump myself sideways and take the shock on my shoulders. The doors bound open and Simon jumps in and pulls me out of the way.

I collapse against him. 'Well done,' he says, looking at his watch. 'I think we're going to make it.' His tie's up over his shoulder and his hair is everywhere. I'm leaning against his chest and his shirt is fairly damp from sweat. 'I must reek,' he says. 'I've been running since South Wimbledon.'

I hold onto him until the thing stops and we have to start running again.

'Have a brandy.'

'No, thanks.'

'Good for shock.'

I shake my head.

'I'm having one.'

'Get me a Coke - no - get me an orange juice.'

'Okay.'

The steward comes to us and Simon orders for us both. I kind of turn my head and close my eyes. I just don't want to have to talk to anybody. When he leaves I take a big gulp. It's tasteless stuff, orange coloured water with pips thrown in. Still, it feels good going down. I'm ravenous.

'She's going to be alright.' Simon takes my hand. His hand feels suffocating around mine. I don't think I've been breathing enough since Leswin Road.

I shake him off irritably. I say, 'You don't know that. Nobody knows how she's going to be. We'll just have to wait and see.'

He hunches down in his seat, rucking up his jacket at the back, and has some of his brandy and soda.

Poor guy. 'Look, I'm sorry. You've been great. It's just…'

'It's okay.'

'No, it's not. I just felt patronised. I'm okay, really.'

'Okay. Fine.'

'Give me your jacket and I'll put it up top.'

He puts his brandy on my tray and leans forward, undoing his seat belt. This gives him just enough room to wrestle out of his jacket. He lets out a little groan of comfort and undoes his shirt button, sliding his tie off. 'Can you put this in your bag?'

I'm still folding his jacket in the overhead compartment. 'Give it here, I'll tuck it in your suitcase.' I lean down to look at him. 'You can change in the toilets, if you want. I've got more comfortable clothes here.'

'After dinner.'

'Okay.' I shut the thing and slide back in under my tray. The orange juice tastes better now.

'So,' I say, 'How was your day?'

He gives me a little half-grin. 'Well, I can't say it's been boring. My review was this morning.'

'You didn't tell me.'

'I didn't know.' He touches his nose gingerly. 'I'll bet this is going to swell up again with the air pressure.'

'What happened?'

'It just gave a kind of twinge.'

I shake my head impatiently. 'I mean your review.'

Simon tries very hard not to look pleased with himself, but fails. 'I've been offered a new position. Taking care of all the New Media stuff. They're going to give me another four grand. And I've had a bonus, too, another grand.'

'That's fantastic!' That brings his salary up to just over half of mine. 'Well done!'

'It's pretty exciting. They were planning to take my picture for the bulletin, but now they're going to wait until I get this thing off and the stitches out.'

'Charlie Maddock will do that for us. Helen's brother. He's a plastic surgeon.'

'Okay.'

'That's great about New Media.'

Now how am I supposed to tell him? I sit there, wishing everything didn't have to be so hard.

Simon sucks on an ice cube. Maybe he won't even ask about my day. He often doesn't.

'How did Quentin take it?'

I've almost been dozing, staring at my orange juice glass. Its been a bit much, this day, to be honest. And I'm not that good at dealing with stress any more. I've got used to Cat's approach to life. When things get difficult, have a nap.

'Maggie?'

I turn to face him. His right eye has faded down to a light purple, but the left still looks fairly hideous. My hands never did discolour, but the knuckles are so swollen I can't take off my rings at night. What are people are going to think?

His eyes themselves regard me carefully. No bullshit, I remember. 'He's offered me another job to stay.'

'What did you say?'

'I said I'd think about it.'

He starts to say something, but instead reaches down and shoves up the armrest that separates us. He puts his arm around me. 'What's the job?' he asks into my hair.

'New Media. Reporting to the board.'

I can feel his ribs shake before I turn to look at him laughing. 'Well, it would be, wouldn't it?' he asks me. 'And how many millions will you be making?'

The little light dings for turbulence and I put my seatbelt back on. 'I didn't ask.'

'Are you going to do it?'

'I don't know what I'm going to do.' If I angle my legs in just the right way, I can lean back on his chest. I do this, and, after a moment, he puts his arms around me.

'What about the book?'

I groan. 'Fliss wants to change it all.'

'Take it somewhere else.' He holds me tight. 'Really, Maggie, we've got enough to live on, now, just with what I make.'

'It's not that simple. I've signed a contract. And I don't want to let Fliss down. And anyway, if I really want people to find out about all this, then the larger the market the better.' I close my eyes. 'I guess. I don't know.'

Simon kisses the top of my head. 'So tell Quentin to take a hike. Write your book.'

'What if I can't do it?'

He shrugs. 'Then we live on my salary. But I think you probably can, or Fliss wouldn't have bought it.'

'Fliss was on cocaine. She would have bought the sweet menu.'

We're silent for a moment. The plane bucks a little underneath us. Some people make worried sounds about it.

Simon says, 'It doesn't matter to me, Sweetie. You do what you think is best.'

I swallow. 'If this book takes off, I'll be gone a lot for awhile. Reading and things. You know. Radio shows. Signings.' Tears come up behind my eyes.

'Shhh,' he says. 'Shhh.' He pats me as I cry into his shirt. One of the buttons is right under my mouth and I find myself nibbling at it, as if it were a teat that will give me comfort.

'I'm so scared. All of this and,' my voice breaks, 'now Mom.'

He holds me tighter. 'It's all going to be alright,' he says. 'It's all going to work out fine. I know it is.' He sighs. 'It'll all be okay. It's just... It's just that we don't know how yet.'

Simon holds onto me and kisses my head again, pressing his lips to the bare parting.

He's right. I know he's right. It really will work out fine. It just looks scary because we don't know how everything works. We don't know how anything works.

I shift my shoulders around so that I can hold Simon, as well. Then I close my eyes, and reach out for the light.

Acknowledgements

The book you hold in your hand would never have existed without the help of the following people:

Andy Wadsworth, my husband, who didn't mind my distraction, mood swings, neglect and lack of income;

Richard Kerridge and Tessa Hadley, who let me into Bath Spa Creative Writing MA, and Philip Gross, Jeremy Hooker and all the rest of the faculty and staff who nurtured and supported and instructed me (and still are);

The Creative Writing MA class of 1999, bless them, who put up with me. All the people of Galilee, the Jordan River valley and Jerusalem, who gave me the feel for Saint Rock;

The ever-helpful staff of the British Library Humanities One Reading Room, who put up with my methods;

David Riding from MBA Literary Agency, who saw something in this novel and never lost hope, even when I did;

All the editors and marketing directors at the big publishing houses, who provided the stone I honed the text against;

Debbie Hatfield at Allison & Busby, who had plenty of courage and enthusiasm for both of us when I had lost mine;

All the staff at Allison & Busby and their sales force, who worked so hard to get this book into the shop you bought it from;

My baby daughter, Olivia Wadsworth, who probably thinks that proof pages inevitably accompany all forms of nourishment;

The trade and their press and buyers, for taking the risk;

And you, Gentle Reader, who invested your time, money, and trust.

May the light shine for you all.